THE DEIMOS VIRUS

Predators of Darkness Series: Book Five

LEONARD D. HILLEY II

For my wife, Christal, our two children, and our two grandchildren. My love always.

Chapter 1

Deimos Moon Life Station

DEATH CREPT silently through the stainless steel corridors inside Deimos Life Station. Disease was his breath and decay, his fragrance.

Dr. Frank Carter sat at his desk, speaking into the life station computer microphone, recording his final log. His wavy black hair was unkempt. He needed to shave. Weary, he spoke with little emotion, in the dullest monotone.

"We had no compassion for the dying; no remorse for the dead. Their deaths ended the burning torment pulsing through their diseased bodies."

His voice cracked.

Dr. Carter paused and sipped water. He lingered a few moments to gather his composure and rubbed his tired eyes. Finally, he cleared his throat and continued his report. "We called it an alien virus, but we're the aliens. We're the invaders. The virus was Deimos' response to rid itself of us, its human infestation."

Carter sighed. "Computer, end recording."

"Yes, Dr. Carter," the computer replied.

Carter stood and grabbed his stainless steel briefcase. Glancing around the lab, he became overwhelmed. Silhouetted memories from when the room was filled with other scientists and nurses replayed in his mind. He could almost see them interacting. His mind fought the building emotions welling deep inside him. Then, his gaze rested on the small framed picture on his desk. He sickened from loss and heartbreak. His knees weakened. A soft whine of agony pierced the otherwise silence in the room.

Carter's eyes heated with tears. His chest muscles constricted, making breathing difficult. A lump in his throat made swallowing nearly impossible. His loss was too difficult to accept. Would the pain ever lessen? He doubted it could.

Picking up the picture, his hands shook. Frozen in time, from the previous New Year's Eve party, was his nurse and lover, Wanda Myers. She sat beside him. Confetti and balloons fell in the background. They smiled broadly, clicking their champagne glasses while gazing lovingly into one another's eyes. She'd been the one, he remembered. The one he'd love forever.

He loved how her blue eyes sparkled whenever she laughed, and that night he'd never seen her happier. Hell, he'd never been happier than when the photo had been taken. But a few days afterwards, tragedy struck and their world crumbled around them. Every plan, hope, and dream they shared was gone.

"I'm so sorry, Wanda," Carter said. "If I could go back and stop it, I would."

Wanting to hold her, to kiss her again, he set the picture on the desk and turned it face down. His chest hurt. His heartbeat increased. Never had he ached like this. He took several deep breaths to prevent himself from having another anxiety attack. His mind raced back to several days earlier when the unexpected catastrophe struck the moon station, killing all the inhabitants... all except him.

THREE DAYS EARLIER:

WEARING a yellow HazMat suit with a micro breathing apparatus, Dr. Carter stepped into the infirmary. Sheet-draped corpses occupied fifteen beds, lining the far wall. At another bed, Wanda sat beside an infected female patient.

The sick woman's tired eyes searched the room. She was disoriented, not really seeing what was happening around her. Or so he thought. When she noticed him, her gaze held the slightest glimmer of hope.

Carter walked over to them. Wanda met his eyes, and Carter forced a tired smile. Through the thick plastic face-guard of her HazMat suit, she smiled, but her eyes revealed the saddened horror of watching another colleague die.

Carter sat on a stool beside the woman's bed, took a syringe, and thumped the side until all the air bubbles drifted to the top. He pushed some of the liquid through the needle to expunge the collected air bubbles, not that the precaution was necessary or even mattered at this stage of the disease. Death was inevitable.

The patient glanced weakly, opening her mouth to speak, but no sound came. Her empty gaze reflected the loss of any hope she might have had left. Yellow lesions blistered her purple-mottled skin. Carter injected the needle into a swollen vein in the woman's arm.

"What'd you give her?" Wanda asked.

"Potassium cyanide."

"What?" Wanda's eyes widened. "That'll kill her."

Carter replied, "She's dead anyway. We all are. At least she won't suffer like the others."

She frowned. Her blue eyes fixed on his. "These Hazmat suits won't protect us?"

He started to speak, but then his eyes widened before sadness claimed them.

"What's wrong?" she asked.

Yellow blisters welted on her cheeks. He wanted to tell her she'd be okay, that everything would work out, but he couldn't bring himself to lie. The evidence in the room proved otherwise. Sixteen corpses. Once the blisters formed, death followed within hours.

Wanda stood. Perspiration beaded her furrowed brow. Her blonde hair was soaked with sweat. "We're going to be okay, right? The suits... they'll protect us?"

"No," Carter said, shaking his head. "Unfortunately, the virus had already circulated through the ventilation system before we ever suited up."

"So we're infected, too?"

"Yes. I'm afraid so," he replied, refusing to make eye contact. "Incinerating the dead bodies was the best precaution we took, but we'd already been exposed."

"Have you contacted Boyd Grayson in California about the outbreak?"

"What's the point?"

"To help us find a cure."

Carter shook his head. "There's no cure, Wanda. I've tried all of the antibiotics and antivirals we have, and even the strongest steroids to help boost their immune systems. Nothing has aided the patients at all. *Nothing*. Not even momentarily. Whatever this retrovirus is, it's vicious. It's more dangerous than HIV and spreads through the body more rapidly than Ebola. I've never seen anything like it."

"I know. But Grayson might have suggestions or he can contact scientists to analyze and unscramble the DNA structure of this virus."

"Our welfare on Deimos has never been Grayson's primary concern. The gem mines on Deimos and Mars are his top priority." Carter stood and pulled a sheet over the dead patient. "We're not worth any more than the dead rats in our laboratory."

Tears crested in Wanda's eyes. "You're probably right."

Carter's jaw tightened. The gentleness of his eyes blazed with sudden anger. "You *know* I'm right. The Deimos Life Station and the Olympus Mons settlements are that madman's dream. His greed is what has killed us."

"Oh my God," she whispered. Instinct brought her gloved hand to the protective face shield of her HazMat suit as though she'd cover her mouth with her hand.

"What's wrong?"

Horrified, she pointed. "Your face."

Carter ran to the sink and looked in the mirror. Yellow lesions blistered his cheeks. Sweat beaded his brow and dripped from his damp black hair. He yanked off the helmet.

"No!" she gasped.

"It doesn't matter anymore, Wanda," he said, examining his face in the mirror. "I'm going to die. You're going to die. It's useless."

Wanda unzipped her helmet and flipped it back. "I feel sick."

She collapsed to her knees and vomited. Seconds later, she fell to her side and desperately extended her feeble hand in his direction.

"Please, help me," she said.

Staring in the mirror, Carter noticed her lying on the floor. Tears filled his eyes. He turned, grabbed another syringe of potassium cyanide, and knelt beside her.

"Please, Frank," she whispered, "help me. I love you. Please."

Carter sat on the floor and cradled her head on his lap. He plunged the needle into her jugular and squeezed the poison into her bloodstream. Her eyes revealed her sudden surprise and terror. Her expressions indicated nothing less than complete betrayal. He rubbed and caressed her cheek until her breathing stopped.

"I'm sorry," he whispered.

Carter stood, picked her up, and carried her to an empty bed. After he set her down, he gently closed her frozen eyes, and kissed her forehead.

"If I survive," he said, "Grayson will pay with his life for what happened here."

A couple of hours later, Carter placed Wanda's body on the incinerator roller tray. After kissing her cold blue-tinted lips, he shoved the tray into the furiously hot flames. Still sick and weak, he struggled to close the heavy door. When he finally sealed the door, he pushed a button and the fire roared louder.

He turned and headed out the door with her I.D. badge clenched inside his fist. Suffering from intense vertigo, he leaned against the wall as he walked until he reached his office. He glanced at her badge. Through blurred vision, he stared at her photo. He staggered to his desk. Frustrated and filled with regret, he tossed her badge on the desktop with fifty-five other badges.

At the computer, he touched the screen and brought up the staff list of former life station occupants. Next to Wanda Myers' name, he clicked, "Deceased".

Carter grabbed a vial, a new syringe, and sat on the edge of a bed. He withdrew 2 cc of potassium cyanide. Tears streamed down his cheeks. Angered, with spittle spraying from his mouth, he seethed, "Grayson, I wish I could inject this into you and watch you die. Suicide's never been my option, but I refuse to suffer like the others did."

Resting his elbow on his upper thigh, he steadied the needle, preparing to insert it into a thick vein. The doors at the side of the room hissed open.

"What the—?"

No one else remained alive inside Deimos Life Station. He was the sole survivor, or at least, that's what he thought. Too weak to fight or run, he lowered the syringe and waited. His tired eyes tried to register what was standing before him.

Right inside the doors stood a short, dark-skinned female alien. Her sleek olive skin was unblemished. Her large oval eyes held no emotion. She spoke telepathically. "I can heal you."

Surprised and too weak to protest, he dropped the syringe. It bounced and clattered across the silver floor. She moved stealthily to him, almost gliding, and his shock subsided. She seemed peaceful, and if she could actually heal him, he'd willingly allow her.

Her hands were odd. Each had three long, slender fingers. Her mesmerizing eyes were black like obsidian. He felt comfort in her gaze, almost hypnotized by the endless blackness that reflected his image and the room around him. The alien eased him back on the bed. His body grew limp. Her touch held warmth, which surprised him since her scaly skin looked reptilian.

She undressed him, but no expressions crossed her face. His skin was covered with yellow, pus-filled lesions. He wanted to hide under a sheet because his appearance mortified him. When he looked up, his eyes stared immediately into hers. Strangely, he found peace there. He didn't resist and surrendered to her will and desires.

Carter never felt such repulsion and exotic pleasures at the same time. But the price to survive was worth this humiliation. He'd sacrifice almost anything to survive the virus so he could seek his revenge.

He attempted to think of the happier times because he didn't want her to read his thoughts and perhaps offend her. With her ability to speak to his mind, she was probably able to discern his thoughts as well.

Closing his eyes, he thought about Wanda before the virus infected her. He tried to imagine that he was having sex with her instead of this alien, which brought some added comfort.

The alien caressed his face. Her touch soothed him, making his mind lighten into an ecstasy dreamlike state. She interlocked her three-fingered hands with his fingers and straddled him.

When he opened his eyes, no pain or pleasure showed on her face. While she slowly rode him, he wondered if she desired to have a child to merge their species, or perhaps she wanted to form a new race to kill Grayson's human invasion into her realm of space. He didn't know her intentions, as she never disclosed her reasons, but he didn't care. He simply wanted to live. Living was the only way to exact vengeance.

The alien placed her six fingers against his temples. Her fingertips glowed. Warmth flowed through him. His body relaxed, and she climbed off.

When Carter and gazed into her eyes, she spoke to his mind. "The plague can no longer harm you. You are immune."

"How can I repay you?" he asked.

"Kill Boyd Grayson. Make him suffer like these have suffered."

"With the virus?"

She nodded. With a gentle touch of her fingers, she caressed his cheeks. "Sleep. When you awaken, you'll become stronger and more vigilant."

Carter awoke the next morning, and the alien was gone. He listened carefully for sounds. But silence inside a space station was never absolute. It wasn't a vacuum, void of noise. The LED lights offered no sound. The ventilation system hissed softly. A thermostat clicked, moments before heat susurrated through the vents. He rose and did a quick search of the laboratories, offices, and sick bays, but she was gone.

As she promised, he was stronger and mentally alert. The lesions and his fever were gone. Since she had healed him, he swore to carry out her mission and kill Boyd Grayson. After all, it was the least he could do, and he'd promised Wanda, too. Grayson needed to pay for the deaths of the doctors, nurses, and prisoners who had died inside the Deimos Life Station.

One vial of the virus was enough to kill everyone inside Grayson Enterprises on Earth. Carter took two.

He gently packed the two vials labeled, *Deimos Virus*, into a foamed-lined stainless steel briefcase. He took the New Year's Eve picture and walked down the cold silver-walled corridor that led to the landing bay.

Carter set the briefcase and the picture on the seat of the shuttle and suited up. The shuttle could only transport him to the Olympus Mons settlement on Mars. It wasn't built to withstand a six to seven month trip to Earth. Somehow, he'd have to find a way to stowaway on an earthbound ship to carry out the alien's request.

Carter sat in the pilot chair and flipped different switches and control knobs. Various lights flashed and glowed across the console. After the computer acknowledged his destination and fired the booster rockets, flames flared from the rocket exhausts. The shuttle vibrated roughly, and after several minutes, the thrusters slowly settled into a more rhythmic hum.

Excitement rushed through Carter. It'd been months since he last visited Mars. Although this time, his arrival must be absolutely discreet, so Grayson wouldn't discover that Carter wasn't amongst Deimos' casualties. If Grayson knew Carter was alive, it was unlikely Carter could successfully carry out his vengeance. To reach Grayson, Carter needed to blindside the billionaire. Grayson's security forces were the best trained on Earth, Mars, and the moon. Being a ghost, at least on the computer's records, was Carter's only way to get close to Grayson without being noticed.

The landing bay doors parted at a snail's pace. The bright reflection of Mars loomed like a small reddish marble far in the distance. He marveled at the sight, thinking back to his interview with Boyd Grayson years before. The thought of seeing Mars and being so far from Earth enthralled him with such a temptation, that for days, all his mind focused on was the thought of becoming the chief medical examiner on Deimos.

After the landing bay doors fully opened and locked into place, Carter pressed one last button. "Destination Mars" flashed on the computer screen. The shuttle lifted and drifted through the bay doors.

A smile spread across Carter's face. He gently patted the briefcase and said, "How much are you willing to pay to spare *your* life, Mr. Grayson?"

Chapter 2

Olympus Mons Mining Pits (Two days later)

DEEP INSIDE THE GIGANTIC, long dead volcano shaft of Olympus Mons, one hundred prisoners mined in a circular room that spanned several hundred yards from its center to the outer edges. Half of the men swung heavy pickaxes while the other half used large scoop shovels. They dug and shoveled the reddish-brown soil into long sifter machines. These massive sifters clacked and vibrated, separating the Martian soil from the valuable gems, known as MarQuebes.

Armed guards with laser rifles patrolled the outer edges of the enormous mining pit. Approximately one hundred yards above, another line of guards stood along the narrow ridge path at critical vantage points.

The mindless miners dug, scooped, and flung dirt. Their in sync rhythm was mechanical, like well-oiled machines, and they never missed a beat. Sweat mixed with dust formed reddish mud, coating their faces, arms, and clothing. They continually repeated the process without mumbling a single word or complaint. The miners blinked methodically, never making eye contact with one another or glancing away from their assigned tasks. Their eyes were glazed over, no emotion registered on their faces, and their movements didn't appear any differently than how a programmed humanoid acted. In fact, they were more like machines than humans.

Magnus Knight, a massive black miner, scooped a shovelful of dirt and tossed it into the sifter. Then another and another. Sweat dripped from his bald head, beaded on his brow, and dripped into his eyes. Although the salt stung, he resisted wiping it away. The other prisoners mined without pausing, without glancing around or slowing their pace, and it pained Magnus to keep up, but he did. Something was wrong with the other miners but what exactly he wasn't certain. However, the constant shoveling weighed upon him, but he told himself to keep pace with the others. Keeping up while trying to regulate his breathing grew harsher with each passing hour. He feared he'd pass out long before their shift ended, and they were sent back to their cells.

He wondered how these miners maintained their stamina, never tiring or breathing hard, but all he could do was mimic them. Since none of them ever talked or even cursed beneath their breath, he never tried to converse with them. He was afraid to do anything other than mine, due to the armed, patrolling guards. The worst part about his ordeal was that he didn't remember how he arrived at the mines, but physically and mentally, he couldn't continue this charade much longer.

Magnus had actually *awakened* two days earlier, or at least, that's how he chose to define it. He didn't have any clue how long he'd worked alongside these other hypnotized slaves because he wasn't sure what the date was. All he recalled was the sudden, severe headache that brought his vision slowly into reality.

Heavy breathing, shovels scooping, and the loud rattling of the sifting machines were the first sounds to welcome him from his deep, hypnotic daze. At first, he thought he was having a nightmare, but his mind processed his surroundings and adapted at a rapid pace.

The awakening caused him to pause for a moment, but then he kept shoveling. He wondered what prompted him to continue scooping dirt rather than questioning what he was doing or trying to walk away. But after overhearing two guards talking, he learned about the computerized chips that controlled the prisoners.

He realized that perhaps he had shoveled the red gritty soil for so long that his body continued doing whatever his mind was programmed to do. Muscle memory, as some termed it. He supposed habit or involuntary instinct had saved his life.

While Magnus shoveled, he continually studied the other prisoners around him. For hours, he waited for someone to talk to help take his mind off the menial physical labor, but no one ever spoke. He watched and observed the guards with causal side-glances while he copied the actions of the other prisoners. To escape, he understood he'd be alone in such an attempt since the others were controlled to total silence. Even if he spoke to them, none could assist him. He doubted they'd hear his words at all.

An odd groan caught his attention. Using peripheral vision, Magnus noticed a miner drop his shovel. The man clamped his hands to the sides of his head. His eyes bulged. His face flushed red, his head shook, and he screamed. His loud scream could be heard over the thundering machines. Although concerned about the man, Magnus kept shoveling like the other unalarmed prisoners. While scooping shovels of dirt, he watched the crazed miner without turning his head. It was difficult fighting his curiosity, but he'd trained himself to never react out of haste. Remaining somber didn't alert the guards that he wasn't controlled like his coworkers. He was safer doing what the other zombie-like prisoners did.

The wild-eyed miner stepped out of the line. Froth foamed at the sides of his mouth, and without any further hesitation, he tore into a sprint.

The guard closest to this prisoner punched buttons on a small handheld device, rather than attempting to physically stop the man or shoot him.

Guards along the perimeter raised their rifles. But before they captured him within their sights, the miner ran headlong, driven by pain, and flung himself over the ledge into the waste pit below. Magnus didn't have to see the man's body to know the man was dead. The drop to the bottom was over fifty feet. This sudden drama didn't draw any attention from the miners working around him, either.

"Dammit!" A guard shouted into his jacket transmitter. "Jenner! We've had another Sleeper Chip malfunction!"

"Copy that, Eddings," Jenner replied. "I'm on my way."

Sleeper Chip? Is that what they call it? Magnus kept his head down and kept shoveling.

Eddings stood at the ledge, overlooking the pit. Jenner ran through the line of miners and stopped beside Eddings. He peered down at the bottom of the pit and shook his head.

"That's the second one this week," Eddings said.

Jenner nodded. "I know. The upgraded chips have been shipped from Earth, but it'll be months before they arrive."

"That may be too late. If every chip malfunctions, we'll lose control of the prisoners. We're already outnumbered six to one. Without these chips, there'll be no way to keep the prisoners in check. We'll be dead."

"Let's hope these chips hold out until the new ones arrive."

An emergency alarm wailed, followed by the command, "Guards, send all prisoners to their cells."

When the alert echoed through the mining shaft, perimeter guards pulled out handheld computer devices and typed commands into them. The prisoners dropped their picks and shovels. Magnus assumed the small devices sent radio frequency commands to the Sleeper Chips, which signaled direct commands to the prisoners.

He dropped his shovel and stepped into the long single line. While they marched to their cells, Magnus stared straight ahead, imitating the other prisoners. He wondered about these *Sleeper* Chips and the programmers that controlled them.

When Magnus had been a Texas state prisoner, he and other inmates were offered work releases from their sentences if they chose to work on Mars. To become the first inhabitants of the red planet, even as miners, seemed more an honor than a punishment. They were informed that they would have tracer chips implanted so they could be tracked, in case any of them escaped. The last thing on Earth he remembered was being taken to the infirmary to have the tracer chip implanted at the base of his skull. Apparently, the tracer chips were *more* than ordinary tracking devices.

Although the question lingered in his mind, he guessed these chips were responsible for the near zombie comatose actions of the miners. How else could people maintain the muscle-straining deterioration caused by mining nearly twelve hours a day with only a short lunch break? Without their mental faculties, the miners would never revolt. Hell, they couldn't even complain. They had no idea of their aches and fatigue. And what disturbed Magnus even more was the amount of control the guards held over the prisoners, and to what extent they used such power.

After the prisoners entered the long corridor, Magnus stopped at the third cell on the right and waited. The thick glass door to his cell opened. He walked into his tiny room, stood at attention, and waited until the door closed. Once the door hissed shut, he released a long sigh, his shoulders slumped, and he nearly collapsed from exhaustion. His tight shoulders, arms, and the back of his neck pulsed with muscle spasms. Heat radiated off his skin. His lower back hurt in ways he couldn't adequately describe in words. The thought of sleep tempted him, but a heated shower was even more inviting. Not only would the hot water soothe his aching muscles, he could wash away the sweat and grime embedded into his pores.

His thick hands were covered with old callouses and new blisters. Grit was packed beneath his cracked, chipped fingernails. It hurt to close his hands into fists.

From beneath the bed, soft chattering arose. A pink nose poked from the edge and little narrow eyes stared with excitement.

"Digger," Magnus said with a chuckle. After a couple of seconds, the critter slinked across the floor and nuzzled against his muddy pants leg.

He pulled a bent metal can out of his pocket. "I saved you some tuna, Digger."

The gray-striped ferret chattered. Magnus placed the can on the floor beside his bunk. Digger licked the tuna juice and nibbled the meat.

Magnus arched his back. Several loud pops ran along his spine. He turned his head each direction and popped his neck. After stretching, he sat on the edge of the bunk and rubbed his aching right shoulder. He smiled at the ferret. It was nice to have something to talk to after his long day of mining, especially since none of the other miners spoke. Of course, Digger didn't *talk* but he was good at listening and soothing to pet.

"Sure am glad I found you," Magnus said. "Man, I hurt all over. I don't know how much longer I can keep doing this."

Digger busily lapped the tuna and juice from the can. The ferret never looked up. Instead, he devoured the food.

Magnus smiled and laughed. "Don't you worry. It's all yours. No one's going to fight you over it."

The ferret had come through a hole into his cell the previous day, and the best Magnus could guess, the electricians were using ferrets to run electrical line from room to room and through narrow places where humans couldn't possibly fit. Apparently Digger broke free of the harness line attached to his collar and never turned back.

"At least you got free of your captors, buddy."

Magnus placed his elbows on his knees and rested his head in his hands. After a few moments, he closed his eyes and rubbed them. He drifted between sleep and reality.

"I've got to find a way to escape and get back to Earth, Digger. Neither of us belongs here."

The ferret looked up and regarded him for a moment with an inquisitive stare.

Magnus laughed. "Don't worry, Digger. I ain't leaving you behind. You're coming, too. They probably worked you as hard as us miners, didn't they? No telling how much electrical line you ran through these tunnels, but we're going to get out of here somehow."

He picked Digger up, stroked the back of his neck, and then he looked into its eyes. The ferret rubbed its nose against his massive hand. He scratched between the ferret's ears, and Digger closed his eyes. "Oh, you like that, don't you, boy?"

Dark shadows moved outside the glass door. Magnus tucked the ferret under his bunk. "Stay under there and don't move. We have visitors."

The only people that roamed the halls were guards, but none patrolled after the prisoners were locked inside their cells. He wondered why they were there. The ferret? Had they come to take Digger?

Sadness crept into Magnus' heart. His eyes moistened for a moment, but he fought to regain his composure. Any slip of emotion when the guards entered his cell might give him away. He couldn't allow that. He swallowed, took in a deep breath, and exhaled slowly. Then he relaxed. Seated on the edge of the bed, he focused his attention on the door.

He gave the same blank stare like he did while mining and waited for the door to open.

Chapter 3

The prisoner cell doors were secured with three different locks, but only one needed to be unlocked to open the door. Two locks were electronic—a computer panel that required a code, or a magnetic swipe card—and one deadbolt lock that required a key. Occasionally the electrical conduits and connectors flickered off, causing a loss of power. To prevent prisoners and guards from being locked inside a room, the bolt locks remained a necessity. Staff, mechanics, and other personal could use a palm-print scanner to access their own rooms.

Outside Magnus' door, two guards stopped. Cain, the taller of the two, lifted his mirrored face-guard and looked at Matt, who held a computer notebook.

Cain said, "You sure this is the right room?"

Matt looked at the cell number and then the notebook. He nodded. "Yes. Magnus Knight. Computer shows his chip has malfunctioned. We need to take him to the infirmary to have it replaced."

"Door code?"

"9-3-5-8. Or use your key card."

Cain shrugged and typed the numbers on the keypad. The door opened with a hiss.

"This shouldn't take long," Matt said, looking at his computer notebook.

DIGGER STUCK his nose out from between Magnus' large boots. Magnus gently pushed Digger beneath the bunk and put his feet together to keep the ferret hidden.

The door opened.

"Dammit," Magnus whispered.

The two guards stepped into the cell, and Magnus stared ahead blankly, unblinking.

Matt frowned when he looked at Magnus. "His chip seems to be working fine. What do you think?"

"Yep, he looks as dumb as the rest of the miners." Cain laughed and waved his hand before Magnus' eyes. Magnus didn't blink. "You think the computer made a mistake?"

"Doubtful, but someone may have categorized another prisoner's chip number as his by accident."

Matt shook his head. "Damn. If that's the case, it'll take hours to find the right prisoner."

"I know. That'd delay my later plans."

"With Jessica?" Matt asked with a sly grin.

"Oh, you know it."

Cain reached to take Magnus' right wrist. Digger chattered and scampered past Magnus' boots and across the floor.

"Hey!" Cain said, "That's the ferret the electrical engineers are looking for. How'd he get in here?"

Matt shrugged. "There's no telling. Grab it!"

Cain ran after the ferret. A few seconds later, he had cornered Digger. Cain's thick hand moved to grab the ferret, but Digger dodged and rolled into a ball. Cain grabbed Digger, and the ferret clamped its sharp teeth into the soft flesh between Cain's right thumb and index finger.

"Dammit! It bit me!"

He dropped Digger, and the ferret scampered away.

Matt reached for his laser pistol. "I got him, Cain."

Magnus leapt to his feet and yelled, "No!"

Matt's eyes widened. Before he could turn to aim the pistol at Magnus, Magnus' huge fist struck Matt in the chest and launched him in the air. He slammed against the wall and dropped unconscious on the floor.

With blood dripping from his hand, Cain pulled his gun, but Magnus moved extremely fast to be such a large man. Magnus knocked the gun to the floor and punched Cain hard in the gut. The air expelled from the guard's lungs, sending him to his knees. He leaned forward on his hands and knees, heaving for air, and his face flushed dark red. The veins in his forehead swelled.

He gasped and sputtered. He placed his hand against his throat, and his eyes filled with fear. The man couldn't breathe.

"Oh, God," Magnus whispered. He rushed to Cain and patted his back, trying to help Cain breathe. "Relax, man. Give it a few seconds. You'll be okay."

Drool dripped from Cain's mouth. He shook his head. Magnus formed a fist and pounded the center of Cain's back several times. He took in another sharp breath, panted, took another breath, and finally, his breathing started to stabilize.

"See?" Magnus said. "You're going to be okay."

"You son of a bitch," Cain said between breaths. He forced himself to his feet and scrambled to get the gun off the floor.

Before Cain reached the gun, Magnus tackled him. Cain groaned. In spite of Magnus' massive size and weight, Cain continued to reach for the gun.

"Get... off... me," Cain said.

"Afraid I can't do that, sir," Magnus said.

Cain stretched until his fingers touched the laser pistol. Magnus slapped the gun away. It spun across the floor and skidded to the edge of the bunk. In desperation, Cain swung his elbow and almost struck Magnus' jaw.

Magnus shook his head. "I can see there's no point trying to reason with you."

"You're a prisoner. I have no desire to discuss *anything* with you. Now, get the hell off!"

Cain struggled to work free of Magnus' incredible grip but wasn't successful. Cain's eyes stared past Magnus and then Cain smiled.

"My gun's there," Cain stammered. "By the bed."

Magnus glanced over his shoulder and noticed Matt trying to stand.

"I tried to help you," Magnus said. "You probably would've died if I hadn't."

"Hurry, Matt!"

Magnus shook his head. His huge fist came down and knocked Cain unconscious. Magnus rolled and came to his feet before Matt fully gained his balance.

"Sorry about this," Magnus said, staring into Matt's frightened eyes. Magnus swung a hard right. Matt slumped to the floor a second time. Magnus shook his fist from the pain and grimaced.

Digger cautiously crept from beneath the bed and chattered.

"Sorry you had to see that, Digger."

Magnus grabbed Matt's ankles and dragged his body into the small shower stall.

"Damn," he said. "So much for taking a hot shower."

He returned and took Cain by the shoulders and pulled him into the bathroom. Since Cain was the larger of the two guards, Magnus stripped off the man's uniform. Even though Cain was larger than Matt, Cain was still *much* smaller than Magnus.

Magnus slipped into the coverall uniform and zipped up the front. The uniform was tight but manageable. Searching through the front pockets, he found a set of handcuffs and the security key card for the doors. He searched the other guard's pockets and removed his set of cuffs. After several minutes, he placed the two men back to back and cuffed their hands together. He stuffed their mouths with socks.

Even if they awakened, they'd have a nearly impossible time of maneuvering to get out of the tiny shower, so they couldn't get to the door. He hoped that gave him enough time to find a way back to Earth, which seemed quite an impossible feat in itself.

Magnus ran water in the sink, soaked a towel, and quickly washed the mud and grime from his face, neck, hands, and arms. Removing the dirt from the most visible areas prevented someone from readily concluding that he was an escaped miner. He paused for a moment while washing the thick red dirt from his neck. Turning his head slightly to the left, he noticed the slight bulge at the base of his skull. He ran a finger across it. A Sleeper Chip? According to the two guards, his had malfunctioned, which explained *why* he was awake and no longer a mental prisoner to the control devices the guards carried.

Thinking about the man that had flung himself into the mining pit, he wondered why he had not undergone a similar fate. And why had it taken the guards two days to realize his chip had stopped working?

He shrugged and washed away more Martian soil. He reached to turn off the water and noticed his grimy fingers. No guard's hands were this filthy. All it took was for one person to notice the reddish muck coating his hands and fingers to draw immediate suspicion. He couldn't deny he was a miner. The evidence damned him.

Magnus stuck his hands under the faucet. The cool water stung his cracked skin and the runny blisters. Even his fingernails ached when the water broke away the grit from beneath them. In spite of the pain, he washed off as much dirt and grime as possible. After drying his hands, he examined them. The swollen cuts and blisters needed some antibacterial ointment, but he didn't know where he might find some.

Glancing at the shower, Magnus realized he needed to hurry. Time was not a factor in his favor. Eventually guards or supervisors would start looking for these two guards. He didn't have many options and little time to act.

Although the area outside Olympus Mons was undergoing terraformation by the introduction of hardy plants capable of adapting to the Martian environment, the terrain was still too harsh for humans to survive without wearing habitat spacesuits. The oxygen levels weren't high enough to travel without an oxygen pack, which greatly limited the distance one could travel outside Olympus Mons. And food? Nothing was edible on the planet except for packaged processed foods. Once he left the mines, access to the food packets was gone.

Magnus picked up Digger. "Come on. We can't stay here."

Digger tilted his head and looked at him.

"How should I know where we'll go?" he asked. "*You* know the corridors better than I do."

Magnus took Cain's helmet off the floor and squeezed it over his head. It was too tight, but he needed to disguise himself the best he could. Before Magnus swiped the key card to open the door, he noticed his reflection on the thick glass. He looked ridiculous. The uniform was tighter than he imagined, and should he happen to approach another guard, he was certain to be stopped and questioned about the size of his uniform.

The snug sleeves pinched into his biceps whenever he bent his arms. One wrong move and he'd probably split the seams along his shoulders, down his arms, and across his chest. He tried holding in his muscled stomach, but even that didn't help.

Magnus swiped the key card and the door hissed open. Before stepping into the corridor, he looked both directions. Confident the long pathway was clear, he stepped out. He placed Digger inside the pouch pocket. The ferret curled into a ball and went to sleep.

Uncertain where to go, Magnus followed the corridor in the opposite direction of the mines. He marveled at the polished round corridor where the tunnel-drilling machines had bore out the passages that now housed prisoners. The red walls were smooth like glass. Anchored on the ceiling about every twenty feet were LED lights. Whenever the lights struck the walls at the right angle, the embedded MarQuebes glittered. He placed his huge hand against one and shook his head. These gems were what the prisoners slaved away and killed themselves for in the mines.

Around a sharp bend in the hallway, a glass door shook and rattled. Magnus stopped. The floor beneath him wasn't vibrating, so it wasn't a tremor. However, the glass door continued rattling. He eased closer and noticed the door kept changing colors—from silver to blue to green to red and alternated in different flashing patterns. Over the entrance—which *wasn't* a prison cell with a narrow door but a much wider set of doors—was a sign: **The Vortex**. His curiosity got the best of him, so he slid the guard's key card through the reader.

The doors hissed opened, and he walked inside.

Hard rock music pulsed. He shook his head. Dozens of people, off duty guards and staff members he assumed, were dancing. Along the left side of the room was a large bar with a long beveled mirror behind it. Two rows of various whiskies, vodkas, and tonics set beneath the mirror. A few of the bartenders poured quick shots for the people seated at the polished bar while another bartender grinned and talked to a young lady seated on a tall stool.

Off duty men and women drank and laughed while others danced mindlessly to the music. Those who drank heavily were already staggering. The dancers were lost in their moves, probably letting their minds drift back home to Earth. At least that's what he guessed. While mining was rigorous for him, since he awakened, the other prisoners weren't even aware of their labor. The guards had nothing to do because the prisoners were like machines and didn't require much attention. In a way, the prisoners seemed better off than the guards because they were oblivious to their surroundings.

Magnus watched a bartender pour a quick shot for a guard slouched against the bar. The man downed it. Magnus hadn't drunk any liquor in over a year. After the unusual day he'd experienced, plus his aches and pains, the timing couldn't be better. He stepped past a couple of dancers and walked to the bar. None of the dancing males and females paid him any mind.

Magnus grinned, sat on a bar stool, and ordered a shot of whiskey.

Chapter 4

Olympus Mons

BEFORE THE SHUTTLE neared the landing bay doors, Dr. Carter pulled his visor down. Harvey usually made the bimonthly trips to Mars for supplies, so no one expected Carter's arrival and he planned to keep anonymity.

Carter's role as Deimos' chief medical examiner required him to be on duty 24/7. Seldom was he allowed the luxury to visit and seek entertainment at Olympus Mons. Not that the getaway mattered, because he and Wanda shared private moments whenever time allowed. But now she was gone.

The landing bay doors opened. Carter's fingers tightened around the metal briefcase handle. He was thankful the computer was the flight navigator, so he didn't worry about crashing the shuttle during landing.

It was a shame the shuttle couldn't make the entire flight to Earth. Had it been capable, he'd have made the journey. The flight to Earth took approximately seven months. He didn't have enough provisions on Deimos to sustain such a journey, and the small shuttle wasn't insulated properly to shield for longer periods of radiation. The ship certainly didn't have enough fuel or oxygen to last more than a few days.

When the shuttle docked inside the landing bay, Carter waited for the cockpit signal to flash and the shuttle door to unlock. After the lock unsealed, he flipped the door lever and pushed it open. He stepped out, kept his visor down, and headed for the corridor on the other side of the bay.

Standing near the computer panels, a brown-haired woman watched his approach. She stood five-four, and her brown curly hair flowed down her back. Her mechanic jumpsuit didn't diminish her athletic figure. Her brown eyes studied him with skepticism.

Carter pretended he didn't see her, so he didn't pause his stride as he walked past.

"Wait," she said. "Harvey! You forgot to sign—"

Carter stopped and turned slowly.

Following him, she lifted a clipboard and presented it. "You forgot to sign the landing chart."

Frustrated, Carter lifted his face-guard. "I didn't forget."

"Dr. Carter?" she said with a surprised, interested smile. Her eyes brightened.

"Hi, Sylvia. It's been a while," Carter said in a low voice. He flashed a flirty grin and a quick wink.

Sylvia's freckled face reddened as she flipped back her hair. "I certainly didn't expect to see *you*. Why didn't Harvey fly the shuttle?"

Carter leaned close and placed a finger to his lips. "Shh. No one must know I'm here. Understand?"

She shook her head. Her brown eyes studied his with keen interest. "No. Why the big secret?"

In a hushed voice, Carter said, "I can't tell you here. The mechanics and guards might hear."

"So?"

"I can't. Okay?"

Sylvia glanced at her watch and nodded. "Okay. My shift ended fifteen minutes ago. Come to my room. It's quiet. We can talk without worrying about anyone hearing."

Carter nodded and lowered his face-guard.

THE VORTEX

MAGNUS SAT at the bar with his mirrored face-guard partially raised. Even though the suit was three sizes too small, no one seemed to notice him. It was hard for him to accept that he sat in their midst without being seen. They were more interested in drinking, dancing, and playing board games or cards than anything else. He felt like an invisible giant.

He took another shot of whiskey and tilted it back. The warmth ran down his dry sore throat, which eased the pain a bit. Hours of shoveling red dirt caused him to cough up muddy phlegm, which was another reason he wanted to leave Mars. Even a healthy, muscular man like himself couldn't maintain the toil he and the miners suffered. Most of the men laboring beside him in the mine looked aged, tired, and frail. He reasoned the intense labor, without adequate rest, played a significant role. None of the men chosen for such tasks were weak and frail. Their intense labor beat them down, lowering their immune systems. Constantly breathing in the dust and grit wasn't healthy, either.

After Magnus downed his third shot, he felt less pain from the grueling labor he'd endured for weeks. His mind relaxed, too, which was something he longed for. But he knew this effect was short-lived. He needed to be on the move soon, find a shuttle to stowaway on, and head home. The longer he waited in one place, the easier it was for them to find him.

He tilted his head from left to right until his neck popped several times. He sighed from the relief. How long would it take for his muscles to loosen after the countless long hours of rigorous mining? Although the chips prevented miners from feeling pain, it didn't alleviate overworked muscles from possibly tearing or spraining. The wear and tear continued, regardless if they had any knowledge of their labor. Whenever injuries occurred, there wasn't any work stoppage. They shoveled or swung picks until a guard noticed a miner's trauma, provided they ever noticed at all.

The only pain radiating through Magnus now was the blaring music from the large speakers. He was glad to have the numbing shots of whiskey, but he couldn't stay in this bar much longer. The angering beat blasting and bouncing off the walls grated his nerves. If he allowed that to continue, his aggravation might make him too edgy to tolerate even the minor annoyances of potential drunks asking too many questions.

For his safety and perhaps that of others, Magnus decided to leave The Vortex to explore the corridors. The only places he had seen until his discovery of The Vortex were the mines and his small prison cell. He wondered what else he might learn about the prison planet.

He stood and headed for the door.

"Hey!" the barkeeper said. "Pay your tab!"

"Sorry," Magnus said, returning to the bar. His hands grew wet with sweat. He didn't fear the man because Magnus was twice the barkeep's size. Few men ever intimidated him. However, he couldn't afford any direct attention from the patrons seated around the bar. Off duty guards and officers were armed. Should an argument catch their attention, they might quickly identify him as not one of their own.

Nervously, Magnus wiped his hands on the uniform. He wasn't sure how to pay the bill. He stood at the edge of the bar and put his hands inside his pouch pocket where Digger slept.

"What's your problem?" the barkeeper asked. "You haven't drank *that* much. Your badge."

"Huh?"

"Let me scan your badge."

"Oh!" Magnus said, handing it to the barkeeper. "Sorry about that. It's been one of those days."

The man ran the card through the scanner. "There. See? Cain Meadows?" The barkeep suspiciously looked at Magnus for a long moment before handing back the badge.

Magnus slid the badge in his pocket and turned to leave.

"Cain?"

Magnus paused and looked over his shoulder.

"You putting on some weight or something?"

"They gave me the wrong size uniforms this week."

The barkeeper laughed. "Yeah, go with that. That'd be *my* excuse, too."

Magnus frowned. "It's true. And it hurts like a mother in some places."

"I imagine so," the man said with a slight grimace. "I guess you're near to busting out the seams."

Magnus feigned a laugh and walked to the door. Talking too much would definitely give him away, especially if this man actually *knew* Cain personally. The barkeep would figure out the ruse within the matter of minutes. It was best for Magnus to stay away from people, if he could help it.

Outside in the corridor, he decided to keep going farther from the mines and the prison cells.

The narrow corridor broadened into a wider area that looked like the construction crew might eventually drill an intersecting corridor to function as a crossroads, which would open more mining pits, prison cells, and storage facilities. The two sides not yet completed were dark and unlit. The voices of a man and woman approached beyond the unfinished intersection, so Magnus darted into the shadows to avoid being seen.

Chapter 5

"I need to return to Earth," Carter said, glancing at Sylvia.

Sylvia laughed. "Don't we all?"

"I'm serious, Sylvia. I need to return immediately without anyone learning of my departure."

She stopped walking. Her smile faded, and her brown eyes narrowed with concern. "Why? What's wrong?"

"Everyone on Deimos is dead."

"What?"

Carter placed a finger to his lips and shushed her.

"You're serious?" she whispered.

He nodded and looked away, remorseful.

"How, Carter?" she asked. "What happened?"

"A deadly virus killed them all."

"God, really?"

"Yes."

Sylvia took his resistant hand into both of hers. She squeezed. Nervously, he looked at her.

She asked, "How'd you survive?"

"Good fortune, I suppose. For some reason, I'm immune to the disease."

The pain in his eyes brought tears to hers.

"I'm so sorry, Carter," she said. "To see everyone around you die... God, I have no idea how to cope with that."

Carter closed his eyes and shook his head. "To be honest, I don't know that I'll ever recover."

"Come on," she said softly. "My room's down the next corridor."

Carter and Sylvia headed down the tunnel. After they passed where Magnus hid in the dark crevice, he crept out and followed from a distance where he could still hear their conversation without them noticing him.

Sylvia asked, "Why do you want to return to Earth without anyone knowing?"

"I can't leave Deimos for three more years," he said.

"Why not?"

"My contract with Grayson Enterprises doesn't expire until then."

"Mine's much longer than that," she replied. "But due to the circumstances, can't you request a temporary reprieve on your contract?"

Carter chuckled. "With Grayson? Are you serious?"

Sylvia shrugged. "It doesn't hurt to ask, does it? You're not a prisoner, after all."

"Our contracts bind us here. I've found no loopholes in the legal jargon, so we might as well consider ourselves prisoners."

"I never looked at it like that because I'm serving out my sentence as a mechanic. But, the boredom gets to me sometimes."

"I know. When Grayson first hired me, I was so excited," Carter said. "To live so far from Earth and actually see our home planet in the night sky... I fantasized about that as a kid. And for a while, I loved my job and its duties. I truly did. But after everyone on Deimos died, I've no desire to stay. To be free of my contract, Grayson needs to think I died with all the others."

"Take me to Earth with you."

"What?" Carter shook his head. "I can't."

"Why not?"

"I'll have a hard enough time escaping by myself."

She smiled. "I know the landing bay's layout and controls quite well. You'll *need* me to get aboard an earthbound shuttle."

"I don't know," Carter replied.

Sylvia stopped outside a frosted glass door. With an air of excitement, she said, "We're here. This is my room. But before you say no to taking me with you, please hear me out."

She squeezed his hand and slowly released it. She stared into his dark eyes until he finally nodded.

"Okay."

"Good," she said.

Sylvia pressed her hand against an identification scanner to open her door. "Come in and let's figure out a way we both can escape."

Carter followed her into the room. The door slid shut.

From the shadows, Magnus stepped outside Sylvia's door and leaned closer to listen.

SYLVIA'S CHAMBERS resembled a small studio apartment, except the walls were carved out of the drab volcano. Fewer MarQuebes were polished in her walls. She grabbed a pair of sweat pants and a sweatshirt from a drawer and walked across the room to change. Carter sat on the edge of her bunk with the silver briefcase resting on his lap.

She slipped out of her mechanic jumpsuit, stood in her underwear, and smiled over her shoulder at Carter to see if he was checking her out. His attention focused on the briefcase. She sighed with awkward disappointment.

On the three previous occasions she'd seen Carter in the landing bay, she found herself attracted to him. She liked his chiseled chin, his dark eyes, and his self-confidence. Although they never exchanged more than cordial greetings, the occasional look of possible intimate interest between them intensified each time he visited. She was drawn to his charisma. His mannerisms were more gracious than her coworkers and he never displayed a judgmental attitude of her status.

Seeing his evident pain, Sylvia wanted to ease his mind and her loneliness. While she smiled at him, wearing only her bra and panties, the chemistry she hoped to find didn't materialize. Most men would've considered her actions an obvious invitation for intimate exchanges, but Carter didn't glance her direction.

His dark eyes didn't reflect an interest in pursuing more than causal conversation about returning to Earth. His haunted eyes revealed more important matters pressed on his mind. With all he'd suffered on Deimos, she understood.

Embarrassed by the awkwardness she placed herself in, she dressed quickly and stepped closer to the bed. "Okay, let's say you decide not to take me. How do you plan to escape from Mars and return to Earth?"

He shrugged. "I'm not certain. Do you have suggestions?"

"Of course, but they all include *me* leaving with you."

"I'm serious."

"So am I. Getting aboard a shuttle without being seen or shot by the guards is our biggest challenge." She pulled her hair into a ponytail.

"I assumed *that* much."

Sylvia smiled. "You don't understand. Personnel shuttles from Mars to Earth leave once a month. The ore cargo ships leave for Earth twice a week."

"Perhaps we should leave on a cargo ship instead of a shuttle."

She shook her head and grinned. "Nope. That's impossible. Cargo ships are computer operated. No pilot. No seating compartments at all."

"So?"

"It's a seven month trip. Cargo ships don't have oxygen, food, or cabins."

Carter sighed. "Okay, so when does the next shuttle leave?"

A sly smile crossed her face. Excitement grew in her voice. "You're in luck! Tomorrow. Several of our top officials are set to return to Earth at Grayson's request. To board requires a high clearance badge and *you* have one."

"I can't use mine without Grayson knowing I'm still alive."

"A simple solution."

"What?"

"Why not inform Grayson about the viral outbreak? I'm sure he'd reassign you to another post, or quite possibly renegotiate your contract due to traumatic stress. Actually, that qualifies as PTSD."

Carter shook his head. "No. He'd cover it up. He's probably preparing more men and women to be flown to Deimos anyway. Besides, I don't want him to know I'm coming."

"Why not?"

"It's personal. He must suffer the consequences for the deaths on Deimos."

She frowned. "How do you plan to do that?"

"There are ways."

"So you're plotting revenge?" she asked.

A man's shadow moved on the other side of her door.

Carter rose. "Someone's outside your door."

Concern furrowed her brow.

"You expecting anyone?"

She shook her head. "No."

The door hissed opened. Sylvia gasped. Magnus entered wearing the tight helmet with the visor down. Seeing the guard uniform, Carter shook his head in disbelief and looked at her with an astonished, hurt expression.

"You set me up? How could you?"

"No," she replied, moving to stand beside him. "Honestly, I don't know *why* he's here. I want to leave Mars, too. So—"

"As do I," Magnus said in a deep voice. He struggled and finally pried the tight helmet off his head. "Perhaps I can assist you."

Sylvia stared at Magnus with suspicion. "You're a guard. Why would you want to help us?"

Magnus laughed softly. "Actually, I'm a prisoner."

"If you're a prisoner," Carter said, frowning. "How'd you get that uniform?"

Magnus unzipped the front of the jacket. Digger poked his head out and looked around. "It's a long story, but to save little Digger, I had to knock two guards unconscious. I took this uniform from one of them."

Digger slinked from the pocket and stepped onto Magnus' huge hands.

"Oh," Sylvia said, "he's so cute! May I?"

He nodded and handed Digger to her. "Take him to the shower and turn on the water. He loves that."

"Really?"

Magnus nodded.

"Okay," she said with a broad smile.

Carter sat on the bed. "You're wanting to return to Earth, too?"

"Yes."

"If you leave," Carter said, "you'll forfeit your work release contract with Grayson Enterprises."

Magnus chuckled, shook his head, and sighed. "The work release is bogus bullshit, man. No prisoner will live long enough to ever claim their freedom on Mars."

"What do you mean?" Sylvia asked. "There are a hundred prisoners in the mines. Our contracts grant us freedom and property ownership once we fulfill our obligations."

"It'll never happen," Magnus replied.

She frowned. "I don't understand."

He smiled. "Well, we're all prisoners in more than one way. Whether or not we choose to accept it."

"I don't follow, either," Carter said.

Magnus pointed at the base of his skull behind his right ear. "Look. Right behind my ear."

Carter rose and looked at the small lump. He inspected the bulge by rubbing two fingers across it. "What's that?"

"When we were prepped to board the ships to Mars, they told us they were placing tracer chips in us, in case anyone escaped after we arrived. They could find us easier."

"So it's a tracker chip?" Carter said.

"Technically, yes," Magnus replied. "That's what they *told* us. But it's not what they are. It does far more than simply track our location."

"I don't understand."

Magnus sighed. "Look, I don't know when I arrived on Mars, and I don't remember anything after the surgeons in Texas prepped me for the implantation. That is, until two days ago when this chip malfunctioned. I awakened to find myself mining."

"Malfunctioned?" Carter asked.

Sylvia frowned. "What do you mean by 'awakened'?"

Magnus nodded. "From what I've gathered, these chips control what actions the miners do. The guards use some kind of handheld devices and type in different commands to give us orders. Perhaps they originally used the chips to ensure no one revolted, but they're abusing the miners to increase work production with unauthorized, extremely long shifts. Twelve hours or more, by my estimation, but none of them even know what we're doing. After my chip stopped working, it was nearly impossible for me to keep up with the others."

"Have you talked to any of them?" Carter asked.

"The other prisoners? No. They don't talk or interact. They work like they're programmed to do without complaints. No obvious aches or pains. The chips override the brain's reasoning, which enables them to work past total exhaustion."

Carter rubbed his stubbled chin, deep in thought.

"You left Deimos, right?" Magnus asked.

Carter nodded.

"What about the prisoners there? Did they have chip implants?"

"I never spent a lot of time with the miners. Well, that is, until they contracted the virus."

"Nothing unusual about them?" Magnus asked.

"Now that I think about it, yes. Even during the most painful stage of the disease, they never voiced a complaint. They succumbed to fever and pneumonia but never complained or even talked. They withered away but seemed to do so peacefully."

"And you didn't think that was *odd*?"

Carter shrugged. "Not at the time because I knew they were hardened prisoners. I simply thought they were tougher than the rest of us."

"No one's *that* tough."

Carter ran a hand through his black hair. "I suppose not. But this explains a lot about how the disease spread so quickly."

"How's that?"

"If they were controlled by chips, the prisoners kept working even after they were infected. By the time guards noticed the prisoners' infections and sent them to the infirmary, they were already contagious. Ordinarily they'd have been quarantined, but the infirmary never received them until after we knew they had the virus."

"The chips are apparently programmed to suppress pain and resistance to authority," Magnus said.

"Their medical charts didn't contain a record of when they received these chips," Carter said. "Not that I found, but I was more concerned with their previous vaccinations and prescriptions."

"Another chip malfunctioned earlier today," Magnus said. "It didn't end well for the man."

"What happened?"

Magnus explained the man's extreme pain and how he hurled himself into the mining pit, apparently to rid his agony. "The only good thing was it shut down the mines for the remainder of the shift. Honestly, I don't think I could've kept going much longer."

"I don't understand how you survived a few hours," Carter said. "And you *really* don't remember boarding the shuttle to Mars?"

"I don't remember *leaving* the prison infirmary."

"What's the last thing you do remember before they implanted a chip into you?" Carter asked. "Did anything unusual happen?"

Magnus' eyes searched as he thought. Finally, he nodded. "About a week before I was chosen for the Mars work/release program, a man came to the prison and requested to see me. I'd never seen him before. He never gave his name. He told the guards he was my new attorney, which was a lie, but it got him inside to see me."

"What did he want?"

"He offered me a warning."

Carter frowned. "A warning? For what?"

"Somehow he knew about these programmer chips. He promised to prevent them from controlling me."

"How?"

"He brought an expensive leather briefcase. I thought he might have papers and files about my court case records. Instead, he opened the case and showed me a syringe. He told me the injection would prevent the chip from exerting mind control over me."

Carter took in the information. "Any idea what was in the syringe?"

"He said it contained microchips that would short out the control chip."

Carter looked at Magnus incredulously. "And you *let* him inject you?"

Magnus shrugged his massive shoulders. "At the time, I didn't figure I had much choice. Besides, what else did I have to lose? I was in prison serving a life sentence. If the injection killed me, that's an early parole."

Carter smiled. "That's one way to look at it. This man must've had some credentials to convince the guards he was your attorney, wouldn't he?"

"You'd think so. The only things he had were his expensive suit and the briefcase. I guess since he *looked* and acted like an attorney, they didn't do any additional background checking."

Carter chuckled softly. "So apparently, the injection worked."

"Yep. Next thing I know," Magnus said. "I'm shoveling red Martian dirt and free of the chip's control."

"So you've not been controlled for two days?"

"That's right."

"How have the guards not noticed?" Carter asked.

"I'm good at playing dumb, I guess. I noticed how the miners closest to me behaved, so I kept doing what they were doing. The hardest part was trying to maintain their pace. Almost felt like I was going to die a couple of times."

"I can't imagine."

"You'll see. Once we're close to where they're digging, watch how they behave. The wear and tear of their demanding schedule is killing them, but they haven't any idea. Most look twenty years older than they actually are. Hell, I already look five years older than when I left Earth, but I *feel* thirty years older. My muscles and joints ache so deeply that I wonder if I'll ever gain full mobility again."

"So you must have done one hell of a performance to keep the guards in the dark."

Magnus gave a slight nod. "I did. But after my chip malfunctioned, the main computer sent a report showing it'd lost my signal. That's why the two guards came to my cell tonight. They were going to have a new chip replace this one. When one guard tried to kill Digger, I had to stop them."

Sylvia's laughter echoed in the shower. "He does love the water!"

"Told you he did," Magnus replied in his deep, rich baritone.

"Why would they want to kill the ferret?" Carter asked.

"I'm not certain they were actually going to kill him. One of the men tried to catch Digger, and Digger bit him. The other guard reached for his gun, so I stopped them before they overreacted. They seemed a bit trigger happy."

"Can't blame you for that."

Magnus smiled and his eyes softened for a moment. "The little guy's been the only one I could talk to, before running into the two of you."

Sylvia giggled.

Carter studied Magnus' gentle eyes and demeanor. "Why you?"

"What do you mean?"

"Why'd this man choose you over all the other prisoners?"

Magnus replied, "Maybe he knows I'm innocent? I'm not sure. By helping me, I suspect he believes I'll help him destroy Grayson Enterprises."

"Is that what you plan to do?" Carter asked with interest.

"Well, not exactly. I want justice. I want the people who framed me to pay for their crimes. The only way that'll ever happen is if I get back to Earth."

"I see."

"*Why* do you want to go back?" Magnus asked. "I've heard bits and pieces of your conversation with Sylvia, but I'd like to hear it from you directly."

"All my friends and colleagues died on Deimos."

"From the virus?"

Carter nodded. "I'm the only one that survived."

"And you hold Grayson responsible?"

"Yes."

Magnus studied the coldness in Carter's eyes for a moment. "Why? He didn't cause their deaths."

"He should've researched the environment better. The virus came from the mines. That's why everyone died. And Wanda—" He choked back tears and looked away. "I lost her."

"I understand your loss and how resentment can fester from such tragic disasters. But how exactly do you plan to get revenge?"

Carter's hand rested on the briefcase. "I'd rather not go into the specifics yet. First and foremost, we need to steal a shuttle. That's the only way we can leave Mars."

Magnus nodded. "Agreed. There's another uniform in my room that should fit you."

Sylvia returned with Digger wrapped in a wet towel. She grinned at Magnus.

Carter looked at her. "Do you think we could pose as guards to get aboard the shuttle?"

"Guards seldom get on the shuttles," she replied. "It's rare. Being close to a shuttle would automatically draw scrutiny from the perimeter guards."

"Maybe," Magnus said. "But all we need is enough time to get aboard."

"They'd stop you before you ever got inside," Sylvia said.

"Then who's going to pilot the shuttle?" Magnus asked.

"Me," she said. Her eyes brightened with excitement. "I know how to set the controls and the coordinates."

"How do you know that?"

"I'm a mechanic, so I have access to all the manuals. When I'm not repairing something, I spend a lot of time reading those books."

Her statement caught Magnus' immediate attention. "Since you're a mechanic, could you get Carter and myself some mechanic coveralls?"

"Sure. Why?"

"Guards might draw suspicion by being near a shuttle, but a group of mechanics wouldn't."

Her smile widened. "That's true. But you'll need the guard uniforms to get into the storage room at the landing bay. That's where they keep the jumpsuits. You'll want to blend in, so disguising as mechanics is a great idea."

Carter rested his elbows on the briefcase. "Dressed like mechanics, we won't have a problem getting to the shuttle, but once we reach Earth, we're going to need money."

"I have money I can access through an ATM when we land," Sylvia said.

"Using your earnings from here?" Carter asked.

She nodded.

"No. Any funds we've earned through Grayson Enterprises will be frozen. We won't have any access to whatever money Grayson's paid us."

Magnus said, "He's right."

Sylvia frowned. "Why?"

Carter replied, "Once we leave the landing bay, Grayson will know who took the ship, or at least he'll check the surveillance cameras to discover who we are. We'll be surrounded when we land in California. I guarantee that."

She smiled. "We *won't* have to be aboard the shuttle when it lands."

Carter frowned. "What?"

"Are you suggesting parachutes?" Magnus asked.

"There are emergency chutes, but there's never been a reason to use them. I can set the shuttle for autopilot and slow its velocity. When we reach the right altitude, we jump near a city where we can hide."

"That might work," Magnus said.

Carter nodded. "True. But it still leaves us stranded without money."

Magnus clapped his hands together with such force that both Carter and Sylvia jumped. He smiled. "I know how we can get more money than all three of us could ever earn from Grayson during our contracts."

"How?" they asked in unison.

"It's why the miners are slaving in the pits. It's what I was mining for. The MarQuebes. They're the most desired gems on Earth."

"Where do they keep them?" Carter asked.

"They're locked in the storage corridors on the other side of the mines. I've watched other workers push carts full of those stones down that corridor. And now I have a security key to get inside." Magnus grinned.

Carter frowned. "Are you certain that key will access the storage units?"

"I don't see why it won't," Magnus replied.

"There's always the chance the guards are only allowed access into certain areas based on their security levels."

"We won't know unless we try."

Carter sighed. "And if it doesn't, we're right back where we are now."

Magnus shrugged. "If we can't use the key, we'll brainstorm some more. We're bound to find a solution."

Carter looked at Sylvia. "Are there cameras in the corridors?"

She nodded. "Yes."

"It's a chance we have to take," Magnus said to Carter. "But you'll need the other guard's uniform in my cell."

Carter stood with the briefcase. "Then let's go get it."

Magnus smiled at Sylvia. "Do you mind taking care of Digger while we go?"

"Not at all," she said, scratching behind the ferret's ears. "It's nice to have a pet. We were supposed to get to place orders for cats and dogs, but our supervisors seem to have forgotten about that."

Carter shook his head and frowned. "I doubt the animals would survive the trip from Earth to Mars."

"That's true, I suppose."

"Thanks, Sylvia," Magnus said. "Come on, Carter."

Magnus opened the door, and he and Carter entered the hallway.

Chapter 6

Magnus and Carter stepped briskly, yet cautiously, along the corridor, hoping not to be seen by other patrols or off duty staff members. They didn't need any confrontations.

Carter wore his helmet with the visor partway up. Once he put on the other guard's uniform, they'd be less suspicious wandering through the corridors. However, that didn't make Magnus any more confident of going unseen.

According to Sylvia, surveillance cameras were along the corridors, but he didn't see any. Carter looked at the floor as he walked to avoid the chance of an overhead camera recording an image of his face.

Carter breathed rapidly, and completely lowered his visor. His hands trembled so badly Magnus wondered if the doctor might hyperventilate or pass out before he could get the suit. He looked like a frightened cat dropped inside a cage full of angry dogs.

"How far is your room?" Carter whispered.

"A ways yet."

Carter sighed. "I know wearing the suits will help conceal our identities, but shouldn't we take their guns, too?"

Magnus glanced at Carter. "Do you know how to use a gun?"

"No."

"There's your answer then. If you carry a gun, you'd best be prepared to use it. Without one, we won't be considered as hostile."

"Okay. I'm nervous. I've never done anything like this."

Magnus chuckled. "And you *think* I have?"

"Well, you are a prisoner."

"So?"

"Why were you in prison?"

Magnus shook his head and kept walking. "It's a long story. I'll tell you another time when we're not constantly looking over our shoulders."

Carter nodded. "Okay."

Magnus stepped to a smaller tunnel to the right. "Come on, let's go this way. It's quicker."

Carter followed without question. This narrow tunnel was darker, which comforted Magnus a bit more but seemed to set Carter on edge. His paranoia was getting the best of him. He brushed away invisible cobwebs, ducked when there weren't any obstructions, and gasped when he thought something had flown at him.

"Keep moving," Magnus whispered.

"I am. You're certain this path is safe?"

"Safer to keep us hidden from cameras and guards, but there's nothing here that should alarm us. Other than humans, there aren't other living creatures here."

"You never know."

"So you believe life might exist on Mars?"

"As a doctor and a scientist, I'd never rule it out," Carter said.

The short path circled around and led to the open mining pit. Magnus stopped at the edge of the door. His eyes widened with surprise.

"What is it?" Carter asked, in a near whisper.

"Here's where I mined. I never knew another shift worked after ours ended."

Carter edged beside Magnus where he could see.

Rows of miners swung picks while adjacent rows used shovels to scoop the loose volcanic soil. The sifter machines rattled and hummed. Large front loaders scooped the outer edges of the mine where drillers were carving out new passages.

Carter shook his head. "Damn."

"Yep. It's worse than my words described. But you're a medical doctor. I know it's hard to discern from this distance, but notice how none of these men ever slow their pace. They don't interact. Hell, even the guards are bored."

The patrols around the perimeter stood in pairs with their laser rifles slung over their shoulders. They talked in causal conversations, and some smoked. None were on high alert. And if any noticed Magnus and Carter, they never reacted to their presence.

"Come on," Magnus said. "We're almost there."

Magnus turned down a wider corridor where he walked daily and stopped outside his room. "Well, here it is. My palace."

They stepped inside the cell, and the doors shut.

Magnus walked to the shower and looked in the stall. The shorter man frowned with evident fury and spite. His face was flushed red from trying to yell for help while struggling with the cuffs. The other guard was still unconscious and not moving.

Magnus shook his head and looked at Carter. "I hit him a bit harder than I intended. Is he breathing?"

Carter knelt and felt for a pulse. "Yeah, he's breathing. His pulse is strong."

Magnus sighed. "Good."

Magnus got the keys to the handcuffs and leaned over the conscious guard. "I'm going to take the sock from your mouth. Unless you want to sleep like your friend there, I suggest you stay quiet. Understood?"

Matt's jaw clenched tightly and his eyes narrowed even more.

"Do you understand?"

Matt nodded.

"Good." Magnus pulled the sock free.

Matt said, "You're going to pay severely for this."

"Uh-uh!" Magnus said, pointing his huge thick finger. "Think about what I said, and look at Cain. I don't want to hit you again, but you best believe I will if you force me. Don't make me feel worse than I already do because he hasn't roused yet."

"You know you two are going to die for this, right?" Matt hissed. Spittle sprayed from his mouth.

Magnus formed a massive fist and reared back. Matt cowered and closed his eyes.

"That's better," Magnus said. "I'm unlocking your cuffs. One wrong move, and I'll drop you worse than I did before."

"All right. Fine. What do you want?"

"I want you to strip of your uniform and hand it to my friend there. That's it. Nothing more."

"Hell no!"

Magnus gave an even grin. His eyes narrowed. "Voluntarily or involuntarily, you'll give up that uniform."

Matt rose to his feet, glanced at Cain, and turned his cuffed wrists to Magnus. His eyes lost their hostility when Magnus neared and towered over him. A sense of renewed respect and fear reflected in the guard's eyes.

Magnus unlocked the cuffs and took a step back. He halfway expected Matt to attempt to fight or charge, but he didn't. He unzipped the uniform, slipped out of it, and placed his hands out to be re-cuffed.

"No, behind your back," Magnus said.

Matt obeyed.

Magnus clamped the cuffs tightly behind Matt's back, seated him against Cain, and then he interlocked Cain's cuffs around Matt's.

"Thanks for your cooperation," Magnus said with a smile.

Matt opened his mouth to reply, and Magnus stuffed the sock into Matt's mouth.

He patted Matt's cheek. "And I didn't even have to ask."

The look of contempt reclaimed Matt's gaze.

Magnus tossed the uniform to Carter. "Pull that over your clothes. We need to hurry before these men are reported missing. Once they're found in my cell, they'll begin searching for me."

Carter hurried and pulled on the uniform. Magnus handed the helmet to Carter. "Put this one on and lose your pilot helmet. Hurry up and let's go."

Chapter 7

Grayson Enterprises, California

SENATOR RALPH JOHNSON pulled his silver Cadillac with mirrored windows through the security gate. He drove along the winding blacktop to the rear parking lot until he reached his reserved parking spot.

The senator stepped from his car, brushed his pants with his hands, and closed the door. Pressing his thumb against the car security panel, he said, "Doors lock."

The doors audibly clicked into the locked position. The horn beeped and the computer set the alarm. Johnson nervously glanced at his golden Rolex, sighed, and walked up the concrete sidewalk.

God, he hated coming here, but only because of Boyd Grayson. Everything else about the property was pleasant, and if he came for any other reason, he'd have taken the time to enjoy the walk.

The sidewalk cut through a most brilliant, lavishly landscaped quad. Bright orange-red leaves on the spreading Japanese maples were breathtaking. The concrete path curved and meandered through a slender forest of weeping cherry trees, lilacs, palm trees, and hardy junipers. Two large brown squirrels bickered over a shriveled cherry, but dispersed when Johnson's hard-soled shoes clicked his approach.

In the entire glorious splendor of Grayson's landscape, Johnson held a bitter taste in his mouth. His stomach churned badly. Acid burned the back of his throat. No matter what Grayson's empire looked like on the outside, it reminded him of nothing less than the glossy peel on a rotten apple—spectacular to behold, but inside it was filled with putrid, runny goo.

He hated visiting Grayson, but keeping his seat in the California Senate meant he must appease the wealthy entrepreneur and his unusual political demands. Without Grayson's financial support, Johnson held no hope of being elected simply because he was an old man. People wanted someone younger, more popular, and much better looking. He entertained retiring, but he liked the cameras and luxuries as much as anyone else in southern California did. He'd rather die in office than lose his socioeconomic status.

The harsh noon sun struck the towering brass columns with silver-mirrored windows, forcing Johnson to put on his dark shades to shield his eyes. Even with the shades, the intense glare stung his eyes, making him cup a hand above his eyes because it was impossible to look directly at the building. Grayson's need to shine was even incorporated in the architecture of his enterprise.

Where the sidewalk leveled with the building, a row of gigantic, polished MarQuebes—each weighing over a ton—were centered as attractive centerpieces to grace the building entrances. The MarQuebes were the first gems discovered from Grayson's Mars exploration. The stones were dark like rubies but when held into direct light, they revealed their inner purplish hue. The blend of contrasting colors made them a prized stone. Since Grayson was the first and *only* man to land and stake a claim on Martian mining rights, he controlled the market without fear of competition.

Johnson paused outside one of Grayson's many gift shops where tourists bought small bottles of Martian soil, pebbles, and rocks. On Mars, these were worthless garbage, but to tourists, these prized novelties sold for untold millions. He shook his head in disgust. Were there items people would *not* buy?

Grayson invested billions into his Mars excavation projects and reaped one thousand times more than what he spent. With these endeavors, though, not one soul in Congress ever dared breathe the words aloud, but they understood that Grayson *owned* Mars, Deimos, and the crashed remains of Phobos. His status wrought power, numerous friends, and a vast number of jealous enemies.

Johnson climbed the narrow cement stairwell, stopped, and wiped sweat from his brow. Excited children ran around the retired Vortex Shuttle, which was the first successful vessel to journey to Mars and back.

Other youths played virtual reality space battles on the laser tag field. Another school field trip, Johnson thought. *For a price*, of course. Everything connected to Grayson Enterprises came with a price. Nothing was free. Not even water. No water fountains existed inside Grayson Enterprises. If anyone wanted water, the vending machines were the only way to acquire it.

Johnson despised Grayson as much as he possessed a treasured need to be considered his friend. Grayson's greed ran deep, and Johnson's desire to feast from the table of plenty overwhelmed his rationality to flee and reclaim his soul. Grayson's money lined Johnson's pockets. The senator understood that no one stood in Grayson's way. Opposing Grayson brought painful repercussions, physically or financially. Or both. Sometimes, even death.

Several of Grayson's most outspoken opponents had disappeared without explanation. No conclusive evidence ever surfaced to set the blame on the tycoon. Money silenced a lot of people—prosecutors and judges alike. Johnson didn't know a single person who'd ever crossed Grayson and walked away unscathed.

Johnson kept his sunglasses on while he walked past several schoolteachers. He couldn't tell from their expressions if they recognized him or not, so he ignored them. He had better things to worry about than hearing more complaints from parents who insisted he do something about funding the state's educational system. Sadly, most parents placed the blame on the wrong groups. The more money given to the schools meant the less the students actually learned. School administrators tended to give themselves raises, install unnecessary testing programs, or simply squander the money on other projects rather than inject the money into hiring better teachers or buying educational books. However, no one ever understood those correlations. By the time parents finally figured it out, Johnson would be long dead and gone; provided they ever figured it out at all.

Keep dangling the carrot and the ignorant mule will follow.

In his golden years, Johnson realized he was one of the dumb mules. It was far too late to free himself from his political harness.

Entering through the front brass doors, Johnson was greeted by two security guards. These were massive muscled men, wearing dark shades and visible earpieces. They kept their suit jackets open, revealing their guns. Their massive sizes intimidated Johnson more than their guns. He doubted these men ever *needed* to use them.

Johnson stepped through a metal detector. The green light cleared him. He placed his palm against the print scanner. A line of green flashed across the panel.

A computerized voice stated, "Welcome, Senator Johnson."

Johnson turned, grumbling a few obscenities. A guard stepped beside the senator and escorted him to the elevator. When the silver doors opened, Johnson stepped inside where another guard waited.

After the doors closed, he offered a nervous nod at the solemn guard. The man ignored his kind gesture and stared straight ahead at the doors. His silence chilled Johnson. With the giant standing beside him, the small elevator made Johnson claustrophobic.

"Perhaps," he thought. "It's time I retired from politics. Stress will kill me sooner than old age can claim me."

Anything was better than facing the pressure of visiting Grayson. He imagined the amount of horrendous pain these bodyguards could inflict should he ever piss Grayson off. Knowing Grayson, death wouldn't come fast.

The elevator opened. Another muscled guard waited. Johnson stepped on the plush carpeted hall and reluctantly followed the man. At times, he wondered if Grayson sponsored his own bodybuilding gym as well as his space conglomerate businesses. He didn't recall ever seeing any guard that weighted less than three hundred pounds.

The guard turned left at the intersecting hallway, and Johnson followed without hesitation. At the far end of the hall, Grayson's gorgeous brunette secretary, Beatrice, sat. They stopped at her desk.

Without looking up, she said, "Mr. Grayson will see you, Senator Johnson. He's been expecting you."

He nodded, looking past her. Large tinted windows opened to the most brilliant, panoramic view of the blue ocean. The sensation of being on top of the world ran through him. A place Grayson considered his godly throne.

Johnson glanced at Beatrice, but she didn't even acknowledge he was still standing beside her desk. She watched the security display screens where cameras spied at the end of each hall, the elevators, and even at the helicopter liftoff pad on the roof.

"This way, sir," the guard said.

Johnson followed. The guard opened the door, let him pass through, and shut it. No guards stood inside the room. He often entertained the idea that Grayson didn't want his security team to know exactly how cunning he was. Of course, they were probably paid to *ignore* any of Grayson's shrewd activities.

Johnson crossed the room and stood before the desk. Grayson stood from his desk chair and extended his hand.

"Good you could make it," Grayson said.

A puzzled expression crossed the senator's face. "I see you've heightened security."

"Yes. I have my reasons."

Grayson turned to the window. He folded his arms and watched the waves crashing on the shore. Several seagulls hovered and admired their reflections in the glass. Grayson took a deep breath.

"I must admit," Grayson said. "This view's the only reason I prefer this office over the one in my New York high-rise. So peaceful. The tranquility flows like a meandering brook. Don't you think? This is probably better than your stuffy office paid for by your constituents."

Johnson wrung his hands. His impatience and frustration had built during his long hot journey from the parking lot. In exasperation, he blurted, "Sir, what do you need? I do have *other* appointments today."

Grayson turned on his heel and faced Johnson. His muscular jaw tightened. The frown on his face made his blue eyes icier, meaner. His tailored Armani suit displayed his muscled arms, chest, back, and shoulders. Grayson was bigger than his largest guard.

"Do you now? Are they as generous in funding your cause as I?"

Johnson looked at Grayson's feet. He feared sparring eye-to-eye with Grayson. "No sir. I'm sorry. They're not *that* important. My secretary can reschedule them."

"Good. That's what I thought."

"What do you want?"

Grayson smiled. "I need more prisoners for my mining operations on Mars. The preliminary projects are going well. With more prisoners, we'll be able to establish the settlements quicker."

"More? That's *impossible*. I've freed as many prisoners as I possibly can to prevent more ethical protests from the civil rights organizations."

Grayson shook his head. "It's a shame when prisoners have more rights than their victims."

"They're still people. Besides, training and medical exams are expensive."

"Since when have you worried about the finances? I cover all the costs. I always have."

"You dispatched one hundred new men for Mars last month. They should arrive in about six months. That will put you close to two hundred prisoners on Mars once they arrive. Seventy men were released to you last year for your Deimos project."

Grayson nodded. "I know. Something's amiss on Deimos."

"What do you mean?"

"I've not received any communication from Dr. Frank Carter in over a week. Perhaps their satellite transmission is on the fritz. I don't know. But I need to train another seventy men, just in case."

"They may be prisoners, but need I keep reminding you? There's the issue of human rights. Why not hire qualified laborers? Why use only prisoners?"

"Prisoners are more dedicated to their labor."

Johnson frowned. "I'd think them more apt to rebel."

Grayson shoved his thick hands into his pockets. "To the contrary, none have ever rebelled."

"I find that hard to believe."

"Why?"

"Over ninety percent of the men you sent to Mars were the most ruthless murderers on death row. They were the worst of the worst. I'm surprised you even requested them."

Grayson shrugged. "They have more freedom on Mars. Such liberation has produced loyalty and their gratitude for having a second chance increases their drive to work even harder. They're not confined to small cement block enclosures with metal bars. And should they escape, where are they going to run?"

"Yes, but given that they're enclosed in the bunkers and mines, who's to say they won't rebel and start killing one another? Or your guards?"

"They know their place. But even if they escaped the mines, the brutal terrain of Mars would kill them. They're safer remaining workers."

Johnson seated himself across from Grayson's desk. "How can you be so confident they'll stay submissive?"

"They're under constant surveillance and guarded by men with high-tech laser weapons and sound blasters. Taking another hundred prisoners for Deimos won't be a problem."

"A hundred? You said seventy."

"Any number above seventy won't be a problem. The more violent the men are, the harder they work. Besides, they have the pride of being the first Earth inhabitants on Mars. They get to see the sun from a different angle and watch the Earth travel across the sky at night."

"I'm aware of your popular selling point for recruits."

Grayson's eyes narrowed. "Your son enjoys space travel, right?"

The senator ignored the question. "Mr. Grayson, exactly *what* are you trying to accomplish?"

Grayson frowned.

Johnson cleared his throat. "I thought your goal was to settle Mars and establish a civilization."

"It is."

"Why not start recruiting *qualified* people, who *aren't* violent, to go to Mars and settle instead of requesting more prisoners?"

"We must set the groundwork first. Why endanger decent, honest people with the drudgery required to establish housing and businesses? You know as well as everyone else that our prison system is an overflowing burden. A large percent of *your* voters consider them a tax burden on society. And since capital punishment is no longer an option, the problem continually gets worse. I remove them by employing them on Mars. They're paid excellent wages and will be deeded land once we've succeeded in settling outside the mines."

"So you're proposing to later settle decent people with the ex-cons inhabiting Mars?" Johnson asked. "I don't believe you'll find too many eager volunteers wanting to neighbor with the type of criminals you're enlisting to do your groundwork."

"Even the worst of men can be broken through manual labor," Grayson said.

"Careful," Johnson replied. "I've already persuaded the council to believe that you aren't enacting slave labor."

Grayson laughed. "Whatever it takes."

"I'm serious."

"So am I," Grayson said with an intense glare. He stepped to the edge of the desk and pointed his finger at Johnson. "Keep me happy and your seat in Congress remains safe. Understood?"

Johnson tucked his chin to his chest and stared at the floor. "Yes, sir."

"Get me one hundred fresh prisoners in no less than two weeks. Can you do that?"

Johnson loosened his tie and cleared his throat. "Sir, I'd really like to help you, but—"

Grayson's jaw tightened. Anger burned in his narrowed eyes. "But *what?*"

The chilling tone made the senator visibly shake. He ran a hand through his silver hair. "Sir, the Prison Release Committee wants to see the results of how well the prisoners are doing. The ones you *already* have. They won't allow more prisoners until you've proven the work environment is safe enough for the miners and no riots have occurred."

"More politics?" Grayson asked.

"You might say that."

"That's *your* area of expertise. I'll tend to my own affairs. You get me more prisoners."

"Must I remind you that's it's far too early for me to approach the committee and request more prisoners?"

"Tell them I'm expanding," Grayson replied.

"They're not fond of your mining projects as it is. They believe you're monopolizing the Martian frontier, making it impossible for others to set up claims."

Grayson folded his arms and looked at Johnson. "I planted my flag on Mars before anyone else, using only *my* funds. I never asked or borrowed a single cent from anyone else. They're more than welcome to send their own missions. Until they do, what I claim is mine."

Johnson sighed. His face flushed red. "No one *owns* a planet."

"Senator, I've not had any lines of little green men with picket signs protesting my endeavors on Mars. The only opposition I have is from jealous business people on Earth. Men too cowardly to take the chances I've taken, and these are the same individuals who believe I should offer them my ships, services, and funds to get them to where I've already settled. Since I have no competitors, why should they worry about *my* operations?"

"They believe you're exceeding your authority," Johnson replied.

"Authority? Over what? There's no other authority on Mars. So make my request known."

Johnson shook his head. "I cannot."

"Senator, it's wealthy people like me who line the pockets of politicians like you with money so you can misdirect your voters into believing you're doing what's in the best interest of the country. That's how democracy and capitalism has worked for decades, is it not?"

Johnson shook his head. "That's not true."

"No?" Grayson said with his thick arms crossed. His murderous gaze was calloused, cold. "It's how our government operates. You know it. It's media manipulation. People believe what they see on the news or read on the Internet. So the media runs with fake catastrophic events like onshore terrorism, the collapse of skyscrapers, and school shootings to get stricter laws passed to take away personal freedoms. And people are so blind and naive that they believe the government has the best solutions to everything. They readily hand over those rights, too."

"You sound like one of those conspiracy theorists, Mr. Grayson."

"*Theorist?* Senator, I'm a part of those conspiracies, just like you and all the other wealthy lobbyists making congressional members richer. We're setting up a new world through science, laws, and money."

"What's your point?" Johnson asked, exasperated.

"The point is I have more than adequately compensated you for the little favors you've returned to me. Like the prisoners to help set the population on Mars."

"As I told you, sir, I cannot do it."

"Cannot or *won't?*" Grayson asked.

"Does it really matter at this point?"

"Need I remind you that you work for me? Or shall I release that video to the press?"

Nervousness quaked Johnson's stomach. His eyebrows furrowed. He gazed at Grayson with sudden curiosity. "What video?"

Grayson took a controller, pushed a button, and the large flat screen in the corner of the room came on. Behind the curtain at a political rally, the camera zoomed in on Johnson making out with a young, well-shaped brunette, who was possibly in her early twenties. Her blouse was fully unbuttoned and Johnson worked to remove her bra while kissing her.

Johnson shook his head and closed his eyes. His heartbeat increased. How had he been so foolish? Now, he totally understood why the girl had come onto him and never rejected his advances. Grayson had hired her... for *this*.

Grayson hit the pause button. "Need I show you more?"

"For God's sake, no. Turn it off!"

"I'm not certain exactly how God plays into all of this, but I don't think Mrs. Johnson would be too thrilled to watch this on the evening news, do you? The online tabloids would have a day with it, too. They tend to be quite brutal. Do you wish for her to learn of your... indiscretions?"

Johnson loosened his tie even more. His face paled. "No, sir."

"Don't forget *who's* in charge here, senator. Understood?"

"Yes, sir."

Chapter 8

Magnus and Carter left the cell and followed a long dark corridor. Magnus worried they'd run into more guards, but they never did. At first, he thought the absence of patrolling guards was odd, but the more he studied the situation about the Sleeper Chips, the less he worried about encountering any guards at all.

"Why should they need patrols?" he reasoned. The men guarding the miners did so without worrying about the workers rebelling or rioting, so there wasn't any need for regular patrols.

Magnus became more at ease.

"I see you," a female voice whispered through the speaker inside Magnus' snug helmet. "Who are you? What'd you do to Cain?"

Magnus stopped walking and looked around the corridor. He couldn't find any overhead cameras. His nervousness spiked.

"What's wrong?" Carter asked, turning around.

Magnus motioned Carter to remain silent.

"Who's this?" Magnus whispered with his visor down.

"Boony."

"What makes you think I'm *not* Cain?"

The lady chuckled. In a soft voice, she said, "I watched Matt and Cain enter your cell. Only you came out. That uniform's a *tad* too small on you, but not necessarily in a *bad* way. You seem to have a better muscular build than Cain or Matt."

Uneasy, he looked along the ceiling for a camera.

"Who's your companion?" she asked.

"I'm afraid I cannot reveal that to you."

"Why not?"

"We hardly know one another," Magnus replied.

"You hardly know him or me?" she asked, teasingly.

"Honestly? Neither of you."

Boony laughed. "Well, I know your location and every move you make. You can't hide. I can have a team of guards on you in minutes."

Magnus nodded. "You could, yes. I don't doubt that for a moment. So why haven't you sent them for us?"

"You intrigue me."

Magnus chuckled. "How's that?"

"You're a prisoner, unlike the others, making rounds with a man I do not recognize. Yet, you wish to keep his identity a secret? There's not much to entertain us in the security center, so I'm curious: what's your next move?"

"Actually, I'm kinda curious about that myself," Magnus replied.

Carter lifted the mirror face visor on his helmet slightly. "What are you doing? We need to keep moving."

"He cannot hear you?" Magnus asked.

"Not unless I want him to, and I don't at the moment," she replied.

To appease Carter, Magnus started walking.

"Ahh," Magnus replied, "I see."

"So where are you heading now?"

"Where's the element of surprise, if I tell you?"

Boony sighed softly. Magnus liked her sultry voice. It was comforting and almost intimate to hear her whispering in his ear.

"According to the floor plans, you're heading to one of the vaults where MarQuebes are stored," she replied.

"Then I'm going the right direction."

"Hmm, once a thief, always a thief, eh?"

Magnus shook his head. "Never stolen a thing until today."

"Then why are you in prison?"

"I'd rather not say."

"Why not?" Boony asked.

"Because you wouldn't believe me."

"Try me."

Magnus and Carter turned into another corridor. The overhead lights were brighter. He noticed the surveillance camera and nodded.

He said, "I was framed."

Several seconds of silence separated them.

Magnus shook his head. "See? I knew you wouldn't believe me."

"Sorry," she whispered. "Another tech stepped in the room for a few seconds. He's gone now."

"Ahh, okay."

"If you're innocent, how'd you manage to get sent to Mars? Usually we only get the worst prisoners. You must have been framed for something horrible."

"Not that severe a crime actually," Magnus said.

"Then why'd they send you here?"

"A judge wanted to keep me silent."

"Now, you have me even more intrigued."

"I'm full of surprises like that."

She laughed.

"Nice I can keep you entertained," Magnus said.

Boony said, "Tell me. What good are these stones to you?"

"They've no value on Mars. They're rocks."

"Then *why* do you want them? Do you intend to escape from Mars?"

"You want me to further incriminate myself?" he asked.

"Magnus Knight? Is that correct?"

Magnus held his breath for a moment. She held every advantage. He couldn't see her and didn't know if only she was watching him, or if others were watching, too. If so, they might be closing in on him.

"Yep. That's me."

"Good. I wanted to make certain."

Magnus frowned. "You didn't really know?"

"Sometimes it's easy to get the rooms mixed up. It was the last time Cain and Matt reported in."

"Shit," Magnus said.

"What's wrong?"

"Their absence will have other guards coming soon."

"No," she whispered.

"And why wouldn't it?"

"Because your uniforms are tagged with tracers and you're both active."

"Oh."

"According to your chart, your sleeper chip malfunctioned. Wow."

"What?"

"You act fast for someone that's only returned to the real world for two days."

"What do you mean?" he asked.

"You overtook two guards, stole their uniforms, and now you're planning to steal MarQuebes and escape from Mars?"

"Few other choices to make," he replied. "So, yes, it's crossed my mind."

"As it has many of ours," she replied.

"What?" Magnus asked. "You don't like the accommodations?"

"It's not as glamorous as the virtual tour they gave me."

"At least they *gave* you a tour. I got a shovel and an orange jumpsuit as consolation prizes."

She laughed. "I suppose you're right. It could be worse. I imagine it was a rude awakening for you, huh?"

"It wasn't good, and it could've been much worse."

"How?"

Magnus told her about the man that killed himself when his chip had shorted out.

"Oh, God. We got the report for that, but I'd hate to have seen it."

Carter walked ahead of Magnus and reached the vault door first. He pulled the door lever, but it didn't budge.

He faced Magnus. "Can you open it?"

"Patience," he replied.

Magnus slid the guard's card but the computer denied access. He took the key ring and tried each key. None of them worked.

"Sorry," Magnus said. "I can't open it."

"Damn," Carter said. "What do we do now?"

"Not sure."

A few seconds later, the vault door panel glowed. The lock clicked loudly, and the door opened.

Perplexed, Carter looked at Magnus. "How'd you do that?"

Magnus shrugged.

He whispered to Boony. "Was this your doing?"

"Of course."

"Why?"

"I'll allow you to keep moving until I find more information about your prison sentence and why you were sent to Mars."

Magnus opened the vault door wider. "I don't have time to go into the details right now."

"You don't have to," she replied. "I can research everything about you on the computer. I have access to all your records and everything you've done while on Earth."

"I'm an open book, eh?"

"Not yet. But soon. Don't spoil the ending for me."

Magnus chuckled.

Boony sighed. "Whatever you need to do in the vault, do it fast. Anytime someone enters a vault, it's logged, so you don't have a lot of time."

He took a deep breath. His stomach ached like he'd been kicked in the gut. He worried guards might see the open vault and investigate.

"I'll hurry," he said.

"You'd best. My shift ends in fifteen minutes. Take what you need and get out so I can secure the door."

Magnus shook his head. "You realize you're now an accomplice, right?"

"Shh. I won't tell if you don't," she replied.

"Are you going to turn us in?"

"Not unless I find out you're lying to me."

"I'm not," he said. "I swear."

"Let me be the judge of that after I read your records."

"Fair enough."

"Now hurry."

Chapter 9

Inside the vault, Magnus removed his helmet. Mesmerized by the glittering array of gorgeous stones spread across the grading table, he gasped. Jewelry and gemstones never interested him before. But looking at these stones, he understood why someone could become greedier.

When Magnus glanced at Carter, he was greatly disturbed and slightly taken back. The glint in Carter's eyes became darker, lustful, and sinister; something Magnus never expected to see. If a snapshot could capture what pure greed looked like, Carter's facial experiences matched.

Grabbing a handful of the stones, Magnus poured them from hand to hand. The rattling sound was equivalent to shaking a bag of glass marbles. On the center tabletop were open trays of stones not yet sorted. The far wall was lined with rows of small cabinets. Each drawer filled with MarQuebes was labeled according to the carat size. He doubted all the stones were catalogued. It didn't seem possible.

Carter set his briefcase on the table and picked up a MarQuebe. He examined it beneath the lights. The ruby-red stone flickered. Its inner deep violet hue shimmered as he turned it in the light. "They leave them out in the open like this?"

"Why not?" Magnus asked. "It's not like the prisoners will steal them. Except us, of course. But even if others gained the freedom of their minds and robbed a vault, they'd either be shot on sight or die once they made to the outside hostile terrain."

Carter stared at the gems. "I'm a bit worried about getting shot myself."

"We'll be careful. Once we get the mechanic jumpsuits, we'll escape."

"I'm not so certain," Carter said.

"Don't let your nerves get the best of you. Our lives depend on our ability to remain bold and calm."

"How many MarQuebes should we take?"

"Two dozen should be more than enough," Magnus replied. "Don't take any of the largest stones though."

"Why not?"

"Uncut stones are going to raise questions, anyway. Anything more than two to three carats will draw suspicion from a jeweler or pawn shop owner."

"That makes sense, I suppose."

Magnus admired his handful of stones. "But we're only going to succeed by keeping out of sight and under the radar."

"It's worked so far," Carter replied.

"Mind if we store the stones in your briefcase?"

Carter shook his head. "No. There's no room."

Carter grabbed the briefcase and tucked it against his side.

"Okay. Not a problem." Magnus eyed Carter with suspicion.

Magnus counted twenty-four of the best-colored stones and slid them into his pocket.

MAGNUS PEERED out the vault door with Carter slightly behind him. Before stepping out, he forced on the tight helmet. Outside the vault, he shoved the door closed.

"I'm signing out for the night," Boony whispered in his ear.

Although Magnus didn't know her, and they'd only talked a few minutes, he ached at her sudden departure. He liked the mystery of talking to someone new and unseen, the euphoria in learning more about her. He found himself filled with disappointment. He might never hear her voice again. His chest felt heavy.

He almost pleaded for her to stay on the mike, but before he could ask, she said, "You could meet me at The Vortex in a half hour if you'd like."

Eagerness overshadowed any worry that she was setting him up. He loved the softness of her voice, the sultriness whenever she teased, and more than anything, he wanted to put a face to the beautiful voice. He hoped not to be disappointed. Usually people fell for one another at first sight, but with her voice... he really didn't care what she looked like. She'd already won his interests.

"That sounds great. How will I recognize you?" he asked.

"I'll come to you," she replied.

"Very well."

"Heads up," she said.

"What?"

"Guards are changing shifts. You and your secret friend need to get out of the tunnels *now*."

"Where should we go?"

"Damn," she whispered.

"What?"

"I have to go. My supervisor's coming up the stairs. Hurry and hide."

Sudden bumping static crackled in his ears. She apparently yanked off her headset. The transmitter went dead.

"Come on," Magnus said. "We have a problem."

"What?" Carter asked.

"Guards are heading our way."

"How do you know that?"

"Trust me. They're coming our direction."

Carter looked both ways down the tunnel. "Which way are they coming from?"

Magnus shook his head. "I'm not certain."

"There's nowhere to hide."

"This way," Magnus said, heading for the darkest part of the tunnel.

"If you don't know which direction they're coming from, how do you even *know* they're coming?"

"I just do," he replied.

Carter shook his head and grunted.

Magnus hurried to the left side of the tunnel. He wished Boony had told him from *which* direction these guards were coming.

He ran his hand along the polished corridor wall. Voices echoed ahead of them. Others from behind. He and Carter were caught in the middle.

Magnus winced. Had Boony set them up?

Chapter 10

Jonas Walker entered the surveillance office. His short spiked, silvery hair resembled the blunt quills of a hedgehog. His gray eyes studied Boony. She fumbled to remove her headset and set it on her desk, wrecking her short sleek hairstyle in the process. When his eyes greeted hers, she replied with a nervous smile.

"Boony?" he said with a firm stare. "Is everything okay?"

"Fine, sir. I'm heading out for the night."

Humor teased at the edges of his narrowed eyes. His deep wrinkles revealed his wisdom. "Big night planned?"

She pursed her lips and nodded. "Oh, of course. Going to cruise the midway for a while. Maybe stop and window shop at the mall. Eh, you know, those girly type of things."

Jonas chuckled. "So all was quiet tonight?"

Boony nodded. "Nothing stirring."

A light flashed on a console across the room. He went to check it out. "Who entered the vault in Corridor 10?"

She shook her head. "No one. Why?"

He sighed. "Someone did. I'll replay the film footage to see."

"Don't waste your time. That door occasionally sends out a false alarm."

Jonas frowned. "I know. It *did*, but I updated its alarm program last week."

"Most electronics don't work too well on Mars."

"We still experience some minor glitches, but they've improved since the new techs arrived a few weeks ago."

Boony gathered her pack and other belongings together. "That's helped. How's Derek? Is he still out on the Martian terrain?"

Worry furrowed Jonas' brow. He nodded. "He should almost be finished with the radio receivers at the Phobos Crash Site. He's a brave young man."

"Your grandson's braver than anyone else stationed on Mars."

"Being too brave can get you killed before your time," he replied.

"Not Derek. He's the only one who can successfully do this mission alone."

Jonas sighed. "That's what I keep telling myself, but I've not heard from him in three days."

Boony stood at the door with a sad expression on her face. She tried to be reassuring with her eyes and voice. "Probably another sandstorm. Those produce static and block our communications via transmitters."

"I know. That's another possibility," he replied.

"I'm sure he's okay."

"Thanks for your optimism. Enjoy the rest of your evening."

She forced a smile and left the computer control room.

After the door closed, Jonas shut his eyes, fighting frustrated tears. Being the head security supervisor over the computer techs, he wanted to protest his grandson's voluntary request to set up the radio receivers at the Phobos Crash Site. But he couldn't show favoritism, and in spite of his own selfish qualms, he okayed Derek's request.

Derek had left the safety of Olympus Mons alone. Perhaps not totally alone. But no humans journeyed with him. Instead, Derek traveled with his team of robotic humanoids he'd built and programmed, which troubled Jonas. Derek argued the robots could withstand the rugged, bitterly cold terrain without suffering any human casualty.

Except the possibility of yours, Jonas thought.

It was a grandfather's painful duty to stress about his grandson's welfare, especially on such a dangerous mission so far from their only base. This worrisome situation was another reason Grayson didn't allowed families to come to Mars together yet. Should tragedy arise, it weighed heavily on people, making them less productive. However, Grayson allowed Jonas to bring Derek to Mars for several reasons.

More than thirty years earlier, when Jonas was almost forty, he worked for the CIA. His duty to the government didn't go unnoticed. Actions he took on the job placed his life and his family's lives in jeopardy. He'd unraveled an inner threat within Congress to secretly overthrown the sovereignty of the U.S. Constitution, so many radical political opponents vowed to destroy him and his aligned colleagues in the CIA.

Jonas was taken into the identity protection service, but his son Samuel, refused to comply. Stubbornly, Samuel continued his political bid for the senate, believing that if elected, he could stop the radical uprising inside Congress, but his opportunity never came.

Samuel was shot and killed during a campaign speech. Jonas knew the assassination was carried out by the corrupt antigovernment officials he'd exposed in Congress. But since he assumed a new identity, and was no longer in the CIA loop, he couldn't prove it. He held the suspicion that they killed Samuel in the hope of drawing him out of hiding. Whether true or not, his opponents weren't finished.

Almost a year later, Samuel's wife was killed in a car bombing in D.C., but due to what could only be described as a miracle, Derek survived, unscathed. He was an infant. Investigators could find no feasible explanation for why the blast didn't kill Derek.

Jonas emerged from hiding to get his grandson, and in doing so, the men that wanted him dead attempted to kill him. Only instead of their setup to bring Jonas to them, Jonas turned the tables and crippled their faction by permanently removing their strongest leaders. It was the first time Jonas actually approved of government drone assassinations on U.S. soil.

Grayson learned about Jonas' bold determination to fight against political opposition in order to protect his family. He was so impressed that he hired Jonas to oversee the security firm at Grayson Enterprises. Jonas took the offer without hesitation and was no longer seen in the public eye. He and Derek were safe. Grayson's buildings were more fortified than any organization Jonas previously supervised.

During the time Jonas worked at Grayson Enterprises, Derek's keen interest in computer programming and robotics flourished. Grayson paid for the entire robotic engineering training Derek needed. By the time Derek was twenty, he had patented several humanoid prototypes. Grayson was fascinated and offered Derek the chief engineering job on Mars.

Derek readily accepted, and Jonas insisted he journey to Mars as well. Grayson allowed it, but only if Jonas resided as the head of security at Olympus Mons.

In retrospect, Jonas never regretted moving to Mars with his grandson because it was a new frontier where few individuals would ever reside, at least during what was left of his life. It was also less likely that his remaining enemies could threaten them.

Jonas looked at the Martian weather map. Were the sandstorms the reason he'd lost contact with Derek? Or was it something worse?

The Phobos Crash Site was thirty-five miles northwest of the Olympus

Mons Aureole, slightly southeast of Lycus Sulci. The site was in its earliest developmental stage. Grayson Enterprises mandated new incoming prisoners would be stationed there once electrical power and living quarters were properly established.

Jonas was dead set against the idea, but Grayson believed Phobos might contain different gemstones than Olympus Mons, or more valuable ores. Jonas worried Phobos might have high levels of radiation, and that might be causing interference with the radio waves.

Frustrated, and not wishing to continue stressing over a situation he had no control over, Jonas fidgeted with the vault door's control panel. When he played back the video feed, he found the camera angles weren't positioned like they should be. Instead, they focused on the ceiling. The footage showed the blurred image of smooth rock. This image remained for almost ten minutes.

What occurred during those ten minutes? What role, if any, had Boony partaken? Had she shifted the cameras away from the vault door?

He hated to assume she had anything to do with this because she was his most loyal, dedicated tech. He'd ask her later if Curt or Phillip had been in the office while she was on duty. They were two people he didn't trust. He wouldn't put it past them to steal from the vaults.

Jonas sat at the desk and put on his headset. He tuned the adjustment on the computer and increased the volume. "Derek, if you can hear me, please respond."

He waited fifteen seconds and repeated the message.

No reply.

Not even static.

Jonas typed in commands for the orbiting satellite and zoomed in for a ground scan of the Phobos Crash Site. With so many boulders, craters, and intricate holes surrounding the crash site, it was unlikely the camera might accidentally locate Derek.

He sighed and tried via transmitter again.

Nothing.

It looked to be another long, agonizing night. He never imagined a grandson could stress him to age even faster. The love for a family member was never easy, and the absence of his grandson made him wish he were young enough to trek out to ruins to search for Derek.

HIGH ATOP a narrow ridge overlooking the Phobos Crash Site, Derek Walker sat hunched against the base of the short radio tower, shielding himself from the abrasive wind-pelleting grains of red grit and pebbles. His form-fitted smart-suit was the newest technology he and his engineering team had invented, but he was the first to test it during one of Mars' harshest sandstorms.

The light suit allowed more agility and flexibility, but the cruel windblown grit might actually damage the suit. The sand pelleted off his domed space helmet, severely reducing his visibility. It was useless to stand and work on the radio tower when he couldn't see what he was doing.

"Dammit," he whispered. "This storm's in for a long haul."

Even without the storm's interference, he didn't have any means to communicate with his grandfather at Olympus Mons. His transmitter malfunctioned nearly twenty miles into his trek after he stepped down from his Mack flatbed truck to brush away the excess sand on the solar panels. After clearing the panels of debris, he inspected his robots and other mechanical supplies for the turrets. Then he noticed the vehicle's radio antenna was bent and disabled by the unrelenting winds. Without realizing it, the blowing grit jammed into his suit's radio transmitter and shorted it out, leaving him without any way to contact the base at all.

After he discovered the damage, he was only ten miles from the Phobos Crash Site. The drive itself wasn't difficult. Rather than turning back, he drove to the site to finish connecting the communication radio towers along the ridge left by the previous technicians. Although they never constructed any roads, the natural fault lines along former lava flows provided decent, almost smooth grooves, which were adequate, natural roads. Every now and then, abrupt shallow drop-offs or protruding large rocks interrupted large sections of these roads. Such obstructions were nuisances and prevented them from driving at fast speeds.

Due to the rugged terrain and the truck's draining batteries, Derek left his transport truck about a hundred yards away and continued on foot through the swirling dust storm. He figured if he got the towers fully activated, he'd be able to contact his grandfather and let him know he was safe. But until the winds died down, he remained at the mercy of the unforgiving weather. He couldn't do anything except wait.

Waves of reddish sand and silt formed a small dune on the other side of the radio tower. Derek' five robots stood lined together, forming a small wall to block and protect him from the whipping windblown debris. It helped but wasn't one hundred percent efficient.

Time would tell if he survived this maddening ordeal, and whether or not his robots were sturdy enough to function on the Martian terrain. A part of him held more hope for the robots than he did for himself. In only two years, he'd suffered more depression than he ever had on Earth. Dying alone, where no human could hear him scream, seemed a fitting end to an otherwise bland life. Strangely, though, his five robots stood by, doing everything they could to protect him from death. Even though he never programmed them to exhibit loyalty or behave in such a protective manner, they stood at attention, watching over him as though he were family. And *that* troubled him most of all.

Chapter 11

The guards approached Magnus and Carter from both ends of the tunnel. Carter stood too terrified to move.

Magnus pulled him against the wall and into a natural volcanic opening, which was barely wide enough for Magnus to squeeze inside, but they managed to conceal themselves moments before the two squads passed one another in the main passageway.

Magnus pushed his back against the curved opening. The wall behind them cracked. He shoved harder and the brittle wall shattered, revealing a strange series of natural spiraling steps that led upward.

"Come on," Magnus whispered.

A concerned expression crossed Carter's face. "Where's that go?"

Magnus shrugged. "I've no idea, but let's find out. It's safer than wandering along the corridor until after the guards reach their stations."

Magnus headed up with Carter close behind. The stairs ended along a narrow ridge, which overlooked the miners below. The view was spectacular, and the men below resembled tiny figurines.

"How'd this path get here?" Carter asked.

"This must be a natural occurrence from when the volcano had been active."

"How do we get down?"

"I'm hoping it somehow connects to one of the bored tunnels. Maybe we can find a set of stairs leading down."

They walked another forty feet, and the path narrowed. The temperature increased. Blinding yellow lights glowed through the narrow cracks at the edge of the path, which seemed to be the source of heat.

"What's down there?" Magnus asked.

Carter shook his head. "I don't know."

Magnus knelt and crawled close to one of the cracks. The harsh bright lights made him squint. After a few moments, his eyes adjusted. "I'll be damned."

"What?"

"It's a greenhouse. Probably a couple acres of tomatoes, corn, and other vegetables."

"Yeah," Carter said, nodding. "I read about that project over a year ago. The vegetation increases the oxygen levels inside the mines and provides fresh vegetables to feed everyone. The leftover greens are used for small game animals like rabbits and poultry."

"That's not a bad idea."

"They plan to expand it each growing season."

"I discovered something else that's interesting."

Carter frowned. "What?"

"All the greenhouse workers are women."

"Women? Seriously?"

Magnus stood and dusted off the red dust on his knees. "Yep. I wonder if they're female prisoners?"

Carter shrugged. "I don't know. They could be. There weren't female miners on Deimos."

"Come on. I think I see a way back down."

Carter eagerly followed. Around a small corner, a set of manmade steps led down.

"Told you," Magnus said. "Looks like they've been doing some construction. They may eventually use this path."

"It almost looks like something already *has*."

GRAYSON ENTERPRISES

"MR. DONALD PARKS," Grayson said. "I didn't expect to see you any time soon."

"You wanted me to report whenever I retrieved new information."

"I did."

Donald straightened his striped tie. The narrow pupils of his dark eyes resembled small polished, obsidian stones. He was thin, about five-nine, and his face was tan. He worked for the CIA but for the right amount of money, he reported essential information to Grayson about his ongoing mission projects to own Mars.

Grayson smiled, opened a Cuban cigar box, and offered one to Parks. Parks gladly accepted.

"Please, be seated," Grayson said with a charming smile.

The agent sat, cut off the cigar's tip, and puffed it while Grayson extended a lit match.

"Ah, nice!" Parks said, grinning.

"So what's the information?"

"For starters, the rumors are true. China sent a rocket to Mars."

Grayson frowned. "When?"

"Approximately one year ago."

"A year? No one ever informed me."

"According to the UN Space Council, no one has to."

"I see." Grayson puffed his cigar. "Seems someone's keeping me out of the loop."

"Not me."

Grayson laughed. "Of course, not *you*. Otherwise, you'd be elsewhere hiding and not sitting in my office."

Parks chuckled but his face expressed relief that Grayson wasn't accusing him. "Senator Johnson, perhaps? His son's one of the shuttle pilot inspectors."

"Yes. I know. I'll tend to that matter later, but I sincerely doubt Johnson possesses the backbone to oppose me. What did the Chinese send to Mars?"

"We don't know. It was a secretive mission."

"Obviously."

Parks puffed the cigar. "From the information I've gathered, whatever they sent was in response to your meeting with them a year ago."

Grayson's firm brow rose, which indicated a flinch. Something few people ever witnessed while talking to him.

"So you remember the meeting?" Parks asked.

"I do."

"What'd they want?"

"They wanted to use my landing base at Olympus Mons for free, so they could deliver their supplies until their settlements were established and running smoothly."

"I take it... you denied them such access?"

"Of course. What they consider collaborating, I consider leeching. I see no benefit opening my base to pave an interplanetary road for them."

Parks exhaled smoke. "I can't say I or anyone else could blame you. But, for what it's worth, you have the tendency to piss off a lot of people around the world."

Grayson shrugged and then grinned. "I do, but I didn't make all my money for others to squander."

"I wouldn't expect for you to."

"What did they ship to Mars?" Grayson eyed Parks with keen suspicion.

Parks shook his head and grinned. "Not a clue. I wasn't lying when you asked me the first time."

"Surely you've some idea."

"No, but I'm working to uncover more information for you."

"Work faster and there's a million dollar bonus for you."

Parks smiled. "I'm on it."

Chapter 12

Sylvia stepped outside her door. Magnus explained and showed Carter how to use the guard's key to enter the room.

"See?" Magnus said. "It's not that difficult."

"I'm glad you're back," Sylvia said, holding Digger. "I was worried the guards might've captured you."

Magnus scratched the ferret's ears. "You mind watching him a bit longer?"

Sylvia nodded, but appeared slightly worried. "Sure. What's wrong?"

"Nothing," he replied. "I... uh... need to check some things."

Carter walked past and placed his briefcase on the bed.

"Okay," Sylvia said. "But come back. You're more than welcome to stay here tonight."

"I'll be back. That way we'll be together when we head to the maintenance storage room in the morning."

"Sure."

Magnus rubbed the ferret's neck and pointed his thick finger. "You behave yourself, Digger."

The ferret rubbed the side of its head against Magnus' hand. Magnus chuckled, turned, and headed down the corridor. After he was out of sight, Sylvia let the door slide shut. When she turned around, Carter was staring intently at his feet.

"Is everything okay?" she asked.

Carter didn't respond. His eyes were frozen in an eerie trance. She nudged him. He shook his head and looked at her.

"You all right?" she asked.

He nodded. "Yeah. Sorry. I'm tired."

"Go take a shower. You'll feel better. We can sleep afterwards."

Carter stood, took the briefcase, and walked to the small bathroom. "A shower sounds great."

"You can leave the briefcase on the bed."

He shook his head. "No. No, I can't."

With concern, she watched Carter. He mumbled and staggered to the shower. He set the briefcase outside the shower, glanced at her, and turned on the water. He didn't step into the shower until she broke his intense glare.

Uneasy, Sylvia busied herself by sorting through her clothes in one of the drawers. The shower curtain slid across the rod with a harsh scraping sound. She dared a glance at the shower. His clothes covered the briefcase. She wondered what was inside the case that he didn't want her or Magnus to discover.

Carter was awfully protective of the case. Whenever she asked about the case, his abrupt behavior made her uneasy. He wasn't the same as she remembered several months earlier; but then, he'd witnessed the deaths of those on Deimos. Was that why he acted aggressive and paranoid? With such mental trauma, she'd give him a pass. When they reached Earth, maybe he could talk to a psychiatrist to grasp control of his emotions.

By being his friend and showing compassion, he might recover somewhat from the early stages of PTSD. She worried his symptoms might get even worse before lessening. She hoped to help him heal so his emotions wouldn't darken and become destructive.

Sylvia decided not to ask about the briefcase for now, but that didn't lessen her curiosity about what was concealed inside.

Chapter 13

Magnus immediately regretted re-entering The Vortex. The pounding music wasn't so bad, but the harsh flashing strobe lights hurt his eyes and sickened his stomach. He used his hand to partially shield his eyes.

Totally exhausted from his two fully conscious days of mining, he realized how worn down he was physically and mentally. Were it not for the seductiveness of Boony's intriguing voice, he'd have skipped coming to The Vortex altogether. But he wanted to know what she looked like.

Since he didn't plan to be on Mars beyond the next day, he didn't have any alternative, if he ever wanted to meet her. And he *did*. If her appearance was half as beautiful as her voice, he entertained the thought of *not* returning to Earth, provided they hit it off. He was willing to ignore the horrible pulsating music and blinding lights to satiate his curiosity, at least for a while.

Stepping through the doors, Magnus didn't stride straight for the bar. Instead, he lingered near the entrance in case guards rushed to take him into custody. Although the crowd held different faces than earlier, these people acted exactly like the others. They danced, drank, or played games. None reflected a determined desire to arrest anyone. Although guards, they were captives trapped inside a different type of prison.

After enduring five minutes of the nerve-grating music, no one approached. The grating music started to grow annoying and agitating. His head ached. He squeezed his eyes closed, hoping to shut out the music, drive away the pain, but it didn't help. The stress of trying to ignore the music caused his neck and shoulder muscles to tighten even more. At that moment, he'd have given one of his most expensive MarQuebes for an hour massage or for *anything* capable of lessening the pain.

"Are you okay?"

Magnus opened his eyes and stared down at the dainty Asian woman. She stood about five foot tall. When she smiled, cute dimples appeared. Her smile was more seductive than her honey-rich voice whispering through the earpiece. Her dark eyes glistened with interest and excited him. Her short, bobbed hair was highlighted with streaks of blonde.

"Boony?" he asked, lifting his visor slightly.

She nodded.

"You're much smaller than I imagined," he said.

She gave a flirty smile. "Perhaps it's that you're so much *larger* than everyone else?"

Magnus chuckled. "That's true, too. It tends to be a problem, no matter where I am."

"Care for a drink?" Boony asked.

He shrugged. "Sure."

"Come with me. I already have us a table."

Nervousness reflected in his eyes. He glanced ahead, watching her graceful, yet alluring walk. Her legs and buttocks were shapely. He blushed, fighting his temptation to rudely stare while she walked.

"Don't worry," she said, glancing over her shoulder. "I didn't bring anyone with me."

Magnus released a pent up sigh, but the fact she brought up the subject didn't add to his confidence. His skepticism kicked in. If she was trying to put him at ease, she'd kept him partially suspicious. After all, why bring it up unless to have him completely lower his guard?

Boony walked through the dancers. He followed close behind. The strobe lights washed over half drunken men and women. Occasionally, due to his size, Magnus rudely squeezed between people in order to keep up with her.

While Magnus moved through the off duty guards and officers, he made subtle side-glances. Misery set in their eyes, and for a moment, he thought that maybe the prisoners actually had the better end of the deal on Mars. The Sleeper Chips prevented prisoners from experiencing depression, pain, homesickness, and total exhaustion. The true prisoners were the ones retaining their full mental capacity and understood their surroundings. They knew despair and realized they were imprisoned on the red planet for the better part of their lives. The majority of them might never see Earth again.

Such knowledge explained why they drank heavily to escape reality. They might have the freedom to come and go, but they were stuck inside Olympus

Mons. Few were allowed the clearance to venture outside the massive volcano. Low-level guards were stationed permanently inside Olympus Mons.

Boony sat at a table near the edge of the dance floor. A mirrored wall blocked part of the throbbing vibration of the music. Magnus took the seat across from her. He sat at an angle where he could see her but also where his use of the mirror prevented anyone from sneaking up from behind.

"Don't trust me?" Boony asked, playfully raising her eyebrows and beaming her cute smile.

Magnus frowned. "Let's just say, I'm overly cautious."

She winked. "Understandable."

He folded his large aching hands together and studied her face. Her beauty was something he wished he could behold for hours each day. Her eyes hinted mischief, but nothing in her gaze indicated she was someone he couldn't trust. Either that, or she was excellent at suppressing her emotions.

"Well?" she asked, breaking the growing silence.

"What?" Magnus asked, shaking his head.

Boony smiled, offering a shrug. "I didn't take you for the silent type."

Magnus took a sharp breath and glanced around at other people. A few seconds later, he met her eyes again. "Did you check out my background information?"

"Yes."

"And?"

"I can't comfortably say you're fully innocent, but I can say the circumstances behind the charges are a bit shady."

"I told you."

She smiled. "As would any other prisoner in the mines *if* they could speak."

A waitress stopped at the table. "Can I get either of you anything?"

"Martian Mudslide," Boony said.

Magnus gave her a strange look and half grinned.

She smiled. "It's good."

He chuckled. "If you say so, but I've tasted enough mud on Mars. No way I'd entertain the thought of ordering a drink to remind me of it."

Boony's eyes brightened, and she laughed.

"And you, sir?" the waitress asked.

"Cold beer in a bottle is fine."

"Very well."

After the waitress walked away, Boony said, "So how do you plan to get to Earth?"

He shrugged. "Still working on the details."

She shook her head.

"What?" he asked.

"No need being so secretive, Magnus. We both know there's only *one* way you'll get off this planet. The real question is, '*How* do you plan to succeed?'"

"I know. But I'm not comfortable directly discussing this with security personnel. Sort of a breech of confidentiality."

Boony folded her small delicate hands and formed a bridge to rest her chin. "You think I'll tell my superiors?"

"Why would you not?"

"Maybe I'd like to see if you're successful."

"Why?"

"If you can pull it off, there's hope for the rest of us."

"You'd abandon all of this splendor?" he asked, waving his huge hand toward the dance floor.

"In a nanosecond."

Magnus leaned closer. "How tight's your security?"

"Depends on which department you're referring to. Most guards are lazy. They're not motivated because the prisoners offer no challenges. Techs like me, watching the cameras, get bored. We find something else to do instead of staring at inactive footage. That's why you intrigued me and why I wanted to know what you're up to."

"So we have a good chance?"

"Taking a shuttle?" she asked.

Magnus nodded before wishing he hadn't. Being tired and caught in her gaze, he spoke without thinking. Perhaps that was her plan. Offering him tidbits of information to gain his trust, and in return she'd gain knowledge of what his plans were.

Boony grinned, reached across the table, and patted his hand. "I told you our *weaknesses*. I didn't disclose our strengths."

"And that is?"

"Jonas Walker."

Confused, Magnus frowned. "Who's he?"

"Head of security. He's an ex-CIA agent."

"On Mars?"

Boony nodded. "Yes."

"Wow."

"Grayson's known to hire the best in any field."

"Apparently."

The waitress brought their drinks and set them on the table. Boony handed the lady her badge. "Charge the drinks to me."

The waitress scanned the card and handed it back.

"Enjoy," the waitress said, turning and heading to another table.

Magnus took a sip from the bottle. The cold beer felt good going down. He couldn't believe how raw his throat still was from inhaling the Martian dust. The whiskey earlier had helped numb it for a while. The cold beer soothed in a different way.

He watched Boony stir her drink with a plastic straw. Her movements were as delicate and graceful as the beauty of her face. Although less than a third of his size, she didn't seem intimidated by his massiveness, which aroused his curiosity about her. Did she have a laser pistol aimed at him under the table? Although small in stature, he assumed she was a trained expert in hand-to-hand combat. He had not completely disregarded the possibility that other security officers might be seated nearby ready for her signal to arrest him.

Magnus set down the beer bottle. "Is he a retired agent?"

"A great agent never stops being an agent."

"I suppose not."

"He's also the oldest person on Mars."

"Really?"

She nodded. "Yes. In his sixties."

"Odd."

"Why's that odd?"

"I'm surprised he passed the physical to take the flight here."

"He's in great shape for his age. His mind's sharper than yours and mine combined."

"So he's the one to avoid?" Magnus asked.

"You can try."

Magnus leaned back in his chair and stretched. His backbone popped and cracked. He sighed with relief and seconds later, he rubbed his tired eyes.

"You look exhausted," she said.

"The mines will do that."

"I imagine so."

Magnus studied her eyes. "The mining pits are death sentences. Regardless of what promises the prisoners received for their labors on Mars, no one will cash in. The only farm they'll buy is the plot they get buried in."

"You really believe they won't live that long?"

He nodded.

"Why?"

"I tell you what, Boony. The next time you get a chance, go look at them. They're aging faster than we normally do. It's from the unending intense labor. Hell, they're being worked nonstop without breaks. I estimate most will die in the pits from sheer exhaustion."

Her eyes narrowed. "The majority of them were the worst murderers and rapists on Earth. Do you really think they deserve *lighter* sentences or the freedom to settle on Mars?"

"So you're okay with the deception?"

"At least they'll pay for their crimes, unlike those on Earth who sit in jail cells watching television or working out all day."

Magnus nodded. "I see your point and for the most part, I agree. But what if others are here like me and were framed? I was sent to Mars so I couldn't get my charges reversed."

"I'm still researching your case. I promise to find everything I can."

"Will you tell Jonas about our plan?"

Boony stared intently into his eyes. She held the top of her glass and stirred her drink with her index finger. Her expression indicated her skepticism and yet, she wanted to trust him. She pursed her lips, considering her words. Finally, she said, "No. I won't."

"Why not?"

"Boredom? It might do our security team some good to have someone shake them awake."

Magnus smiled. "You could leave with us."

She cocked an eyebrow and then shook her head. "No."

"Not a risk taker?"

Boony smiled. "Don't want to be a fugitive for the rest of my life."

"A fugitive?"

"You'll be stealing a ship that's worth millions of dollars."

Magnus sipped his beer. "I understand, but it seems there's more to it than that. Something more holds you here."

"There is."

"Like what?"

Her eyes never left his, but he never felt uncomfortable staring into hers.

Boony replied. "I won't betray Jonas. He's like a father to me, which is something I never had on Earth."

"By not telling him our plan, isn't that betrayal enough?"

She shook her head. "Not the way I view it. Things need to be shaken up around here to make others realize their duties are required."

"And if I die?"

Boony looked away. "Well that... that'd make me very sad."

Magnus grinned and chuckled. "I won't be too happy about that either."

She grinned and immediately her eyes were drawn to his. "How do you do that?"

"What?"

"Find humor in everything."

"Survival tactic, I suppose."

"It's a good one," she said.

"That's how I survived my childhood in Dallas. There weren't too many options growing up with an alcoholic mother and an absentee, deadbeat father."

"But wasn't it family problems that got you here to begin with?" she asked.

"I guess you could say that. But it's more complex than that."

She nodded. "Sounds like we share a familiar background."

"You, too?"

Boony straightened in her seat and crossed her legs. She stared at her drink and chewed her lower lip. "I grew up in an orphanage. Never knew my parents. Ran away when I was twelve. I learned to protect myself very early."

He watched her pouty lips as she spoke. When she grew silent, he could see her world of emotions swirling in her eyes. For someone so small, she possessed so much strength and more character than anyone he'd ever known.

"I probably would've been a delinquent, had it not been for a lady that took me in. She helped me get into a good school and later she helped me with college. She turned my life around."

"Do you still communicate with her?" Magnus asked.

She shook her head. Tears glistened in her eyes. "No. She died some years back, which is why I decided to take the opportunity to come to Mars. I didn't have anything else on Earth, so this seemed a logical choice. Nothing tied me down there."

Magnus nodded. "Yeah, I can see that. My decision was a bit different. I didn't have any choice. My hands were tied in my coming to Mars. Well, *cuffed* actually."

Boony grinned, sipped her drink, and watched the erratic dancers nearby. "Do you dance?"

"Do you value your feet?" he replied.

She shook her head and smiled. "If you succeed in whatever plan you have, I'll miss you."

"Really?" Magnus asked, flattered. "We hardly know one another."

Boony shrugged. "All the same, you're the most interesting person I've met in a long time."

"Thanks. And if we fail?"

"Let's not discuss that outcome. Remember. Don't spoil the ending for me, okay?"

"I'll try not to." Magnus finished the beer. "What do you think our chances for success are?"

"Evaluate the information I've given you. Your success depends on how well you make decisions during your escape on whether you'll succeed or not. I've told you all I can about the security without truly betraying Jonas. The rest is up to you."

"Very well."

"So, who's the man you're trying to help?" she asked.

"I've told you all I can about him."

"I suppose we're at a information standstill, huh?"

"Looks that way."

Boony said, "How well do you know the man?"

"No more than I really know you."

"And you'll fully place your life in his hands?"

He shook his head. "No. I'd never drop my guard around him."

"So you don't trust him?"

"I'm still questioning his motives, but right now, he's the only ticket I have to get to Earth. That's what I'm betting on, more so than him."

She smiled. "I see."

Magnus returned the smile. "However, if I had to fully trust someone, you're the sure thing."

"Oh?" Her face reddened. "And why's that?"

He shrugged. "There's something in your eyes and smile that leads me to believe I'd be safe."

"You don't have any doubts you might be wrong with such an assumption?"

"I suppose a minor second-guess might gnaw at the back of my mind from time to time. But, it'd be worth the risk."

"How so?" she asked.

"Young lady, I've never seen anyone more beautiful than you."

She gave a sly smile. She blushed and covered her eyes. "Some of the most attractive things in the world are also the most dangerous and deadly."

"That's true, too. But I wasn't speaking only about your physical beauty. Your personality—"

She shook her head and raised a hand, motioning him to stop talking. "Let's not go this direction."

"What do you mean?"

"If you weren't attempting to escape, or if we were on Earth and met, I'd love to get to know you on a more personal level. But, with what you need to do, and what might happen, this can't benefit either of us."

Magnus shook his head. "I didn't mean anything like that."

Boony finished her drink and stood. "Good luck to you, Magnus. I hope your endeavors are worth the risk."

Before he could reply, she slipped through the dancing crowd. He sat a few minutes longer, thinking about her. If he intrigued her, she'd taken his mind hostage. Her sudden absence made him profoundly lonely. Even though her demeanor was pleasant and her eyes and smile made him want to trust her, he still cautiously eyed others on the dance floor and those seated at nearby tables. The abrupt coldness in her voice and quick departure made him uneasy. He half expected guards to approach the table, but ten minutes after her departure, no one approached. Not even the waitress.

The thunderous music seemed much louder after she left. And worse, his heart was lonelier than he wished to think about. Digger had given him *something* to talk to, but Boony's introduction had given him a human connection filled with anticipation and renewed hope, which was something he missed most of all.

Carter wasn't a friend. Like he had told Boony, Carter was an associate who held the same mutual goal—to escape Mars. Magnus understood that, even if Carter didn't. He knew he couldn't place full trust in Carter, nor did he want to. Once they got to Earth, Magnus planned to go his direction to settle a debt long overdue. What occurred to Carter afterwards? He'd have to wait and see.

Chapter 14

Jonas sat at his desk and stared at the computer monitor. The Martian weather map indicated Boony's prediction was correct. A dust storm covered the region where Derek was supposed to be working. From the speed of the winds and the size of the storm, the worst should sweep past the Phobos Crash Site in less than a half hour. Since night had fallen, the dust storm made visibility even worse.

Another downfall with these sandstorms was the excessive production of electrical static charges. The static affected radio communication from one station to the next, and most likely was the reason Derek had not contacted him.

Jonas typed commands to the Grayson Satellite to use the high-powered cameras to see where his grandson was, if possible. Derek was resourceful. No doubt, he'd found shelter under a rock cliff; which, combined with the layers of blowing sand and silt, made the likelihood of spotting him via satellite impossible. But Jonas hoped one of his grandson's robots might be in the field and located.

Jonas zoomed the Martian positioning camera over the Phobos Crash Site.

Nothing large moved.

The grainy satellite feed was difficult to filter.

Jonas typed a few more codes, and a green dot lit up on the computer screen. He breathed a sigh of relief because that was Derek's tracer chip, so his grandson was there. The light, though, didn't guarantee he was alive. It only showed his position and not his vital status.

Taking a deep breath and exhaling slowly, Jonas sought to calm his nerves.

Eight red dots appeared on the screen, which alarmed Jonas. These dots were moving from the west toward the Phobos site. Derek only had *five* robots. Nothing else should be on the Martian terrain. Through the grainy footage, he couldn't obtain a clearer image.

These eight dots were on the Lycus Sulci ridgeline directly north of Derek's position and seemed beelined to Phobos. What the hell were these *things* heading Derek's direction?

Jonas clung to the hope these unidentified images were Derek's robots. He hoped the extra dots were simply a glitch due to the sandstorm. But with all the misery he'd endured over the years, his luck was never fortunate. Then, as if Fate wanted to add to his misery, Derek's five robot detectors lit up on the screen. Their lights were blue and positioned around Derek's signal.

Derek's favorite color was blue, so he programmed them to appear blue on the map. Whatever the red dots were, they weren't Derek's creations, giving Jonas more worries. What else was out there?

Jonas picked up the transmitter. "Derek. Do you copy? Over."

Static.

"Dammit."

The position of the five robots indicated they were surrounding Derek to protect him. Jonas marveled at his grandson's creativity. Three of the five robots were masculine while the other two were feminine. Each was designed with a distinct personality, which unnerved Jonas on occasion. They weren't androids, at least not in their outward appearance. They looked like mechanical people in their structure.

Derek grew up an only child. After his parents were murdered, Jonas did his best to fill their gaps, but Derek became introverted. He spent his time reading and researching and seldom interacted with Jonas or children Derek's own age.

Had Derek deliberately created his five robots to be the types of friends or playmates he longed for during his youth? Derek favored two of his robots the most: Isaac and Bradbury. Their bond, odd to consider it such, was similar to the affection brothers and sisters held for one another. Kurt, on the other hand, never interacted with Derek, except on occasion. Like an outcast, he distanced himself from Derek and the other robots. Octavia and Ursula maintained feminine qualities but were reserved, like elderly librarians with cold, straightforward personalities.

Derek fashioned the female robots to exhibit attractive facial features, but their personality traits were something Derek might have longed for in a protective and encouraging mother. They lacked any forms of playfulness or sensuality.

How were these robots faring in the current weather conditions? With whatever approached their location, could Derek's robots adequately protect him?

Without any way to contact Derek, all Jonas could do was watch the red dots move closer to the Phobos Crash Site. Whatever danger these things possibly represented, Jonas couldn't do anything except wait and hope for Derek to contact him soon. The dust storm was now the *least* of Jonas' worries.

DEREK SHOOK off the red sand covering his smart suit. The winds had died down, but dust sieved downward from the atmosphere like flour through a giant sifter. He wiped away a thick coat of red silt from his helmet's visor, not that it aided his vision much more in the darkness.

After shaking off dust and grit from his sleeves, he turned and leaned against the metal radio tower. His wall of robots resembled clay statues. He punched a few commands on his left wrist computer control panel. The robots whirled and turned. Sand and silt spilled off them, forming little smooth pyramid dunes around their feet.

Derek didn't understand why his grandfather worried about his need to explore the Martian frontier. With no predators or political enemies on Mars, exploration was safer than a jungle on Earth. The frigid nights and rugged terrain were his greatest dangers. The temperatures were gradually warming and should increase over time, as the terraformation of trees, grasses, and various lichens and fungi flourished.

The Carson Terraforma Project had introduced plant species from Earth to seed the Martian terrain. Each shuttle or ore ship entering the Martian atmosphere dispersed millions of fertilize-coated seeds from compartments, after they descended into the jet stream. Seeds from the hardiest tundra plants on Earth were part of Phase I. Once these plants became established, they released more oxygen into the atmosphere. Scientists hoped, over time, the climate would warm enough to initiate Phase II. Plans were underway to introduce small game after the smaller mossy plants matured, but this phase might not occur during Derek's lifetime. The time between the first and second phases could take several hundred years.

He understood his grandfather was overly cautious since Derek's parents had been killed, but that occurred on Earth. He didn't have to worry about any assassination attempts on his or his grandfather's life. His family's former enemies couldn't touch them on Mars.

"*No Martian drive-bys here, Grandpa.*" He chuckled.

Derek couldn't connect the first radio tower until the sun rose. Connecting all the towers would take several days. He imagined Jonas was upset about the radio silence, but once Derek connected the first tower's aerial signal, he could contact Jonas to let him know he was okay. Once the radio towers were properly established, techs were to deliver twenty missile turrets to the ridge overlooking the Phobos Crash Site as a defensive front.

Against what?

Grayson possessed the only settlements on Mars. Derek couldn't fathom any direct competition in the near future. No other space entrepreneur or national space program possessed the necessary funds to get to Mars. Did Grayson intend to permanently prevent others from staking claims on Martian territories before they even had a chance to venture here?

From what he knew about Grayson, probably.

In a way, Derek understood Grayson's line of thinking. Grayson had invested nearly his entire fortune into establishing his Mars settlements. His large projects could have bankrupted him, but he took those risks anyway. He supposed the tycoon wanted to earn as much profit off his endeavors as possible without others cashing in on his claim. But from what Derek gathered, Grayson's wealth had increased over one thousand percent since his Mars exploration. That was a substantial amount of profit, and Grayson wasn't finished reaping his rewards.

Derek held several patents for his robotic inventions in the A.I. sciences, so he understood how others sought to gain profit off another person's work and ideas. Patents were short-lived, which eventually gave someone else a chance to use the technology for their own profits, after the inventor gained his head start in the industry. But Grayson's situation was completely different.

Grayson's actions reflected his need to own and *rule* the planet. Thus, the future construction of the missile turrets.

"*Derek!*" one robot said.

Derek turned in response. The robots could speak, but during their trip to the crash site, they'd been quiet, perhaps allowing Derek time without outside intrusions. Their voices sounded more human than robotic when they spoke. He often bantered with them, but never had one initiated the conversation with him. At first, he was intrigued by their self-evolving A.I. advancements, but lately, this disturbed him more each day. Their deductive reasoning and problem-solving abilities increased at such a rate that his students would be greater than what he'd programmed for them. And if this evolution progressed much further, he feared he might have to shut them down. That is, if such a capability remained.

"Yes, Isaac?" he replied.

"*Western horizon. Enemy encountered.*"

"What? Trying to tell a joke again, Isaac? We don't have any enemies out here," Derek replied, shaking his head.

"*Enemies approach, Derek. Prepare to take cover.*"

Derek rushed up the sandy slope and tapped the front of his helmet visor. The fiber-optic display glowed to life. He clicked the night vision button and the dark Martian terrain brightened before him. Silt continued to fall, but not so heavily to obscure his visibility.

About four miles out, he saw them. Eight strange, manlike beings were moving their direction.

What the hell?

Robots? From this distance, it was impossible to tell. They could be cyborgs for all he knew, but whose?

"Shit!" Derek said. "Camera, zoom in."

The lens zoomed in on the intruders. So closely, in fact, they appeared to be standing only a few feet away. These weren't men. They were robots but far more advanced than the ones he'd created. He scanned closer. Each robotic soldier either carried a military grade automatic weapon or a similar weapon was fused to its right arm. Their metallic arms housed small laser blasters, too. Their right eyes glowed crimson red. When he saw the red, he flinched and took a quick breath. Heat-seeking detectors? The robots turned their heads back and forth, apparently scanning the terrain.

"Assassin robots?" he whispered, even though the cyborgs couldn't hear him. "*Who* sent them?"

"*Information unknown,*" Bradbury said, stepping closer.

"It doesn't make any sense."

"*Why not?*" Isaac asked.

"They're scanning the terrain for heat sources. The only *living* being here is me."

Derek watched their approach. Fear prevented him from looking away. In seconds, the answer to his own question became evident. A Chinese flag was painted on each robot's right shoulder. The paint and metal were resistant to the outside weather, preventing the windblown dirt and silt from caking on the outer surface of the emblem.

"Chinese-made?" Derek said.

"*Seek shelter,*" Isaac said.

An odd sensation flowed through him. His robot possessed more insight than he did at that moment. They realized Derek's danger, but Derek's curiosity encouraged him to watch these robots instead of hiding, in the same manner killer tornados mesmerized storm chasers until the last second before rushing to safety.

Derek's inquisitiveness quashed his common sense.

Isaac was correct. Derek needed to hide. His position atop the ridge line made him vulnerable. Exposed, he stood an easy target for these robots or cyborgs. His best place for shelter was inside a crevice or a broken tunnel within the Phobos remains. Jonas expressed his concern that the rubble might be radioactive, but neither Derek's suit or his robots detected any radioactivity at the crash site.

Another alternative was to get to his abandoned vehicle. But with nightfall, the solar batteries might not have enough charge to return to Olympus Mons. Should those batteries completely drain, he was stuck inside the vehicle. The metal cab was not thick enough to withstand the assault of these Chinese robots' weapons. They'd easy pierce the doors and kill him.

His best chance to survive was to find a recess tunnel into the Phobos ruins and hide, which wouldn't be easy in the darkness.

A few geologists had began mapping the perimeter but since he wasn't a geologist and he didn't have direct communications with Olympus Mons at the moment, he didn't have access to their map layouts.

Eventually the Phobos ruins would be mined for minerals and possible gems. Geologists assumed the ores and minerals weren't any different than the ones on Mars and Deimos. For Derek, he saw no logical sense to set up a base-camp at the crash site prematurely. He figured Grayson hoped to find rare gems like the MarQuebes, plus expand his territorial claims by stationing people outside Olympus Mons.

When the next prisoners arrived, they were scheduled to be stationed inside the Phobos ruins, but that was impossible since no proper shelters had been erected. Several trucks had driven to the ruins, loaded with machinery and supplies for the prisoners to use once they arrived, but without housing, no one could survive the current elements.

"*Now,*" Isaac warned. "*I must insist, Derek, that you—*"

"In a minute," Derek replied.

"*You don't have a minute,*" Octavia said in her stern motherly tone. "*Unless you wish to die.*"

Derek glanced her direction. Her stern robotic stare held no patience. To add to her authoritative expression, she rested her hands on her hips, expecting him to head for safety immediately, without question or further argument.

He shook his head and suppressed a smile.

In that moment, he realized something else about himself. He didn't really want to die. No matter how much depression he suffered on Mars, he wanted to live. He also needed to live so he could warned everyone in Olympus Mons about these Chinese cyborgs.

Derek turned his attention to the ridge. The eight armed cyborgs marched away from their positions. Their pace was slow but unfaltering. The harsh winds and sands didn't disrupt their movements. Their destination seemed to be where Derek and his robots stood. At the rate these assassin robots travelled, he estimated their arrival at the Phobos site could take at least forty minutes or longer.

"*Octavia's right,*" Bradbury said. "*You don't have much time.*"

Derek shook his head. "Bradbury, not you too?"

Bradbury tweeped an odd sound. "*We cannot afford to lose our creator. It's our responsibility to protect you.*"

Derek smiled. He studied the parked dump trucks and flatbed trucks near the Phobos ruins. The turrets and supplies were hidden beneath tied down tarps. The vehicle doors were probably unlocked. Hell, why lock them?

He considered hiding inside one of the cabs. The cold metal doors were much thicker than his vehicle but not thick enough to conceal his body heat from the robots' heat-seeking devices. They'd find him.

The cyborgs must have detected his position and that was why his robots urgently demanded he find shelter.

Derek began his descent from the ridge to the Phobos remains with the aid of infrared vision. Even with such technology, his path was covered by the various layers of dust and grit, making the terrain deceptive. One misstep could plummet him off the cliff to his death. A quick death was better than other alternatives. He might break his ankle, leg, or get wedged between rocks and die a horribly slow death.

Each step must be taken carefully. Once safely at the bottom, he could find a place to hide.

Derek punched commands on his wrist console. The robots turned. Their joints whined and cranked. They walked ahead to guide him, leading the way down to the Phobos ruins, and pointing out the dangerous parts of the terrain.

During his slow descent, he realized he might fare better by adopting his grandfather's worry-streak. Or, at best, presume dangers existed where none should be. Now, more than anything else, he wished he could talk to his grandfather. The chance to do so might never occur again.

Chapter 15

Carter stared at the bathroom mirror. The briefcase rested on the edge of the sink. His head throbbed, and the room grew dark. Overcome by dizziness, he gripped the sink to prevent falling.

"Are you almost finished?" Sylvia asked.

"Yeah," he stammered.

"You've been in there for quite some time."

"Sorry."

"No, it's okay. I wanted to check on you."

Carter shook his head. In the mirror, something moved behind him. He turned. Nothing other than the hovering cloud of shower steam was behind him.

Facing the mirror, he caught a glimpse of the alien's large dark eyes staring at him. He squeezed his eyes shut. When he looked again, she was gone. He wiped condensation off the mirror. Leaning closer, he stared into his eyes. Everything *seemed* normal.

With his right index finger and thumb, he peeled his eyelids wider apart. Other than partially bloodshot from fatigue, he didn't see any signs of jaundice or strange dilations of his pupils. He closed his eyes and massaged them gently, until bursts of bright colors intensified behind his eyelids.

Looking in the mirror, Carter rubbed his cheeks. He needed to shave. Not that it really mattered. By the time the seven-month trip to Earth was over, he'd have a full beard and long shaggy hair, which might prove to be a blessing for disguise. He expected, without doubt, that Grayson Enterprises would try to capture him, Magnus, and Sylvia at almost any cost. With longer hair and a beard, no one could readily recognize him.

Wiping his brow with a damp towel, his hands shook. Chill bumps pimpled his back and arms. He shuddered and patted his face dry. Anxiety overshadowed him.

Outside the door, Sylvia laughed and talked to Digger. He wished he could laugh with such a carefree attitude, but he doubted he'd ever experience true happiness again. Life was short. His only true happiness had died a few days earlier.

Carter looked into the reflection of his sad eyes. "Wanda, I'm so sorry. I'm sorry for everything."

<hr />

SYLVIA'S DOOR opened and Magnus entered. She sat on the bed, stroking Digger's neck. The ferret's eyes closed with obvious content.

"Welcome back," she said.

Magnus glanced around the room. "Thanks. Where's Carter?"

"Still in the bathroom. He's been there since you left."

"Showering?"

She shrugged. "Who knows?"

Magnus shrugged. "If I had the opportunity, I'd shower that long, too."

"The water stopped forty-five minutes ago."

"He's been through a lot. Maybe he needs time to cope."

Sylvia forced a smile. "I suppose."

Carter opened the bathroom door and stepped out with the briefcase. Steam billowed out behind him.

"Everything okay?" Magnus asked.

Carter nodded. "Yeah. I'm tired and need to sleep."

"That's a good idea," Magnus replied.

"Yes," Sylvia said. "We need to get to the mechanic shop *before* the guards change shifts and that's *early*."

"Why's that so important?" Carter asked.

"The night shift guards will be exhausted and less alert."

"So will we, if we don't get some sleep," Magnus said. "I'll take the floor."

Sylvia got a blanket and tossed it to Magnus.

Magnus stretched out on the cold floor and sighed. "The hard floor should help my aching back."

Carter sat on the edge of the bed and stared at the floor. His eyes became distant.

Sylvia pulled back the blanket on her narrow bed and eased on the mattress. "You take that side, Carter."

He didn't answer.

"Well, when you're ready." She pulled the blanket over herself and closed her eyes.

CARTER SNORED LOUDLY until Sylvia finally shook him awake.

"What?" He rubbed his eyes.

She beamed a smile when he finally looked at her.

He frowned.

"Get dressed," she said.

"It's morning?" he asked.

"Hell," Magnus said. "If I'd known you'd sleep this long, I'd have taken a *longer* shower."

Carter sat on the edge of the bed and shook his head. His eyes were heavy, fatigued. He put on the guard uniform. He took his briefcase and met Magnus at the door.

"You okay, Carter?" Magnus asked.

He nodded. "Yeah. I don't understand why I'm drained."

"Space lag," Sylvia said. "It'll be even worse by the time we reach Earth."

Magnus said, "I never thought about that, but seven months... yeah, that's gonna tax us pretty heavily."

"We'll spend most of the trip in Hyber-Sleep," she said. "We should set our sleep timers for a month and awaken for three or four days to exercise before inducing sleep for the next month."

"I don't remember my journey to Mars," Magnus said. "We must've undergone some kind of transitional stages. Surely, they don't put prisoners in the mines to work immediately."

Sylvia said, "They gradually exercise them over a two-week period before placing they start mining. That's probably not enough."

"Muscular atrophy would be my concern," Carter said. "Any idea how guards and officers cope with these trips?"

"Exercise bikes and machine weights are aboard the shuttles," she replied.

Magnus said. "That'll help."

"The officers who come to Mars must wait eight months before they can shuttle back to Earth," Sylvia said.

"Really?" Magnus asked. "Why?"

"Something to do with bone density," she said. "Space travel causes bone mass loss. Back to back flights could increase the chance of osteoporosis."

They stepped into the dark corridor. Magnus pulled down his helmet visor, as did Carter. The corridor was eerily quiet.

"Hurry," Sylvia said in a quivering nervous voice. "We need to get to the mechanic room before this place gets busy."

She walked between Carter and Magnus. She made it appear as though they were escorting her since she was an hour ahead of her work schedule. Should they encounter security guards or were being watched through the surveillance cameras, their accompaniment made her arrival look official.

Sylvia's breath escaped her nose and mouth in little clouds. The corridor seemed colder than normal. She hugged herself.

The closer they came to the landing bay, the brighter the corridor became. Under the LED lights, the polished walls were magnificent to behold. The brilliance of the small MarQuebes infused in the walls was mesmerizing. The imbedded stones resembled an array of shiny ruby-red and blue twinkling stars.

"Remain calm if any guards head our direction," Sylvia said. "Don't engage in conversation because it might give you away."

Magnus nodded.

Chapter 16

Carter didn't acknowledge her words. They were *already* being watched. Not by the overhead cameras or the guards, but by *her*, the female alien that saved his life. He sensed her. She was closeby.

Each moving shadow caused his heart to accelerate. Had his mind melded with hers during sex? She only spoken telepathically to him. Yet, he continued seeing her from the corner of his eyes. He hoped the farther he got away from Deimos, the safer he became. Her touch lingered on his skin, and she intruded his mind, possibly listening to his thoughts. How long would she pursue him? Was Earth far enough to break her bond?

MAGNUS GAZED at the lights as he walked. He focused on the cameras, hoping Boony was watching, but his transmitter remained silent. His mind and heart ached because of her absence. Such feelings were premature. They'd only spoken for an hour, but he missed her. He loved her candor and honesty the best. She hadn't betrayed him by turning them over to Jonas, which she could easily have done.

Without warning, his skepticism overtook him.

"*Yet.*"

A whole team of security guards could be waiting to take them into custody once they arrived at the landing bay, or easier, they'd be shot down. He doubted the latter. Most likely, they'd have Sleeper Chips implanted and live out their contracts as mindless slaves.

He refused to allow that to happen, even if it meant forcing the guards to kill him in order to spare Carter and Sylvia. After two days of mining without the Sleeper Chip's control, he didn't want Sylvia or Carter to suffer years of grueling torture. Even if they weren't aware of their labor, he didn't want Grayson to earn one dime from free labor.

The uneventful walk to the mechanic shop didn't alleviate anyone's apprehension. Sylvia nervously slid her key card through the scanner. The first time it didn't scan. Her hand shook. With wide eyes, she ran the card a second time and waited, holding her breath. It hesitated longer than normal, checking her status, but finally, the light turned green and the door unlocked. She sighed and pulled the lever. The door widened. Magnus looked over his shoulder while Sylvia and Carter stepped through.

He wanted to engage in conversation with Boony again, but he feared someone else might be on the other end of the line, and not her. Reluctantly, he closed the door.

Sylvia motioned them to follow. She slid Digger from her tool pouch on the front of her mechanic uniform. He curled over the bend of her elbow and sniffed the air.

"I'm not certain how to hide him," she said.

"We need a small box, but he should behave inside one of our suits until we get inside the shuttle. It's warm and dark, so he tends to sleep more than he's awake," Magnus said.

"Okay," she said. "I hope so. We can't afford to draw attention to ourselves."

"Don't I know it," Magnus said.

Rows of toolboxes, various engine parts, and repair manuals covered one side of the room. An overhead rail system held a shuttle engine above a grid metal floor with oil traps beneath it. Parts of the engine were disassembled on the floor.

Sylvia slid open a narrow door. Inside the closet, dozens of mechanic jumpsuits hung on a metal rack.

"In here," she said, "find one that fits."

Magnus squeezed past her and took several of the larger uniforms off the rack and held them against his chest. He shook his head. The uniforms were too small. He kept moving down the rack until he found one much wider and longer than the others. He doubted any mechanic stationed on Mars was anywhere near his size. Quite possibly no other mechanic, guard, or prisoner equaled his mass.

Inside the small closet, he unzipped the tight guard uniform and shed it. He welcomed the sudden coolness of the room. The snug uniform was like a sauna sweat suit, trapping his heat against his body and soaked with his perspiration.

Magnus found a towel and wiped the excess sweat beneath his armpits. He enjoyed the cooler air for several minutes, letting the heat rise off his body. Realizing he couldn't delay any longer, he pulled on the red and silver jumpsuit and zipped it to his neck. He liked having a roomier suit.

He grabbed the small guard helmet and pried its transmitter and components out without damaging the wires. He wasn't certain it still worked, but he hoped it did. If Boony were to contact him, she'd probably connect to same transmitter as the night before.

Sylvia leaned into the closet and rapped softly. "Hurry. Carter needs to change."

"Sure. I'm done." He stepped past her, allowing Carter inside.

Carter stared blankly.

"You awake?" Magnus asked, looking at the briefcase. He placed a gentle hand on Carter's shoulder in passing.

Carter replied with an agitated grunt and closed the door.

"Something wrong?" Sylvia asked.

Magnus shrugged. "Maybe he needs some coffee or something to eat."

"Shit," she whispered. "We need breakfast. Wait here and take Digger."

"Where are you going?" Magnus asked.

She smiled. "Vending machines. Best use some of my earned cash before it becomes inaccessible on Earth."

"True."

"Please make certain Carter hurries." She looked at his watch. "The shift change is in a half hour. I'll be right back."

She rushed to the other end of the mechanic room and exited into an adjoining room. Amongst all the supplies, tools, and other odds and ends, Magnus found several fifty pound sacks of dry ferret food. He grinned. They couldn't carry an entire bag aboard the shuttle, but he could hide ten to twenty pounds of feed in a large toolbox.

He hadn't given much thought in feeding Digger during the flight, but he guessed the shuttle's rations contained an ample supply of canned tuna. He hoped the ship was equipped to house and feed ferrets.

<hr>

SYLVIA HURRIED to the break room. She slid her badge through the machine's reader. She bought a dozen different types of cakes, chips, and nuts. The shuttle stored enough food and drinks to supply more than two-dozen people, so they'd be okay on their journey to Earth. They needed to eat now because she wasn't certain how long it'd take to get aboard.

For her to successfully fly out of the landing bay... that was another factor altogether. And thinking about what she needed to do, her anxiety spiked.

Could she actually pull this off?

The guards should be exhausted from working their long night shift. Someone stealing a shuttle was the last thing they'd ever expect, so the element of surprise was their greatest asset.

Sylvia scooped the snacks in her arms and headed to Magnus and Carter.

She thought about Carter. She'd slept beside him during the night while Magnus slept on the floor. Carter was handsome, and she wanted to become intimate with him, but he fell asleep without even talking to her.

During the night, she wrapped her arms around him, feeling his warmth and his pulse. He slept, unmindful of her embrace. He didn't seem interested in her, and that disappointed her. If he failed to express any interest soon, the trip home was going to be extremely long and lonesome.

Carter didn't slept well. He mumbled and tossed all night, which was probably part of why he seemed so aggravated this morning. She wondered if she could do something more to comfort him.

Sylvia returned to Magnus and presented all the snacks in her hands. "Pick something."

"Sugar rush, eh?"

"It's the best I could find. Sorry." She cringed, scrunching her freckled nose.

"Not a problem." He took a chocolate muffin.

"He's *still* in there?"

Magnus nodded while unwrapping the muffin.

She shook her head. "Does it take men that long to change?"

"It didn't me, and I've got a *lot* more area to cover."

"He took an extremely long time in the shower last night. Not actually showering, either. Why would any man stay so long in the bathroom?"

"No comment," Magnus said.

"You don't think—"

"I don't know, don't care, and don't want to discuss it." He shoved half the muffin into his mouth.

"Oh, God! I wasn't referring... I didn't... mean *that*." Her face flushed bright red. "Dammit, I really embarrassed myself."

Magnus chewed with puffed cheeks, tried not to grin, but failed. Pieces of the muffin and icing spilled out. Magnus cupped a hand beneath his chin and caught it. He finished the muffin and released a long, loud laugh. Tears formed at the edges of his eyes.

"I didn't mean that the way it sounded," she said, still bright red.

"It's okay."

"No. Since everyone he knew on Deimos had died, that maybe Carter was... *crying?*"

Magnus' smile drained. "That's possible, Sylvia. Carter kind of comes and goes. I've noticed that myself."

She sighed. "Do you think he'll ever open up to me?"

"In what way?"

"I've given him blatant hints that I like him, but he never reacts like I hope."

Magnus patted her shoulder. "It's like you said. He's the only survivor from Deimos. He watched everyone die. That has to weigh heavy on his soul. Perhaps, he's afraid to get close to you because he's lost so much, and if you two hit it off, maybe he's afraid you might not be around long either."

Her eyes saddened. "Maybe I'm rushing things too quickly."

"The journey gives you months to get to know one another."

"We'll either hit it off or hate one another by the time we get there."

Magnus grinned. "There you go. At least it's a good sized shuttle."

"For three of us, it is."

Chapter 17

Carter set the briefcase down and looked through the coveralls. He was apprehensive about heading to Earth. He thought about the deadly virus. He almost wanted to shove the briefcase in a corner and forget about it. Taking the virus to Earth meant he had to kill Grayson. He hated that his colleagues had died. Grayson needed to answer for their deaths. But, Carter didn't think he could commit murder.

He took a pair of coveralls and wrapped the briefcase tightly and tucked it under a bench.

"Dr. Carter, *what* are you doing?"

Carter gasped. He looked around, but he didn't see her. He recognized the alien's voice, but *how* could she reach his mind from this distance?

"Where are you?" he asked.

"Don't let that concern you. *Do* what you *promised* me."

He closed his eyes and held his breath.

"Do it," she said. "Or suffer repercussions. You're only alive because of me."

"I know."

Carter swallowed hard. His mouth was pasty. He grabbed the briefcase and unwrapped it.

Someone rapped on the door.

Carter almost screamed. He jumped and faced the door.

"Yes?" Carter asked.

"Please hurry," Sylvia said.

"Okay," he replied. "I'm almost finished."

Carter found a suit his size and exchanged one uniform for the other. He hurried to the door and glanced at the rack of uniforms. He half expected to see her shadow, or something emerge, but nothing happened.

MAGNUS SCANNED THE LANDING BAY, amazed by the massive room.

"Come on," Sylvia said to Carter. "We're running behind."

Carter rubbed his eyes and grabbed his helmet. "I'm sorry. I should've gotten more sleep."

"You can sleep *plenty* on the shuttle."

Static burst on the transmitter wire. Magnus inserted the tip in his ear.

"Heads up, big man," Boony said through his earphone.

Magnus turned with a grin and walked away from Carter and Sylvia. Excitement swelled inside his chest. Hearing her voice eased his apprehension.

"You're up early. What is it?" he whispered.

"They found the guards in your room and now, they're looking for you."

"Shit!"

Carter and Sylvia turned toward him.

"What's wrong?" Carter asked.

"Nothing. But Sylvia's right. Let's hurry."

"Here," Sylvia said, handing them each a small toolbox. "Helps you play the part."

Magnus took the toolbox and then picked up the larger one he filled with ferret feed. Carter put on his helmet, tucked the silver briefcase under one arm, and carried the toolbox in his other hand.

"Let's go." Sylvia headed to the doors on the far side of the mechanic room. The automatic doors opened and the landing bay came into view.

Ten guards with bored expressions on their faces stood along the inside perimeter of the landing bay. Their guns were slung over their shoulders.

"You're right," Magnus said, looking at Sylvia.

"About?"

"The guards look wiped out."

She smiled. "They're like this every morning. They've not had a day of excitement since they've been here."

"That changes today," Magnus said with a grin.

Carter studied the guards. At first, he didn't appear nervous. His unconcerned gaze changed when he noticed their weapons. "How often do you think they practice shooting those rifles?"

"Probably never," Sylvia said.

Carter fidgeted with his collar. "I can't say that makes me feel any better."

"Just remain calm," Magnus said.

Sylvia stepped through the doors with Magnus and Carter behind her. When they neared the center of the landing bay, two armed guards turned and marched their direction.

Carter nervously glanced at Magnus. Magnus gave an encouraging wink and a slight nod. They stopped to allow the guards pass uninterrupted. The guards never paid any interest in them. After the guards passed, Sylvia led Magnus and Carter to the front of a silver shuttle, which was named: **Percival 3000**.

Sylvia whispered, "Pretend to fix something while I set the controls for take off."

"How do we get the landing bay doors open?" Carter asked.

"They'll open soon enough. A cargo ship's scheduled to depart this morning. We'll follow it out."

Magnus opened a side panel and set down the two toolboxes. "Go set the controls."

Carter stood close to Magnus. "Are you sure we didn't need those weapons in your cell?"

"No," Magnus replied. "I was framed for murder. If this fails, I can plead my case better if I don't fire back."

"I wish I had your nerves of steel."

"I'm more nervous than you think."

"You hide it well," Carter said.

"Remember, worrying never changes anything. It never solves a problem. Sometimes you must face danger head on."

The landing bay gates unlocked with a loud snap. The massive doors separated and slowly widened.

Carter crawled under the shuttle, pretending to inspect the landing gear.

"Magnus," Boony said. "Jonas issued an APB search for you."

"No alarms?" he whispered.

"No. The guards are sweeping the corridors and each prisoner's cell. When the guards change shifts, they'll scan each person's tracer chip to make accurate identification."

"Thanks for the heads up, Boony. I'm going to miss you. I wish things were different. Perhaps sometime in the future, whenever you return to Earth, we can meet again. I'd love to learn more about you."

"Do what you need to do, Magnus. If I suspected you lied to me, you'd have been taken into custody last night."

"I'm aware of that."

"Don't make me regret my actions," she said. "Make right what was wronged to you. This might be your only chance."

"No, if I stayed on Mars, I'd never get the chance. I'd die in the mines."

Boony released a soft sigh. "That's true."

"Thanks, Boony. I greatly appreciate this."

"Be careful. Should fate want our paths to cross again, nothing will prevent it. So do me one favor?"

Magnus smiled, thinking of seeing her in the future. "Sure, if I can."

"Don't ruin the ending for me, okay? For what it's worth, we all deserve a happy ending in life."

Magnus wanted to say more but the cargo ship propulsion engines ignited. The sound was relentless. He tucked the transmitter inside his vest pocket.

The landing bay gates opened wider and the bay's temperature plummeted within a moment's notice. *Percival 3000* was painted deep maroon on the silver shuttle. It was parked approximately a hundred yards to the side of the massive cargo ship.

Sylvia leaned through the shuttle door and waved them to her. "We're set. Get aboard!"

The outside harsh winds and cold air swept into the landing bay in a deafening rush. Fierce gusts swirled red dust across the metal flooring. The perimeter guards lowered protective goggles and turned their backs to the gushing air and loose debris.

Magnus and Carter grabbed their toolboxes and closed the compartment door. They hurried into the shuttle. Sylvia hit the liftoff preparation button. The door lowered and sealed shut.

Sylvia returned to the cockpit and sat in the pilot's seat.

Magnus took one of the two co-pilot seats and Carter eased into the other. Carter regarded Sylvia with a curious stare. Magnus assumed he gave her the same stare. After all, their escape and lives depended on her getting the shuttle through the gates safely.

Sylvia took a deep breath, giving them nervous side-glances. She seemed uncomfortable having them watch her. Their presence was added pressure she didn't need. Sylvia held her finger over the engine's start button as the heavy cargo ship inched toward the landing bay gates.

"What are you waiting for?" Carter asked, watching the landing bay activities on the large monitor screen. "*Hit* the button."

She shook her head. "No. We must wait until the cargo ship passes through the gates first. If I start the engine too soon, the guards will be on us in seconds. We'll never escape then."

Carter rolled his eyes. "The guards aren't even facing our direction."

Sylvia turned, partially frowning. "They will be once the air stabilizes and reaches equilibrium. The only reason their backs are turned is to keep the grit and sand from striking their faces. Believe me, it's painful and can slice open your skin."

Magnus leaned forward. "After that cargo ship leaves the bay, will we have enough time to clear the gates before they close?"

"Of course. The shuttle's much faster than the cargo ships."

Carter frowned. His hand clenched tighter on the briefcase handle. "Then why not go out first?"

Sylvia glanced at Magnus. "Do you think we have enough time?

He smiled. "More than plenty, provided this shuttle's as fast as you boast."

Frustrated, Carter said, "You certainly have enough time to outpace it."

"I agree," Magnus said. "The cargo ship is moving like a snail stuck on flypaper."

Sylvia pressed the ignition button. Fire blasted from the rear boosters. She flipped several more switches. The undercarriage boosters blasted, lifting the shuttle.

A guard turned and noticed the shuttle rising. He pressed the emergency button on the wall to shut the landing bay gates. Red lights flashed. A horrendous alarm squalled with a shrill louder than the roaring winds and the engines combined. The half-awake perimeter guards turned and fumbled with their laser rifles.

"Damn," Carter said. "Now you have their attention."

"I told you the engines would put them on alert. Hold on!"

Sylvia increased the throttle speed, but the gate began closing. Two guards rushed in front of the Percival 3000 and aimed their laser rifles. They fired. She screamed, winced, and jerked to the side, shielding her face with her arms. In the abrupt movement, her hand knocked the steering mechanism. Carter rushed from his seat to stand beside her.

"They can't hit *you*," Carter said, placing a hand on her shoulder. "That's only a screen feeding us the outside camera views."

Although the deflective shields of the shuttle could repel the blasts, Sylvia's reflexes caused her to jump. She accidentally pulled the steering handle to the left. The rear of the shuttle scraped the nose of the cargo ship, which pivoted the end of the shuttle to the right.

"I'm sorry," Sylvia said. "I thought they were going to hit me, but—"

"Watch out!" Carter said. "We're going to smash the gates sideways."

Sylvia strained with every bit of her strength to gain control of the steering handle, hoping to realign the ship into a straight exit through the gates, but she didn't have enough strength. More guards rushed ahead of them, firing as they approached. The blasts bounced off the Percival 3000, and the gates moved closer together.

"I can't control the shuttle!" Sylvia shouted in desperation.

More guards fired. The blasts hit the side of the shuttle. The shield panel lit up.

"Critical," flashed on the screen.

"We can't take many more hits," Sylvia said with tears brimming. "The shields are overheating and getting weaker."

Carter pointed at another panel. "The shields aren't even up."

He pressed the button, making the force field barrier surround the ship.

"Thanks," Sylvia said. "That helps, but I'm not strong enough to straighten this shuttle out. I can't pull us back on track. If we hit sideways, we're stuck, and they'll capture us."

Magnus rose from his seat and grabbed the handle. With his strength, he moved the steering handle easily. Cutting hard to the right, he readjusted their position and pulled the shuttle into a straight path toward the exit.

"Boost the speed," Magnus said.

Sylvia pushed the acceleration lever to full throttle. The rear rockets fired and the shuttle thrust forward, dead center of the gates. Four guards rushed and stood between the shuttle and landing bay gates.

Magnus pulled the steering handle enough to prevent hitting the guards and killing them but the shuttle remained low enough to intimidate them. Before they could fire, the guards flung themselves down on the metal floor. The shuttle coasted over them. The guards rolled and rushed to the perimeter to avoid being fried by the booster exhausts.

The gates narrowed, but the Percival 3000 was already three-quarters of the way through the gates. By the time the gates closed, the shuttle should be in the Martian atmosphere, but would it completely clear the gates in time?

"We're going to make it!" Sylvia said, squeezing Magnus' shoulder.

"Hang on," Magnus said. "We're going to have some impact."

The gate scraped the edge of left shuttle wing.

Sylvia gasped, watching the monitor. Magnus turned more to the right and tilted the shuttle to the side. Sylvia pushed the accelerator lever harder, until she was at full throttle. Her action was more hopeful than anything else.

In seconds, the shuttle flew past the closing gates. The gates slammed shut with an echoing rattle.

"You did it," she said softly.

Magnus smiled and shrugged. "*We* did it."

"At least we don't have more lasers to worry about," Carter said.

Sylvia said, "Yes."

Magnus stood from behind the steering wheel and motioned her. "Sylvia, it's all yours."

"Once we get in orbit, I'll let the computer take over."

Carter stepped away from Sylvia.

Sylvia's hands shook as she took the controls. She smiled at them. "We . . . we did it."

Magnus nodded.

She mouthed, "Thank you."

Carter plopped in his copilot seat and shook his head. "That was much easier than I expected."

"*Nothing* easy about that," Magnus replied.

"We're still alive," Carter said, placing his hands atop the briefcase.

Sylvia replied, "That counts for something."

"No," Magnus said, "it counts for *everything*."

She gave Magnus a relieved glance. "Thanks, again."

"Not a problem. I'd say this part was a lot easier than what awaits us on Earth," Magnus said.

Carter responded with a stern glare. "What do you mean?"

"Grayson will be waiting for us."

"Well, hell, I know that."

"But the thing is," Magnus said, "Grayson has seven months to prepare for our arrival. Seven months is a hell of a long time to make plans. No telling what he'll have in store for us."

Sylvia's face paled. "Magnus, can we please talk about something else? I'm already so nervous that I'm sick to my stomach. Let my nerves calm for a few days before we discuss that."

"Sure. What would you like to talk about?" he asked.

"If you could relive your life and do it differently, what would you choose to do?"

Magnus picked up Digger and rubbed the ferret's ears. "Well, Mars would *not* be in the picture."

Sylvia laughed. "Yeah. I'd rethink that decision, too."

"As would I," Carter said.

Chapter 18

Jonas stared at the landing bay, surveillance screen in disbelief. "Grayson's prized shuttle has been stolen!"

Fuming, he stormed to Boony's desk. He stopped inches from her and she looked up, meeting his angered stare.

"Did you see that?" he asked. His face flushed red, making his silvery hair almost glow.

"Yes," she replied in a near whisper.

"Find out *who* they are!"

"Yes, sir." She spun her chair around and opened her computer. "I'll look into it."

"No, don't *look* into it. I want their identities immediately, like yesterday!" He ran his hands through his hair and shook his head. "Dammit! I can't believe I've allowed this to happen."

"This isn't *your* fault," Boony said.

He thrust his finger at the surveillance camera screen, which was replaying the Percival 3000 leaving the landing bay. "As head of security, anything of *this* magnitude *is* my fault. *How* do you think Grayson will view this? I'll be at the top of his shit list now."

"But you're not to blame." She looked at him with concern, but kept her voice quiet. "Calm yourself, sir, please. Things only get worse if you have a stroke or heart attack."

Jonas gritted his teeth. Heat rose up his neck, making his face redder. She had a point, like always. He made fists, took a deep breath, and exhaled an agitated growl.

Boony smiled. "Jonas, everything's going to be okay. This isn't your fault."

"Boony," he sighed and rubbed his temples. "Derek's silence has preoccupied my thoughts. I've overlooked my duties and obligations, worrying about him. I allowed things to slip past unnoticed. No one has a higher rank on Mars than me, so I take full responsibility."

"Anyone in your situation would've sought to find a lost loved one, sir."

"No."

"Yes, they would."

"I can't allow that as an excuse, Boony. I can't. Not in my case. This is why Grayson's dead set against family members working together on Mars. Had I not been so wrapped up about Derek's safety—"

"Jonas, it's *okay*." She placed her hand on his arm.

Jonas bit his lower lip. Her eyes searched his. He kept waiting for her to flinch, to look away, but she didn't. "Have you seen anything remotely unusual on the monitors over the past few days? Anything at all?"

Without hesitation or any change in her voice, she shook her head. "No."

He studied her eyes for several seconds and turned away. Crossing his arms, he said, "To steal a shuttle took time to plan. This didn't happen on the spur of the moment. See what you can find on the surveillance videos and report it to me ASAP. Meanwhile, I have the unique privilege to inform Grayson that his newest multi-billion dollar shuttle was stolen. The Percival 3000 was the first in his latest fleet design. He'll be sorely pissed."

"I'm sorry, sir," Boony typed the commands to download the past day's video feed.

"Not as sorry as those thieves will be. When it comes to theft, Grayson's the worst enemy anyone can have."

"I'm on it, sir."

"Pull up facial recognition and compare their images against the records of the Olympus Mons residents. Check for everything. Guards, prisoners, workers, and even my security personnel. All of them. Without exception. Understood?"

"Yes, sir."

Jonas exited the office door, letting it slam behind him.

BOONY SIGHED WITH SLIGHT RELIEF. Fear rose inside her. Not because she'd lied to Jonas. He believed her. Otherwise, if he suspected any dishonesty on her part, he'd have arrested her without any further directions or questions. She worried about Magnus. Had he fully anticipated the possible repercussions for stealing Grayson's shuttle? She couldn't warn Magnus without Jonas intercepting her communication. From here out, he'd probably eavesdrop on every conversation inside Olympus Mons.

While she pretended to search the camera videos, she deleted all her voice transmissions with Magnus. She erased the entire footage of her and Magnus at The Vortex, though she felt regret in erasing that memory. She was glad Magnus escaped. She hoped he somehow avoided Grayson's vengeance. He deserved to get the justice against those who had framed him.

GRAYSON STOOD and stared out his penthouse office window at the crashing ocean waves. They didn't soothe him like normal. Anger tightened his face. He listened intently to his Bluetooth attached to his right ear.

He recorded his reply. "You're telling me the Percival 3000 was hijacked, Jonas? By whom?"

The worst part about communicating with officers on Mars was the long delay in feedback. A radioed message took approximately fifteen minutes to get from the speaker to the listener and vice versa. A lot could happen during that half hour. Emergencies could end tragically without one party knowing what had happened to the other.

After thirty minutes, he received Jonas' reply.

"Yes. Minutes ago. By the time you receive this, approximately forty-five minutes ago. I don't know their identities yet. Once I get that information, I'll update you."

Grayson pulled the earphone and tossed it across the room. His hands tightened into muscled fists. His inner rage made him want to hit something, anything, but nothing in his office could satiate that need. He picked the earphone up off the floor and marched from his office. He went to his small gym where a heavy punching bag hung. By the time Jonas contacted him again, Grayson could dent a huge chunk of his aggression away.

He changed into gym clothes and struck the bag hard. He hoped whoever had stolen the shuttle could fly it properly. The worst that could happen was the shuttle exploding on entry due to pilot error or it crash-landed. Either was bad for him, but merciful to those aboard. Mercy they didn't deserve. Should they successfully land, they'd experience far more agony than imaginable.

AFTER THE PERCIVAL 3000 broke free of the Martian atmosphere, Sylvia set the autopilot controls.

"We're all set," she said. "The shuttle's destined for Earth."

"That's good," Carter said.

"Except for the waiting," Sylvia replied.

"True," Magnus said. "But there's nothing we can do about that."

He set Digger on the floor.

"Where are you going?" she asked.

Magnus turned. "I'm going to see what's inside the shuttle. That should busy me for a couple of hours."

"Mind if I tag along?" Carter asked.

"Not at all."

Sylvia scooped up Digger. "I'm coming, too."

They walked down the center aisle of the twenty-seat crew compartment. Each seat was ergonomically designed for the prolonged space hibernation. On the armrests were feeding tubes that connected to I.V. machines.

"I don't like the idea of this," Sylvia said.

"What?" Magnus asked.

"Inserting our own I.V. needles."

Magnus glanced at Carter. "Why worry about it? We have a doctor on board."

Carter nodded. "Not a problem. I'll set you both up."

"I didn't think about you being a doctor," she replied with an embarrassed grin.

Above the plush passenger seats were shatter-resistant capsules that lowered and sealed around the hibernating occupants. The enclosures were made with radiation protection shields and maintained their body temperatures ten degrees below normal, placing the sleeping passengers into hypothermia, which dropped their metabolic rate seventy percent.

Sylvia sat in one of the seats. "These are the most comfortable seats I've ever seen."

"Probably aids sleep," Magnus said.

"Must we sleep so long during the trip?" she asked, pressing her head against the plush headrest.

"We have to," Carter said.

"Why?"

"Because we'd go stir crazy if we didn't. Sleeping most of the trip helps maintain our sanity. We'll be comatose. The shuttle's computer monitors our vital signs and feeds us intravenously."

"Seriously?" she asked.

Carter nodded and sat beside her. "Didn't you do this when you left Earth?"

Her brow furrowed as she thought. "Honestly, I don't remember the trip. Before I arrived at Grayson Enterprises to board the shuttle, I was extremely nervous. We drank juice or something, but... that's the last thing I actually remember."

Carter stared into her eyes. She smiled and for the first time since he'd left Deimos, he returned the smile. "Yes. Trust me. It's not that bad. I researched everything about space travel before I signed Grayson's intimidating contract. I didn't want to take unnecessary risks. Luckily, Olympus Mons' settlement was already settled when Grayson requested me to join his Deimos Project."

"I didn't know enough about the trip," Sylvia said. "A part of me didn't even care because I didn't have a choice. I wanted my prison record erased. On the plus side, the high pay rate was too tempting to pass up. Sadly, if what Magnus says is true, I've lost everything I've earned."

Carter gave her a reassuring smile. "Don't worry about money. We'll have far more money than that with the MarQuebes we took."

From farther back in the shuttle, Magnus yelled, "Hey, guys! Come check out what I found."

Carter and Sylvia hurried through the crew compartment and rushed to where Magnus stood in one of the storage rooms. Magnus turned around with a strange device that resembled a UPC scanner.

"What's that?" Sylvia asked.

Magnus smiled. "It's a scanner that detects our tracer chips. It'd be a good idea to see if you and Carter have chip implants."

"Why would we?" Carter asked.

"Your question should be, 'Why wouldn't you?' You underestimate Grayson. He keeps tabs on every employee on Mars and probably on Earth, too."

"I'm a doctor. He's no reason to implant a chip in me."

Sylvia said, "I probably have one due to my record."

"What'd you do?" Magnus asked.

"Petty theft and bank fraud. Nothing severe compared to the majority of the prisoners, but I still probably have one. Since I had great mechanical skills before my sentencing, Grayson offered me a great deal. My record will... *would* have been expunged after my three year contract ended."

"*If* he kept his end of the contract," Magnus said.

"You don't think he would've?"

Magnus shrugged. "He'd have figured out some way to convince you to extend it."

Her brow furrowed and she looked at Carter.

Carter nodded. "He's probably right. I don't trust Grayson at all."

Magnus turned on the scanner and ran it across her arm.

Nothing.

He proceeded to scan her head. The detector's red light turned green and the scanner beeped. Small text scrolled on the screen, indicating she had an active chip.

"See? I have one," she said.

Magnus nodded. "I figured you did."

"What do we do?" she asked.

"Either we deactivate it or cut it out. Otherwise, Grayson will know every move you make when we reach Earth."

Carter frowned, studying the scanner, and then he looked at Magnus. "Can't you deactivate it? I don't have the proper equipment to surgically remove it. And should she suffer an infection during Hyber-Sleep, she could die before we get to Earth."

Magnus turned and walked to a shelf. "There's another device here with a strong enough magnet that might make her chip malfunction."

Carter said, "Why'd they have all of this gear on this shuttle?"

Magnus shrugged. "Maybe for prisoner transport. They possibly need this equipment for when a chip malfunctions. I honestly don't know. But from what one said, a lot of chips are shorting out."

Magnus set down the scanner and took the magnetized device and turned it on. He placed it near the chip at the base of Sylvia's head.

"Will this hurt?" she asked.

"I hope not," Magnus said.

He turned up the magnetic frequency. She squinted and groaned.

"You okay?" Magnus asked.

Sylvia nodded. "Yeah, I'm okay. It hurts a little, like a slight headache. It's also getting warmer."

After several minutes, he shut off the magnetic device. He took the scanner and ran it across the back of her head. The scanner showed the chip but revealed it as inactive.

"It's dead now," Magnus said. He turned to Carter. "Let me check you."

"Sure, why not?"

Magnus ran the scanner across Carter's head and then scanned from head to toe.

"You're clear," Magnus said.

"So I don't have one?"

"Not according to the scanner."

Sylvia felt the lump at the back of her head. "Strange I never noticed it was there."

"At least it wasn't a Sleeper Chip like mine," Magnus said. "I wonder how many days I spent mining without ever knowing it."

"That must be like a nightmare," she said.

"It would be if I obsessed about it. Time loss and not knowing exactly what happened during that time; yeah, it could drive you insane, worrying about it. I'm glad that the man gave me the microchip injection. Otherwise, I'd still mining."

Sylvia smiled. "You won't have to do that ever again."

"Damned straight," Magnus said. "I won't let them take me alive. They'll have to kill me before I'll be chipped again."

"That's a bit extreme, Magnus," Sylvia said. Sadness claimed her face.

"Not to me it isn't."

Carter returned to the hibernation seats and sat in one. "Time for us to settle in for a long nap? Some hibernation sleep? Seven months is a long time."

"No, not yet," Sylvia said. "Our trip just started. Can't we wait a few weeks before we undergo hibernation?"

"I don't see why not?" Magnus said. "What do you think, Carter?"

Carter shrugged. "That's fine by me, but what do we do for entertainment?"

"Well," Sylvia said, "They have access to thousands of movies. Some officers talked about that when I repaired some hardware inside the cabins. There's also a digital library, if you'd rather read. Puzzles and—"

"To those who have stolen the Percival 3000," a voice said over the intercom. "Return the shuttle to Olympus Mons and your punishment will be less severe than what you'll face on Earth. You know Grayson's reputation well enough to know I'm *not* exaggerating."

"Shit," Magnus whispered.

Sylvia glanced from Carter to Magnus. "What do we do?"

"Where's the transmitter?" Magnus asked.

"In the pilot's cabin."

"Let's go."

Chapter 19

Jonas returned to the security office after sending Grayson the message about the stolen shuttle. In a way, he was thankful for the fifteen-minute delay in communication. The thirty-minute gap in their conversation helped Jonas mentally brace himself for Grayson's explosive fit of fury. A few shots of whiskey also helped.

A guard stepped into Jonas' office. He stood six foot tall and was thin. His hair, eyes, and skin were characteristic of someone from the Middle East.

"What is it, Zeke?" Jonas asked. "I'm rather busy at the moment."

Zeke eyed the whiskey bottle, nodded. "Did you not get the report?"

"Which report?"

"I set it... *there*, on your desk, under you laptop," Zeke replied, pointing.

Jonas picked up the folder and opened it. He looked at the picture profile. "Magnus Knight?"

"Yes, sir. He incapacitated two guards yesterday after his shift."

"And I'm learning about this *today*?"

"We found them a little while ago. They were cuffed and gagged inside his shower. He stole their uniforms."

Jonas frowned. "He apparently stole the Percival 3000. Where are the two guards?"

"In the infirmary. According to the report, one's still unconscious. Critical condition. The other one should leave within a few hours."

Jonas nodded. "Come with me."

He left his office with Zeke and walked down the stairs to Boony's desk. She was going through facial scans on the computer. He expected Grayson's message at any time. At least he'd discovered one thief's identity, but he wanted more information before he replied to Grayson.

"Boony, patch me through to the Percival 3000's intercom."

"Yes, sir." She typed in several commands. "You're connected."

"Come in, Percival 3000," Jonas said. "Channel's open. For now."

BOONY SAT AT HER DESK, evaluating the video feed. Once the facial recognition software identified Magnus' and Sylvia's faces, she had no choice but to reveal their names. Not doing so made her more of a conspirator, even though she really couldn't deny playing a role by allowing Magnus to escape.

Jonas wouldn't hesitate to make an example out of her, so no one else inside Olympus Mons would ever attempt any similar, insubordinate action.

She imagined she'd end up in the mines like Magnus, or perhaps worse. While the computer scanned faces, she maintained her normal nonchalant attitude.

"Percival 3000. Come in," Jonas repeated.

Boony's computer sounded its recognition alert. Jonas turned and looked at the computer screen. When he saw the face, he took Magnus' picture from the folder and set it before her.

Jonas pointed at the screen. "That's a match. Boony, get me the information on Magnus Knight *now*. Everything you can find."

"Yes, sir." She bit her lower lip and typed additional search commands.

Jonas connected to the bridge of the shuttle. "Magnus Knight? Care to reply? I know you're aboard. The evidence speaks for itself. Being silent doesn't change that fact. Cooperate, or you're facing more severe consequences."

Boony printed out Magnus' bio. Secretly, she hoped Magnus made it to Earth safely. He was a giant of a man, but his heart seemed kinder than his intimidating appearance portrayed. Some people weren't photogenic. Magnus was one of those people. Had Magnus been ruthless like the hardened prisoners, he'd have killed those two guards. But he held the mildness of a true gentleman.

The computer screen beside hers froze with the next identified culprit.

Jonas' face turned red. "Shit!"

"What is it?" she asked.

"Sylvia Perkins? She's one of my best mechanics. She's the last person I'd suspect to do something like this. Her sentence was short, and she scored favorably on each of her conduct reports. Are you certain that's the correct match?"

Boony shrugged. "The facial recognition indicates it's her."

Jonas gritted his teeth. "You think you know someone—"

Boony stared at the screen, keeping her composure, partially feeling guilty of the secrets she kept from Jonas. If he found out, would he forgive her?

———

MAGNUS LOOKED at Sylvia and Carter with slight confusion. "How'd he find out so quickly?"

"Hard to say," Sylvia replied. "But cameras are everywhere in the mines, corridors, and the landing bay."

"I know, but I expected a longer delay." He closed his eyes and shook his head. Boony mentioned the guards had been discovered, so they quickly identified him.

Magnus pushed the transmitter button. "This is Magnus."

"You overtook the two guards in your cell yesterday. Is that correct?"

"Yes, sir, but it's not what it seems."

"You think I should believe a prisoner who just stole Grayson's prized shuttle?"

"I understand how it looks," Magnus said. "But if you—"

"It's not how it looks, son. It's *exactly* what it is. What I don't understand is how you convinced my best mechanic to help you?"

Sylvia leaned close to the intercom. "He didn't convince me. I chose to go on my own. Magnus came into the picture *afterwards*."

Magnus frowned, placing his index finger to his lips.

"No," Sylvia said. "What he's saying about you isn't true."

Jonas said, "Look, there's no way I can go after you. I'm sure you're aware of that. So let me appeal to your better judgment. That is, if you are fortunate enough to *possess* any rationality at all."

Magnus' jaw clenched tightly. His eyes narrowed.

"Magnus," Jonas said in a milder tone. "I don't know if you've ever heard about the things Grayson's done to those who've betrayed him in the past. I know his relentlessness. I've *seen* it. Even if he gets his ship back, and you somehow escape, he won't stop hunting you. He won't rest until he makes each one of you suffer. So, I'm placing this offer on the table. It's a one time offer."

"I'm listening," Magnus said.

"Bring back the Percival 3000, and I'll explain your cooperation to Grayson. You'll remain out of his reach here on Mars. I'll make certain things go back to normal for you."

"Normal?" Magnus replied. "No deal. I'm not going back to the mines."

"You signed a contract," Jonas said in an aggravated tone. "I have a copy in your file."

"I never signed away my rights to lose my mentality, sir. Never. None of those miners took their contracts to become mindless slaves. That deceptive information was never disclosed to *any* of us, which in a court of law is considered fraud."

"So you're an attorney now?" Jonas asked.

Magnus chuckled. "No, but that's what you and Grayson fear the most, isn't it? If we get to Earth and expose what he's doing, what's *really* going on, you'll go to prison. I suppose that's a huge stain on a legendary ex-CIA officer, huh? How many humanitarian laws has he broken to put more money into his filthy pockets? Your compliance makes you an accessory."

Jonas didn't respond.

"And since you willfully continue to support Grayson," Magnus said, "I can't trust we'd be any safer returning to Mars."

"You're making a huge mistake," Jonas said. "Think this through."

"I've thought this through. Listening to you has made it that much clearer. When we get to Earth, Grayson Enterprises will crumble. I'll make it my life's mission to let authorities at all levels know the despicable treatment these miners suffer. The media will go into a frenzy reporting this. I'm certain the U.S. Supreme Court will find it appalling enough to shut down his operations. Most likely, he'll get prison time for his crimes and you will, too."

Anger rose in Jonas' voice. "Without mind control over these prisoners, there'd be no possible way to control them. These men were the most ruthless killers on Earth, and *you're* the perfect example. Within a few days of having the freedom from your Sleeper Chip, you stole Grayson's most expensive shuttle."

"No, sir. Don't place me into the same category as those other miners. I'm nothing like them. I didn't kill those guards—"

"One of them's in critical condition. If he dies—"

Magnus sighed. "How bad is he?"

Jonas didn't reply.

Carter nudged Magnus. "He might be lying to you about that."

Considering the possibility, Magnus nodded. He continued talking to Jonas. "Look, my criminal charges on Earth pale in comparison to what these other prisoners did. I was framed for a murder I didn't commit."

"If that's true, prove yourself to me," Jonas said. "Return to the landing bay. I'll investigate the charges against you. I have ties on Earth in highest security levels with the FBI *and* the CIA. We can examine your case. I promise you won't return to the mines until they've fully evaluated all the evidence."

Magnus looked into Sylvia's worried eyes. Carter shook his head.

"Sorry, sir, but I'm not that trusting of your promises," Magnus said.

"If you won't do it for yourself, do it for Sylvia," Jonas said in a milder tone. "Her contract was short, almost over. Have her return the ship, so she can finish her original sentence without penalty."

Sylvia shook her head. "No. I'm in this with both of you. I don't trust him. Don't believe him."

"She says, 'No deal.'"

"Fine," Jonas said evenly. "You'll discover your true danger *after* it's too late. Even though you can't find it in yourselves to trust me, I have your best interests in mind. You have another passenger on board. Who is he?"

Magnus smiled. "I'm sure with your great investigative skills, Mr. ex-CAI, you'll figure it out."

Magnus pressed the button and turned off their connection.

Chapter 20

Jonas shoved his hands into his pockets. He frowned and shook his head. He met Boony's eyes. "How the hell did he find out I was in CIA?"

She held her breath and shrugged.

Jonas sighed. Worry furrowed his brow. How did he tell Grayson? Rubbing his tired eyes, he said, "I thought with Magnus' intelligence, he'd listen. I tried to appeal to his rationality."

Boony held Magus' records. "His college scores were quite high. His I.Q.'s right near the genius level. You probably shouldn't have started with direct threats. The anger and tone in your voice placed him immediately on the defensive."

Jonas nodded, running a hand through his spiked hair. "You're right. But my old interrogating habits are hard for me to break. Even as I've gotten older, I still prey on my ability to coerce cooperation. It's a big flaw and probably why Derek and I have butted heads so often."

"Maybe the two of you are too much alike."

Jonas forced a tired smile. He chuckled. "Well, there's that, too."

"But Magnus never had a record until the murder that he swears he was framed of committing. It's possible, don't you think? He might actually be innocent?"

"It happens, Boony, but over the years, the majority that hold the excuse about being framed never proved it in court."

"Isn't it difficult to do that from *inside* a prison?" Boony asked.

"Yeah, I imagine so. But even if it's true, if he's really innocent, he's like a guppy in a shark tank. Grayson will tear him apart."

"Have you seen his size?" Boony asked. "He's another shark for Grayson to deal with."

"Boony, I've worked with Grayson over a decade. Grayson's made a lot of enemies during his lifetime, and he's not old. That's why his team of security guards could put Olympic powerlifters to shame with their build and size, and Grayson's larger than any of them."

"That may be true, Jonas. But remember, Magnus has knowledge and intellect on his side."

"You don't achieve Grayson's wealthy status and sit at the top of the Forbes' Billionaire List by being stupid. Grayson's a genius. He's invented a lot of things and reaps much more than he's invested."

Boony smiled. "I don't doubt that. But there's still a big difference between Grayson and Magnus."

"What's that?"

"Grayson has everything to lose. Magnus has nothing left to lose."

Jonas grinned and cocked an eyebrow while studying her. "I'm beginning to think you're on Magnus' side?"

"If he's truly innocent, I hope he succeeds in whatever he plans to do. I tend to root for the underdog, sir. That's where I put my money. And if he's not guilty, more power to him. No intent to offend or excuse the theft of the Percival 3000."

"None taken."

Boony returned to reading more of Magnus' file.

"Do you really think he might be innocent?" Jonas asked with a furrowed brow.

"There's always that possibility, like you said. Did you read the report when he took down the two guards?"

"Not yet. I found out a few minutes ago. He hurt one of them pretty badly."

Boony frowned. "Well, I don't know about that. Who knows what really happened when the guards entered his room? Things get out of control sometimes. Magnus is big and might have accidentally injured the guard. But the thing that sticks out to me the most is he didn't take their weapons when he could've easily done so."

"That's true."

"If he were a vicious killer, he could've killed a lot of people with those weapons. The guards first, but he didn't. He could've killed guards all the way to the landing bay, so there's the strong possibility he's innocent."

"Email me a copy of his file. I'll see what my former colleagues in the States can find out."

"Sure."

"Have you discovered anything about the mystery passenger?" Jonas asked.

Boony shook her head. "Nothing yet, sir."

"Keep me posted. Time for me to face the music. I need to inform Grayson about the two we have identified." Jonas headed to the door.

"Wait, Jonas. I found something."

He turned on his heels. "What? Do you know who is he?"

"No. But he was stationed at the Deimos Life Station."

Jonas frowned. "Then why the hell did he come here?"

"I don't know."

"Find out," Jonas said, walking toward her. "Can you pull up his image?"

"Not yet. All I have is the footage when he landed. But he kept his helmet visor down and avoided cameras directly."

Jonas rolled a chair next to hers and sat. "Show me what you have."

Boony replayed the footage of Carter exiting the Deimos shuttle.

"Odd," Jonas said.

"What?"

"He deliberately tried to conceal his identity the second he landed."

"Looks that way," she replied, nodding.

"Zoom in on his briefcase."

She did.

"Doesn't seem out of the ordinary," Jonas said. "But I wonder what's inside."

"There's really no way of knowing."

"I'm more concerned about him than I am about Magnus."

"Why?"

"He arrived on Mars unannounced, wants to keep his identity secret, and fled with two prisoners to get to Earth."

Boony nodded. "That does seem suspicious."

They continued watching the video footage. Dr. Carter carried the briefcase and causally tried to leave the landing bay when he was stopped.

"That's Sylvia," Boony said. "She seemed genuinely surprised at his arrival."

"Hmm," Jonas said. "That still doesn't tell us *who* he is."

"I know."

Jonas pointed. "He signed the landing sheet. Contact the landing bay. Find out who signed it."

"On it," she replied. She tapped an extension number on the console. "Hey, Barry. Help me out. Who signed the landing sheet yesterday when the shuttle from Deimos landed?"

Boony glanced at Jonas. "He's checking."

"Good. That's good."

"Really?" she said into her microphone. Disappointment showed on her face. "Thanks."

"What is it?" Jonas asked.

"The signature isn't legible."

"Very suspicious."

"I think so, too."

"Connect me to the Deimos Life Station."

She pushed several numbers on the computer panel to connect their radio frequency to relay communication with the chief security station supervisor on Deimos.

Heavy static came over the speaker.

"Something's blocking our frequency," she said with concern.

"Does that happen often?"

"I've never experienced it before. It seems deliberate."

"Damn."

"Sorry I can't be of any more help."

"You're doing a great job," Jonas said. He stood. "Keep looking. Surely he removed his helmet *somewhere*."

"I'll let you know the second I see his face and have the facial recognition scan for his identity."

He sighed. "I'll let Grayson know what we know. The day keeps getting brighter and brighter."

"After you contact Grayson," she said, "worry more about contacting Derek than this shuttle. The Percival 3000 is Grayson's concern now. Not ours."

"I know. But Grayson won't see it that way."

Boony smiled. "What's it matter? He's on Earth."

"Trust me. That's still too close. I've seen him at his worst, and this incident will set him off like nothing else ever has. Keep me posted."

"I will."

"I'll be back soon."

Jonas exited the security office.

BEFORE BOONY DELETED the footage of her and Magnus talking in the Vortex, she wanted to watch it one last time.

Although Magnus was a giant of a man, he seemed timid and somewhat nervous when she had spoken to him. He possessed an honest smile. His demeanor was gentler than most men she'd met. He was certainly kinder in his mannerisms than the cocky guards that came onto her in The Vortex. Something about him made her want to believe he was innocent. His smile beamed warmly, which was even more rare for her lately.

"Safe travels, Magnus," she whispered, hitting 'delete' and wiping their video existence from the camera records. "I hope you find the justice you seek."

When the video disappeared, she stared at the monitor attached to the outside cameras at the Olympus Mons Landing Bay, which gave her a spectacular view of the night sky with the brightest array of stars she'd ever seen. On Earth too many streetlights glowed in the cities. The glare, along with pollution, prevented one from seeing star clusters clearly. A part of her hoped the population on Mars never exploded like it had on Earth.

As Boony stared at the night sky, she regretted not taking Magnus' offer to return to Earth. By staying on Mars, she was jeopardizing her own freedom should Jonas ever discover her hand in helping Magnus steal the shuttle.

"Be safe, Magnus," she whispered.

Chapter 21

Derek scanned the hillside where the strange Chinese robots had stood. He could no longer locate them, even though the harsh winds had died and the red dust and silt had settled. His night vision offered no real advantage.

Their sudden disappearance made his heart race. Given the treacherous terrain along the Phobos rocky ledges, how could those robots move so fast? Fear crept into his mind. A chill shot through him. Where had they gone? Were they watching him?

He wondered if he'd ever see his grandfather again.

Despite his robots pleading for him to hide hours earlier, he ignored them. Instead, he stopped at a radio tower near the bottom of the slope and attempted to finish connecting the wiring before seeking shelter, which now he viewed as a grave mistake.

His robots made him aware of an opening at the side of the Phobos debris. He estimated he still had plenty of time to rush to it whenever the cyborgs came into view.

While he worked briefly on the radio tower, Octavia and Ursula scouted in opposite directions. Bradbury and Isaac stayed near Derek, scanning the area for the robots. Kurt was nowhere to be seen.

Once Derek realized he didn't have enough time to get the radio workable, he untied a tarp on a truck bed and looked beneath it. Missile turrets. Three of them.

When Derek first learned Grayson wanted to set turrets around the Phobos perimeter, he believed Grayson intended to keep Mars all to himself.

But now, after discovering the heat-seeking robots closing in, perhaps Grayson was preparing for the inevitable. Other countries like China might eventually invade Grayson's settlements and kill his citizens to shut down his operations.

By the time Grayson sent replacements, other countries might've already stolen and settled his bases at Olympus Mons and the Phobos Crash Site with their occupants. Recapturing zones he considered his own required military strategies. With the majority of the inhabitants controlled by the Sleeper Chips, his miners turned militants would be under the control of only a few individuals. Should the opposition kill those who dictated the prisoners' commands, the prisoners became easy bait and would be killed without any resistance. Or worse, the enemy took control and used the miners as combatants against Grayson's reinforcements.

Grayson had other projects in the works on Mars that no one on Earth knew about. Not only was he building his own steel industries on Mars, he was ready to start his own mint for Martian currency to get away from the U.S. and U.N. monetary control. Backed by his trillions of dollars, he was his own bank.

Although no prototype coins had been sketched, Derek knew enough about Grayson's ego to realize the coins would have Grayson's facial image stamped on them. Derek was surprised Grayson hadn't plastered large banners with his image or erected statues of himself inside Olympus Mons yet.

Derek didn't believe Grayson was a true dictator at heart. Grayson's ideology proved the man was getting closer to setting up a throne on Mars where he could rule his new civilization. However, Mars didn't have the luring extravagances like the ritzier places on Earth. If Grayson wanted to make an appearance to astound his resentfully jealous competitors, he couldn't do that on Mars. Such places didn't exist on the red planet, nor did Derek believe they ever would within the next three lifetimes. Grayson needed to remain on Earth where the other wealthiest aristocrats lived so he could witness their expressions as he rubbed his success in their faces.

Derek pulled back the tarp off the truck and studied the unassembled turrets. Since the turrets weren't set up and connected to a command station, they were useless. He didn't have the means to craft a weapon from the parts.

"Damn," Derek said.

Every guard posted in Olympus Mons was issued laser rifles and laser blaster pistols. He'd been given one of each by his grandfather, but he didn't bring either weapon with him. Of course, he never expected he'd *need* a weapon since no viable life forms roamed the Martian terrain.

Derek tapped the air filter on his helmet. Loose dirt and grit rained from the mouthpiece. He imagined how badly the sandstorm could tear someone apart and kill them without a protective helmet and an insulated suit. The red sand and grit were more abrasive than mid-grade sandpaper and sharp like needles.

Isaac and Bradbury stood to each side of Derek while scanning the rocky terrain. Derek's inspiration for naming his robots came from the sci-fi tomes he'd spent most of his youth devouring. Isaac was named after Isaac Asimov who had written, *I Robot*, which inspired Derek to work diligently on building robots. Bradbury was named in honor of Ray Bradbury and *The Martian Chronicles*. Of the five robots, these two were his favorites.

Octavia was positioned to the west within view, and Ursula stood slightly to the east. Kurt was at the radio tower on the ridge line with his back to Derek.

"Do you see any of the enemy robots?" Derek asked.

"*Negative. Nothing to report,*" Isaac said.

Bradbury said, "*Still, you need to find shelter. The threat of danger has not passed. It's inevitable they'll seek confrontation.*"

"I realize that Bradbury."

"*And yet, you continue to ignore us. Ursula and Octavia are coming your direction. Best you find shelter before they arrive.*"

"Give me five more minutes," Derek said.

"*The enemy's still out there,*" Isaac said.

Derek glanced around. "Are they headed for us?"

"*Negative. There's still no physical sign of them,*" Bradbury said.

"They cannot disappear."

"*Logically, no,*" Isaac said. "*But they've gone stealth.*"

"Stealth?" Derek said. "Cloaking devices?"

"*Quite possible,*" Bradbury replied.

That wasn't something he'd even considered. "Come on, let's head to the crash site."

A red laser sliced through the air and grazed Derek's shoulder. He winced in pain, dropped, and rolled in the red soil. His eyes searched the area while he clutched his burning shoulder. Smoke rose above the melted suit material and his blistered skin.

Looking around, he didn't see anything other than his robots.

Bradbury rushed to him, grabbed and lifted him, and carried Derek toward the small opening between two giant slabs of rock in the Phobos crater. Another blast fired, but Bradbury's back shielded Derek from further injury. The robot continued running, unaffected by the deflected laser.

Isaac followed Bradbury, but he ran in strategic sidesteps as he attempted to locate their metal enemies. Octavia and Ursula positioned themselves at the truck's flatbed. Motionless, they scanned the terrain.

Derek held his shoulder. His enemy combatants must have re-cloaked themselves, which was technology he'd researched but had yet to master its utilization for his robots. He never considered he'd need such technological advancements for his AI.

The thought prompted him of what his grandfather once told him. "Prepare for the unexpected at all times."

Sound advice, but now he wished that he'd equipped his robots with anti-cloaking devices to shatter the stealth ability of these foreign robots. Since his robots should've been the only ones on Mars, he never made such upgrades.

Bradbury carried Derek near the blackened edge of the massive, seven-mile high mountainous side of the Phobos remains. Feeling nauseous from the increasing pain in his shoulder, he'd barely noticed the tunnel leading into the rock wall.

Another laser blast struck Bradbury and glanced off, striking the rocky ground behind them. Bradbury moved to a tunnel-like opening and carried Derek inside. He didn't know how deep the tunnel was, but once inside, they were trapped and weaponless. Not exactly the way he pictured his death to be.

Chapter 22

Grayson's huge bare fists pummeled a three hundred pound punching bag. The vinyl bag covering sank with each crushing blow. Some of the seams were ruptured. Had he been hitting a man, his victim's insides would be mush.

Sweat beaded his brow and his face flushed crimson. His white undershirt was soaked. A normal routine last thirty minutes, but with the frustrating news of escaped prisoners stealing the Percival 3000, he was still going strong after forty-five minutes.

He stopped hitting the bag when his earphone beeped. His chest heaved. Grabbing a towel off a weight machine, he wiped streams of sweat from his face and the back of his neck.

A guard handed him a chilled bottle of water. The message on the earphone held no real urgency with the long delay between Earth and Mars. Most of his anger had subsided. He wanted a few minutes to cool down before listening to Jonas' update.

Grayson had always worked hard for his money. His empire existed solely because of his shrewd nature, but mostly because he willingly took risks whenever necessary. As he had told Senator Johnson, Grayson never begged or borrowed a dime from anyone. His monetary status as one of the richest men in the world came from intuitional gambles; not from outside sources. If he could do it, he figured anyone with half a brain should be able to repeat his success.

He hated when people thought they were entitled to benefit from someone else's hard work without lifting a finger, breaking a sweat, or bleeding an occasional drop of blood. Whatever happened to virtue and integrity?

So many wanted to benefit from his Mars settlements but none wanted to contribute their funds without begging his assistance. And now, a prisoner on Mars had stolen his prized shuttle, the Percival 3000.

Grayson wiped his face one last time. He took a deep breath and tossed the towel into a hamper before attaching the earphone and clicking the playback button.

"Mr. Grayson," Jonas said, "We've identified two of the three hijackers. One's Sylvia Perkins, a mechanic. With her extensive knowledge of the shuttle's controls, she's probably the acting pilot. Magnus Knight's a prisoner whose Sleeper Chip malfunctioned. He overtook two guards that were attempting to replace the chip. Currently, we don't know the third person's identification. All we know is he resided at the Deimos Life Station and shuttled to Mars, so it shouldn't take long to identify him. After his arrival, he joined Sylvia and Magnus. We're not certain if they conspired prior to stealing the shuttle or if that was how the opportunity arose for them. I've had no success contacting the Deimos Life Station. Communication seems blocked. I'll continue to update as I get information."

Grayson turned off the message. His mind raced, but overall, the rigorous workout helped alleviate his stress. Besides, what more could he actually do before they reached Earth? Upon their arrival, though, he'd unleash hell on these thieves. Until then, he had plenty of time to figure out an appropriate punishment—one that satisfied his need for revenge while ensuring these individuals never double-crossed him or anyone else again.

Chapter 23

Grayson sat at his desk, deep in thought, with his huge fingers bridged. He listened to Jonas' latest update for the third time. What caused the technical problems, blocking communication with those on Deimos? Who was the third person aboard the Percival 3000 that had left Deimos? Surely, the two connected.

His concentration was interrupted when he noticed his newest intern standing beside his desk. The brunette was physically fit, wore a tight miniskirt with net stockings, and a low cut top. He'd been so engrossed in evaluating the problems on his space frontier that he didn't know how long she'd been standing there.

Meeting her dark eyes, he cocked a brow. She smiled with a hint of flirty mischief and curled a strand of her hair with her index finger.

"Misty," Grayson said. "Find all the staff and personnel files for the residents stationed at Deimos Life Station and bring me a hard copy. Print a full list of the Deimos prisoner files, too. Then run further background investigations for each of them. I need this brought to me within the hour."

"Sure." She nodded, winked, and ran her tongue across her lower lip. "Is there anything *else* I can do for you, Mr. Grayson?"

He read the intent in her eyes and shook his head. "No."

Misty looked somewhat disappointed. "Are you sure, Mr. Grayson? There's nothing else you'd like me to do?"

For a moment, Grayson studied her. "There's one thing."

"Yes, Mr. Grayson? What's that?" An eager smile curled her plump lips.

"Invest in suitable professional attire, not floozy outfits. You're working in a respectable office, not on some street corner. Understand?"

Misty's face flushed red. She nodded, her high heels clacked loudly, and she hurried to the door. The bodyguard politely opened the door. She glanced at Grayson and forced a smile, hoping he was watching her. He wasn't. A dejected sigh escaped her mouth, and she left.

The guard closed the door.

Grayson shook his head. "Damn. I'm beginning to wonder if the employment agency's sending me dedicated interns or *groupies*."

The guard chuckled.

"Henry," Grayson said. "I'm not joking. I expect workers to act and dress professionally."

"Sorry."

Grayson waved him off. "Don't be. She's an attractive young lady, but if she wants to move past her internship, she has to prove she can do the job. Looks and dress are important but secondary. Intelligence and work ethic are primary."

His desk intercom buzzed.

"Yes, Beatrice?" Grayson said.

"Viktor Baskov is here to see you."

"Send him in."

Henry opened the door. Viktor walked in. He stood six four, thin, but rugged. His pocked face held no emotion but his solemn eyes were menacing. He walked stiffly across the room. This man was difficult to read, and with all the recent events on Mars and Deimos, Grayson didn't need additional problems.

Grayson stood and motioned to the chair in front of his desk. "Please, have a seat, Mr. Baskov."

"Thank you," Viktor said in his thick Russian accent.

"Can I get you something to drink?"

"No, thank you."

Grayson frowned. "You sure? I have vodka."

"Maybe a little."

Grayson motioned Henry. Henry walked to the bar to pour the drink.

"Cigar?" Grayson asked.

Viktor shook his head. "No time."

"How can I help you?"

"You know dat thing you wanted Parks to investigate?"

Grayson nodded, and his eyes narrowed.

Henry handed Viktor the drink.

Viktor nodded his appreciation. "I have information."

Grayson grinned, but couldn't hide his surprise and curiosity. "Okay?"

"You give me money dat you promised Parks for dis information?"

"Of course. Not sure why Parks hasn't gotten back to me, but why do *you* have this information?"

"He snoop 'round with wrong sort of people."

"Is he dead?" Grayson asked.

Viktor sipped the vodka and shook his head. In his deep voice at a near whisper, he said, "Oh no, no. He's not dead, but probably wishes so."

Grayson's eyes narrowed. "Okay, so *why* are you here?"

"To give you dat information you seek. But I need your word that I get money."

"Certainly."

"De whole million dollars?"

Grayson nodded.

"Good. Den. You have problem. Big problem."

Grayson's slight smile faded. Concern furrowed his brow. "What kind of problem?"

"Chinese sent rocket to Mars about a year ago."

"That's *not* new information to me. I'm well aware of that."

"I know," Viktor said. "It's da package that went with de rocket. Dat be your problem."

"Package? What kind of package?"

"Seems Chinese have sent robots to Mars."

Grayson frowned. "What?"

Viktor nodded. "And not an ordinary kind of robot. They sent heat-seeker Dra-0100s."

"So these robots are on Mars right now?"

"Yes."

"For what purpose?"

Viktor cleared his throat. "My guess is to... uh, kill your people."

"All because I refused to allow them to use my landing bay?"

"Seems so."

"Shit," Grayson said.

"Told you, it big problem."

Grayson leaned back in his chair and crossed his arms. His jaw tightened as he waited for Viktor to continue.

Viktor offered an even smile. "But Chinese possibly have deeper reason. You know how they are. Soviet Union has had contention with them for years."

"I don't know about that. The Soviets have been quite chummy with the Chinese lately."

Viktor frowned and shook his head. "No. Only for public show. While we display our friendship to the world, mainly to show threat to U.S., deep down, we hate one another. At one time in history, Soviets battled U.S. in space race. That mellowed over time. Not so much with Chinese. They wish to dominate every market. They see you making fortunes and want their share."

"Then they should find their own way. I owe them nothing."

Lifting his right forefinger, Viktor replied, "This is a web of conspiracy, Mr. Grayson. Chinese have wanted to control international markets for decades. Now, interplanetary as well."

"Damn." Grayson stood and turned to the tinted window. He ran a hand through his hair. "I've no way to stop them from destroying what I've invested so much time and money to preserve."

"There is way," Viktor said.

Grayson turned and faced him. His eyebrows rose with keen interest.

Viktor smiled. The expression looked foreign on this man's hardened, scarred face. He'd witnessed a lot of bad events during his lifetime, killed a lot of people without second thoughts or remorse, and most likely would continue doing so provided people paid enough money to hire and keep him on their good side.

"You have a way?" Grayson asked.

"For da right price, we find a way."

"And what is the 'right price'?"

Viktor formed a bridge with his fingers and thought. "First, the million dollar for information 'bout robots. Once that clears bank, I give you call with *additional* price."

"Mr. Baskov—"

"Please, call me Viktor."

"Viktor. You know my money's good. I'm the richest man in the world."

"Ah, yes, Mr. Grayson. Dis I know. But I don't work alone. I must discuss with my contact and see what's necessary. Understand?"

Grayson's jaw tightened. After a few seconds, he nodded. "I understand."

"You see. We don't have de necessary device to stop those robots. To get it, we must steal it."

"From the Chinese?"

"Yes. This requires substantial cash upfront. Most loyal people give information if price is right. This avoids... de more violent options."

Grayson nodded and met Viktor's devious grin with one of his own. "Okay. How soon will you have an estimate?"

Viktor rubbed his chin, thinking. "Two days. I get you price in... two days. Deal?"

Grayson extended his hand to shake Viktor's. Viktor shook Grayson's hand firmly.

"Deal," Grayson said. "Beatrice, my secretary, will set up the direct deposit for the million dollars at her desk."

"Thank you, Mr. Grayson. It has been pleasure."

"Not so much for me," Grayson replied.

"How's that?"

"Bad news is never a pleasure."

"Ah," Viktor said, nodding. "Dis is true. But we turn your bad news into *good* news. I assure you."

"I look forward to hearing back from you," Grayson said.

Viktor turned at the door. "Two days. I call in two days."

Chapter 24

Boony stepped into the infirmary to talk with Dr. Lee. The two guards Magnus roughed up were sitting in the waiting room. The information she'd been given was that one of them was still unconscious and in critical condition. Someone had gotten incorrect information or lied.

Since Magnus was a prisoner, it made sense for the guards to exaggerate their injuries in the report. These two guards were probably embarrassed a prisoner bested both of them. Magnus had crushed their egos, so they must've hoped other guards would make Magnus suffer whenever they cornered and captured him. But since Magnus had escaped, payback was impossible.

She recognized the two guards from The Vortex. Both had hit on her without success on several occasions. Their looks weren't what turned her off during their initial approach. Their arrogant attitudes did. Both men were handsome, but the all cocky, stuck on themselves stances signaled she could do much better than them.

Matt's right eye was swollen and dark purple. Cain's arm was in a sling. Based on Magnus' size, their injuries were milder than she imagined. He could've easily put these men into comas, or much worse, if he'd intended. He only did what was necessary to subdue them without inflicting serious or permanent damage in order to escape. He held back, at least partially.

A malicious convicted murderer trying to escape wouldn't leave living witnesses. Even Jonas talked about how these miners were the most vile, ruthless people on Earth. From what she'd seen, Magnus didn't fit that profile.

Who framed Magnus on Earth and why?

With more research, she hoped to find out.

Boony walked to the desk where a redheaded woman sat. Her name tag identified her as Mary.

"I need to speak to Dr. Lee."

"Sign in," the woman said, sliding a clipboard across the desk.

"I'm not here for an exam, and I don't have time to wait," Boony said. "I need to ask him a couple of questions."

"About?"

"It's confidential and *doesn't* concern you."

"You must still sign in," Mary said.

Boony frowned and rested her hand on her gun. "Why don't you get Jonas Walker on the phone?"

Mary stared at the gun and then met Boony's cold hardened gaze. The fierceness in her eyes made Boony's stature of little significance. It was an almost believable example of an icy glare capable of killing.

Mary's uneasiness was obvious, but before she replied, Dr. Lee peered out from his office. He offered a friendly smile. "Please, come on back."

"Thanks."

After she entered his office, he shut the door and sat behind his desk. He was tall and slender, wore a white lab coat, and round-rimmed glasses. In spite of his graying hair, the glasses caused his Asian face to resemble someone in high school. "What can I help you with?"

"I have a couple of questions."

Dr. Lee nodded. "Sure. What is it?"

"About these Sleeper Chips... what did you find out about the malfunctioned one in the miner that committed suicide? I assume you did his autopsy?"

Dr. Lee cringed. "I did. That was a bit messy."

Boony nodded. "I imagine the fall broke him up pretty badly."

"No. A different kind of messy."

"In what way?"

"When the chip shorted, that's exactly what it did. The tissue around the implant was charred. Almost like a burst of hot energy exploded and burned his flesh."

Boony shivered. "Was he conscious after that happened? No longer under its control, he'd have to be, right?"

"My guess would be... yes. After watching the video feed, and seeing him plummet into that deep pit, he was probably experiencing so much pain. He had no other choice but to kill himself."

"Have any of the other defective chips caused these kinds of reactions?"

Dr. Lee shook his head. "No. We've not had many malfunctioned chips, but with the few that have, most prisoners are simply disoriented. They stop working. The guards notice them right away. With this man, there was no fore-warning at all. No time to get him to the infirmary."

"Any idea why these chips are malfunctioning?"

"From what the techs have told me, the chips somehow misread the directive signals from the CAM-Ls. This friction overheats the receptor, causing the chip to malfunction. None have ever heated so severely as to burn flesh though."

Boony nodded. "Are you aware of the chip in the prisoner who stole the Percival 3000?"

Dr. Lee rolled his eyes slightly, thinking. He shook his head. "Nothing more than the report I read and what the two guards in the waiting room told me when I examined them."

"I'm not certain I'd hold much confidence in what either of those guards told you."

"Why not?"

"Their report indicates one of them is in critical condition."

Dr. Lee smiled. "One was unconscious when he arrived at the infirmary. It was several hours before he awakened."

"But still... that's *not* critical condition."

"Yes. I understand your point."

Boony sighed. "So Magnus Knight's chip somehow deactivated, too?"

"Yes."

"I'm curious about something. How'd he keep guards on the mining lines from realizing that?" she asked.

"I'm not certain. According to those two men, he kept working like the other miners, never showed any sign his chip malfunctioned, and even pretended to be under its control when they entered his cell."

"What set him off?"

Dr. Lee shrugged. "According to them, when they tried to capture the ferret, Magnus attacked them."

"How serious are their injuries?"

"Not bad, really. Bruised up, but nothing serious. Why does this interest you?"

Boony gave an even smile. "Since Magnus helped steal the shuttle, we're trying to find exactly what happened so we can accurately report it to Grayson. You know how a stickler he is for thorough details?"

Dr. Lee nodded. "Oh, yes. Very particular."

"Well, the more we know about the thieves, the better Grayson can prepare for their arrival. One thing in Magnus' favor is that he didn't kill them."

"True, but if he's ever brought back to the mines, he won't live long."

"Why's that?" she asked.

"Those two guards will kill him."

"I see."

Dr. Lee nodded. "They're not very forgiving, especially when it comes to their prisoners."

"Even though he spared their lives?"

"Both are furious about what happened. I examined them. Each grumbled the entire time about how they'd like for Grayson to ship Magnus back so they can make him pay. Can you blame them?"

"I'm certain more details will surface about what happened that night. However, I don't think Magnus will ever return to Mars."

"Why not?"

Boony shrugged. "It's a feeling I have."

"You could talk to Cain and Matt to get more information."

"That's not necessary. I needed information about *why* the chips are malfunctioning so I can understand the drastic differences between Magnus' chip and the miner that killed himself."

"Without a computer tech examining Magnus' chip, we'll never really know," Dr. Lee said.

"I assumed as much, but I was hoping you could provide *some* speculation?"

Dr. Lee shrugged. "I've told you all I know from the medical perspective. A computer technician would be more helpful, I'm sure."

"Thanks. You've been quite helpful," Boony said, turning to leave. She paused at the door. "What's your opinion on one's mental state *after* being released from the Sleeper Chip's control?"

"What do you mean?"

"Once the miners' contracts end and they're released, would any of them suffer depression or perhaps become more aggressive? Anything like that."

"There should be little change."

Boony frowned. "So their minds being in limbo for years won't affect their psychological states once they're released?"

"It shouldn't. Why would you expect it to?"

"You're the doctor. That's why I asked."

Dr. Lee stood. "I suppose what you're suggesting is possible since the chips suppress their thought processes and quite possibly conflicts with the brain's chemical uptake. I guess it could. But no one rightly knows, and everyone's body chemistry is different. No extensive research has been done. The prisoners on Mars are the first to undergo such a long-term usage."

"I know. That's what makes me worry."

"Worry about what, exactly?" he asked.

"If ever the CAM-L control devices stopped working and the guards lost control of the prisoners, we're all screwed."

Lee's eyes widened slightly.

She smiled. "You understand what I'm hinting at. Those prisoners will take over, killing anyone that tries to stop them, including us. There's no safe place for us to hide."

Lee looked at the door as she opened it.

"Since you're with security," he said, "what suggestions do *you* have?"

"If I were you, I'd contact Grayson Enterprises and see how soon the new chips arrive."

He nodded.

Boony left the office and closed the door behind her. Mary glanced her direction but quickly looked away, pretending to busy herself with papers.

Matt and Cain looked Boony up and down with lustful glances. She rolled her eyes in passing.

"I so wish *you* were one of the prisoners," Cain said.

Boony stopped midstride. "Why's that?"

"Oh the things I'd make you do under the control of a CAM-L."

Boony smirked. "That'd be the only way you could ever get near me since I've shot you down so many times before. Even chip controlled, I'm sure I'd reject you."

Cain's hands balled into fists.

Matt elbowed him. "Stop."

She grinned. "No, let him. I *dare* him to come at me."

Cain leaned forward in his chair to stand.

Matt grabbed his arm. "*Don't.* Can't you see her weapon?"

"I don't need my weapon," she replied.

Cain stared into Boony's harsh gaze, read her anger, and eased back in his seat.

"That's better," she said. "I'd hate to give you any more bruises. Looks like you took a nasty beating already."

At the door, she turned and grabbed the door lever.

"Best watch your back from here on," Cain said in a low tone.

Boony didn't reply or look back. She opened the door and exited.

Before the door closed, Matt whispered to Cain. "We don't need any eyes on us from security. What the hell do you think you're doing?"

Boony thought his statement was a bit odd and wondered what it implied. Since she didn't have hobbies on Mars to occupy her extra time, she planned to keep an eye on these two guards for a few nights. While doing that, she could research the events behind Magnus' court case. Maybe she could discover new information to clear his name. Even if she did, Grayson would, no doubt, file charges against Magnus for the theft of the shuttle, which could still put him in prison. However, from what she had learned about Grayson, Magnus would never see a prison should Grayson take him into custody.

She couldn't imagine what type of punishment Magnus faced. Again, she wished she'd left Mars with them, but she had a better chance to help clear him of his charges by thorough research while he traveled through space. The more facts she gathered to prove his innocence, the more likely Jonas might actually help him, too. Jonas didn't seem to like Grayson that much, but Jonas was a man of his word, willing to honor his contract even during unethical situations.

Chapter 25

Cain shook his head. "Don't *ever* put your hand on me."

Surprised, Matt said, "Really? You're threatening *me*? Stop with your macho bullshit. The last thing we need is for her to take any interest in us. Besides, she works with Jonas. Hell, that alone's enough for you not—"

"I don't care *who* she works for, Matt." He rubbed his sore large knuckles.

"Well, you should."

Cain laughed. "That old man? He should've stayed on Earth and retired. We don't need him here, especially not for security."

"Jonas is someone you'd best respect," Matt said softly.

"Oh? And why's that?"

"The majority of the guards hold the man in the highest respect. We'd be taken into custody before we ever get a chance to do anything."

"Phht." Cain shook his head.

"Don't ruin this for us. We have a great thing going, and the last thing we need is for Jonas or that Asian chick to find out."

"She's more talk than she is fight."

"I don't know about that."

"You saw how tiny she is. Hell, she's no match for either of us. She's only brave because she thinks she can hide behind Jonas."

Matt sighed. "She's a lot tougher than you think. You didn't see her apprehend the two drunk guards at The Vortex a couple of weeks back?"

"No."

"Ah, that's right. You were with Jessie that night, right?"

"Yep. She kept me more entertained than anything we could do at The Vortex."

Matt laughed. "I understand. I was with her the next evening, which is why I'm telling you not to ruin what we've got going."

Cain sighed. "All right. There's not too many chipped females under a CAM-L's control."

"Precisely why we need to keep a low profile."

"Gotcha."

THE DOOR behind Dr. Lee's desk opened. He turned with a start. A short, older Asian woman entered the room. She was four feet, nine inches tall, but her fierce eyes were enough to send chills down his back. She crossed her arms and frowned.

"Ah, Dr. Sheung," he said.

"What did she want?"

"Boony?"

"Yes."

Lee turned in his swivel chair and faced her. "She was asking about the Sleeper Chips."

"Why's she interested in those?"

"She wanted to know why they're malfunctioning."

"That's all? Did she ask anything else about the chips?"

Dr. Lee shook his head. "No. Nothing else. Why?"

She glanced at the other door. "I don't trust her or Jonas."

"Her intent seemed sincere."

"Perhaps. But she works for Jonas."

"So?"

"He marches around like he's royalty. He's always poking his nose into everyone's business."

Dr. Lee offered a gentle smile. "It's his job to know what's happening here. He's the chief of security. As long as people aren't participating in shady activities, no one has anything to fear. Right?"

Her eyes darkened and her jaw tightened. Her glare made him flinch and look away. "If she comes back, you tell her nothing."

Lee nodded and refused to make any further eye contact.

She grabbed the door handle behind her without looking, pulled it open, and left. When the door closed, he took a deep breath and wiped sweat from his brow with a handkerchief. She always made him feel uneasy, but he never understood why. Yet, he'd never felt terrified of her or what she might be capable of doing. Until now, he'd never suspected she might have a secret agenda. Suddenly, he didn't like sitting with his back to her door.

———

NIGHT SHIFT WASN'T ALWAYS the quietest time to watch camera monitors because off duty guards and techs crowded The Vortex. With some quick research, Boony found Cain's and Matt's rooms in the C-corridor. Their rooms were only three doors apart. She found the tracer identity codes for their radio transmitters, which allowed her to keep track of them after they were off the clock. Something about them made her uneasy.

Matt was in The Vortex, but oddly, Cain was not. They seemed close friends and two that seldom did anything without the other tagging along.

Typing in Cain's code, the computer pinpointed his exact location. He wasn't even in the C-corridor. Instead, he was in the prisoner bunkers near one of the mining pits.

"Strange," she said, zeroing in on his exact location. "Jessica Hall's room?"

Boony requested the prisoner's record information. Jessica's mug shots surfaced. Other than the woman's weird neck tattoo, she was attractive.

"In prison for... murdering her husband and his lover? Seriously? That's not a bad enough crime to be sent to Mars," Boony whispered.

She continued reading. The husband's lover was a female judge, and he was her bailiff. A bit more intriguing, but still not justifiable reasons to finish her prison sentence on Mars. But no more evidence came up. The rest of her records were sealed.

Jessica was assigned to work in the greenhouse.

"Better than the mines, I suppose."

Boony connected to the corridor camera closest to Jessica's room. The door was visible, but she didn't have any idea what was happening on the other side. With Cain in Jessica's room, Boony only imagined the worst, which disgusted her.

Boony wanted to rescue Jessica, if what she suspected were true. If she were wrong about Cain's intentions and barged into the room, she'd find herself reprimanded and facing Jonas' wrath. None of the guards would ever trust her, either. Simply rushing in Jessica's room on a hunch wasn't a valid reason, even though she wouldn't put it past Cain to subvert Jessica to his perverted fantasies. She needed conclusive proof of her suspicions. How'd she covertly obtain evidence?

Another idea occurred. On duty guards were equipped with body cameras, which was required by Grayson and enforced by Jonas. She figured this was a precaution to prevent theft, especially of the MarQuebes. Since the Sleeper Chips controlled the prisoners, the higher-ups never requested footage concerning the inmates.

Cain openly suggesting he'd like to control Boony with a CAM-L insinuated his lewdness and indicated he most likely was using the device to do unspeakable acts prisoners. Matt rebuking Cain further indicated these two held secrets they didn't want her or Jonas to discover.

Boony searched Cain's files until she located the code to connect to his camera. Her only setback was not having the proper clearance to view his activities.

"Damn," she whispered.

Jonas entered the security office. "Problem?"

Boony glanced over her shoulder and met his tired eyes. He offered a worried smile.

"Any news about Derek?" she asked.

He shook his head. "I'm putting together a search team. What are you working on, Boony?"

She sighed and turned in her chair to face him. "When I talked to Dr. Lee earlier, I had a run-in with the two guards Magnus incapacitated."

Jonas grinned. "A run-in? They were hostile toward you?"

"Cain was overly gender rude."

"I don't follow."

Boony explained Cain's insinuation and what Matt said as she left the office.

"I can see how that's more than disturbing. I hope you got his attention."

"I did, but I think he's up to no good."

Jonas frowned. "Meaning?"

"Okay, I did some snooping and got Cain's and Matt's tracer codes to track their positions this evening. Matt's in the Vortex but Cain isn't."

"Where's Cain?"

"I've tracked his position to a female inmate's room."

"What? Why would he be there?" His eyes narrowed. He apparently concluded the same thing as she.

Boony nodded. "That's the first question I asked. I don't have security clearance to view his activities through his body camera."

Jonas walked over to her desk. "Here. Allow me."

She slid her roller chair aside. He typed his security pass code and the information page popped up.

"There you go. Let's see what he's doing," he said.

Boony slid back over and highlighted the camera icon associated with Cain's badge I.D.

The camera footage immediately came into play on a small inset of the computer screen. Boony right clicked and expanded the footage to full screen.

Boony shook her head. "Oh my God. Unbelievable."

Jonas' jaw tightened. He turned and headed for the door. "Which cell is this? I'm busting his ass right now."

"Wait," Boony said.

"Why? What he's doing is immoral."

On the screen Jessica stood completely nude before Cain. She danced, swaying back and forth like a stripper. The things Cain said caused Boony to mute his mike. Jessica kept dancing, oblivious of him or her performance. Cain fumbled with the zipper on his suit with one hand since his other arm was still in a sling.

Disgusted, Jonas said, "This isn't right."

"I know," Boony said. "Quick question though."

"What?"

"Is there a way to override his CAM-L? Is that even possible?"

"Yes. Of course. Why?"

Boony smiled. "I want to punish him *before* you arrest him."

Jonas took his master CAM-L from his jacket pocket. He typed in Cain's information and badge number. On his screen, he tapped the "override" button.

"It's all in your control," he said, handing the CAM-L to her.

"Watch the screen."

Jessica swayed her nude body closer to Cain. Her transfixed eyes stared into nothingness. She held her hands above her head and pivoted her hips back and forth. Boony unmuted his mike.

"Oh, yeah, baby," Cain mumbled. "That's what I like to see. Come closer, baby. I have something special for you. Like the other night... you know how to make a man feel real good."

Cain reached for her. His hand rubbed her thigh.

"Now," Boony said. "Let's see how much you like this."

A second later, Jessica backhanded Cain hard. The loud fleshy thwack made Boony and Jonas wince.

"Oooh!" Boony said. "That was harder than I expected."

"What the hell?" Cain shouted, rising to his feet. He grabbed his CAM-L off the table and tapped a few buttons. But Jessica spun around and kicked his gut. The CAM-L hit the floor. He groaned, desperately reaching for the control device. "Damn thing... isn't working."

Boony tried to suppress a grin as she typed more commands. Jessica kicked the CAM-L across the floor.

Cain rose, trying to find his composure, partially stunned by what was happening and bent in obvious pain. Jessica's eyes remained distant, her mind still totally controlled by the chip. She continued to sway seductively.

"Calm down," he said, in a hopeful tone. He eased closer to her. "Relax, baby. Everything's going to be okay."

Under Boony's control, Jessica balled a tight fist and swung. The sound of cracking bone echoed. Cain grabbed his nose and blood covered his hand.

"You little bitch!"

"Don't let him hurt her," Jonas said.

"He won't."

"I'm sending guards to her room now." Jonas tapped his transmitter.

Cain positioned himself lower, like he was going to rush Jessica and pile drive her on the bed. Before he moved, Jessica kicked his groin. He gasped and released a high-pitched whine.

"Damn, Boony," he said.

She shrugged. "Part of that one was for his remark to me at the doctor's office."

Cain collapsed and fell on top of his camera. The screen went dark.

"Guards should be there any second," Jonas said. "Do you think Matt's a part of this?"

She nodded. "I believe so. Matt wanted to quieten him. We could wait to see if he shows up at Jessica's room before we arrest him."

Jonas nodded. "We could, but I don't want to chance giving him any such opportunity. I want to know exactly how long they've been doing this. I never expected anyone to do this, but I suppose it shouldn't surprise me. I'll demand better background checks in the future. We don't need perverts having this kind of control over helpless people."

"I agree. But eventually someone was going to take advantage and do this. There are some sick people."

"I know."

"We really don't know what these prisoners are capable of, either," she said.

"That's why I'm glad *we* have the CAM-Ls."

"At the rate the chips are malfunctioning, I'm becoming more concerned."

Jonas sat in a chair across from Boony. "Me, too."

"I expressed this to Dr. Lee."

"What was his reaction?"

"After I explained the violent nature of our prisoners and what they'd do if these chips failed to control them, he became quite nervous."

"He should be nervous. We all should be."

"Jonas?" a voice said over his transmitter. "This is Bert."

Jonas tapped it. "Yes?"

"We have Cain in custody. Where do you want us to take him?"

"Is he conscious?" Jonas asked.

"Barely."

"Bring him to my security office."

"Yes, sir. On our way."

Jonas said, "Bert? How's Jessica?"

Silence.

"Bert?"

"Well, sir, she seems to be doing some kind of odd dance in the nude. She not responding to Cain's CAM-L, either."

"We'll take care of her," Jonas said. "Bring Cain to me."

"Copy that."

Jonas glanced at Boony. "Perhaps you can get her to stop dancing and into bed to sleep?"

"On it."

"Thanks."

Chapter 26

Three days earlier, Bradbury carried Derek as far back into the tunnel as he could. At the tunnel's end, Derek found a small hole large enough to crawl through, but his robots weren't agile enough to follow. He hoped the same was true with the Chinese robots.

Three days was a long time to stay hidden. His only rations were those he'd taken from Bradbury's emergency storage compartment. The pack contained a half dozen high protein bars, a gallon of water, extra oxygen tanks, and strong pain medicine to use for severe injuries. His food lasted two days, and due to the medicine, Derek slept most of the time.

He never favored using pain relievers. The blisters on his shoulder ached from the slightest movement. Normally, he was too restless to sleep long periods of time, but this medicine rendered him unconscious. When he opened his eyes, he tapped the side of his visor to bring up the time. Stunned, he'd slept another twelve hours.

Derek's mouth was pasty. His head felt heavy. He tried to stand but quickly sat down. In the disorienting darkness, everything spun. His stomach sickened. He patted the floor until he found the half frozen water. He uncapped it and took a couple of sips through his helmet's straw device. The cold water hurt his stomach, but he forced himself to keep it down. He was close to dehydration.

The inside of the tiny crevice was chilly, but not nearly as cold as the harsh terrain outside the Phobos ruins.

With the pain meds subsiding, his blistered shoulder ached. Part of his sleeve was melted into his flesh. It was tender and raw to touch, but at least he'd postponed the pain for a while.

Hunger pangs gnawed his gut. More emergency provisions were stored behind the seats in the flatbed trucks. To retrieve them meant leaving the safety of his hideaway. The moment he emerged, he became an open target. He didn't see any other choice. He needed to leave the Phobos ruins and return to Olympus Mons.

His tattered suit exposed his injury to the elements. Being inside the rocky enclosure somewhat protected him from the extreme cold. His arm was slightly chilled, which numbed the pain a little, but he needed to get to the infirmary before infection set in.

Pushing a button on his belt signaled his smart suit to repair the damaged area around his shoulder. The suit's polymers released chemicals that formed thick foam over his exposed skin. The foam gelled together with the surrounding materials and mended the tear.

Derek shivered. Grayson's plans to construct steel mills inside Olympus Mons were genius. The forges would increase the heat inside the dead volcano, elevating the temperature and granting the luxury of not having to wear heavy uniforms. The lack of comfortable clothing was the biggest complaint amongst his colleagues. He agreed. He couldn't remember the last time he wore a T-shirt without an insulated uniform over it.

A sharp beeping inside his helmet caught his attention.

"Dammit," he whispered, reading the gauge on his visor.

His oxygen levels were nearly depleted. Not only did he need to hunt for food provisions inside the truck cabs, he needed a new oxygen tank. He wasn't certain extra tanks were in the trucks, but in case of emergencies, he figured a few should be. If nothing else, he might be able to connect to a larger, reserve oxygen tank to recharge the one inside his suit.

Derek crawled through the small crevice, careful not to place any pressure on his injured shoulder or accidentally scrape against the rocky wall. Even though the repaired material covered his injury, any bump could rupture the blisters. He crawled past two of his robots standing guard and rose to his feet. His robots didn't move.

Bradbury and Isaac turned off their verbal communications to prevent attracting the heat-seeking robots to their location. His robots didn't emit the same heat frequencies as humans, so the Chinese cyborgs had not located and obliterated Derek's prized companions. But since he needed their assistance to get to Olympus Mons, he reactivated their communication signals and voices. Doing so might attract the attention of the enemy robots, but Derek could never make it back to base without them.

After three days of radio silence, Jonas was certain to be frantic and fuming with anger. He tended to show his angry quicker than to reveal his worry, even if it was over Derek's safety.

Derek hoped Jonas had sent a search party, even though Derek was adamant against him ever doing so. Now, though, he hoped Jonas defied the request like he always had in the past.

Had Derek's heated rant with his grandfather gone too far this time? Had his words soured his grandfather to let Derek learn from his mistakes, regardless of the cost? Without the radio towers working, Derek didn't know. He wished he could apologize, as he might not live to see the next sunrise should the cyborgs locate him.

Another worry crept into his mind. Those in Olympus Mons weren't aware of their enemy, and Derek couldn't tell them. Any rescuers sent to find Derek would blindly enter the Phobos Crash Site and could be killed.

Bradbury exited the small cave-like tunnel, followed by Isaac.

"Derek, why did you leave your shelter?" Bradbury asked.

Derek held his shoulder. "My supplies are depleted, and I'm almost out of oxygen."

Derek leaned against a large boulder and steadied himself. His vertigo was off, his vision blurred, and he felt much weaker. Was his lack of energy due to dehydration or was he suffering from radiation?

"Bradbury," Derek said.

"Yes, Derek?"

"Detect radiation levels."

"Processing," Bradbury replied. He extended his arm. A side compartment opened on his forearm and a Geiger counter probe emerged. *"All radiation is within safe limits."*

"Good."

Isaac said, *"Our enemies are nearby."*

The Chinese robots were waiting for him. Being machines, patience wasn't an issue. They were programmed destroyers sent to Mars to kill Grayson's men, but did he know these robots were here?

Doubtful, he reasoned. And a greater reason to get to Olympus Mons to alert his grandfather. At least Jonas could send Grayson a message and let him know about the Chinese invasion on Mars.

Derek dared a glance over the truck's flatbed to see if he could locate the heat-seekers. He located them readily. The sun reflected off their metal armor. He lowered himself but kept his gaze on his enemies.

The robots shimmered several more seconds and slowly *vanished.* They returned to stealth mode.

"Shit," he whispered.

Derek felt doomed. How did one defend against such technology?

Chapter 27

Olympus Mons: Mine Shaft Fifteen

CLARK MIDDONS BRUSHED his long brown hair from his face and pulled it into a ponytail. His scraggly beard helped keep his face warm while working in the mineshaft corridors. If he had his way, he'd still be in the western United States studying the geothermal energy sources in Yellowstone National Park where he could wear shorts and flip-flops. But the money Grayson offered a geophysicist with his experience was far too great to decline. His three-year contract on Mars would earn him enough money to buy a new Jeep and start his own whitewater rafting business—'where every day was a vacation and *not* a chore'.

Clark hammered a metal temperature spike into the volcano wall. A few seconds passed before the gauge provided him the temperature reading.

"Damn," he said, shaking his head.

"What is it?" Shad Templeton asked, walking to Clark. Shad was eight inches shorter than Clark, and probably the shortest man residing on Mars. He glanced up at Clark.

Clark tapped the temperature reading device with his index finger. "I think this gauge is stuck. This can't be right. The temperature's getting warmer?"

"So? We're getting deeper into an old volcano, and much farther from the permafrost."

"I know *that*," Clark said. "But the core temperature reading inside Olympus Mons has been a steady thirty-six degrees, and that's *hot* for Mars. Except for the landing bay where it's always colder. Twenty-six degrees there."

"That's because the landing bay gates never stay shut long enough for the temperature to moderate. The thermal ventilation system has increased the overall temperature of Olympus Mons."

"Yes," Clark said, frustrated. "That's in the tunnels. This reading's from the core rock. It contradicts every former prediction about a cold Martian core. And if it's getting warmer the deeper we go, who's to say we might actually hit a lava pocket or cause an eruption."

Shad laughed and his eyes resembled blue ice. His nose scrunched, which made him look mousy. "Lava? This volcano's been dormant for millions of years."

"As far as we know," Clark said.

"You really think such a possibility exists?"

"It's not *impossible*."

"So it's a myth?" Shad asked, placing his hand against the rough volcanic wall.

"I wouldn't necessarily classify it as a myth. But, think about it. Every report we've had about Mars shows the atmosphere is oxygen poor, which is true, but the oxygen levels *inside* Olympus Mons are much higher than any scientist ever assumed."

Shad shrugged. "I wouldn't get all bent out of shape over it."

"It should be worrisome."

"Why? Who knows what other secrets we'll uncover the deeper into the volcano we go."

"That's *why* we should be more cautious."

Shad laughed. "No life forms have been found. Hell, no *fossils* have even been found."

"*Yet*," Clark said. "That's what we're looking for."

"I hope we do unearth some fossils. Wait, no... this is Mars, so there isn't any *earth*. Right? Do we un*Mars* fossils?" He brushed reddish soil off his boots. "Got a question for you, Mr. Geologist."

"What?" Clark asked.

"If we call dirt on Earth, earth, what the hell do we call dirt on Mars? Oops, I got some *mars* on me. How do you get ground-in mars off your clothing? You have a technical answer for that one?"

"Oh, stop being a smartass."

"Okay, fine. Let's say we find fossils, then what? We've seen nothing indicating life. Other than ourselves, obviously."

"I know, but—"

Shad shook his head. "No tremors. Not even a slight one. Right?"

"That's correct."

"And you worked at Yosemite?"

"No, Yellowstone."

"Basically the same thing."

Clark shook his head. "Nowhere near the same thing, and the locations are half a day apart from one another."

"Okay," he said, rolling his eyes and waving his hands in surrender. "Anyway, you studied for possible earthquakes."

"Yes."

"So no tremors should be a big clue that this volcano is dead."

"Not all formations are the same, Shad. This is Mars, and until we got here, what did anyone really know about the geological formations on this planet? The increasing temperature concerns me, even if it doesn't you."

"You're right. It doesn't concern me. It means I get to wear less clothes," he said with a wide grin. "I might have to make jumpsuit cutoffs before much longer."

"Fine," Clark said, grabbing his pack and slinging it over his shoulder. He picked up his small pick ax and turned to walk away.

"Oh, calm down. Besides, our job isn't to determine the temperature ranges. We're supposed to keep searching for signs of former life, too."

"I know. I *did* mention that earlier."

"Technicalities. *Always* the details for you."

Clark's jaw tightened. "Precise measurements and data prevent errors, which sometimes prove to be fatal because the proper research wasn't performed."

"Well, you keep up with all of that technical stuff, and I'll get back to my drilling machine so we can move closer to the center of Olympus Mons."

They walked past two miners shoveling loose dirt into wheelbarrows. Neither miner noticed them. Both shoveled at the same pace and almost in mirrored reflections of one another.

"Please take it slowly. As a precaution?" Clark said.

"Your reading isn't anywhere near what a hot volcano would read. But if it'll ease your mind, I'll drill *slower*."

Shad climbed into the driver's seat of the giant tunnel-boring machine. He took out his CAM-L device and typed commands into it. The two miners placed their shovels on top of their wheelbarrows and moved out of his way.

"That's sad," Clark said.

"What?"

Clark pointed at the CAM-L control device. "Being controlled by computer chips the way they are."

"Beats the whips and chains, baby! Besides, I'd rather not deal with a murderous convict with mere words. These Sleeper Chips are the best invention Grayson ever developed. Certainly alters the minds of psychos."

"Not *all* of them were psychos. So using those controlling devices doesn't bother you?"

"Shit no. Not in the least. It's nice to know they can send us the absolute worst criminals, and we never have to worry about any revolts. Besides, I'm only one step from becoming a Space Warden. When they establish the next mining camp, I might get promoted even higher than that."

Clark smiled, shaking his head. "Well, don't sprain one of those fingers, buddy. You might get *demoted*."

Shad frowned with a soured expression on his face before adjusting in the seat. He pulled his seatbelt and locked it. He turned on the machine's blinding bright lights.

"Do me another favor," Clark said.

"What's that?"

"Instead of descending at the normal four percent grade, how about leveling forward a hundred yards. I'd like to test the temperature there. If it's not abnormal, we'll return to the four percent, okay?"

Shad shrugged. "Sure, why the hell not?"

Clark had only worked with Shad for two weeks. Already, he was tired of Shad's short man syndrome attitude. Shad always overcompensated for any activity. Even if the task required additional help from his coworkers, Shad insisted on attempting to do the assignment alone, at least until he absolutely proved he couldn't handle it by himself.

The other irritating thing Clark noticed was how the little man loved the power of his CAM-L. He could control six prisoners at a time, each of which was twice his size. The device empowered Shad, making him overly cocky, but Clark knew if the chips ever failed, Shad would flee and scream like a frightened child. His confidence thrived with the knowledge that the prisoners possessed no freewill to challenge his authority. Remove the control aspect, and Shad became bloody chum to a host of violent prisoners.

Clark was a geophysicist and not assigned to any guard duty. He didn't have access to use the mind-controlling device, and he was quite thankful for that. He wasn't someone with the education to properly perform psychological analysis on people, but even he saw the immediate danger the staff and guards faced should the prisoners ever break free of these mind-controlling devices.

He was shocked by the small ratio of guards overseeing the vast number of prisoners when he first arrived at Olympus Mons. He questioned how long before some type of computer glitch released the prisoners. The guards would hold no control of the prisoners. Once that happened, the revolt was nothing they'd ever contain. The guards would be at the mercy of the crazed prisoners, which, as Shad indicated, probably possessed no compassion for anyone else.

Clark looked at Shad. "Have you ever considered the possibility that one day these prisoners will break free of your electronic reins?"

Shad laughed. "That'd certainly add more excitement to my duties. This job's so boring I seldom carry my laser weapon. The CAM-L control is impossible to fail."

"Chips have been malfunctioning lately."

"A few have, but the margin's so slim. It's almost nonexistent."

"Nothing's impossible, Shad. Nothing. You never know what we might find here. Life could exist. Different life forms unlike anything we've ever known."

"This planet was dead long before we reached it, Clark."

"Perhaps, but this volcano's the largest in our universe, and we're still at a high level above the Martian surface. Who knows what we'll find once we dig deeper."

Shad shook his head. "Okay, I'm not a scientist, nor do I ever hope to be. But I have enough knowledge to wonder why you'd think we'll find signs of life *inside* this volcano."

"Why?"

"If the volcano contained flowing lava when it was active, how could life possibly exist here? The temperatures would have killed anything that stepped inside, right?"

Clark hung his pick on his tool belt. "My theory is that living creatures might've moved inside the volcano after the lava cooled and hardened. Probably long before the surface water vanished and the atmosphere thinned. As the outside terrain became too severe to support life, different species might've sought refuge here."

"That's absurd."

"Not really. On Earth, creatures have adapted for thousands of years. Ever heard of eyeless fish and newts that live in the total darkness of caves?"

"Yeah? So?"

Frustrated, Clark shook his head. "Never mind."

Shad started the giant drill. The whining noise forced Clark to insert his earplugs to reduce the sound. The drill cut into the volcano wall. Shavings of rock, small stones, and crushed MarQuebes rained down in cascading dry streams, forming piles of colorful debris.

The drill whirled, cutting a giant circular groove. It made a strange whine as the bit scraped and caught in the wall. The machine shook. The massive drill bit twisted out of its proper alignment. Shad shut off the drill while he maneuvered the tracks, hoping to back the machine up without causing further damage.

"Dammit!" Shad shouted.

Clark turned. "What happened?"

"The drill bit struck something hard and threw itself off track."

"I see that. Looks like your down for the day."

"Hell, even if we have the necessary parts, it'll take more than a few days to fix *this*!"

The rocks beneath the carved out circle rumbled. Part of the wall collapsed, revealing a large opening on the other side of the wall. Shad shifted the gears and backed the machine several yards. The bright lights beamed through the enormous hole.

A warm breeze flowed from the opening, spilling across them. The air held a strong acrid smell, forcing them to cover their noses and mouths with the top of their jumpsuits.

"What the hell?" Shad asked.

Clark set his pick on the side of the machine track and pulled out his earplugs. "I'll be damned."

"What's that?" Shad asked.

"Looks like you've tapped into a large opening. Probably from when the volcano was cooling down."

Shad climbed down from the cab and rushed ahead of Clark to the opening. "I'm checking it out."

"Wait," Clark said.

"Why?"

"Be cautious."

Shad grinned. "Of what?"

Clark pointed. "The ceiling looks unstable and more rocks might collapse."

"Okay, yeah, I see that. But isn't it odd I've tapped into what *looks* like a room of some sort."

"I agree."

Shad hurried to the wall. The opening was about a foot above his head. He climbed the rugged outcroppings until he could look through. He unstrapped a small pickax on his belt and struck the opening to enlarge it. Loose debris pebbled and cascaded down the other side of the wall. Orange light glowed from the other side, illuminating Shad's face.

"What do you see?" Clark asked.

"We've stumbled onto something big," Shad whispered in awe.

"What do you mean?"

"It's much warmer in there."

"Told you the temperature was getting warmer."

"Yeah, but there's a bridge-like structure and a silver door on the other side of it."

"Oh, bullshit!"

Shad looked down at Clark and nodded. "Seriously. I'm not lying."

Clark grabbed a flashlight out of the metal toolbox welded to the drilling machine.

"You won't need that," Shad said. "Between the machine's light and the orange glow in there, everything's visible."

Shad pulled himself into the opening. His feet dangled over the edge.

"Wait up," Clark said, grabbing a handhold and starting his way up the side of the wall.

"I'm going to check it out," Shad said. "I discovered the room. Don't try to hog my glory."

"We should alert Jonas and the others first."

"And let them take credit for my discovery?"

"We don't need to go inside until we have guards or other staff here. We have no idea what might be over there."

"Clark, we've tunneled all this way and haven't found one fossil. Not one. No signs of life other than the door and bridge inside this open chamber. There's nothing moving in there."

"A bridge and door isn't enough evidence that something *might* be alive in there?"

"Seeing is believing," Shad replied. "I don't see anything that's alive."

"Dude, you kept insisting you needed proof. Don't you have enough proof?"

Clark pulled himself higher, trying to get to Shad before he climbed over the wall and down the other side. Shad pulled forward, but Clark grabbed his right foot and held fast. Shad tried to kick free with his other foot but missed.

"Let me go!" Shad shouted, staring down at Clark.

"Not until I see what's over there."

"That's what I figured."

"What?" Clark asked.

"You want to claim this discovery for yourself."

Clark held Shad's ankle tightly. "That's ridiculous."

"Then let me go."

"Let's wait until we have others for backup."

Shad rolled his eyes. "If I see any little green men, I'll *scream* for you."

"Not funny," Clark replied, pulling Shad's ankle.

The rock ledge supporting Clark cracked. The section beneath his left boot gave way and forced Clark to release Shad. Clark grabbed a handhold on the wall to keep from falling.

Chapter 28

Shad pulled himself through the hole before Clark rebounded his position and could grab Shad's foot again. Shad dropped down the other side of the wall and struck the ground hard. The breath escaped his lungs, and for a moment, he was paralyzed in pain, groaning.

Lying on the ground, he looked up at the opening. The bright lights lit the large room. It resembled daylight. The orange glow was a reflection from the machine's light striking the room's ceiling, nothing more.

Shad was much farther from the opening on this side of the wall than he had been on the other. He'd have a long way to climb to get out, but he soon discovered another setback. This side of the wall was smooth like glass. No rough places existed to use as handholds or footholds. Someone would have to toss down a rope to get him out.

Clark peered through the opening. "Are you okay?"

"Yeah," Shad replied, somewhat bitterly. "The fall knocked the air out of me and bruised me up a little."

Shad stood and wiped dust from his clothes. His ankle hurt when he placed weight on it, and tightness increased around his swelling, right knee.

"Think I twisted my ankle," he said, turning on his visor light.

Clark looked down. "Damn, that's a ways down. Can you hoist yourself back up?"

"No. It's too deep and the wall's smooth. You'll need a rope so I can get out."

Shad limped away from the wall. The ground where he stood looked like a dry riverbed, or most likely, it was a dead lava flow.

"WHERE'S the door and bridge you mentioned?" Clark asked.

"Ahead of me. See?" Shad said.

Clark looked, frowned. "No. I don't see anything."

"There!"

"I don't see a door. Only rock walls."

Shad limped forward.

"Turn around and wait," Clark said. "Let me call the engineering office to get a rope so we can pull you out."

"Not until I see what's on the other side of that door."

"There *isn't* a door, Shad."

Shad kept limping, ignoring Clark. "This might be the discovery we've needed."

Clark might have thought Shad's delusional state came from striking his head when he fell over the ledge, but he mentioned the silver door *before* he fell. The path Shad walked was smooth and meandered a good hundred yards before disappearing around a steep mound of rocks. Even with the light shining into this hollow room, no door was visible. No bridge either. If the door and bridge were silver, the light would have magnified or reflected off them.

Were the lights playing tricks on Shad's eyes? Harsh lights could distort images or odd shapes, but Shad was *not* in the blinding glare. He walked with determined steps like he saw something. Did the pungent air contain hallucinogenic chemicals?

Movement stirred on the floor, like tiny reddish undulating waves, rocking side to side. Clark wondered if *his* eyes deceived him. He cupped his hands and shielded his eyes, blocking the harsh light. The movement on the floor continued.

"Shad!" Clark shouted with grave concern.

Shad didn't answer. He kept walking.

"Shad! Get back here! There are moving creatures on the floor. Don't you see them? Armies of them."

"I don't see anything. Stop trying to frighten me."

The rusty red creatures crawled like stick insects. They camouflaged with their surroundings and had they not been moving, Clark would never have noticed them.

The strange creatures moved forward, closing in around Shad. Hundreds of these things moved in streamlines right at him. Their slender legs crept in unison, like soldiers marching abreast and headed for battle.

Shad was trespassing in an unknown enemy's territory. By the time he finally noticed them, they blocked his path to return. These strange bug-like creatures crept around him. The room was filled with a giant hive of weird insects, unlike anything Clark had ever seen.

Shad turned and faced Clark. The growing fear on his face was evident. One of the creatures leapt at him. Shad kicked it before it attached to his leg. Others approached. Shad stomped one of them. He lifted his foot to inspect his kill, but the creature wasn't dead.

Instead, it bounded into the air and latched on his leg. He tried to swat it off, and screamed in sudden agony, as it bit him.

"Shad!"

"Get help!" Shad cried. None of the other insect-like creatures advanced. They simply waited. His hands frantically patted his leg. "I can't feel my leg. I can't move—"

Shad dropped to his knees. His eyes grew wider. A second later, he collapsed face first into the swarm. They covered him, and he offered no resistance. He didn't scream again. The first creature must've injected a paralyzing poison into his bloodstream. They inserted long beaklike projections into his body. They were drinking his blood.

Appalled, frightened, and sickened, Clark glanced around the opening. Thousands of these creatures roosted on the ceiling and all around the opening where he sat.

"Oh, shit," he said, slowly crawling away from the ledge.

Clark flung himself off the wall and landed on the drilling machine. He scrambled around until he reached the steps to the cab.

Once inside the cab, he shut the door tightly, and turned on the engine. Clark played around with the gear sticks and shifted them, trying to roll the borer tip into the hole before the swarm discovered their path to escape. Not familiar with the control sticks, Clark went in reverse, tilted the machine to one side and then back to the other. After several failed attempts, he found the proper combination with the gear sticks to move the tracks forward.

Easing the machine to the hole, he set the round borer bit flush against the opening. He shut off the engine and inspected his progress. The bit filled the majority of the hole, but several open gaps remained where the rocks had collapsed. He couldn't seal the opening completely shut. The gaps were large enough for the creatures to squeeze through.

In less than fifteen seconds, three of the creatures crawled through and scuttled down the rough wall.

"Dammit," he said.

He shut off the bright lights, hoping by doing so, these creatures wouldn't be attracted to the hole. The three insect-like beings scrambled toward him. He grabbed a shovel, flung it overhead, and brought it down in one swift blow. Although he hit the creature directly, it scurried to one side, made a whiny noise, and reared back like a small cobra with forelegs. The metallic exoskeleton protected it from excessive damage. Its large red compound eyes focused on him while it swayed back and forth.

Clark struck with the shovel again, missed, and broke the handle. The creature revealed two fangs dripping with yellowish ooze. Poison. His fate would be the same as Shad's if he were bitten.

Rather than trying to kill it, Clark ran. He didn't view his action as cowardly because if he died, no one in the upper levels of Olympus Mons knew about these things. Everyone in the mines could die within hours if the hole wasn't blocked.

He glanced over his shoulder. How fast could these creatures move? Not seeing them, he returned his attention to the path. He ran into a miner before he could sidestep the man. The miner's pick fell and clanged against a rock. The miner continued swinging as though he still held it.

Clark grabbed the prisoner and shook him, trying to rattle him loose of the chip's control. The man would become food for those creatures if he remained in the tunnel. The violent shaking did nothing to break the chip's grip on his mind. In desperation, Clark smacked the prisoner's face hard.

After hitting the man, Clark braced for retaliation from the muscled prisoner, but he acknowledged no pain. Clark struck the man again and again, hoping for some reaction, but the physical abuse did nothing.

Clark shook the man. "Come on! Snap out of it!"

The prisoner pried free, turned, and went through the motions of mining again.

Tears heated Clark's eyes because he couldn't help this man. He was a prisoner, probably guilty of heinous crimes, but Clark's conscious struggled to accept he'd have to leave the man behind. Now, he realized how important Shad's job was. Without the CAM-L and the codes to access the proper commands, the miners continued doing their last programmed task, regardless of impending danger.

Clark grabbed the man's pick. One insect snapped its claws at him. Instead of running, Clark hoped to kill the three that came through the hole. Maybe he could prevent the miners from dying before he reached Jonas to get help.

Clark ran to the opening. When he reached the wall beneath it, he swung the pick. The metal spike drove through its brain. Its body—now nerve-operated—tumbled off the wall and dropped in front of the drill machine. It hobbled and staggered. A horrid smell drifted from its dying body. Pheromones?

An unnerving clicking sound came from the hole. Their insect claws chinked together with a disturbing, haunting echo. They were coming for him.

Clark ran.

Years before, when he'd worked with a beekeeper one summer, he learned a lot about how certain pheromones worked. With most bees and ants, when disturbed or crushed, they emitted a strong chemical scent to alert their comrades that their hive was under attack. These chemicals sent the hive into an uncontrollable, aggressive frenzy, making them willing to sacrifice their lives to protect their queen. With thousands of these creatures on the other side of the wall, he figured they had a queen or perhaps even dozens of queens. For him to remain at the wall and kill more would only escalate their maddened desire to kill any human near their hive.

Running from these Martian insects was Clark's only choice to survive. He needed to warn Jonas about their discovery. The best they could hope for was to build a wall to block the tunnel. They possessed the proper equipment, but did they have enough time before their encampments were invaded by the hive?

Chapter 29

Derek crawled around the side of the nearest flatbed truck. He didn't want to get too far from the tunnel since the Chinese robots remained in stealth mode. If he suspected they were surrounding him, he hoped he retained enough strength and energy to run inside.

He braced himself against the side of the truck and attempted to stand. Dizziness overcame him and his stomach sickened. He grabbed the door handle to prevent falling.

Derek gently pulled the handle and eased the creaky door open. Layers of dust and silt drifted off the door, forming a small pile at his feet. He leaned into the truck and reached behind the seat. Like he expected, some rations were stored inside metal containers. He pried and ripped off the can's top.

Peaches. Brown but still edible. He climbed on the seat and drank the juice from the can. The seat offered a better view of the terrain around him.

Bradbury stood guard in the direct sunlight, but Derek didn't see Isaac. Bradbury's solar battery packs were charging in the sunlight.

"Bradbury," he said. "Where's Isaac? Report?"

"Forty meters south."

"Why?"

"Perimeter search."

"Are the robots nearby?"

"Negative."

"Where have they gone?" Derek asked, chewing on the gummy peaches.

"They have vanished, but not by stealth," Bradbury replied.

"Have they scouted outside your detection range?"

"*Affirmative.*"

Derek downed the rest of the can. Still chewing, he said, "I don't know if that's good or bad."

"*Perhaps a little of both,*" Bradbury replied.

"In what way?"

"*Good that they're not waiting to kill you. Bad because we don't where they've gone and we might cross paths with them again.*"

"You're right. Knowing their exact location greatly reduced our risks."

Isaac's voice came over Bradbury's transmitter. "*Kurt has been destroyed.*"

"Destroyed?" Derek and Bradbury asked simultaneously. "How?"

"*The Chinese robots,*" Isaac replied.

"*Perhaps it was suicide,*" Bradbury said.

Derek cocked a brow and stared through the window at Bradbury. "Suicide?"

"*He has tried it before,*" Bradbury replied. "*Twice if you count his shower attempt. Or as I like to refer to it, the 'Short Circuit Syndrome'. I warned him that the all-liquid diet wasn't for robots. Of course, Kurt has always insisted on proving everyone wrong.*"

"Isaac, what about Ursula and Octavia?" Derek asked, trying to ignore Bradbury.

"*They're intact and with me,*" Isaac replied.

"Good."

Remorse tightened Derek's chest as he thought about Kurt. Although people viewed them as merely robots, they were much more than that to him. They were family, extensions of himself, and to his amazement, Bradbury and Isaac were evolving into something he never programmed them to become.

Kurt wasn't anything like the rest of the robots. If a machine could suffer depression, Kurt fit that mold. His actions exhibited all the signs of an introvert. He was a solitary robot, and for whatever reason, he didn't blend with the rest of the group. Kurt even understood that. Perhaps, he'd deliberately shied away, despite the fact Derek used the same personality platform for all five robots. Kurt was somehow mentally deficit or broken, compared to his mechanical siblings and busied himself with isolation, ignoring the learning tasks Derek programmed and updated.

No matter what data evaluation Derek used to check the programs to see if they'd been properly installed with Kurt's RAM, which they had, Kurt regarded them as GI/GO, and rejected the information. No visible flaw existed inside Kurt's computerized AI brain. Quite simply, Kurt's personality was what the robot had chosen for himself.

Octavia and Ursula were capable of performing the same tasks Isaac and Bradbury could do, but they hadn't show any signs of evolving to the next level. He wondered why. They conversed quite well but lacked the witty sarcastic remarks their male counterparts often displayed. He believed this deficiency was due to him being a male and not knowing how women talked and interacted, so he failed to properly program such feminine formats into them. Or perhaps, they didn't like him.

The lights on Bradbury's computer panel lit up. He whirled around and scanned Derek's vitals. "*We must get you back to Olympus Mons. Immediately.*"

"I need to complete one radio tower before we leave."

"*Negative. Infection is setting in your shoulder. Your body temperature is too low. You need food and water.*"

"There are probably more supplies in the parked vehicles."

"*Come. Stay close to me,*" Bradbury said.

"Any sign of the robots?"

"*Negative.*"

"What's the status of your battery level?"

"*Thirty-four percent.*"

"You need to charge your battery before we start back or it will be completely drained."

"*It is sufficient,*" Bradbury replied.

"No Bradbury," Derek said, "it isn't. To be fully charged, you need nearly two days of sunlight since we don't have an electrical charging port."

"*We cannot sacrifice that much time.*"

Derek lowered the side truck window and stared at Bradbury. The robot kept his back to Derek and scanned the perimeter for the Chinese robots. Derek reached into a thickly insulated container and removed a bottle of water. Even with the insulation, the water was partially frozen. He took several sips through the straw and his teeth ached. Once the cold liquid hit his stomach, he winced from brain freeze.

Thick layers of sand and silt covered the windshield, preventing him from seeing through the front glass. He turned the key in the ignition, but the hybrid motor made no sound. With the solar panels blocked by the recent sandstorm, he didn't expect the engine to respond. He popped open another can of peaches and chewed another mouthful. The sugary syrup helped revive his energy levels a little, but he was still a long way from total recovery.

Derek held the inside door handle, contemplating what to do next. Since this vehicle wasn't charged enough to start, he figured the others parked nearby were in similar condition. By the time he got to his truck, the solar batteries on it might have received enough sunlight to charge.

"Take shelter!" Isaac said, running toward the flatbed trucks.

A laser shot, striking the side of the truck. Derek pulled the door handle and shoved the door open. He dove to the coarse sandy grit. Peering from beneath the truck, Derek noticed two Chinese robots heading his direction.

Derek rolled, shoved himself to his feet, and staggered a couple of paces, trying to get his balance. Bradbury gripped Derek's elbow and ran beside him. Isaac took a laser blast in the back, which toppled the robot forward. His hand caught the side of the flatbed, preventing his fall. He turned, catching another blast in his midsection. Smoke and sparks rose. Isaac made several odd shrills before slumping to the ground.

"Isaac!" Derek shouted.

Bradbury pulled Derek to the front of the truck. *"Stay down."*

Derek obeyed. He wished he'd brought his laser weapons. He was helpless. Kurt was gone. Isaac was injured, and the severity uncertain. Derek only knew Bradbury's location. Ursula and Olivia could've been destroyed for all he knew. And since the Chinese robots were capable of going stealth, he didn't know how many were there or where they might reappear.

Bradbury left Derek at the front of the truck.

"Where are you going?" Derek asked.

Bradbury didn't answer. The robot slipped around the side of the truck. A few minutes later, Bradbury returned with Isaac. He set Isaac beside Derek.

"Will Isaac live?" Bradbury asked with genuine concern.

The question jarred Derek slightly. His robots didn't consider themselves machines. Their AI insisted they were more than programmed robots. They were *living* beings.

Isaac's front panel was charred. Derek leaned over to inspect the damage. The blast had not melted through the robot's exoskeleton, so Isaac might have only suffered a brief short-circuiting. Derek found the reset button on Isaac's mainframe.

Isaac lifted his head and scanned the area around him.

"Welcome back," Bradbury said.

Isaac looked at his robotic colleague. *"I don't recall leaving."*

Bradbury extended his hand and helped Isaac stand.

Derek rose to his feet and placed his hand on Bradbury's back.

"Do you wish to get to safety?" Bradbury asked.

"Where are the Chinese robots?" Derek asked, looking across the terrain.

"No trace of them."

Derek stood between Isaac and Bradbury. Lasers struck the tarp-covered cargo on the flatbed truck behind them.

Isaac grabbed Derek by the shoulder and pushed him to the ground. Derek sought shelter beneath the truck.

The atmosphere was much clearer with the majority of the sandstorm settled. Visibility was almost at its maximum level. He tapped the side of his visor and searched the area, hoping to find the Chinese robots. They weren't on the hillside near the row of radio towers. He scanned the rugged terrain along the side of the Phobos Crash Site. No sign of them in that direction either.

"*Head back into the Phobos fissure,*" Bradbury said.

"No," Derek said, shaking his head. "We need to get to my truck."

"*The cave is safer,*" Isaac said.

"No. If I go back in, I won't get back out alive. They'll block the entrance and wait until I starve to death."

"*How can you be certain?*"

"They are like you," Derek replied. "They have no need for food or water. It's a waiting game, and they can out-wait me. Besides, we need to warn everyone at Olympus Mons."

Bradbury and Isaac moved to the rear of the truck. Lasers struck the ground where they had stood. Chunks of pebbles and gravels flicked into the air. Some of the grit bounced off his visor.

Derek rolled and glanced upward at the high towering side of Phobos. Red laser streaks shot downward. At least two enemy robots were visible and knew where his position, trying to keep him pinned down.

"What's their firing range?" Derek asked.

"*From what little damage Isaac suffered,*" Bradbury said, "*my estimate is that we are nearly outside their range. Up close, their lasers will slice right through any of us.*"

"They're firing from directly above. We should make a run for those low lying rocks on our west side," Derek said. "I can use those rocks for cover and possibly move farther out of their range."

"*Be careful,*" Bradbury said.

"I plan to be."

Isaac turned and helped Derek stand. "*We'll follow behind you, acting as shields.*"

Derek ran, crouched forward. Lasers zipped past his head and some flicked debris near his feet. But he made it to the low-lying rock wall. A narrow path ran between the wall of rocks and the Phobos mountainous remains. He figured if he followed the path, he was safe from the overhead fire. There was a good chance the path was long enough that he could reach his vehicle without the enemy noticing. That gave him valuable time, and it was the only hope he had left.

Chapter 30

Steven Matthews sat at the bar inside the Vortex, sipping Irish whiskey. Disguised as a guard, everyone assumed him to be Norm Schrader. The real Norm was serving Matthews' prison sentence in the mining pits.

While on the red planet, Matthews' disgust for Grayson had not mellowed. He still despised the man and remained a step or two ahead of the pompous trillionaire. In the same manner Matthews had injected Magnus with micro nanobots in the Texas prison, he self-inoculated the same computerized bots as a precaution should Grayson ever implant a Sleeper Chip in him.

When he worked for Grayson, Matthews became quite privy to Grayson's schemes and the inhumane technology he was using on his prisoner slaves. Of course, Matthews learned this by hacking into Grayson Enterprises' top secret files. Matthews obtained useful information about the chips as well as other underhanded experiments Grayson planned for future endeavors. So he wasn't surprised that Grayson would eventually implant a chip into him once Grayson discovered his true identity.

Although not on a monetary scale, Matthews was Grayson's chief competitor in the world of scientific and technological advancements, but Matthews leaned more toward the evolutionary progressions in genetics. Not exactly Grayson's forte, but Grayson possessed something Matthews eventually hoped to get his hands on—alien DNA.

Matthews had come close to getting those samples, but others interfered. The Lydia clone was one of them, and because of her, Matthews was captured, *twice*. In some ways, he despised her more than he did Grayson.

He stared in the mirror at the nasty scar that ran down his right cheek and beneath his jaw. Had his plastic surgery been allowed to heal in the necessary amount of time, he wouldn't have the scar, but Lydia's brutal assault almost killed him. Naturally, he preferred the scar to death. Without the assistance of his colleague temporarily rendering Lydia unconscious, Matthews would not have been spared. He was alive, and the scar reminded him daily how close to death he'd come.

His disfigurement motivated his vengeful need to kill Lydia if ever he returned to Earth. Matthews couldn't ignore his previous theory. Grayson had hired the clone to kill him. But after Matthews was captured and placed in prison, Grayson changed his mind. Instead, he decided to make Matthews waste away by serving a life sentence as a miner on Mars. In Grayson's twisted mind, that was a better punishment than death. The sentence wasn't exactly punishment. It was vengeance. However, Grayson's underestimation of Matthews gave Matthews an edge and the upper hand once more.

For all Grayson and the Mars security staff knew, Matthews was still mining. He hoped to keep it that way for now.

He often wondered where Grayson obtained the alien DNA. Mars seemed the most logical place, and if Matthews happened to be correct, he could easily take control of the DNA and Grayson's operations on the red planet. Doing so crippled Grayson Enterprises by impeding future wealth-increasing shipments to Earth, which essentially lacerated Grayson's financial jugular vein. A suitable compensation for what Grayson had put Matthews through. Under different circumstances, Matthews believed he and Grayson might have teamed together to become the most dangerous threat to the Earth's overall economic system.

Matthews had stood on the higher ledge of the mining pit when the one prisoner's chip malfunctioned, causing the anguished man to run blindly, jump into the deep pit, and kill himself. Magnus had also witnessed the event.

But Magnus never showed any indication his chip had malfunctioned until later that evening. Matthews was responsible for shorting out Magnus' chip, but he couldn't take credit for the other malfunctioning chips. Apparently Grayson's chips were flawed on quite a large scale, and should they continue to malfunction, Matthews understood the dangers the occupants of Olympus Mons faced. These ruthless prisoners *weren't* people that needed to be free or alive. He understood Grayson's need to control their minds with the chips, but he despised Grayson's ingenuity for making money off their demise and free labor, only because Grayson had thought of it before Matthews.

Matthews hoped he'd have discovered the moment when the nanobots freed Magnus from the Sleeper Chip, but Magnus somehow fooled Matthews and the other guards in the pit. The man was incredibly strong, both mentally and physically, to have continued mining after his chip shorted out.

As a perimeter guard, Matthews didn't receive the notification when Magnus' chip stopped working, so he didn't have the proper authorization to retrieve Magnus. All he could really do was wait at the infirmary for a chance to talk to Magnus before the doctor implanted a new chip, but that opportunity never came.

Matthews was as surprised as everyone else to learn that Magnus had stolen the Percival 3000. Perhaps Matthews' disappointment outweighed his surprise because he would've boarded the shuttle with them to get back to Earth if he'd known Magnus' plans.

Had Matthews tried harder while on Earth, he could've avoided being sent to Mars since he could've tempted Grayson with new technological business opportunities. People like Grayson *thrived* on beneficial bribes. But as a scientist, Matthews was grateful to be here.

Living on Mars wasn't available to everyone. Besides, in a lot of ways, he could do more damage to Grayson while on Mars than he ever could on Earth, especially since Grayson assumed Matthews was mentally out of commission. Grayson most likely wasn't even giving Matthews a second thought, which gifted Matthews with an even greater advantage. By the time Grayson discovered what Matthews planned to do, it would be too late.

He rubbed the scar on his face. Anger stirred.

Norm, who had unwittingly taken Matthew's mining position, didn't possess any scars or blemishes. The only reason Norm was in the mines unnoticed by security or the guards was because the chips were what guards used to identify the prisoners more than mugshots or fingerprints. During the flight from Earth to Mars, Matthews' chip shorted, causing him to struggle inside the Hyber-Sleep machine. His eyes bulged, and he started shouting before he was fully awaken.

As a precaution, one guard was required to remain awake in case the computers failed. When the guard checked Matthews and realized his chip had malfunctioned, he opened Matthews' sleep chamber to tend to him. After the chamber bubble lifted, Matthews removed his I.V. and other connectors, and grabbed Norm with a chokehold until the guard lost consciousness. Then Matthews carefully placed the unconscious guard on the floor in the aisle.

He cuffed Norm and then walked to the ship's infirmary where he found a scalpel and a syringe of Marcaine for local anesthesia. From a drawer he took several large bandages. Looking in the mirror, he injected Marcaine beneath his chip implant, and waited until the area around it numbed. The worst part about the procedure was removing the chip himself. Where the incision needed to be made, he expected to see a lot of blood.

Matthews removed his shirt, opened a bandage, and set it on the sink counter. He placed a towel around his neck and took a deep breath. Using his left finger and thumb, he pressed the chip downward to the softer flesh beneath the base of his skull. Then he took the scalpel and sliced below the bulged skin. The blade cut without resistance. The pressure from his fingers popped the chip partway through the opening. Blood trickled around the chip and seeped into the towel. With another push, the chip slipped through the cut skin and landed on the towel.

He grabbed the open bandage and covered the area, applying some pressure until the blood flow lessened. Then he pressed the adhesive part of the bandage against his head and held it in place for several minutes.

Matthews didn't doubt the pain would radiate as soon as the anesthetic faded, so he wanted to act fast to take Norm's tracer chip out and replace it with a new Sleeper Chip. Somehow Matthews needed to assign the new chip with Matthews' identity. Once they reached Mars, the scan would reveal Norm as Matthews. But inserting a new chip back into Norm's incision didn't go as easily as he had hoped.

The blood made the new chip slick and greasy. Norm's incision leaked worse than his, which made it difficult to see the center of the wound.

Placing the towel against the bleeding slowed the blood loss, but Norm started to stir. Should he fully awaken, he'd struggle, making it impossible to implant the chip.

Matthew grabbed a small tuft of Norm's hair and pulled upward, exposing the hole. He pushed the small curved end of the chip into the widened hole until it was midway inside. Carefully he applied more pressure, partially tearing the opening wider, but he got the chip inside. He took a bandage and stuck it against the wound. He hurried to the infirmary to find a needle and thread before Norm awakened.

He found them and sprinted back.

Norm groaned and attempted to move his cuffed hands without any success. He opened an eye and fastened his gaze on Matthews. "What the hell are you doing?"

Matthews ignored the question. "Hold still."

"No. I'm not holding still. Tell me what you're doing."

"Please. Don't struggle. You're losing a lot of blood."

Norm turned his head so he could see Matthews clearer. "I'm bleeding? How? Why?"

"Seems you fell and hit your head," Matthews lied. "Quite hard, as you've been unconscious for a while."

"That doesn't require handcuffs, now does it?"

"I'm trying to prevent you from making it worse."

"Bloody hell. You're a prisoner, *not* a medic. Now uncuff me and let me up."

"I wasn't *always* a prisoner." Matthews tried to soothe Norm with his rich, charismatic tone. "Let me stitch the wound and get it bandaged. Otherwise, you're going to lose even more blood. And we're not equipped to give you a blood transfusion, are we?"

Norm sighed and grumbled. "Oh very well. Hurry."

Matthews ran the threaded needle through the edges of the incision several times until the wound was closed tightly. "That's better. Let me help you up."

Matthews placed his hand around Norm's elbow and helped the guard stand. He eased Norm into the seat that had been assigned to Matthews. He patted Norm's suit pockets and then he looked at Norm. "Where are your keys?"

Norm offered a slight shrug. "They should be in one of my pockets."

"I didn't find any."

"Check in the officer room. I might have left them on a table or counter."

Matthews offered a slight smile and nodded. "Okay. Sit tight. I'll go find them and be right back."

After Matthews found a set of keys for the handcuffs, he stopped in the infirmary. He opened a glass-fronted cabinet filled with vials. Near the back was a vial of Midazolam. He filled a syringe with the sedative and returned to Norm.

"Did you find a key?" Norm asked.

Matthews nodded. "I found something else, too."

"What's that?"

Matthews jabbed the needle into Norm's leg and injected the sedative.

"What the hell was that?" Norm asked. His face flushed red.

"Relax. It won't hurt you."

"You bastard." Norm attempted to stand, but Matthews placed gentle hands on the guard's shoulders, preventing him from rising to his feet. Norm shook his head and blinked erratically, trying to stay awake. "What was that?"

"Something to make you relax and go to sleep. Trust me," Matthews said with a smug smile. "You *won't* remember a thing."

After Norm passed out, Matthews eased him into the Hyber-Sleep chamber, typed in the proper settings, and then returned to the maintenance supply closet. He grabbed a new CAM-L still in its box along with its programming book. He needed to learn how to reprogram the Sleeper Chip so Norm would react to the computer's commands and so the guards ID'ed him as Matthews.

That process took Matthews several hours to figure out, but with the time it took to reach Mars, he could've taken a couple of months.

"Schrader!" the bartender said.

Matthews jerked his head and glanced at the man, leaving his daydreaming memories behind. It was difficult remembering to respond to an assumed name.

"Can I get you something else?" the man asked. "We close in a few minutes."

Matthews shook his head and beamed a smile. "No. I'm fine. Thanks."

The barkeep chuckled. "You looked sort of spaced out there. Kinda like one of those brainless prisoners."

Matthews offered a slight grin and tilted his head back with a feigned laugh. "Got lost in my thoughts. That's all. The world of imagination is often so much more pleasant than reality. Don't you think?"

"I suppose. What exactly were you thinking about? Going back to Earth? You can't be thinking too much about your current job. Not much for you guards to do except stand around."

"I imagine everyone here thinks about going back to Earth. Don't you?"

"All the time. The only benefit about being a bartender is the tips. Everyone's so depressed about being stationed on Mars that the majority of the workers will be alcoholics before their contracts ever come to an end."

Matthews chuckled and stood. "I could see that happening. Take care. Probably be seeing you again tomorrow evening."

The bartender nodded. "For most, The Vortex is a daily ritual."

Chapter 31

Derek ran along the Phobos ruins until he came to what looked like another cave entrance. It didn't dead end because light was visible on the other end of the tunnel. Before he entered, sunlight shone on the Phobos ruins. The former moon was pocked with craters where meteors had struck it during its space orbit around Mars, which gave the mountain of rock an interesting texture.

Because of Phobos' low density, the moon had shattered almost like an egg when it impacted with Mars. The inside of the porous body contained a vast cavern system, and even though Grayson's space engineers attempted to land Phobos safely on Mars' surface, its exterior couldn't sustain the pressure beneath its own weight.

Derek entered the short tunnel, followed by Bradbury and Isaac. Bradbury remained at the entrance. Isaac stayed close behind Derek. Derek rounded a slight curve in the tunnel and light spilled through the porous ceiling, enough where the floor was visible. At the distant opening, he hesitated.

"Are the robots following us?" Derek asked Bradbury via transmitter.

"They're still in sight, but presently not following."

At least they weren't in stealth mode. Eventually, they'd pursue him again. Programmed to kill humans, they were sent to destroy everything Grayson held dear, and currently, Derek was their chief target. Were the Chinese also sending militant humans in route to Mars within the next few months?

Derek crouched slightly, preparing to sprint from the tunnel opening, when a robotic hand grabbed him. His heart and body jolted. His sudden terror prevented him from screaming. The robot turned him. It was Olivia. Somewhat relieved, he exhaled a long sigh.

"Don't *do* that," Derek said.

"*Derek,*" she said. "*What troubles you? I thought you'd be happy to see us.*"

Olivia and Ursula stood in front of him. Olivia's front panel was burnt from a laser blast, but she seemed fully functional.

"Do you see any of the robots?" he asked.

She and Ursula shook their heads. In unison, they said, "*Negative.*"

The evaluation didn't reassure Derek completely because his robots could not detect stealth cloaking mechanisms. About fifty yards away, parked in a fault trench, was his flatbed truck. The truck set in full sunlight, so the solar batteries should be charged enough to reach Olympus Mons. If they reached the truck without getting shot, they could put some distance between themselves and their enemies.

Isaac stepped behind Derek. Bradbury was running through the tunnel to catch them. Once Bradbury reached them, Derek stood before them like a commander getting ready to give his team instructions. They were robots. Machines. But they stood with loyalty, awaiting his direction. With Kurt absent, they didn't seem quite complete, but in reality, Kurt had been flawed from the beginning, even though Derek never wanted to accept the robot's obvious computerized mental glitch. Their biggest handicap was not possessing any weapons.

Derek looked at his robots with grave concern. "We must reach the truck and return to Olympus Mons to warn them of the invasion. If I die, these enemy robots will kill every human on Mars."

"*We will not fail you,*" Isaac replied.

Derek smiled. Moving forward jeopardized his life but he risked his creations as well. While he doubted the Chinese robots were swift runners, he didn't have any idea how accurately or to what extent the range of their blasters could still effectively cause lethal damage. At a far distance, he was more vulnerable than his robots. Their metal exterior deflected most lasers, while his smart suit did not. The more distance they put between themselves and the lasers, the safer they all were.

He peered at the ridge where the Chinese robots were. He counted four, so where were the others?

The longer he delayed his run for the truck, the more opportunity he allowed the stealthed robots to advance. For all he knew, they might already be within firing range. He must run now or he might never get the chance.

Derek nodded to the robots, turned, and ran toward the trench line where his truck was. Due to his shoulder injury, running fast was impossible. He hugged his arm against his side to prevent swinging it, which made him hobble. The tight blisters ached. The more he ran, the more the surrounding flesh tugged the scorched tender wound.

His boots kicked a small trail of dust as he trod to the beginning of the gulley. He dared a glance over his shoulder. Lasers shot behind him. Grit and small pebbles exploded. Bradbury and Isaac followed Derek closely, running side by side in such a way as to shield Derek from any incoming direct hits.

The laser blasts weren't coming from where the four visible robots stood. Instead, these sliced the air from the line of the short radio towers. The Chinese robots' stealth mode deactivated and revealed their exact location. Without any hesitation they tore into sprints, kicking sand and debris into the air as their heavy bodies increased momentum.

"*Run!*" Ursula said.

Olivia joined Ursula. The two female robots rushed at the first Chinese robot in what appeared to be an attempt to cut it off. Each grabbed one of its arms to slow its swift advance. Laser blasts seared Olivia's back panel in an unrelenting assault until the rapid fire melted the protective panel shielding her circuit boards. Smoke rose. She pivoted to the side. Her hands released the robot, and she dropped on the thick sand.

Ursula refused to let go of the robot. She pulled, yanked, and twisted, but the robot kept going, carrying her without being deterred or slowed by her additional weight. The strength of the Chinese robot was unbelievable. While she tried to deter his pursuit of Derek, the robot tired of her feebleness. Instead of engaging a fight with her, it raised its plasma pistol and fired multiple point-blank shots into her head. Sparks flickered. Her robot body jerked with fiery spasms. She released her hold. Black smoke drifted off her melting wires and circuits.

Derek ignored his shoulder pain and ran faster. His chest felt heavy. Hot tears filled his eyes and meandered down his cheeks. To everyone else, they were robots, machines composed of electrical components and circuits. To him, they were family. The loss was heavy, painful. He ached inside. Besides his immediate remorse, anger welled inside him. Even though he wasn't a violent person, he wanted vengeance.

He ran faster. Isaac's and Bradbury's heavy footsteps thudded behind him. He wanted to reach the truck, not only to save himself, but also to ensure that his last two robotic friends weren't destroyed. But what if the truck wouldn't start?

Derek's right foot skidded on a small pile of loose gravel. He lost his footing, stumbled, and fell to his hands and knees on the coarse rocky gully. Chips of red pebbles imbedded into his gloves but didn't cut through its protective material.

He winced and muttered words under his breath. Liquid oozed and pain radiated down his injured shoulder. His blisters had ruptured, but he couldn't inspect it until he reached a medic at Olympus Mons. *If* he reached Olympus Mons.

Both robots looped their arms around Derek's elbows and lifted him to his feet. They didn't allow him the chance to run along beside them. Instead, they carried him the final ten yards to the truck.

Lasers glanced off the truck's windshield.

Derek ducked at the truck's grill and crept around to the driver side door. More lasers struck the truck. Other than melting spots of paint, the thick metal withstood the assault. For now...

He grabbed the door handle and swung open the door. The robots were approaching fast. He turned the ignition key.

Nothing.

Again, he tried.

The engine belts turned once, then stopped.

Bradbury and Isaac climbed onto the flatbed and brushed away more silt and dust from the solar panels.

Derek watched the robots running from the other side of the gully. He closed his eyes. They'd be on them in less than a minute.

Bradbury hammered his fist against the roof of the cab. *"Try again."*

Derek took a deep breath and turned the key. The engine started.

"What did you do?" he shouted.

"I connected the solar charger to my adapter."

He shook his head. That wasn't something he'd have thought to do. He knocked the vehicle into drive, revved the engine, and made a wide turn in the rocky channel. A barrage of laser fire assailed the truck. Once he turned the truck and straightened out, he pressed the accelerator. Isaac and Bradbury clung to the railing across the truck cab.

Thick rolling sheets of dirt billowed behind the truck. Looking into the side view mirror, Derek watched the four robots disappear into the wall of dust. He was partly relieved. He'd survived the first encounter with them, but he wasn't at the base yet. He left a trail for the robots to follow. Releasing a sigh, he held hope of seeing his grandfather again. His losses made his heart ache, but at least, two of his robots remained operational.

The top of the roof hammered twice.

"Yes?" Derek asked.

"Isaac is no longer active."

Derek looked over his shoulder through the rear glass. Isaac's left hand clung to the cab rail, which kept his limp upper body from dropping onto the truck bed. The lower half of his body lay on the flatbed. Oil and hydraulic fluid pooled beneath him.

He grieved. Only Bradbury remained intact.

Derek could revive Isaac after reconstructing him in the engineering garage, but it would take quite a bit of time to do so. That is, if they prevented the Chinese robots from invading their encampment. They needed to permanently destroy the robots before the robots killed them.

Chapter 32

Watching movies for several days was more boring than Magnus and Sylvia ever expected. While they watched movies, Carter spent most of his time researching Hyber-Sleep and its possible side effects.

Magnus expressed how stir crazy the shuttle was becoming, even with movies, games, and exercise. Carter suggested they start their first month's hibernation cycle to see how well they adapted after awakening.

Magnus thought they should stay awake another week, but after discussing the situation at length with Carter, Magnus reluctantly agreed to enter hibernation.

Carter lectured his medical understanding about how Hyber-Sleep affected their reactions, their cognitive abilities, and their overall strength. Understanding those results early in the trip allowed Carter to estimate the best time to awaken them so they could rebuild their mental reflexes and strength. They needed to be refreshed and strong prior to entering Earth's atmosphere. They held no doubt Grayson would do everything to arrest or possibly kill them.

Carter gave them high mineral drinks to flush their colons before they were hooked inside the Hyber-Sleep chambers for the first month.

Magnus sat and shook his head. His hands squeezed his stomach. "Man, that's some rough stuff."

"You should've warned us about *that* procedure ahead of time," Sylvia said.

"It's unpleasant but necessary," Carter replied. "You can't harbor solid waste inside your intestines during hibernation. The toxins are dangerous, and you don't have the ability to go to the restroom."

"I understand." She winced and held her stomach. "I think."

"I might opt to remain awake the rest of the trip now," Magnus said. "Rather than go through that again. Talk about losing your shit—"

Sylvia laughed and snorted.

Carter smiled. "Not hibernating is an option. I'm not sure what you'd entertain yourself with though."

"Books," Magnus said.

"Okay. We'll discuss it after this sleep session ends. We need at least one month to test for muscle loss and weakness."

"That makes sense," Magnus said. "But we might need to be awake in case Grayson tries to negotiate a new deal with us?"

Sylvia nodded. "I agree."

"No," Carter replied. "Grayson won't offer any deals this early in our departure."

"Why not?" Sylvia asked.

"Why should he? He'll wait until we're closer to Earth. Seven months is plenty of time for Grayson to scheme. My guess is he won't offer us a deal at all. He owns the ship, and essentially, like Magnus already stated about the miners' contracts, such agreements were phony. His actions imply that he *owns* us, too. Why negotiate with someone you already believe is your property?"

Magnus shrugged. "I agree that's the way he probably views prisoners, but I'm not so certain he thinks that about his guards, staff, and scientists."

Carter sighed. "When I first signed on, I believed that, too."

"And you don't now?" Magnus asked.

"No."

"What changed your mind?" Sylvia asked.

"Laying the groundwork for a Martian civilization will take decades. Probably a couple hundred years," Carter replied. "I've thought a lot about what Magnus said about the prisoners' health. The prisoners are aging at a rapid rate due to being overworked without getting adequate food and sleep. They aren't aware of what's happening, so they can't protest or revolt. Magnus is right. The majority will never live long enough to reap the monetary promises Grayson promised. Even if they did, they'll be too feeble to work their land."

"That's a shame," Sylvia said.

"Perhaps," Carter said. "But with their violent backgrounds, would you ever want to see them without Sleeper Chips controlling them?"

Sylvia shook her head. "No."

"Eventually, those chips will fail," Magnus said. "My chip deactivated because of outside help, but the other miner killed himself because his chip was defective. The odds are that many more chips will short out."

"I agree," Carter said. "Grayson has money, and while most of his goals are usually achieved, he rushed the development of the Sleeper Chips because he wanted to stake his full claim to Mars. The chips should've been tested much longer."

Magnus stared at the hibernation seats. "Are you ready to induce us for our long naps?"

"Yes. Pick a seat," Carter replied.

Sylvia and Magnus sat while Carter administered the setups for their first month of hibernation. Carter programmed the vital sign monitors and unraveled the feeding tubes. Sylvia looked extremely nervous.

Carter's brow furrowed as he tightened different attachments.

"I'll be right back," Carter said. "I need to get sterile I.V. needles."

Magnus nodded.

"I'm sorry to inform you," Carter said, "but if you thought the enemas were bad, the worst part is inserting the catheters."

"Shit," Magnus said with an intense wince. "Never thought about that. *Definitely* staying awake the rest of the trip after this."

Carter left the passenger cabin, and Sylvia looked at Magnus. "I'm nervous. Are you?"

"A little."

"What are you going to do about Digger?" she asked.

He shrugged. "Actually, there's a room for housing pets. Since maintenance uses ferrets to squeeze through those narrow passages, they transport them aboard these shuttles. He's going to be okay. Tons of food and automatic watering spigots. He's set up like a king."

"Good."

"He'll get lonely and fat over the next month."

"Poor little guy. How do you think we'll feel after a month of sleep?"

"Our minds might be refreshed," Magnus said. "Not sure how our bodies will react though. I imagine our thinking will be a bit foggy, too, like waking up with a bad hangover. At first, it'll be hard to find the motivation to exercise or do anything. At least we're not staying sedentary the entire trip. That'd be too hard on us."

"You're right."

Magnus smiled. "I'll be happy when we reach Earth and get back to our normal lives."

"Do you think we can ever return to normal?"

"I don't know, but I'm going to try my damnedest."

Carter returned with two packages of I.V. needles and catheter tubes, but he didn't have his briefcase. He ripped open each plastic bag and after several minutes, he was ready to insert Sylvia's I.V. She trembled when Carter rubbed alcohol on the back of her hand with a cotton ball. She took a deep breath and closed her eyes.

"Don't be so worried," Carter said.

She nodded but kept her eyes squeezed shut.

Carter looked at Magnus. "I have the computer set to awaken you in thirty days."

"Aren't you going into hibernation mode, too?" Magnus asked with a puzzled expression.

"Yes," Carter said, nodding. "I meant... us. We'll awaken in thirty days."

"You sure you'll be able to do that by yourself?" Sylvia asked.

He gave a hesitant smile and nodded. "Yes. That won't be a problem."

Sylvia's nervous eyes stared into Carter's. "Are you certain we're going to be okay?"

"The computer monitors everything," he replied. He placed a gentle hand on her cheek and smiled. "Should something happen, the computer will awaken us."

"Good," she said with slight relief, but her frightened eyes exposed her doubt in fully trusting what Carter said was true.

Magnus stared at Carter with the same scrutiny.

After Carter set her I.V. monitor and the computer commands, he turned his attention to Magnus. He inserted the I.V. needle and typed in the commands for his seat. The overhead enclosures lowered. Metal clamps locked around Magnus' and Sylvia's wrists, perhaps to reduce any extra movement during the hibernation stage. Suffering a nightmare might cause the dreamer to fling up his arms and unknowingly disconnect the I.V. needles, thus a reason for the added precaution of securing them to the seats.

Carter faced them. "You should start feeling some drowsiness in a few minutes. That's the sedative taking affect."

Magnus closed his eyes. He pictured Boony and her smile the night they talked over drinks at The Vortex. He thought about how pleasant a month of sleep would be if she were the one occupying his dreams. Although he didn't really talk to her as long as he wished, he was thankful to have met her. He liked that he had gained her trust enough for her to let him continue his mission for justice, or at the very worst, carry out his ultimate revenge.

His heart raced when he thought about delivering the justice his enemies deserved. He didn't want to let down his ex-girlfriend's cousin, Darnell. Since Boony generously helped his escape, he didn't want to let her down, either. He swore never to give her up even if Grayson captured and tortured him for answers. He chose not to dwell on that possible outcome because he didn't plan to get caught.

Magnus hoped his hibernation dreams weren't interrupted by nightmares of what might happen once they reached Earth. Upon awakening, he feared how things in their lives might have already changed. He possessed a growing uncertainty in what Carter was doing, what his true agenda was, and if the doctor was being truthful. But he agreed Grayson wouldn't offer them any deals. Quite possibly, Sylvia's plan to use parachutes before the shuttle landed wasn't something Grayson even expected. At least, he hoped Grayson wouldn't.

As Magnus' eyes grew heavier, he wanted to tug out the I.V. needle, but the wrist clamps prevented him from doing so. He couldn't do anything until the computer brought them out of hibernation.

He glanced at Sylvia. She was already asleep. Perhaps due to his large size, the sedative took longer or he simply needed a higher dosage. Movement caught his attention on the other side of Sylvia. It was Carter. The doctor didn't have another I.V. needle and didn't seem to be getting ready to join them in the hibernation phase.

"What the hell are you up to?" Magnus thought, fighting to keep his eyes open.

Carter crossed his arms and stood watching Sylvia and Magnus. His eyes were strangely dark, sinister, and an odd smile spread across his lips. Quite disturbing was the best way Magnus could describe it. Carter wasn't prepping himself at all, and that disturbed Magnus more than the fear of possible nightmares. At this particular moment, Carter's intent was far worse than anything the Sandman might deliver.

Carter stared at them a few moments more, turned, and headed down the aisle. Seconds before Magnus' eyes shut in sleep, his last thought was to get free of the hibernation chamber. He flexed his arms and desperately tugged, but the metal restraints didn't budge.

"Where the hell are you going?" Magnus thought as he faded from consciousness and drifted into the hibernation stage. He no longer expected Boony to dominate his dreams. Nightmares of what Carter might do while they slept haunted him.

Jonas sat at his desk and rubbed his tired eyes. He'd hardly slept for days. Derek's long silence worried and sickened him. The red dots on their satellite surveillance cameras nights before indicated unsettling news that perhaps an alien force was moving in to surround and kill his grandson. However, the next day, no trace of these intrusive beings appeared on the radar grid. Perhaps they'd only been glitches in the system or due to his exhaustion, they were nothing other than a mirage.

Boony entered the security office earlier than normal.

"Morning, Jonas," she said with a broad smile.

"Morning."

"You look exhausted. Still no news about Derek?"

"No."

"Go get some sleep, sir. I can handle everything here."

"I've tried. I can't stop worrying about him."

Boony nodded. "I understand. Why not send out a search party to locate him?"

"No. Well, I assembled a team, but Derek was adamant that I didn't. He said that he was sick of me treating him like a child. After he left, I realized that's exactly what I've done his entire life. He's a man, and he needs his independence. If I send a search team, and he's okay, he'll be insulted and angrier than ever. That'll broaden the gap between us."

"I see his point."

"I see it now, too. After losing my son and Derek's mother, the hardest thing was letting Derek become a man."

"That's understandable."

"When you have children one day, you'll understand."

Boony smiled. "I'm sure I will, but with the likelihood of prospective suitors for me on Mars... I don't see that happening."

"No?"

She shook her head.

"You never know. Love finds you when you least expect it."

Boony smiled. "I'm not sure I want it to find me. At least not here. I don't know that I'd want the worry and responsibility of having children. I wasn't exactly the model teenager. And even though I made a lot of bad decisions, my parents still gave me a *lot* of drama for wanting to move to Mars."

"They did, huh?"

"Yes."

"How'd you get them to comply?"

Boony shrugged and smiled. "I didn't. I left."

Jonas' eyebrows rose. "Really?"

"Yes. They were always overbearing and never let me do what I wanted, so I had no other choice except to leave. So it's good you've decided to let Derek live his life."

Jonas nodded.

BOONY TURNED to her computer and sighed. She hated lying to Jonas, but he was in such mental anguish over Derek. She pitied him, which was a shame because he was the strongest person she'd ever met. He was solid and his mental edge was like sharpened steel. So, if a lie helped him overcome his needless mourning, it was worth it.

Of course, if he ever looked into her background, he knew she was an orphan, a delinquent, and was blatantly lying about her past. But she wanted to ease his mind. He was the type of man she wished she'd had as a father. Since his job demanded keen focus, her little lie wasn't too great a crime.

"How are we handling the theft of the shuttle?" she asked, changing the subject.

"That's in Grayson's hands now. There's nothing we can do."

"Okay. If there's anything I can help you with, please let me know."

"Thanks. Keep trying to contact the Deimos Life Station at least once an hour."

Boony nodded. "Not a problem. I can do that."

"What we cannot afford is a similar incident like the theft of the Percival 3000. That's a wakeup call for how we operate the security team. I'd really like to identify the man from Deimos. That'd narrow down a lot of factors. However, not knowing means we don't know if there are others hiding in the shadows to steal another ship or bags of the MarQuebes or do something even worse."

"That's true."

"The surveillance video only showed him exit the Deimos shuttle, didn't it?"

Boony nodded. "Yes."

"Never anywhere else?"

"Everywhere I located him on surveillance video, he always wore the helmet. He never took it off, so he was aware of our cameras."

"He covered his tracks quite well," Jonas said. "I still think he had ties with others besides Sylvia."

"That's possible."

"We have a few shady guards, as we discovered. I should've been paying more attention. God knows I don't have the extra time to do that."

"Did you check the Deimos shuttle log?" she asked. "He'd have had to access the computer, wouldn't he? Even if we can't read the physical copy, the computer has his log."

"I already had a tech scan for that information."

"Nothing?"

Jonas shook his head. "No. The man cleared the computer. Wiped it clean."

"Damn. He must have some tech background. Most people leave tracks somewhere."

"He didn't."

"Well, Jonas, there's something else I need to tell you."

Jonas frowned. "What's that?"

"The last time I was at The Vortex, I overheard some guards talking about the shuttle theft."

"And?"

"They're viewing Sylvia as a hero."

"A hero, huh?"

Boony nodded.

"That's when you realize you have problems. When those standing on the right side of the law begin to think a thief's a hero, they've lost all rationalization between right and wrong. They're not far from stepping across the line of good and becoming what they were trained to fight against."

"I know."

"If those on Deimos view the shuttle pilot in the same light, no telling what kind of chaos is happening inside that moon station."

Boony felt uneasy. Who was the man with Magnus? While Magnus seemed trustworthy, and she truly suspected he was innocent, had he been duped into helping a more dangerous individual make his way back to Earth?

She took a deep breath. "Seems we might have a lot more to be concerned about than we thought?"

"No. Grayson does. It's his ship. Since they're headed to Earth, it's his mess. I expect he has plans on how to clean it up."

"Surely this concerns you, though?"

"Of course it does, Boony. But look at me. My grave will be here on Mars. I'm too old to journey to Earth. This was a one-way ticket for me."

"You're not *that* old."

Jonas chuckled and shook his head. "I'm not about to put my body through the strain of space travel for another seven months. It's not worth it."

She smiled. "It was rough on me, too."

"See? Wait another forty years and reconsider that statement."

"Oh, now—"

The security door flung open. Clark leaned inside the doorframe, bent forward with his hands on his knees, trying desperately to catch his breath. Jonas rose and pulled his laser blaster. Clark's eyes widened and his face grew paler. He waved his hands in surrender, panting, letting them know he didn't mean any harm. He couldn't breathe. Sweat rolled down his face. A half-minute passed before he could breathe calmer.

"What is it?" Jonas asked, lowering his weapon.

"We're got a major problem in Shaft Fifteen."

"What kind of problem?"

Clark panted and wiped sweat from his face. "We have found life on the planet. But it's not a good discovery. They're deadly, and there's far too many of them for us to stop."

Chapter 34

"Life?" Jonas asked. He gave a puzzled glance at Boony. "What the hell are you talking about? What kind of life?"

Clark nodded. "Strange insect-like creatures. They killed Shad."

Jonas frowned. His eyes narrowed as he studied Clark. "These creatures *killed* him?"

"Yes," Clark said. "They *bit* or *stung* him. They possess very toxic venom. He dropped to the floor and was paralyzed in less than a minute. They... I *think* they drained his blood."

"How many creatures are we talking about?" Boony said, walking toward the door.

"Thousands."

"Thousands?" Boony asked. Her eyes widened.

Clark nodded vigorously.

"Why haven't we seen these things before?" Jonas asked.

Clark stepped away from the door, grabbed a swivel chair, and plopped down. Boony handed him a bottle of water. Sweat rolled down his pale, frightened face. He twisted off the lid and downed the water.

Panting, he said, "Shad was operating his drilling machine to lengthen the tunnel. The next thing we knew, the giant drill bit bent and was knocked off its track. The hole in the wall cracked open. Chunks of rock collapsed. He tapped into a large room."

"What do you mean a room?" Jonas asked.

"It's an enlargement, like the big open areas you find inside some cavern systems on Earth. Shad went inside the room. I tried to stop him. These creatures are all over that chamber. The ceilings. The walls. The floors."

"Wait a minute. Why'd he go inside if those insects were in there?"

Clark took a deep breath and exhaled. "We didn't see them. They are well camouflaged. They're the same color as the floor and walls. They blended in so well that I barely noticed them, and by the time I did, Shad was surrounded."

"What possessed him to go inside alone?" Boony asked.

"I tried to stop him. I really did. He was so possessed with discovering something to make a name for himself that he shut out my logical arguments and any rationality. I had grabbed his ankle but lost my footing. When I let go, he dove to the other side of the wall. I tried to convince Shad to come out, but he swore he saw a silver bridge and a door. I didn't see either of those structures."

"Had he been drinking?" Jonas asked.

"No. Not that I could tell."

"Did he hit his head when he fell?" Boony asked.

"I don't know. But there was this pungent chemical odor."

"What do you make of that? Could it have clouded his judgment?""

"It was harsh. I suppose there's the chance that it might have caused him hallucinations, but he could've struck his head in the fall."

Jonas grabbed a laser rifle from the gun rack and handed it to Clark.

Clark shook his head. "I don't think these weapons will harm them."

"Why not?"

Clark explained how he'd struck one with the shovel but the impact didn't hurt it. The pick only worked because he happened to strike it in the exact spot between its jointed segments.

"Any ideas about what you think *might* kill them?" Jonas asked.

"Heat? Or maybe extreme cold. I really don't know. Their exoskeletons are like strong metal, which might prevent almost any tool from penetrating their outer crusty layer."

Jonas pressed the button for the corridor intercoms. "Shaft Fifteen is in a state of emergency. I need all guards and off duty guards to take flamethrowers and fire extinguishers and meet me at the platform that overlooks the tunnel. Under no circumstances should anyone head into Shaft Fifteen until I get there. This is a Level Four emergency."

After he turned off the intercom, he looked at Clark. "How many of these creatures are we dealing with again? Thousands?"

Clark nodded.

"You're certain? Shock sometimes makes us see things that aren't there."

"Trust me. That's probably an *underestimated* number."

Jonas frowned. "Do you think the corridor in Shaft Fifteen might already be infested?"

"I hope not. I tried to seal the opening with the giant drill bit, but part of the wall had collapsed."

"In other words, gaps large enough where they can still get through?"

"Yes, sir."

"Come on," Jonas said to Clark.

"What about me?" Boony asked.

"Watch the surveillance feed. Keep an eye on the corridors. Make sure everything else is running smoothly. Keep trying to contact Deimos Life Station."

"Yes, sir," she replied. "But do note that there are no cameras in Shaft Fifteen."

"I know. We're going in blind."

GRAYSON SAT BEHIND HIS DESK, frustrated with the events that had unfolded during the week. His hold of the vast wealth of the Martian terrain was threatened. He realized how fragile his grip on the planet was becoming. Future applicants for Grayson Enterprises would be required even more thorough background checks and additional screenings before being interviewed. The ones in place were already quite detailed.

Beatrice paged him.

"Yes," he replied.

"Thomas Quaid on line one."

"Thanks, Beatrice."

Grayson tapped the button on his desk. "Yes, Thomas? What have you found out?"

"Two of the occupants on the Percival 3000 are in hibernation. Not sure what the third person's doing."

"Can you override the computer system controls on the shuttle?"

"Negative, sir. I've tried every code. The shuttle computer continues to deny me access."

Grayson frowned and thought for a moment. Thomas was his head computer-programming engineer, and if anyone could hijack and take back the shuttle, he was the man.

"How's that possible?" Grayson asked.

"One possible explanation is that since the hibernation mechanism is in place, the computer has blocked all outside communication to prevent hackers, which in our case would be us, from taking over the shuttle. That's a precautionary code you had me build into the system, which merely keeps the passengers safer."

"I see. Any other possible means?"

"The other possibility is someone aboard has tampered with the control system to reject outside interference. However, there's something else I can try."

Grayson's eyebrows rose. "What's that?"

"I might be able to hack into the nuclear propulsion engine computers."

"So?"

Thomas laughed softly. "I can boost the speed of the engines to have them back to Earth in six months instead of seven."

"Will they detect that?"

"Doubtful. I can set it to gradually increase over a two-day period."

"Do it," Grayson said with a broad smile.

"Consider it done."

Chapter 35

Carter sat inside the passenger cabin. He held the opened briefcase on his lap and stared at the two vials of deadly virus. He took the vials in his hands and studied them in the faint fluorescent lighting. So much power. Enough to wipe out worlds, and he possessed it. A smile curled his lips as he pictured the mighty egotistical Grayson pleading for his life.

"Why aren't you asleep like the others?" the female alien said inside his mind.

"I'm planning my strategy."

"There's plenty of time for that. You need rest, too."

"I'm fine."

"Grayson has vast intelligence. Without sleep you'll not have a sharp enough edge to contend with him."

Carter set the vials into the cushioned interior of the briefcase, closed it, and then locked it. He leaned back, closed his eyes, and pictured her dark oval eyes.

"Is killing him truly necessary?" Carter asked.

"It's the only way," she replied. "Without him, the damaging construction on Mars will stop."

"Others will come."

"Not with the same magnitude he has. They'll start fresh with fewer funds, less people. Perhaps they won't come at all. Grayson's death might frighten others not to risk Mars exploration."

Carter sighed. "I don't know that I can do this."

"I know you better than you know yourself. You *will* do this."

Startled by her angry tone, Carter opened his eyes. His breathing increased, in spite of his tightened chest. His eyes searched the passenger compartment. He half expected her to materialize in front of him. Where had the passion in her voice gone? Why had she allowed vengeance to completely possess her?

He stared at Sylvia inside her plastic hibernation bubble. She slept so peacefully. He thought her facial features were more angelic than human. Perhaps death blessed some better than others.

He waited several more minutes for the alien to speak, but she was gone. He no longer felt her presence.

The computer would awaken Sylvia and Magnus in thirty days. During that time, Carter needed to map his plans for when they arrived on Earth.

CLARK FOLLOWED Jonas with three armed guards. Heading into the narrow dark tunnel worried Clark more than the others, but only because he'd seen the deadly creatures. Jonas ordered the half dozen guards responding to his call to remain at the top of the corridor while he inspected Clark's discovery.

Jonas must not have believed his report about how large an infestation existed on the other side of the wall, or else, fewer guards arrived than what should have. More might be on their way, but he guessed a lot of them had gotten drunk and passed out in their quarters.

Clark carried a fire extinguisher because he wasn't trained to use laser rifles. Besides, a laser weapon probably couldn't harm these strange insects anyway. He doubt Jonas' flamethrower or their fire extinguishers would be any more effective.

Nearing the boring machine, Clark's apprehension increased. He never consider his three-year contract might actually cost him his life. Of course, the space flight to Mars was a great risk, even though Grayson Enterprises had never lost a shuttle or space barge. For Clark, to study the Martian volcano was an achievement that any adventurous geophysicist could ever hope to be assigned. His geothermic evaluations thus far were enough to launch a lucrative scientific career back on Earth. Had he uncovered fossils, his fame would've soared even higher.

The actual discovery of living creatures on Mars broke any previous aspirations he'd ever daydreamed. Any book he wrote and published was guaranteed an international bestseller. Every news channel and talk show host would request to interview him. The major and minor universities would invite him for guest lectures, request him to work on possible research projects with them, and quite possibly NASA might even offer him a job. The possibilities were endless.

Clark's accomplishments meant nothing if he died though. The worrisome part was fulfilling the last two years of his contract. Regardless of his discovery, he was stuck on Mars. Those were his obligations. Grayson would never allow him to back out, especially now.

With his initial eagerness to sign the contract and invest in his future business on Earth, his outlook and notoriety in science now deemed itself far greater. He'd never sought the limelight. He always shunned it. But the possibility of making millions of dollars more than his current contract drew him like a moth sought a candle's flame. Now, he understood Shad's stubborn behavior and why his colleague had walked blindly to his death. Vainglory to amass great wealth was deadly in almost any quantity or environment. Clark needed to remain alert and not make premature stupid decisions.

Shad's misfortunate death actually benefited Clark. Even though Shad was irritating to work with, his untimely death granted Clark the sole discoverer of these Martian insects. Since the insects killed Shad, the story of the deadly creatures became a more intriguing tale to divulge during interviews on the radio and television.

The underlying euphoria of impending fame burned in Clark's chest. When he realized the depravity of his excitement centered around Shad's death, he silently berated himself for allowing such moments of glee.

Another thought occurred to Clark. Since he couldn't leave Mars for two years, Grayson held every opportunity to reveal the discovery of these insects to the world. Jonas couldn't remain silent.

People had died, so Jonas was obligated to report the deaths to Grayson, which included the reasons for their demise. Grayson couldn't claim he discovered these creatures, but he could lessen Clark's importance in receiving all the glory. By the time Clark finished his work contract and returned to Earth, the news would have settled into obscurity. Old news was essentially no news.

Jonas checked the fuel gauges on the flamethrower before they descended the lightless sloped corridor where the insects hid in darkness. The flamethrower could spew blistering waves of fire more than forty yards. Jonas decided it safest if only he carried one. This prevented accidentally engulfing one another in flames should someone panic and get trigger-happy. But they only had one chance should the insects attack and overpower Jonas. Since the other guards were equipped with extinguishers, they wouldn't have enough time to unharness Jonas' flamethrower if he died.

Shad succumbed to the insects' toxin in a matter of seconds. Clark was leery of advancing into the dim corridor where the insects were.

Jonas and the guards flipped on helmet lights to brighten the path ahead. No jagged rocks disrupted the smooth, polished sidewalls of the corridor, giving the insects no easy place to hide. However, the center of the corridors was where miners scooped the spilled debris from the tunneling machine into piles to wheelbarrow out.

The three accompanying guards appeared overconfident and egotistically macho. They lacked any real concern about the creatures. Perhaps they didn't believe there were any creatures. Their attitudes changed the instant they found the first dead prisoner.

The miner lay facedown on a pile of loose dirt. His shovel was about a foot away. Horror reflected in each guard's eyes. Jonas winced with disgust. Now they became attentive to their surroundings and mostly toward the shadowed regions ahead.

Dozens of little crimson, encircled holes dotted the back of the prisoner's orange shirt. The insects had stabbed him with their proboscises and drained his blood.

The miner hadn't felt a thing. The Sleeper Chip made him oblivious of pain. How long it had taken for the prisoner to collapse? Was it as quickly as Shad?

Fear gripped Clark. Only three insect-like creatures scuttled after him, but in the amount of elapsed time, it was possible for dozens more to have squeezed through.

"Check him, Gary," Jonas said to the guard nearby.

Gary stiffened at the mention of his name. "Seriously? I mean no disrespect, but no way he's alive, sir."

"If there's the slightest chance he's alive, we need to know."

Gary swallowed hard and looked at the other guards. They were apprehensive. Their tough machismo was gone. Like Gary, Carter knew there wasn't any need to check the man's vitality. The prisoner was dead. Gary stooped to one knee anyway, felt for a pulse, and when he looked up at Jonas, he simply shook his head. "He's dead."

"Okay. Stay alert," Jonas said, aiming the nozzle of the flamethrower ahead of them.

Jonas and the guards walked past the dead man. Clark cautiously stepped around the corpse. This was the *only* time he actually considered someone with a Sleeper Chip to be fortunate. The man had not suffered any pain or fear before his death.

The drilling machine's metal plates reflected in their lights.

Jonas signaled his men to stop. "Watch the center line of debris. Apparently, these creatures blend with their surroundings."

"Yes," Clark said. "They're the same color as the rock and walls."

"Hold your ground, men," Jonas said. "I don't see any prisoners. As a precaution, I'll scorch the line of debris, in case those creatures are hidden."

The guards nodded and backed away.

Jonas turned the lever and ignited the fuel as it gushed through the nozzle. He hit another switch and roaring flames sprayed in a long stream. The heat was instant. The running flame wall rushed across the debris pile. The adhesive in the gaseous mixture caused the fire to cling to the rubble. It continued burning several minutes after he shut off the valve. Flickering flames danced.

At first, his effort seemed more a waste of time than anything else, but then two insects skittered across the tunnel floor. Engulfed in flames, they emitted high-pitched squeals. After running several yards, they stopped moving. Their bodies deflated and curled inward. Their appendages shriveled.

Clark smiled with a bit of relief. *So they can die.*

Jonas walked to the two smoldering insects. He tapped one with the toe of his boot. It didn't move. Its legs drew inward. Kneeling, he took it by the leg and picked it up. The thing was at least twelve inches in length, probably longer before the flames dehydrated it. An awful smell permeated from its corpse.

"Jonas!" Gary shouted. "Behind you!"

Jonas dropped the insect and turned. Two more swiftly approached. Their legs clicked as they skittered his direction. He flicked the ignition switch on the flamethrower, but nothing happened. Fumbling around with the switches, he engaged the proper combination flow, hit the ignition again, and a stream of fire blazed across the ground. The two creatures tried to escape but weren't successful. The flames engulfed their tiny bodies. Their internal organs must've sizzled inside their metal-like exoskeletons.

One creature scurried from a dark corner seeming intent on attacking Jonas from behind. A guard pulled his fire extinguisher pin and sprayed a frosty white mist over the creature. Instead of harming the insect, the cold retardant angered it. It reared its forelegs and spat greenish goo. The liquid struck the guard's cheek. He screamed and wiped away the acid along with a couple of layers of his skin. He growled, took the fire extinguisher, and tried to smash the insect into the hard floor.

"No!" Clark shouted.

The insect leapt backwards. The extinguisher clanged against the floor, and the insect flung itself through the air, landing on the man's leg. It bit him. The man gripped the insect in his hands and flung it down the corridor. Seconds later, he dropped and fell on his side, unable to move.

Jonas aimed the flamethrower and scorched the insect before it could reach them.

"Okay," Jonas said, "fire works but the cold doesn't."

"Perhaps you should categorize that as *extreme* heat kills them, and the cold pisses them off," Clark said.

Jonas nodded but didn't hint a smile. "You're right. That's probably a better assessment. Is Roy still alive?"

Gary knelt beside Roy. He placed two fingers against the man's throat. "His heartbeat's steady, and he's breathing. Who knows how he'll react to the poison?"

Jonas sighed. "Call the paramedics to haul Roy to the infirmary and have the guards at the top of the tunnel get their asses down here."

"Copy that," Gary replied.

Jonas pointed at the other guard. "You stay with Roy until the paramedics arrive. Gary, you stick with me."

"Yes, sir."

"Clark, you're a scientist, right?" Jonas asked.

"Yes, but a geophysicist, why?"

"Take these critter carcasses to your lab for evaluation."

Clark shrugged. "Sure, not a problem."

"You said only three had gotten into the tunnel."

"Yes, that was before I ran for help." He pointed. "But, like I told you, there are gaps where the giant drill bit doesn't line flush with the wall anymore."

Jonas stared at the hole. "We have to seal that off."

Gary stood to the left of Jonas while Clark followed to the right. Fifty feet from the drilling machine was another dead prisoner. Jonas shook his head and kept moving.

Three more insects hid under the drilling machine and between the tracks. Jonas raised the flamethrower. Instead of the insects attacking, they rolled into tight balls.

"What the—?" Jonas said, lowering the weapon.

"Not sure," Clark said. "Looks like they're trying to shield themselves from the flame."

"How could they have that kind of intelligence?"

"Some insects and creatures have more sense than humans."

Jonas grinned. "I can't argue with that. But balling up won't help them, will it?"

"Probably not. The flames magnify their core temperature causing their internal circulatory system and organs to boil."

"In your opinion, what do you think we should do?" Jonas asked.

"Wait to see what they do. If they charge us, torch them."

After a minute, one of the insects slowly unrolled. It cautiously nudged its companions. The other two stretched out. Their large compound eyes studied Jonas, Clark, and Gary. They extended their forelegs and lowered their heads submissively.

"What do you make of that?" Jonas asked.

"Can't be certain," Gary said.

Clark whispered, "It looks like they're surrendering or bowing."

Gary frowned. "They're bugs."

"On a planet we know little about," Clark said.

"That's true," Jonas said.

"How do we know we can trust their surrender?" Gary asked.

Jonas shook his head. "We can't. Proceed with caution. It'd help if we had a safe way to transport them. Not only do they have a toxic bite, they spit acid quite accurately."

"Wait. Use this." Clark took a heavy plastic container from his geology backpack and handed it to Jonas.

"You expect *me* to get them inside this?" Jonas asked.

Clark held the container. He looked from Jonas to the three creatures on the reddish floor. They remained relaxed and spread out. Clark's best guess was that they were exposing their vulnerability. It seemed their only way to communicate their surrender. He decided to gamble and walked to them.

About a yard away from them, Clark hesitated and slowly removed the lid. They remained still, so he set the container on the floor in front of them and backed away.

The three men watched the Martian insects. After a minute, the insects marched to the container and crawled inside.

Jonas exchanged a surprised glance with Clark and Gary. "I never expected that."

Clark eased near the clear container and cautiously placed the lid on top and secured it. The creatures made no attempt to attack or struggle to get out. They acted docile. Knowing that thousands more of these creatures were beyond the hole in the wall, he remained skeptical. The prisoners near the drilling machine were dead. Were these insects baiting them into a trap?

"Do you feel comfortable carrying the container?" Jonas asked.

In opposition to his nervous stomach, Clark said, "I suppose."

"Should they try to escape, throw the box as far as you can. I'll torch them."

Clark nodded, knelt, and grabbed the box. He stared at the Martian insects. The creatures looked armored with a metal coating. In spite of their deadly poisons, they were fascinating critters.

Jonas said, "Before we head back, I'll check around the drill machine once more. Gary, call some tunnel-drivers to seal off that opening. Make certain they bring the other two flamethrowers. We can't allow any more to get through."

"On it," Gary said. He tapped his earpiece and stepped away to talk.

Jonas rounded the side of the drill machine, slowly, cautiously, with the flamethrower nozzle held ready to spray flames. His finger tightened on the trigger. He scanned around the machine's tracks, and the hole where the giant drill bit pressed against the wall. He walked completely around the machine.

He shrugged. "Nothing."

From the cab of the drill machine a high-pitched screech made Jonas turn fast. An insect flung itself from the cab with its legs outstretched. The jagged ends of its legs were like little daggers. Jonas pulled the trigger. A wall of fire blasted but seconds too late. The creature struck the side of Jonas' armored shoulder and bounced into the air.

"Dammit!" Jonas shouted.

Gary took his laser pistol and fired at it. He missed. The laser flung bits of stone and pebbles into the air. The creature scurried into a dark recess of the tunnel. Jonas turned and lit up the dead end corner with massive flames.

For some reason, after seeing thousands of them on the other side of the wall, Clark expected more to skitter down the walls and surround Jonas, but this seemed to be the last one, other than the three inside the container.

Jonas increased the gas pressure on the nozzle and the flames loomed farther out. He sprayed the fire from the left side of the corner and moved to the right. The insect ran outside the fire's range and tried to wedge between the rocks, but the wave of fire caught up, engulfing it. The little thing squealed and ran a few yards before flipping onto its back and dying.

"I think that's the last one in the tunnel," Jonas said. "Get those three back to the laboratory."

On their way up the corridor, Gary paused where the one guard knelt beside the paralyzed man. "How's Roy's condition?"

"He's still alive. He's in a comatose state."

Clark looked at Roy. His eyes were frozen. He couldn't blink. Had it not been for his shallow breathing, Clark would've assumed him dead. He gently slid his hand over Roy's eyes to close his eyelids.

"Get a gurney here ASAP to take Roy to the infirmary," Jonas said into his transmitter. He glanced at Clark. "Do an analysis of the toxin so we can develop an anti-toxin. With as many in the next room as you say, we're doomed without a way to counteract the poison."

"I know."

"Hell, these three are a great risk to keep them alive."

Clark stared at the creatures. They reminded him of thorny stick insects he'd seen in the zoo. None of the species on Earth were armed with poison though. Their round eyes stared at him, but he didn't know what intention they held, if any. While he thought it odd these creatures were capable of intentional malice, they displayed their understanding of surrendering in order to escape being fried to death. Were they capable of communicating?

Perhaps. It was also possible they were buying time and waiting for an opportunity to escape into the general population. Three were capable of killing or incapacitating dozens of people before Jonas could isolate and eradicate them with the flamethrower.

These three didn't seem a threat though. Shad had attacked one first. In doing so, he reaped their wrath. However, the prisoners posed no threat at all and were killed.

The guard glanced nervously from Jonas to the drilling machine and then looked at Jonas again. "Please hurry."

Jonas nodded. "Trust me. I don't want you down here any longer than what's necessary. We have to seal that hole. Once we do, I'll have another team block this tunnel farther up, just in case."

"Sounds good," Clark said.

Jonas said, "How quickly can you run those critters to the laboratory?"

"Without falling?"

"That'd be preferable."

Clark gave a nervous grin. "Yep. Probably in ten minutes or so."

"Then do so. The faster you and the other scientists get to work analyzing their toxin, the better we know how to deal with them."

"Yes, sir."

Chapter 36

Derek drove through the gulley at thirty miles per hour. Billowing dust clouded a trail behind him. Bradbury held the cab rail while standing on the flatbed.

Derek planned to rebuild Isaac after they reached Olympus Mons. He wished he could circle back and get Ursula and Olivia and repair them, too. He grieved at his losses, but he was still alive. Without their sacrifices, he'd be dead.

It'd probably take the Chinese robots more than several days to arrive at Olympus Mons. He hoped in that amount of time their engineers could construct a protective barrier to keep the robots from entering the volcano. Keeping the robots out wasn't enough, though, with the power of the their laser weapons. They could perform devastating and crippling damage by destroying arriving or departing shuttles. If successful in cutting off future supplies, the citizens of Olympus Mons would eventually starve.

The more distance Derek put between himself and the enemy robots, the more his fear diminished. Olympus Mons towered. In fifteen minutes, he'd be safe. His optimism wavered, but at least his outlook was better than it was hours before, or so he tried to convince himself.

He didn't realize he was caught between two dangers—the pursuing robots and a Martian insect infestation. Lives were in danger, including his own, but without radio communication, he didn't have a clue... yet.

GRAYSON WATCHING the tide rolling in from his office window.

His earphone vibrated.

"Yes?" he asked.

"Boyd Grayson?"

"Who's this?"

"Viktor. I told you I'd call in two days. It's been two days."

"How'd you get my personal number?"

Viktor chuckled. "Let's say... we find way."

Grayson's jaw tightened, but he offered no reply.

"It's test... to prove we have technology to help you... with your problem on Mars."

"How much will this technology *cost* me?" Grayson asked.

"Four million dollars."

Grayson remained silent. Extortion was the first word that came to mind. Were the Russians in cahoots with the Chinese? Although that seemed likely, he didn't want to immediately draw such a conclusion.

"Mr. Grayson?"

"That's a hell of a lot of money, Viktor, for something you're proposing will work. I'd like more definite proof this technology works effectively *before* I hand anyone that kind of money."

"Yes. Four million is... lot of money. But how much more will you lose when those robots kill your miners on Mars? Much more than dis? Correct?"

"Possibly. But I need proof what you're saying is factual."

"What? You not trust me? After I give you previous information?"

Grayson sighed. "I already had a man working on that."

"He got himself into much trouble."

"And maybe you interfered with what Parks was doing, Viktor."

Viktor grew silent for a long minute. "So no deal?"

"Proof first, Viktor. Prove to me it'll work. If you disable those robots, I'll readily pay you the amount you're asking."

"Like I told you de other day, we need funds to act. These men won't risk lives for nothing."

"I won't give out money for nothing, either. I tell you what I'll do."

"What's dat?" Viktor asked.

"I'll pay a retainer of two hundred thousand. That should be enough money for you to travel, steal, or whatever it is that your men plan to do. Are you willing to work with me like that?"

"I don't know."

Grayson ran a hand through his hair. "I gave you one million dollars for simple information. Information I hired another man to find. For all I know, he might have already received that information and you coerced him to give it to you. You know I pay for useful intelligence and technology."

"But dis... it's far more dangerous."

"Okay, then. I guess I'll find another way of dealing with my problem. When I find Parks and if he tells me that you stole the information from him, you'll see a different side of me. So, anyway, thanks for getting back to—"

"Wait," Viktor said. He took a deep breath. "We start with de two hundred thousand. That be good start. We can work with you."

"Fine. Send someone by my office, and we'll get you the money."

"Yes, yes. Soon."

Grayson disconnected the call and shoved his hands into his pockets. The eagerness in Viktor's voice to take the retainer made Grayson even more skeptical that the Russians were trying to extort him. He needed to find Parks and get the truth concerning how Viktor gained knowledge of the Chinese robots. Viktor could be playing against both sides, and if so, Grayson expected to see more problems. Not only on Mars, but at each of his facilities on Earth.

He'd already heightened his security forces inside Grayson Enterprises by doubling the number of bodyguards. For some odd reason, that didn't seem enough.

Grayson glanced at his guard. "Henry, I want you on high alert."

Henry frowned. "Expecting trouble?"

"Could be. Remember the Russian from the other day?"

Henry nodded.

"There's a good chance he's not being on the level with me. Perhaps he has something underhanded planned."

Henry interlocked his huge fingers together and cracked his knuckles. "I'll inform the other guards."

"Thanks."

"No problem," Henry replied with a slight grin.

Henry opened the door and left.

Grayson sat behind the desk and stared at the door, deep in thought. Matthews came to mind. Grayson wasn't certain why he thought about his former rival in the technological world, especially since Matthews was no longer a threat.

Grayson grinned, picturing Matthews working the gem mines on Mars. Then his mind shifted to Lydia.

He'd hired Lydia as a bodyguard but after he refused to let her kill Matthews, she vanished. None of his high-tech hackers could find her. She seemed to have disappeared without a trace, which sorely disappointed him. Having her on his team would've been a great asset. She was ruthless, cold, and unforgiving. The perfect qualities he favored in an assassin. Perhaps her inability to forgive had become a deep-seated grudge and why she never returned? His broken promise concerning Matthews' fate had soured her. Was she was an enemy he needed to worry about? Mercenaries often kept secrets but always worked for the highest bidder. Should she return to Grayson Enterprises, either she or he would be dead. No amount of money could grant him a truce.

Grayson's enemies seemed to increase daily. Some evolved from false accusations, jealousy, or competition. In the business world, it was expected, but Grayson took it personally, often slamming his attackers via the media, which seldom gained favoritism from anyone. Many times, people outside the media, who were sick of hearing about him, wished he'd go away. He loved disappointing them by keeping himself in the headlines, but even he wasn't foolish enough not to know his welcome in the public eye was worn out. He opted to maintain a lower profile, but the outside world's interest in his activities didn't diminish. For some odd reason, whenever someone tried to hide in the shadows, others speculated, often inaccurately, about why he shunned the limelight, and attempted to draw him out into the open.

Being extremely wealthy put a bad taste in a lot of people's mouths. They ridiculed the rich with scorn, insisting the wealthier people were the reason so many others were poor. Grayson wondered if these people ever listened to the nonsense spewing from their own mouths. Probably not. And any amount of reasoning fell on deaf ears, much like little kids sticking their fingers in their ears and blabbering loudly so they couldn't hear a word being said to them.

Most people's minds were already settled about various topics. These viewed debate as a trap, but not listening to or considering the opposite viewpoint lessened the chances for rational thought. A closed-minded society was dangerous. Instead of reaching mutual understandings with those of different views, people yammered to talk louder than the only rational person in the room. Should the opposition utilize the same tools, they were considered abusers and tyrants and racists while the original perpetrators feigned innocence as *poor mistreated* victims. Almost in an instant, radical bullies became victims. Their rules for others didn't apply to themselves, which was hypocrisy in its purest form.

This was why Grayson chose to remain silent in the political world. Using his money and power, though, Grayson got Senator Johnson to do his bidding for him, which was working quite well, thus far. However, Johnson was old and the burden of answering Grayson's demands weighed the senator down. Grayson figured Johnson would attempt to find a way to worm out from Grayson's control.

In the early days of Grayson Enterprises, Grayson never fathomed being wealthy garnered such negative public appeal. He didn't understand how a man that had earned his own fortune owed everyone else a piece of his wealth.

When he attended college, other students held the same ambition to make names for themselves, to earn and fight their way in the world, as he did. They worked hard to achieve their dreams. They fought to be successful. But not today. Too many had been coddled, dependent, and felt entitled. They stood with their hands outstretched, demanding to get what they deserved when they had yet to do anything. *Reap what you sow, and if you refuse to plant anything, don't ask for handouts.*

"Everyone should be required to read *The Grasshopper and the Ant*," Grayson thought. He often wondered, "*Where did these bums come from?*"

The worst tragedy, Grayson thought, was that other governments outside the U.S. were doing the same thing to him. They wanted entitlements. They expected funding handouts from him. And when he refused, these people whined to politicians that the rich people needed to pay higher taxes. Funny, he reasoned. Most politicians were rich due to their own corruptions and yet, the same accusations never were directed at them.

They had an unspoken motto. *It's not fair that you are settling Mars, and we're not.* And they'd do everything, *except* honest work, to pry it from his grip.

Grayson shook his head.

Since he explicitly chose not to let them piggyback, they decided to destroy everything he possessed. No logical reasoning existed in their avaricious behavior, but he refused to give in to their demands. Their actions meant war, and he had plenty of money to fortify his possessions. If that meant it was necessary to kill individuals who got in his way, he'd never flinch or bat an eye. He expected a lot of dead people in the near future. He didn't plan to be amongst the casualties.

Chapter 37

Derek pressed his foot on the accelerator. The motor roared. Dust continued billowing behind him. About thirty yards from Olympus Mons, he eased off the gas pedal and geared down. As he neared the side metal garage door where other utility trucks and Caterpillar flatbeds were stored, he blared the horn.

He slammed the brakes, coming to a screeching halt, but continued blowing the horn until the metal door slowly eased open. Two guards rushed outside with laser weapons in hand.

"Derek?" the one guard, Adam, shouted. He slowly lowered his weapon.

Who the hell were they expecting? Derek shook his head, rolled his eyes, and bit his tongue to keep from cursing.

At first, Derek thought the question was the stupidest thing Adam could have asked, but then he thought about the Chinese robots and wondered if Grayson had alerted Jonas about the robot invaders. Or a rescue team might've been sent to find Derek and got lost. If so, the guard's question was valid. He rolled down the side window.

"Yeah, Adam," Derek replied. "It's me."

The guards motioned him to enter the gate. Once inside, Derek shut off the ignition and got out.

"Contact Jonas for me, Adam," Derek said. He walked to the rear of the flatbed to inspect Isaac's remains. "I lost all communication. Tell him I'm back and to meet me in the infirmary."

Bradbury stepped to the edge of the flatbed and jumped to the garage floor.

"Sure," Adam replied.

Derek looked at the other guard. "Paul, did any other teams leave Olympus Mons?"

The guard shook his head. "No."

"Seal the door and keep it shut. Get five or six more guards to guard this entrance."

Paul frowned. "Why? What's the problem, and what the hell happened to your robot?"

"We have enemies on Mars." Derek held his injured shoulder.

"What?"

"I encountered eight Chinese robots or they could be cyborgs. They're armed with dangerous weapons near the Phobos Ruins."

"Are you shitting me?"

Derek showed them the repair in his suit. "No, I've the injuries to prove it."

"For real?" Paul's brow tightened, and he suppressed a half grin, as though Derek was joking.

Derek's nose flared. He was losing his patience. "Have I ever had much of a sense of humor?"

"Well, no, but we're hopeful."

"I'm certainly not going to start now. Eight enemy robots. They destroyed Isaac and my other three robots." He paused to clear his throat. "The remains of my other three robots are still out there. The enemy robots are heat-seekers, which means they were sent for one reason. To kill us."

Paul looked stunned, but within seconds, what Derek said sank in. He rushed to the metal door, pushed the computerized lock mechanism and sealed the door. Without hesitation, he tapped his chest transmitter and requested backup.

Derek stared at Isaac's remains and fought tears. "Bradbury, stay with Isaac."

"Where are you going?"

"To the infirmary to get my shoulder patched."

JONAS LEFT Mineshaft Fifteen and headed to the interrogation room. He'd rather spend more time helping seal the hole in the wall, but the situation with Cain couldn't wait.

For weeks nothing eventful had occurred, and then, within a few days, all hell had broken loose inside Olympus Mons. Perhaps that wasn't the best cliché he should have used. With his current luck, he wouldn't be surprised to find a fiery pit deeper in the massive volcano.

He took a deep breath and pushed the door open.

Jonas glared at Cain in the small 4 X 4 interrogation room. This was the first time Jonas confronted a guard over a crime, but this was too appalling to ignore.

Cain sat handcuffed to the metal table. His battered face was a dozen different shades of purple and grayish black. He refused to make eye contact with Jonas, from shame or fear, or quite possibly both.

"How long have you been raping Jessica?" Jonas asked.

Cain looked down but refused to answer.

"Dammit!" Jonas slammed his palms on the metal table, making a loud *Thwack!* He pointed a stern finger at Cain's face. Cain tilted his head enough to see the finger. "You're going to tell me, or I swear, you'll have far worse disfigurations than you have right now."

"Is that how the law is conducted on Mars?"

"I *am* the law, smartass! There isn't any authority above me on Mars. So, if you wind up dead... that's your final judgment. There's no appeal process on Mars."

Cain offered a pathetic shrug. "So kill me."

Jonas unsnapped the knife on his belt and slid it from the sheath. The blade gleamed beneath the LED light. "As you wish, but I was in the CIA a long time ago. When we wanted answers, believe me, we found ways to extract the information from punks like you. You might die, but trust me, it won't happen quickly."

"Oh? So you're like, gonna cut off my fingers one at a time? I don't think you have it in you, Pops."

An evil smile crept on Jonas' face. His eyes glistened. "No, it's not going to be like that. Rape is a despicably heinous crime and deserves the worst of punishments. It won't be your fingers I cut off."

Cain leaned back and stiffened in his chair. Even though his eyelids were puffed and swollen, he attempted to open them wider. Fear reflected through the narrow slits. He saw the knife's sharp blade and visibly shook. He swallowed hard. Jonas' threat was clear. Cain didn't need to question the implication. He understood exactly *what* Jonas was threatening to cut off.

"How long has it gone on?" Jonas asked.

"Three months."

"Every day?"

Cain shook his head. "No, sir. Not that often."

"How often?"

"Twice a week, maybe. Seldom three."

Someone rapped on the door.

Jonas turned and opened it. "What?"

Boony jumped back, her eyes staring at the shiny blade.

"I'm a little busy, Boony. What do you want?"

"Sir, I thought you'd like to know Derek's back, and he wishes to speak with you in the infirmary."

The anger vanished from Jonas' face. He slid the blade into its sheath. Blinking slowly, he looked at her. "He's in the infirmary? How is he?"

"I don't know his condition. I didn't see him, but Adam called from the garage and gave me the message. You need to go see him."

"Of course," he said, pulling the door closed. He placed a hand on a guard's shoulder. "Keep an eye on Cain. Don't let anyone else in that room. Understood?"

"Yes, sir."

"Thanks, Boony."

She smiled. "I'll walk with you. Are you okay?"

"Better now that Derek's returned."

"In regard to Cain, I mean? You had out your knife."

"What he did is inexcusable, Boony. Nothing else in my career has ever infuriated me quite like this."

"I'm repulsed by what he and Matt were doing, but don't lose yourself and overreact."

"I won't lie," Jonas said. His eyes were fierce. "I want to kill him, slowly, and make him feel pain."

"I understand. I'm thankful she was under the chip's control. She didn't feel any pain, and she won't remember what happened."

"No. Don't you see? Those are arguments he's going to try to use in his own defense."

"I'm not saying it's okay. I'm not trying to minimize the situation at all."

"Maybe not, but it sounds almost like you're making the ordeal less than what it was."

Boony placed her hand on his arm and shook her head. "No, Jonas. If anything, to me, it's far worse. She couldn't to defend herself. She couldn't fight back. She was silenced without any choice to do whatever degrading act they wanted her to do. Cain and Matt diminished and violated her as a human."

"Trust me, they'll pay dearly for this."

"For what it's worth, I think Cain's behind the whole thing. I don't think Matt's innocent, but his punishment shouldn't equal Cain's. That's my two cents."

"Noted."

They took the final curve in the long smooth tunnel and stopped at the infirmary. Boony looked at him and smiled. "I'll leave you to speak with him alone. Please tell him I'll stop in later to see him."

"Sure."

"I'm glad he's okay."

"Me, too."

Boony turned and headed down the corridor.

Jonas stood outside the infirmary and hesitated. Tears burned his eyes and his throat tightened. Emotions washed through him. The sternness and fury he held for Cain diminished. Even though he and Derek exchanged a heated argument before Derek left, Jonas felt no anger about their disagreement. Instead, he held great relief and gratitude in knowing his grandson was alive. The greatest treasure he valued in life was the young man inside the infirmary. Only Derek could soften the old man's heart in ways that baffled Jonas. He was never a sentimental person, until the first day he held Derek as a newborn.

Before Jonas entered the infirmary, he checked his uniform and cleared his throat. He'd never shed a tear in front of Derek before. Jonas was not a hardened man, but he kept a stolid expression the majority of the time. Some called it his poker face. But due to getting choked up moments before, he doubted he could speak without a shaky voice.

Jonas took a deep breath and stepped into the infirmary. Derek lay on an adjustable bed with the back raised so he could sit upright. A nurse tended his blistered shoulder.

Derek gave a slight grin when he saw Jonas. "Hey, Grandpa."

Jonas swallowed hard, trying to rid himself of the solid lump in his throat. "Derek."

"I suppose I crossed that line, huh?"

"What line's that?"

"In our argument. I carried things a bit too far."

"Let's not—"

"That's why you didn't send a rescue team out for me, right?" Derek asked.

"Actually, I was getting ready to."

"It's okay. I was wrong, and I'm sorry. You were right. I shouldn't have gone alone."

Jonas sighed and stepped to the side of the bed. "Really, I was going to come after you. I've been worried about you since the day you left, but I tried not to be. I've been selfish and wrong. You're a man, and you should make decisions for yourself. You'll make mistakes. Everyone does. I have. Mistakes are how we learn and what shape us. It's time I accept you're an adult."

"Thanks. But, you *were* right. I almost got killed after I lost communication due to the harsh winds and coarse grit. My transmitter failed. That's why I never got in touch with you. I couldn't. I tried several times each day."

Jonas forced a smile. A tear trickled down his cheek. He ignored it. "What happened to your shoulder?"

"That's why it's urgent I talk to you. There are eight Chinese robots out on the Martian terrain. They're heat-seekers, armed with laser weapons. A laser blast did this to me."

"What? Chinese robots?"

Derek nodded.

Jonas ran a hand across his spiked hair. "I saw other activity on the satellite map near your position. I thought it was a glitch. Never considered anything like that."

"They're probably in route to our position. They destroyed four of my robots. Three of their bodies are still at the Phobos Ruins. Only Bradbury's alive and functional."

Alive. Jonas smiled slightly. "Perhaps, once you heal, we can send a team out to retrieve them."

"Not until we figure out a way to destroy the Chinese robots."

"We have encountered an interesting problem inside Olympus Mons, too."

Derek frowned and winced when the nurse snipped loose skin around his burst blisters. "What?"

Jonas told Derek about the strange creatures Clark had discovered and Shad's death.

"Damn."

"Yes. We captured three of them."

"Do you think they're a threat?"

"They're deadly. Their poison paralyzes the victims almost immediately. Exactly how much of a threat they are to our population, we're not sure yet. Clark, the geologist, took them to the laboratory for evaluation. But there are a couple of things I do know about them."

"What's that?"

"They're quite intelligent. The three we took realized the flamethrower could kill them, and they readily surrendered. That's the good thing."

"What's the bad thing?"

"They outnumber us by thousands."

"Shit."

Jonas nodded. "Yep. We're standing in a deep pile of it."

"No kidding."

"Get some rest, Derek. We'll figure it out. Right now, I have some pressing issues to attend to." Jonas smiled. "Glad you're back safe. A little torn, but nothing you can't survive."

Chapter 38

Donald Parks opened his eyes to blurred fluorescent lights. His head ached, as did his ribs and right leg. His mouth was dry and pasty. He was hooked to an I.V. Other beeping machines were at the head of his bed. A television show played from the other side of the room.

He wasn't certain why he was in a hospital. His knuckles were bruised and swollen. Now that he was awake, pain radiated throughout his body.

Parks closed his eyes and tried to remember. It hurt to think. A redheaded nurse came in his room to check his I.V. She was short, plump, and wore 'Hello Kitty' scrubs. Her name tag identified her as Sara. Her overly cheerful persona made his head hurt even worse.

"Why am I here?" he asked weakly. "I guess, more importantly, *how* did I get here?

"Oh, you're finally awake. You've been here a couple of days. To be honest, I was getting worried. The doctors were, too," She beamed a smile and grabbed his chart at the end of the bed. "You're listed as John Doe. The note says that you had no identification when you arrived in the ambulance. Do you know your name?"

He nodded and winced from the pain of doing so. "Donald Parks."

Sara placed his chart at the foot of his bed. "Let me go get a doctor, so he can talk to you."

"Sure, sweetie. Could I get a cup of ice or something to drink?" He placed his hand over his throat.

"Certainly. I'll be back in a few minutes."

About five minutes later a man walked into the room. The tall thin man wore a nice suit and a hat that hid his burr cut. He wasn't a doctor, and Parks didn't recall ever seeing him before. He handed Parks a cup of ice water.

"The nurse said you're Mr. Donald Parks, is that correct?" he asked.

Parks sipped the water. The cold increased the radiating pain throbbing inside his head, but it did soothe his throat. "Yes. Who are you?"

"Sid Davis. NSA." He took his badge from his suit pocket and showed Parks.

"NSA?"

Sid nodded. "Yes, sir."

"Why? What's wrong?"

"You're in pretty bad shape, Mr. Parks. How'd you end up in this condition?"

"I was hoping you could tell me."

"You don't remember?"

"No."

Sid chewed his lower lip for a moment. "That's a shame."

"I'm not happy about it either."

"I imagine not. I'd hate to arrest a man when he can't give an alibi, but it's happened before."

"Arrest? For what?"

Sid sighed. "Well, sir, we found you in a dark alley with two dead Russians and two dead Chinese men. You were the only one still breathing."

"You think I'm capable of killing four men? Me?"

"I don't know. You tell me."

"I remember nothing."

"For all I know, a dozen or more men were with you in that alley. But all the gathered evidence points directly to you."

"Me? In my condition?" Parks shook his head. "No. I took quite a beating."

Sid held up a computer notebook and flipped through pages on the screen with an index finger. "Appears so, but those four men died from gunshot wounds. The gun we found in the alley has your fingerprints on it. Ballistics matches the bullets to the gun. Oddly, the gun's serial numbers were filed off, so that's why we couldn't immediately identify you. You were wearing a holster, too. You also have gun residue on your hand, forearm, and the clothes you were wearing."

Parks frowned. His mind searched, but no memory of the alley emerged to shed any light on the growing mystery.

"Can I ask you something, Mr. Parks?"

"Sure."

"Other than what happened with the shooting and your assault, do you remember everything else?"

"I suppose. Like what exactly?"

"What do you do for a living?" Sid asked.

"I'm with the CIA."

"In your spare time, you're not a hit man, by chance?"

Parks' mouth gaped. "What?"

"A hit man. You know, gun for hire. An assassin."

"No. I'm like you but I work for the CIA."

Sid's cellphone beeped. "One second, sir."

Parks took another sip of water and then set the Styrofoam cup on the table beside the bed.

Sid turned away. He spoke softly in the phone. After a few minutes, he turned toward Parks and put the phone away. "I'll ask you again. What kind of sideline jobs do you do?"

"I told you. I'm with the CIA. Occasionally, I'll work as a private investigator, but never on any federal level cases."

Sid shoved his hands into his pockets and shook his head. "You see, Mr. Parks. I'd like to believe you, especially due to the nature of your injuries, and since we're both agents. You had the shit beat out of you. I'd like to believe you shot them in self-defense, but I'm... I'm leaning more to the facts that you were hired to kill them. After all, that gun wasn't agency issued. Numbers were removed."

"What? Where did you come up with such nonsense?" Parks grabbed the handrails at the sides of the bed and pulled himself into a seated position. His head throbbed from rising. He was certain he had a concussion. What else hurt that badly?

"Careful now, Mr. Parks. You look to be in a lot of pain." Sid took out a pen and small notepad from his pocket.

"Yeah! Of course I am. How the hell do you come to the conclusion that I'm a hit man?"

"Well, after the nurse told me your name, I called and had my department run a background check on you. Everyone's information is only a few keystrokes away, thanks to the Patriot Act." He grinned. "Anyway... your recent bank deposits are the most damning evidence against you."

"How?"

"You have a recent deposit of one hundred thousand dollars. The week before that, you had the same amount. Now, I can't be certain, but I don't see too many people being able to afford that kind of money for a private investigator. Hell, I work for the NSA, and I *never* see anywhere close to that kind of money."

"Two hundred thousand dollars?"

"Yes, sir."

"Maybe you have the wrong Donald Parks' bank account?"

"No, sir. The photo on file identifies you as the particular Parks with that social security number and bank account. Now, in connection with the money, sir, I have one other question."

"What's that?"

"What relationship do you have with a Mr. Boyd Grayson of Grayson Enterprises?"

"He hires me to investigate, to get background information on people. Why?"

"Using government computers?" Sid asked.

"I use them, but never for classified information. Just routine checks like a lot of employers do for pre-hires."

"That's where those deposits came from? For background checks?"

Parks frowned. "So?"

"Mr. Parks, come now. You're delusional if you think I'll believe that."

"I really don't care—"

"Often Grayson comes across as a very corrupt man. So much so that the CIA, FBI, and NSA all have open cases on him. You're aware of that, aren't you?"

"It doesn't surprise me."

"And yet, you're on his payroll? Mr. Parks, Grayson's a man who's quite capable of hiring a hit man to take out an opponent or benefactor when the relationship has soured."

"Mr. Davis, I'm telling you the truth. He didn't hire me to kill anyone. He's never hired me to do anything like that."

"That's a hell of a lot of money. I can see where the temptation could kick in for almost anyone."

"You checked my background. Did you bother to check my personnel evaluations with the CIA?"

Sid nodded.

Parks said, "Exemplary evaluations."

"They were, yes. But now, not so much. An illegally owned weapon and four dead people are bound to change that."

"I didn't kill them."

"All the evidence shows you did," Sid said.

"Hell, it's not even my gun."

"A convenient loss of memory doesn't help your case, either."

Parks' jaw tightened. "I'm being framed."

"You know what I think?"

"No. But I'm certain you'll tell me."

"Grayson hired you to kill a couple of these people, but something went wrong. You killed these men and thought you could escape the scene unnoticed, but there was another member in one of these two groups who knocked you unconscious. Your medical report indicates you were struck in the back of the head with a blunt object, which gave you a concussion."

"Well, that explains my freaking headache," Parks replied.

"You had the perfect plan to get away scot-free with two hundred thousand dollars, but someone interfered."

"That's a marvelous statement except *I didn't kill them.*"

"Can you prove otherwise?"

"Not at the moment."

Sid scribbled more notes into his small pocket pad. "What exactly did Mr. Grayson hire you to do?"

"That's confidential."

Sid cocked a brow, holding his pen an inch above the pad. "You wish to uphold client confidentiality when you're facing a possible lifetime prison sentence for four murders?"

"It's better than dying quickly."

"You're implying that Grayson would make a threat on your life?"

"That'd be the mildest outcome."

Sid grinned. "Now you're insinuating what I previously stated about Grayson enacting bodily harm or killing people that turn against him is true. Are you not?"

"I'll admit he's underhanded in a lot of ways, but I've never worked as an assassin for him. Not once or ever. I'd be happy to take a lie detector test."

"You know that's not admissible."

Parks frowned. "Why not? We give them all the time."

"True, but in your case there are two reasons why having you take one won't matter."

"What are they?"

"One, your recent memory loss. Two, the CIA trains its agents the proper way to cheat the test and not get caught."

"Then why keep asking me questions, if you don't believe I'll tell you the truth."

Sid smiled. "Because I'm hoping you'll turn the tables on Grayson and help us with our ongoing investigation."

"Look, I'm being honest with you. There's no evidence I could give up that ties him or me to any murders. He's never hired me for that reason."

"Maybe not, Mr. Parks, but there's still something you can do to help us."

"What's that?"

"You have built up trust with him. You're the best person we have to act as an informant since he believes he has a CIA agent in his pocket."

Parks shrugged. "That won't get me off murder charges. From what you've said, there's nothing I can do to overturn the charges since the evidence points right at me."

"It could get your sentence reduced, provided you're able to get what we need."

"A reduced sentence?" Parks shook his head. "No, thanks."

"There might not be any case against you at all, if you get us the evidence we need."

"How's that?"

"I have no idea why you'd be in that alley to start with. Two of the dead men belonged to the Russian Mafia. The other two were connected to a Chinese triad. Maybe you *happened* to get caught in the middle and were fortunate enough to survive. And that's definitely the angle I'd play if I were you."

Parks rubbed his eyes and thought. Making a decision would be so much easier if he could remember exactly what happened in that alleyway. To the best of his knowledge, he didn't know anyone associated with the Russians or the Chinese. That didn't mean he wasn't investigating one side or the other or both.

After a few minutes of getting nowhere with his memories, he said, "What do you want me to do?"

Chapter 39

Jonas returned to the interrogation room, stopping outside the door. When he left Cain, Jonas' anger had taken him to a very dark place, a place where he could kill a man without a second thought or any remorse, and it was a place he'd not ventured in over forty years. He never expected to ever feel that way again.

People like Cain didn't deserve to live, and for some reason, the only justice his type of criminal mind understood came from someone getting on his level and inflicting pain never felt before.

A prison term taught Cain nothing. The battering Jessica inflicted on Cain did little more than bruise his sociopathic ego. And yet, Cain remained smug, unfaltering, and without remorse. Regardless of the punishment, Cain would never have the compunction to admit his faults. Those like Cain never repented. Sadists thrived on reaping pleasure through others' misery, whether mentally or physically. They didn't view the damage as occurring to another human being. They simply never cared.

Jonas entertained the idea of making Cain wait several hours before he returned to finish the interrogation. Jonas glimpsed Cain's fear, the slight crack in his exterior. The longer Jonas left him in solitude, the greater Cain's uncertainty grew. Regardless of an apology or a plea for leniency, Cain knew his impending punishment would be severe. That was enough reason to worry.

Jonas' rage softened after the relief of seeing Derek alive. Shedding tears of joy mellowed him and crying was never a part of his nature. He almost wanted to berate himself for surrendering to his emotions, but he realized he shouldn't be ashamed because Derek viewed the tears as evidence of Jonas' devoted love.

Jonas stared at the closed interrogation room door. Delving back to his previously heated anger wasn't easy, and he'd rather avoid it. But he couldn't be rational and calm with someone as unrealistic as Cain. Anything less than fiery indignation allowed Cain to entertain the idea that Jonas had merely tried to frighten him, being all bark and no bite. Jonas needed to appear more seething and vanquish any doubts Cain might have about how ironfisted Jonas was.

He cleared his throat and entered the room.

Cain sat leaned partway over the table. His body swayed. He was nearly asleep. Jonas slammed the door shut, causing Cain to jerk and glance up.

The moment their eyes met, anger surged afresh inside Jonas. It wasn't an act or a bluff. With what Cain had done, Jonas' disgust made him detest the guard.

Jonas pulled the knife from its sheath in one quick flash. The blade gleamed. Jonas' eyes narrowed. "Now, where were we?"

DR. LEE STOOD at a bed inside the infirmary and watched the nurses attending to Roy, whose paralysis had not lessened. "What happened to him?"

The nurse connecting the I.V. shook her head. She nodded to the other guard.

The guard told him about the insects in Mine Shaft Fifteen. Dr. Lee listened with great intent and genuine concern. Fear furrowed his brow.

"Thousands of them? There are thousands of them? We need some specimens to obtain toxin and analyze it."

"Clark has taken them to the lab."

"So they have caught some of them?"

The guard nodded. "There's a few dead ones, too."

"Good," Lee said. "That's good. Maybe they can get the toxin analyzed soon. We need a strong antitoxin, in case this happens again."

CLARK STARED at the three strange insect-like creatures. Encased inside the thick glass, the creatures never made any attempt to escape. They were quite intelligent beings, for what most people considered *only* insects.

When he first stepped into the lab and set the glass box on the table, the creatures tapped the glass, trying to get his attention. Two of them joined their center legs together and formed the letter, *H*. The other one formed the letter, *I*.

"Hi?" Clark asked. He shook his head. That was a far stretch of the imagination, even for him. It was nothing less than a bizarre coincidence.

Anna, a chemist, approached the table where he stood, looking at the insects. She was five foot four, slender, and her black hair was pulled into a tight bun.

The three insects slightly tipped their heads in a small bow and repeated forming the letters.

"What the hell are those?" Anna asked, leaning closer to view them.

"I found them in Mine Shaft Fifteen."

"Cre-e-epy," she replied.

The trio formed the word, *HI*, again.

"What are they doing?" she asked.

"Looks like they're trying to spell."

Anna laughed and shook her head. "Ah, now, don't be ridiculous. That's the most absurd thing I've ever heard."

"I know. That's what I thought, but look for yourself. See? Those two have formed the letter H, and the other one has made a capital I."

"Coincidence. Nothing more." She chuckled.

"They've done it three times consecutively," Clark said. "The first time, sure, I considered it an accident or a coincidence, but three times is deliberate. They want to communicate with us."

Anna frowned. "What kind of scientist are you?"

"A geophysicist."

"You study rocks and rock formations, right?"

"It's a bit more complicated than that," Clark said.

"Whatever," she said, rolling her eyes. "You ever check the rocks *inside* your head?"

The statement perplexed him. He didn't see any reason for her to verbally abuse and insult him. After all, geology was a science. He often wondered why scientists outside his field viewed geoscience beneath theirs. A geophysicist wasn't someone who simply collected rocks. They studied so much more.

After her insulting remark, the three creatures tapped the glass sharply, catching her attention. They formed an F and a U. Her face reddened, and Clark burst into laughter.

"I suppose that's a coincidence, too?" he asked.

"Go play with your little space bugs, boy, and leave me the hell alone."

"You know what's really weird about that?"

"No, what?" she asked, already giving him a heavy brow.

Clark smiled. "They can read minds."

"Oh, really?" Anna rested her hands on her hips. "You give them that much credit?"

"Yep. Because that's exactly what I was thinking about your rude comment before they formed those letters."

Anna grunted and turned to walk away, mumbling under her breath.

"You don't have to hate me because of my profession."

"That's not why I hate you." She closed her eyes and shook her head. "I'm sorry for being crass. I don't hate you. I've just been under a pile of deadlines, that's all."

"I understand," Clark said in a softer tone.

"Still," she said, "I shouldn't take it out on you or your bugs."

"These aren't like insects on Earth," Clark said with optimism in his voice. "Their toxin's quite potent. They killed several miners. Well, not *these* three creatures, but we killed the others. A guard working with me was paralyzed from a single bite. He died... dozens of them drained his blood."

Her eyes widened. She looked like she wanted to talk, but she didn't seem certain what to say.

Clark said, "It'd help us if you could extract some toxin from the dead insects and analyze the derivatives. We need to develop an antitoxin. Whether or not you like me or my degree, you need to understand these insects outnumber us by tens of thousands."

She shrugged. "You're being serious about all that?"

Clark nodded. "Deadly serious. Jonas ordered men to block the corridor where we encountered them. If that fails, you and I might become victims like Shad. Hell, we all could die."

"Where are those dead bugs?"

He pointed at the cardboard box on another table.

"Okay," she said. "I'll see what I can do."

"Thanks."

"Again, I'm sorry for my rudeness."

"As a geophysicist, I've heard far worse. Believe me. We tend to be the butt of other scientists' jokes." He shrugged. "Why? I'll never know."

Anna smiled. "I promise not be condescending anymore. Your field benefits us here and on Earth. I suppose finding these creatures will help your career?"

He shrugged. "It's possible."

"Don't be modest. If I discovered a new element on Mars that's not on Earth, I'd be leaping and shouting about it. I'd be getting my groove on."

Clark chuckled, watching her do a few moves. "That's what makes being on Mars so exciting."

She smiled. "It has its moments, but once my term's over, this lady's heading back to Earth."

"You don't like Mars?"

"Honey, we left so much behind. Good food, theaters, concerts. Nothing here compares. Red dust, if you look out the bay windows. Hell, the brochure they gave me failed to include the misery part of being here into the proper perspective. The notoriety dies hard. And the cold—" she hugged herself and shivered. "I'm tempted to go home and snuggle any of my old ex-boyfriends."

"It's that bad?"

"When you consider I came here to get *away* from those deadbeats, and now they're starting to *look* attractive? Yeah, baby, it's that bad."

Clark turned his attention to the insects. Although it seemed strange, they were trying to communicate. He went to a counter and rummaged through several drawers until he found a notepad and a pen. Then he unhooked a keyboard from a foldable computer tablet.

He took the items to the tabletop where the insects were caged. He held the keyboard upright with the space bar against the tabletop so the insects could see the keys. The trio of insects studied the letters with keen interest, their little heads tilting back and forth. Finally, one tapped its foreleg against a letter. Clark wrote it down. The insect continued picking letter after letter and the space bar after each completed word. It spelled the following message:

Beware. Only us three, your allies be.

Chapter 40

With an intense glare, Jonas sat across from Cain. Cain's eyes focused on the sharp blade in Jonas' hand.

Cain finally broke the long silence. "So, what's your verdict?"

"Castration's a good start."

Cain halfway smiled, expecting a partial grin from Jonas. Jonas' cold, unrelenting eyes bore into Cain. Cain paled and retracted his smile.

"That's a bit extreme, don't you think, sir?" Cain asked.

"*Now* it's sir? It's amazing how manners surface whenever a severe sentence is enacted."

"You're not serious about actually doing *that*, are you?"

"I said it was a *good start*. *Not* the entire punishment."

Cain swallowed hard. "Look, surely there's some kind of plea bargain for me? On Earth, I'd get an attorney and a chance for a reduced sentence."

"*You're* not on Earth."

"I don't think you'd do it," Cain said. Sweat cropped his brow.

"Are you challenging me?"

"No, sir. I... I can't see you taking a knife to my—"

"Here's the thing, Cain. The reason I can do it is because Jessica was innocent."

"Innocent? She's a damn prisoner!"

"You were her guard, dammit! She might be a prisoner, but that doesn't give you the right to violate her."

Cain noticed the boiling anger rise inside Jonas. "She didn't know it was going on. She has a Sleeper Chip."

"You see? I expected you to go there. The fact that she wasn't aware isn't justification. I come from a different generation than you. Because of my age, it's easy for me to ask, 'what if Jessica was my daughter, and I found out that some scumbag was fucking her without her consent?' For me, there isn't a simple solution that requires only one type of punishment. I'd ensure the person suffered, and in no way would he ever be able to contemplate doing that to anyone else. When I'm finished with you, you'll be reminded every day of your crime and speak several octaves higher."

"Barbaric punishments? That won't set well with authorities."

"And what you did isn't barbaric?" Jonas asked.

"Your punishment far exceeds my crime."

"File an appeal."

"How?"

Jonas stood. "Ah, that's right. You can't."

"So there's absolutely nothing I can do to plead my case?"

"Cain, the *prisoners* here are the worst of the worst. But you're a monster in a different category altogether. You've betrayed everything you were hired to be, and regardless of anything you say, you can't undo what you did. No one influenced you to act like this, which means this was your secret nature that you kept hidden from everyone else. I believe others that personally know you can testify to it because you probably did perverted things to them, but you silenced your victims through threats, fear, and intimidation." Jonas leaned toward Cain and pointed the knife at him. "My guess is that you suffered a similar thing when you were a boy, too. Right?"

For the first time since Jonas had talked to Cain, guilt claimed Cain's face. Sadness reflected in his eyes. He glanced down and nodded. Tears surfaced and dripped on the table like raindrops. The hardness and smugness Cain tried to maintain vanished. His mind shifted back to his earliest memories when he was the victim.

Jonas walked to the door and opened it. In the CIA, he worked as a profiler, amongst other things, and the information he dropped on Cain wasn't mere guessing, it was the typical history and behavior for why some men became rapists. Without even knowing it, HR placed Cain into the ideal situation where he held absolute power over any woman controlled by a Sleeper Chip. The Sleeper Chip was a dangerous tool in the hands of the wrong CAM-L controller. Jonas understood that no amount of rationalization with Grayson would make him abort the use of the chips in the mines, not with the type of prisoners he kept sending.

Grayson might've thought he was doing the overcrowded prisons on Earth a favor by taking the nastiest prisoners into his labor force, but he was setting up the Mars encampments to become devastating failures. Jonas disliked the use of the Sleeper Chips more and more.

Without saying another word, Jonas stepped out and locked the door. While he didn't plan to execute the punishment he'd threatened, he intended to have a chip implanted in Cain and send him to the mining pits.

After losing several miners to the Martian insects, Cain could fill one's place. He disliked that Cain wouldn't experience his punishment, but he couldn't risk the chance Cain might escape. If he obtained weapons, Cain wouldn't hesitate to retaliate.

<hr>

AFTER JONAS RETURNED to the security office, he sent a phone message to Grayson about the Chinese robots Derek encountered, asking what they could do. During the fifteen-minute wait for a response, he called the laboratory where Clark had taken the Martian insects.

"What is it, sir?" Clark asked.

"Did you talk to a chemist about getting a toxin analysis?"

"She's working on it right now."

"Keep me posted."

"Sure. But, you're not going to believe this," Clark said.

"What's that?"

"These creatures are quite smart."

"In what way?" Jonas asked.

"They can spell."

"In English?"

"Yes."

"Bullshit."

Clark chuckled.

"See? I knew that was a joke," Jonas said.

"No. I'm laughing because I can't see people believing it the first time I tell them. But, it's true."

"How's that even possible?" Jonas asked with a frown. "They've not been around us long enough to learn our language, even if they're capable of spelling in the first place."

"In many ways, I wish you were correct about that, sir. But, we're in a lot of danger since you're wrong."

"*Wrong?*" Jonas frowned. "What the hell are you talking about?"

Clark explained how the creatures formed letters with their bodies and then the warning they'd given him. "I'm not trying to alarm you, sir, but if what they're saying's true, the rest of these insects in the corridor and the open chamber are hostile and will attempt to exterminate us the longer we stay here."

Jonas sat quietly for a moment. "Tell the chemist I need her to hurry and analyze the toxin. Express how critical the information is, for all of our sakes."

"Yes, sir. I'll tell her."

Jonas ended the call. The worst part of Mars he'd imagined was the harsh terrain and the extreme cold. Never did he expect to find living creatures or the threat of assassin robots. There was a limit to their defense capabilities inside Olympus Mons. Prisoners greatly outnumbered them, but the Sleeper Chips maintained control, for now, provided no more malfunctions occurred. The insect toxin incapacitated a man in seconds, making them a greater threat since they were *inside* Olympus Mons. Their camouflage and small size helped them hide the cracks and crevices in the walls. Realistically, there was no safe place to hide from them.

Flamethrowers might exterminate a vast number of them, but the insects scrambled quickly. They'd never kill all the creatures before being swarmed and overtaken. He didn't have enough flamethrowers to exterminate a tenth of the insects. Nothing short of napalm could possible destroy the massive nest on the other side of the shaft wall.

Jonas took a deep breath and held it. He didn't remember a time since his son and daughter-in-law were killed when he'd felt this uneasy. Fleeing from Mars in a reasonable amount of time was next to impossible. They didn't have a large enough fleet of ships to send everyone to Earth. Even if Grayson was willing to send transport shuttles to Mars to carry them back—Jonas knew Grayson wouldn't—that was seven months of waiting. And the Grayson's contracts with the prisons prevented him from ever returning them to Earth.

They might be fortunate enough to have adequate room for some staff and guards to board Earthbound shuttles, but not for all. That meant leaving several dozen guards and staff members on Mars. He didn't see any peaceful lottery taking place for those forced to remain behind. They'd fight to get aboard, if the threat of these deadly insects increased.

Since he was the Warden Supervisor and the Head of Security, he was the captain of this ship. He'd willingly stay behind until either help came or everyone remaining, including himself, were dead.

Jonas realized the hundred or so prisoners were food for the Martian insects. He supposed it was a better sacrifice than the alternative, but he didn't like the idea, not even for the worst prisoners from Earth. Yet, he could justify it. Under the control of the Sleeper Chips, they'd never suffer, and with some of their previous outrageous crimes, the majority of the prisoners probably deserved more severe deaths than having their blood drained by the insects.

What troubled him the most was Clark's information. These creatures could communicate. They understood English. So, any communication Jonas gave his guards and staff could be intercepted. Making an advance into their territory to destroy the insects was suicide. These insects would anticipate their approach and react in kind.

These small insects could squeeze through the airshafts, electronic wiring ports, and into narrow crevices along the corridors. Their camouflage gave them a great advantage for surprise attacks. Should they be like other animals after tasting blood, they'd plot to get more.

Jonas sighed and rubbed his tired eyes. The insects were only one of their problems. How did they destroy the Chinese cyborgs? Most likely, they were approaching Olympus Mons. And then, the defective Sleeper Chips. These were all detrimental difficulties he and his staff faced. Being the Security Chief wasn't as secure as it once was.

Chapter 41

Jonas played the voice message from Grayson aloud.

"I received information about the Chinese robots earlier in the week. I've hired a team to go after information on how to destroy them. I'll update you once they retrieve the data."

Boony cocked a brow and looked at Jonas. "So, he already *knew* about them, but didn't tell us?"

Jonas shrugged. "Seems so."

She shook her head. "What a load of BS. Why wouldn't he give us a heads up?"

He sighed. "Maybe he didn't realize how close these robots are to our location? Mars is a huge planet after all."

"But he *knew*, Jonas."

"Don't jump the gun," he replied. "There's one thing I know about Grayson with absolute certainty."

"What's that?"

"He'll protect his investments. That's what we are here. If he says he's looking to find a solution, that's putting it mildly."

"You really think he cares about us that much?"

Jonas shook his head. "No, Boony, not us. His *investments*."

"We're *his* property?"

He laughed. "In a way, that's exactly what we are."

"What a pompous asshole."

Jonas shrugged. "We're the reason he's gained wealth from Mars. Apparently he's pissed off the Chinese government so they're striking at his core. Derek said these robots have heat-seeking technology, which indicates they're here to hunt us down and kill us. Without us, Grayson loses control of his encampments."

"So after we're all dead, the Chinese will send others to replace us?"

"Basically, yes. At that point, whoever resettles this base owns it and everything inside."

"That's sly and underhanded."

"True." Jonas nodded. "Indirectly, we're his best interests here. There's no end to what Grayson will do to prevent a hostile takeover. I've no doubt he's looking for a quick resolution."

"But we may not have that much time."

"Exactly. We need to be preparing."

"How?"

"As soon as the nurse finishes tending to Derek, I'll discuss the alternatives with him."

"Why?"

Jonas smiled. "Because when it comes to robots, Derek's a genius. He might find a way to deal with them ahead of any information Grayson sends."

"I hope he can. I don't have a lot of faith in Grayson's current technology."

"You mean the Sleeper Chips?"

She nodded.

"Well, Grayson hasn't even heard the worst part."

"What's that?"

"Listen," Jonas winked and punched in the code to send Grayson the message. "We've discovered another devastating problem inside Olympus Mons. An infestation of strange poisonous insects outnumber us by the thousands. They've killed one guard and several prisoners. Outside of using extreme heat, we don't have any way to exterminate them. We may have to send guards and crew back to Earth should this situation get further out of hand."

He hit 'send.'

Boony shook her head. "He's not going to believe that."

"You wouldn't?"

"No, of course not. Not without seeing them first. It sounds like a horrible prank."

"It definitely would, if it wasn't me reporting it."

"He'll believe you?"

Jonas nodded. "I've never been one to tell jokes or pull pranks. Grayson knows that's not my nature. I've worked for him too many years. He'll believe me *without* pictures."

Boony marveled. "So after all these years he'd never suspect you to have a sudden thought to pull a shenanigan?"

"No."

"Then your news will certainly cause a bit of panic for him, won't it?"

"Probably. That's another downside about us being on Mars and him being on Earth. Thirty-minute delays in receiving answers to messages. Should we ever experience a catastrophe, that's a hellish eternity to wait. I need to take some digital photos of those insects and send them to Grayson. Then he'll know what else we're up against."

GRAYSON LISTENED to the report about the poisonous insects for the second time. He didn't know how to reply. Fate seemed to be placing a unbreakable chokehold to shut down his operations. Even if he wanted to send reinforcements, they'd never reach Olympus Mons in time.

The only plus side was the discovery of life on Mars, but how'd you report that to the press if the creatures kill all the inhabitants? There wasn't any positive outcome with such a circumstance occurring in the media, especially when most of the news reporters practically hated him and the tabloid shows thrived on reporting anything shedding negative light on him.

Beatrice spoke over his desk intercom. "You have a visitor, Mr. Grayson. He insists it's urgent."

"Who is it?"

"Mr. Parks."

Grayson's eyebrows rose. "Send him in."

About two minutes later, a muscled bodyguard opened the office door and motioned Parks to enter. Parks paused at the threshold for a moment with a nervous expression. He took a step forward with the help of a cane.

"Damn, Parks, what happened?" Grayson asked, coming around the desk to help Parks sit in a cushioned chair.

"The details are a bit fuzzy right now," he replied. He winced and gasped as he lowered into the chair.

Grayson eased back, sat on the edge of his desk, and crossed his arms. "You don't remember anything?"

Parks peered into Grayson's eyes for a moment and quickly looked away. "All I know is what I've been told."

"And that is?"

"An officer found me unconscious in an alley and called an ambulance. According to the hospital physician, I was out for a couple of days."

Grayson studied him beneath a firm brow for several moments. "You remember nothing?"

Uneasily, Parks shook his head.

"Did it have to do with retrieving the information I asked you to get?"

"I'm thinking it did. But, like I said, the details are sketchy."

"I see. In the shape you're in, you didn't have to come all the way down to my office. You could've called."

Parks raised a hand in a wavelike motion like it didn't matter. "I was lucky they allowed me to leave the hospital. Besides, I needed to check in with you. It's safer than using phones. You know that."

Grayson nodded. "Definitely. But in your absence, I have some bad news."

"What's that?"

"Someone else gave me the information I sent you after, and I paid them."

Parks winced. "The whole million?"

"Unfortunately," Grayson said. "Yes."

Parks leaned the back of his head against the cushioned chair, closed his eyes, and shook his head. "To whom?"

Grayson uncrossed his arms and walked to his chair behind the desk. "It's not important."

"To me it might be."

"How's that?"

"He could be the person who did this to me."

Beatrice spoke through the intercom. "Sir, I know you're busy but—"

A male voice cut her off. "Tell Grayson it's urgent I speak with him about payment."

"Grayson," Beatrice said, "he's heading for your office door! He's knocked one of the guards unconscious!"

CLARK STUDIED THE THREE INSECTS. Other than the warning, the insects didn't communicate any further, which frustrated him.

He wasn't delusional. He wrote the letters in the specific order they'd chosen. They never hesitated with their choices. Not once. It was almost like relying on the Ouija board pointer to stop on certain letters. But these were real insects without a chance someone else was manipulating their choices. And now, they were silent.

Jonas and Boony entered the laboratory and approached Clark's table. Jonas took a digital camera and half squatted to get a picture.

"What are you doing?" Clark asked.

"Sending pictures to Grayson."

Clark placed his hands over the side of the glass container, blocking the insects from Jonas' view.

"What are *you* doing?" Jonas asked.

"You can't."

"Why the hell not?"

"Because... Grayson will take the discovery as his own."

Boony said, "You realize our lives are endangered?"

"Yeah," he replied defensively. "I do. But there's nothing on Earth that'll aid Grayson any better in understanding what these things are. Nothing. We're the ones with firsthand knowledge. I'm conducting research, so I can write a scientific report for a journal."

Jonas lowered the camera. "So, what you're saying is you want the credit for yourself?"

"That wasn't what I said."

"It's implied," Jonas replied.

Clark shrugged. His face reddened. "The discovery goes a long way on my resume."

Jonas nodded. "Okay. No pictures. But I have informed Grayson of the danger we face."

"You did?"

"I had to. So if I were you, I'd get busy finding out what you can about them."

"Thank you, sir."

"Care to show us how they're able to communicate with us?" Jonas asked.

Clark swallowed hard. "I can try. After I wrote down their warning, they stopped."

Boony smiled. "That's convenient."

"It's frustrating as hell," he replied. He slid a paper from beneath his laptop to Jonas. "This is the message."

Jonas cocked a brow. "A bit poetic for insects, don't you think?"

Clark sighed.

"Show us what you did," Jonas said. "So I can see. Who knows? Maybe they'll do it again."

Sheepishly, Clark took the disconnected keyboard and held it against the side of the container wall. His face flushed dark crimson. To his surprise, as well as Boony and Jonas, one insect studied the keyboard and started pointing at letters.

"Write it down," Clark said, glancing at Boony.

She grabbed a pen and a notepad.

"I'll be damned," Jonas said.

Boony's eyes widened as she wrote the letters until it stopped pointing.

Clark noticed her troubled expression. "What did they say?"

She read off the message. "In the dead of night, your deaths, our delight."

Chapter 42

Parks gripped his cane tightly and turned in his chair when the man flung open the door. Henry grabbed the man by the lapels of his jacket. The man attempted to head-butt Henry but missed.

In return, Henry smashed his forehead into the man's mouth, cracking teeth and busting his lips.

"Viktor!" Grayson said. "What the hell are you doing?"

"I come for de two hundred thousand."

Parks used the cane to force himself to his feet. He pointed at Viktor and glanced to Grayson. "You know this man?"

Grayson nodded.

Memories started resurfacing for Parks. "He's the bastard that set me up."

Henry's huge hands clamped around Viktor's elbows so tightly the man winced.

"Set you up?" Viktor said in a near whine. "What are you talking about?"

Parks hobbled, steadying himself with the cane, and approached Viktor. "You know exactly what I'm talking about. I went with you to meet the men who had information about the cargo the Chinese sent to Mars. Those two men and two Russians were both killed. I was knocked unconscious and someone tampered with the evidence to frame me so it looked like I killed them."

"De kid, he's crazy. He's lying," Viktor said.

"Am I? Why were you the only one left unscathed?"

Grayson marched across the office and stopped inches from Viktor. "I warned you if you had a hand in Parks' incapacitation, you'd pay severely."

"What you going to do, eh?" Viktor asked.

Grayson grabbed the man's shirt collar and lifted Viktor six inches off the floor. "Henry, check his pockets for weapons."

Henry patted Viktor's pockets and brought out a MP-446 Viking 9mm.

"What's that for?" Grayson asked.

"Protection," Viktor replied.

Henry studied the gun and shook his head. "How'd you get this into the states?"

Viktor shrugged. "As with most other things, well concealed."

"And my metal detectors?"

"Secret I wish not to reveal."

Grayson lowered Viktor to the floor and brought a swift hard jab to the man's gut. Viktor crumbled with a deep intake of air and fell to his knees. "The gun's not going to help you now."

Gasping, he said, "I bring it all the time. Never been problem before."

"That was when I considered you a friend and comrade."

Clutching his gut with both hands, Viktor looked up with a mixture of pain and sorrow in his eyes. "No more?"

Grayson shook his head. "Never again."

Grayson pulled back the trigger and aimed at Viktor's head.

"You're going to kill me? Here? Come Grayson, have heart, eh? I give da information for free."

"And where's this team of yours that you needed the funding ahead of time to do the job?" Grayson asked.

Parks said, "My guess is they're the dead Russians he left at the crime scene with me."

Grayson frowned. "There never was a team, was there?"

The Russian's hardened exterior crumbled. "No team."

"Then why the charades? For money?" Grayson asked.

Parks glared at Viktor. "He has a team."

"I do not," Viktor replied in a firm whisper.

"Sid Davis," Parks said.

The name made Viktor flinch. He took a sharp breath and swallowed hard.

Grayson looked from Viktor to Parks. "Who's Sid Davis?"

"NSA agent. Damn bastard came to my hospital room and tried to blackmail me."

"How?"

Parks grinned. "He wanted me to turn the tables on you."

"I see. Apparently he doesn't know where your true loyalties lie," Grayson replied.

Parks smiled. "He seemed jealous of our alignment and my retainer fees."

Grayson grabbed Viktor's tie and yanked the man to his feet. "Is what Parks said, true? You're working with the NSA?"

Viktor shook his head slightly. "No. Not NSA. Just dis Davis guy."

"What's he after?"

"Da money you paid me."

Parks frowned. "The million dollars."

Viktor nodded but held his gaze at the floor.

"The nerve of that asshole," Parks said, gritting his teeth. "Accusing me of taking bribes and working as a hitman for large sums of money and he's behind this?"

Grayson shrugged. "It still doesn't get me the answers I need."

"Which are?" Parks asked.

"How to stop those programmed Chinese robots from killing my people on Mars?"

Viktor cleared his throat and nervously glanced into Grayson's eyes. "There's no kill switch for dem. No deactivation codes."

Grayson looped Viktor's tie around his hand again and tightened his grip. He placed the gun's barrel to Viktor's forehead. "You knew this and tried to extort four millions dollars from me?"

"No, no. Don't kill me."

Grayson laughed. "Give me a good reason not to."

"I help you."

"No," Grayson replied, shaking his head. "You've helped yourself to more than your fair share."

"No, Grayson, I did not get one penny of da million dollars."

"Sid took it all?" Parks asked.

Viktor nodded. "Yes. He wanted me to get him more money. Otherwise, he deport me to some... unsavory enemies I have. That's why he have me arrange deal with you for codes."

"When there are no codes?"

"Right."

"So we really don't need to keep you around anymore. We dispose of you and go find Sid Davis," Grayson said.

"No, please, you don't understand," Viktor said.

"And what am I not understanding?"

"You have powerful enemies in high places of U.S."

Grayson nodded and shrugged. "Most wealthy people do."

"Not like you think." Viktor shook his head. "Sid Davis hired me. It's who hired him that should make you worry."

"Who's that?" Grayson asked.

Viktor's eyes crossed as he looked at the gun barrel pressed to his forehead. "Put gun away. I tell you. Kill me and you might never know."

Chapter 43

Grayson tucked the gun into his suit pocket. Henry grabbed Viktor by the elbows again.

"So who hired Davis?" Grayson asked.

"No, sorry," Viktor said with a slight grin. "I cannot tell you."

"Why not?"

"It's only insurance I have to stay alive since the trust between us is no more."

Grayson narrowed his gaze. "That wasn't my doing."

"I know. But, I tell you after we get this Davis guy, okay?"

Parks grinned and glanced at Grayson. "I'm all for it."

Grayson returned to his seat behind the desk. Parks limped back to the cushioned chair. Henry dragged Viktor to the other chair and forced him to sit.

Grayson took Viktor's gun and placed it on the desk between him and Viktor. "Davis has the money we wired you?"

"No."

"You already said that he did."

Viktor shook his head. "Before he could have it withdrawn from my account, I had bank freeze my account, telling dem my identity had been stolen. They're to put in new account for me. They also wanted to watch the account a few days for suspicious activity."

"Was this before or *after* you tried to get four million dollars from me?"

Parks simply shook his head in disbelief while looking at Viktor.

"Before," Viktor replied.

"I'm surprised he didn't make good on his threat already," Grayson said.

"He's pissed, eh, but what can he do?"

"Are you serious?" Parks asked. "He's with the NSA. There's no end to *what* he could do to you and never be charged."

"True, if he doesn't want the money. Ah, but, you see the greed in his eyes. He wants money too badly not to wait."

Grayson folded his hands together on the desk. "So what's your next move?"

"I came here for the two hundred thousand—"

"Which you *aren't* getting," Grayson replied.

Viktor gave a slight chuckle. "It's all good. He's to meet with me dis evening to discuss my frozen account."

Grayson looked at Parks. "Couldn't Davis unfreeze the account and take the money?"

"Not without a warrant," Parks replied. "And if he asked for one, he'd need a legitimate reason for requesting it. Doing so, places scrutiny on him. His superiors would keep a watchful eye on him to see where that money ended up. NSA agents don't trust people. Not even each other."

"He won't want warrant," Viktor said. "He wants cash. He thinks I'll bring it when we meet."

"Where's this meeting take place?" Grayson asked.

"Dock 10."

"At the river?"

Viktor nodded.

"Parks," Grayson said, "you want to escort Viktor to that meeting?"

"Gladly."

"Good. Henry, get two more guards to go with them. Make certain they're armed."

"Yes, sir." Henry turned and left the office.

Grayson aimed the gun at Viktor. "This best go smoothly or—"

"All I want's out from Davis' grasp," Viktor said. "I give money back to you in exchange for my life."

"Let's see how it plays out," Grayson replied.

AN HOUR AFTER SUNSET, one of Grayson's bodyguards parked the black four-door car at the end of the dark street near Dock 10. He shut off the engine and the headlights. The front passenger was about as large as the driver. Both men wore earpieces. Parks sat in the backseat with Viktor.

"Here," Parks said. "Place this in your ear."

"What's it do?" Viktor asked.

"Allows me to hear your conversation."

"Ah, yes. Good. You recording it?"

"Yes."

"Good."

Viktor rubbed the back of his head and winced.

"It still hurts?" Parks asked.

"A little."

"It's a tracker chip. Once this is over, Grayson will have his doctor remove it."

Viktor shook his head. "I never meant to betray Grayson's trust."

"Perhaps you can redeem yourself tonight," Parks replied.

"Doubtful. Grayson's *not* a merciful man."

Parks didn't reply, but he didn't disagree with the statement. He'd only agreed to help Davis build a case against Grayson so Davis would stop his threats and get off his back. But now he knew Davis planned to extort as much money from Grayson as possible. He wanted to use Parks to dig up more dirt to blackmail Grayson before Grayson realized what was actually occurring.

A silver Mercedes passed their car and stopped about a block away.

"Is that his car?" Parks asked.

Viktor nodded.

"Okay, go. We're recording and watching," Parks said.

Viktor opened the rear door and pushed it wider. He hesitated emerging from the safety of the car.

The driver looked in the rearview mirror. "We're armed. We have you covered."

Viktor acquiesced an appreciative nod, got out, and quietly pressed the door closed. The street was dark with few streetlights. After Viktor walked away, Parks turned up the volume.

Davis parked his silver Mercedes beneath a streetlight. The car gleamed. Viktor walked down the dark sidewalk until he entered the wide arc of the overhead streetlight that shone like a spotlight off the Mercedes.

Parks wasn't certain if Davis would invite Viktor inside the car or if Davis would get out. But the moment Viktor stepped to the side of the car, Davis swung open the door and got out.

"Where's my money, Viktor?" Davis said, nervously. "You said that you'd have it with you."

"Account still frozen."

"What the hell do you think you're trying to pull?"

Viktor crossed his arms. "Nothing. Bank won't give me money. Told me I have to wait two weeks."

"Two weeks?" Anger rose in Davis' voice.

"If I could give you money, I would. I'd be happy to rid myself of you. Of course, if Grayson ever knew how you used me to double-cross him—"

Davis pulled out his 9mm and steadied it with both hands.

"What?" Viktor asked. "You want to kill me? Go ahead. Definitely no way to get the money den."

Davis lowered the gun, ran a hand through his hair, and shouted obscenities. Viktor stood his ground, unflinching. "What about the two hundred thousand? Did you get that from Grayson?"

"In car."

"You didn't bring it?"

Viktor shook his head. "You joke, right? In a dark street like dis, you expect me to carry briefcase full of money? No. I know places like dis. They bad places. People die a lot here."

Davis sighed and holstered his gun. "All right. Let's go."

"If you like, I could go get it."

"Nah, that's okay. We're already walking. It'll take longer. Besides, you're right. This *can* be a dangerous place after nightfall."

Parks turned down the volume. "How close are they?"

"Half a block," the driver said. He pulled his gun from his holster and shucked a shell into the chamber. He looked at his partner. "Ready, hos?"

The passenger nodded.

They opened their doors and leveled their 9mms at Davis. "Hands up where we can see them."

Davis took a couple of steps backwards and then raised his hands. "You've no idea who you're messing with. Let me get my badge. I can show you."

"Viktor, get Davis' gun."

Viktor reached beneath Davis' jacket and took the 9mm.

"Keep your hands up," the driver said. "That's your last warning."

"You're making a huge mistake," Davis said.

The driver leaned in and turned on the headlights.

Parks opened the rear door and used the side of the car and the door to pull himself to his feet. "We know exactly who you are, Agent Davis."

Davis squinted and leaned slightly forward. "Agent Parks? Is that you?"

Parks grabbed his cane from the backseat and hobbled on the sidewalk. "Yeah, it's me."

"What the hell's going on? Are you working with these goons?"

"No, I'm still working for Grayson. After I found out about your extortion schemes, I figured it was time to turn the tables on *you*, especially after your threats. And after I discovered you killed all four of those men and framed me for it, I did some major reconsideration of your offer. No, I'm not interested in working for you."

Davis stood silent for a few moments. Words failed him. "So what're you planning to do? Hand me over to the authorities?"

Even with two guns aimed at Davis, he held his above-the-law arrogance.

"No," Parks replied. "Grayson's quite eager to speak to you."

In the glow of the headlights, Davis appeared paler.

"Yeah," Parks said. "You see, Viktor's agreed to give Grayson his money back, and according to Viktor, he said Grayson isn't a merciful man. But, of course, with all the research *you've* done, I'm sure you're aware of that."

"No negotiating?"

Parks laughed. "You need to ask? Seems I had no say about my injuries that you had a hand in."

"I was rash in my decisions. I admit it."

Parks stepped up to Davis, reached beneath Davis' sport jacket, and took out Davis' other 9mm. Parks stood toe-to-toe with Davis. "When Grayson's finished with you... let's say whatever's *left* of you, I'll get even."

Davis took a deep breath.

Parks handed a set of handcuffs to Viktor. "Put those on Davis. Make sure they're extra tight."

Viktor tucked the gun behind his belt and obliged while Parks held the gun on Davis. Davis groaned when the metal cut into his flesh.

An Audi sped down the dark street and screeched to a stop beside the black car. Henry opened the passenger door and got out. Grayson stepped out of the driver's side. "Agent Davis."

Davis' eyes widened. "Mr. Grayson. I'd shake your hand, but as you can see, I'm sort of in a bind."

Grayson swung a hard right into the agent's gut. Davis dropped to his knees on the sidewalk, wheezing and gasping for air. When Davis looked up with a glare, Grayson struck the agent's jaw. Teeth cracked. After Davis recovered, his eyes were filled with fear. "As you can see, agent, I'm not in the mood for niceties."

"It's more than obvious," Davis groaned.

"Viktor told me someone hired you on the side to spy on me. Who is it?"

Davis panted. "You've been under federal surveillance for years."

"Let me borrow your cane, Parks," Grayson said.

Parks adjusted his weight and handed the cane to Grayson.

"Thanks. Sometimes, there's a need to beat the stubbornness out of some people."

"Wait," Davis said.

Grayson gripped the cane with both hands like one would with a golf club. "Who hired you?"

"Senator Johnson."

Shocked, Grayson lowered the cane. He couldn't hide his stunned expression.

Davis grinned, in spite of his pain. "See? You think because you have a lot of wealth that you can keep people in your back pocket. People sicken of bullies who try to control every aspect of their lives."

Grayson handed the cane to Parks. He looked at his two bodyguards who still held guns on Davis. "I have the information I need. He's in your hands. Since we're at the docks, you don't have to get too creative."

"I'm a federal agent. Don't you realize the repercussions you'll face for torturing me?"

"Who said anything about torture?" Grayson asked with a cold grin.

Davis' brow rose.

"You failed to understand who you've crossed," Grayson replied. "Dead agents don't talk and can't file charges."

The two bodyguards hefted Davis by his elbows and started walking to the docks. "Dead? Wait. Mr. Grayson?"

Parks looked at Grayson. "You mind if I help?"

"He's all yours. Gentlemen, I don't want to know anything about what you do to him. Make certain his body's never found."

"You can't do this," Davis said, struggling to break free of the two muscle-bound guards.

Grayson grinned and shrugged. "I'm not. They are."

Viktor watched them haul Davis deeper into the shadows of the night. "Mr. Grayson, what should I do?"

"If Davis left the key in his car, have some fun with it."

Viktor gave an aged smile. "No. I mean about us. I never intended to—"

Grayson turned and faced Viktor. Henry stood beside Grayson.

"Let me ask you something, Viktor," Grayson said.

"Sure. Anything."

"Have you at any time ever been approached by Senator Johnson?"

"No."

"Never?"

"No."

"Then how'd you know about Johnson hiring Davis?"

"I overheard Davis' phone conversation."

"And you're certain it was the senator?" Grayson asked.

"Of course."

"But the senator has *never* contacted or visited you?"

"No," Viktor replied.

"Okay. Take the car. Keep the money for your help."

"Da whole million?"

Grayson nodded. "But I want the two hundred thousand in the case."

"Of course. Den things good between us again?"

"Not like they were, Viktor, but since I'm letting you keep the money, you owe me a few favors in the future."

Viktor nodded. He grinned his relief and appreciation. "Certainly. Anything."

The echoes of Davis' screams carried down the dark street. Three gunshots were fired. Davis never screamed again. With obvious discomfort, Viktor looked in the direction. "You not worried someone will call the police?"

Grayson shrugged. "Not really. I own the entire block and Dock 10. Davis apparently wasn't *thorough* with his research."

Viktor gave a sly but nervous grin.

Chapter 44

Hours passed before Jonas received word from Grayson that the robots didn't have kill switches or deactivation codes. Grayson didn't say anything about the strange insects Jonas mentioned, either.

Did Grayson actually believe Jonas had made up a story about Martian insects?

Jonas found Derek sitting at the side of the infirmary bed when he stopped to visit. "How are you feeling, Derek?"

"Better. But I've never known blistered flesh to stop hurting in a short amount of time."

"Burns are some of the worst injuries ever," Jonas said. "So how long before they let you leave?"

"I can go now. Why? Is something wrong?"

Jonas nodded. "Yeah."

"What?"

"Grayson sent an update about those Chinese robots."

"And?"

"There are no kill switches or codes we can use to deactivate them."

"I don't buy it," Derek said. "Any computerized robot has always been designed so they can be shut down in case of malfunctions."

"Robots aren't my specialty. That's why I came to pass along the information."

"You busy?"

Jonas shook his head. "No, why?"

"The Chinese robots showed up on the radar, right?"

"Yes."

"Let's see where they are on the satellite map."

"Sure."

CARTER SAT at the edge of a seat across the aisle from where Magnus and Sylvia slept inside their hibernation chambers. His frozen eyes watched them in a trancelike state. He had not slept in days, even though he teetered close every half hour or so. His mind drifted, lingering on the edge of the nightmare of the female alien who constantly whispered inside his mind. He feared allowing sleep to overtake him, for worry she'd do something.

Magnus was huge, but so helpless while sleeping inside the chamber. His muscled chest and limbs were cramped tightly inside the enclosure. Had he not been sleeping, he'd have complained about obvious pain. No claustrophobic individual would ever allow himself to be shut inside without resistance. But the giant man slept peacefully.

Sylvia's face was almost angelic. Her skin was perfect, unblemished, and she slept peacefully. Her pouty lips occasionally hinted of smiles during her REM sleep. Little lines tugged the edges of her mouth, revealing the cute dimples she displayed during her liveliest moments whenever she was a second from bursting into laughter.

"You have feelings for her, don't you?" the alien asked.

The question jarred Carter from his trance. He gazed around, up and down the aisle, but saw no physical sign of the female alien. He hit his forehead with a closed fist, hard. "Would you get out of my head?"

"I cannot."

"Please!"

For a few minutes, there was silence, followed by a low ringing in his ears. Soon the beeping mechanisms of the hibernation monitors increased. Not that the sounds weren't there before, because they were, but now his mind was no longer zoned into her hypnotic trance. The airflow through the duct system whispered.

Carter sighed, enjoying the moments of her absence. He wondered if she'd stay gone, or if she'd fade from his mind once he killed Boyd Grayson? He was willing to do anything to stop her mental intrusion, even suicide, if it became necessary.

Something soft brushed his cheek, a gentle unseen caress, which sent chills down his back. He flinched and held his breath.

"You're still here?" he asked.

"Always," she replied.

Carter shook his head. Tears burned his eyes. "Please go away."

A gentle soothing laugh echoed near his ear. "Never. I'm a part of you, ever since you gave yourself to me."

"I wish I'd died."

"Don't be... harsh. You *need* me."

Carter rose to his feet. "I can't take this anymore. Leave me alone."

"You're stronger than you think."

"You're tearing my mind apart." Carter walked to the hibernation chamber controls. He tapped his fingers at the edge of the number pad.

"What are you doing?"

"I'm waking them up."

"No, you cannot."

"Why not?"

"They'll die!"

Carter frowned. "You're going to kill them?"

"No. You will. Bringing them out this soon can cause irreparable damage."

Carter lowered his hand to his side.

"You should set your hibernation chamber," she whispered. "You need to rest. Ease your mind."

For several moments, he considered hibernating, but then decided it was best not to. He didn't trust what *she'd* do to Magnus and Sylvia if he were unconscious. He wept and returned to his seat.

The alien gently shushed inside his mind. "It's okay. Relax. Let sleep take you. Everything's going to be okay."

Carter closed his eyes. A few seconds later, sleep overtook him.

CLARK SPENT several hours analyzing the metallic components of the dead insects' chitinous exoskeleton. It was the oddest thing he'd ever studied in a biological laboratory. He never needed to use a diamond-tipped circular blade to dissect an insect's exoskeleton before. These were the most amazing, and yet deadly, creatures he'd seen.

A friend of his on Earth kept venomous snakes, cobras, and Taipans. If bitten, his friend could easily die before receiving antivenin. When asked why he'd keep something so deadly, his friend said he thrived on the thrill and rush of owning a noxious creature capable of killing dozens of people. All that separated them was a thin layer of glass. One mistake in feeding or cleaning the cage meant instant death. Tempting fate brought a similar high, much like an opiate drug, for some people.

Now Clark understood why. He was experiencing the same sensation holding the box with the three insects. He knew what they were capable of doing, and yet he trusted these three *not* to attack. He questioned his own blind faith. Because of their intelligence he lowered his guard, but these creatures were no more tamable than a reptile. Snakes were never pets. They didn't respond to human affection like a dog or cat or other mammals. They responded to the need to eat or self-defense. The reptile occasionally mistook a hand as food entering a cage, which was why many herpetologists were bitten due to carelessness. Such *pets* were unpredictable.

Clark, however, never opened the box of insects. He didn't know if he ever could. He sketched a larger cage outline for the techs to build so the creatures could be allowed more room, but a larger environment might give them better opportunity to escape, depending on how secure the new cage was constructed.

Anna brought a printout of the toxin spectrometer reading and other data sheets. "You were right."

"About what?" he asked.

"Those creatures could kill all of us in a matter of hours."

"What did you find out?"

She spread the data sheets and the reading across the tabletop. "Based on the readings, their toxins contain a vast amount of cnidarian proteins like what the box jellyfish on Earth has."

"How does it numb a person's body?"

"The body goes into shock. From the high levels of these proteins though, I'm surprised Roy has survived this long."

"Why?"

"These proteins cause red blood cells to rupture, which floods the bloodstream with high levels of potassium, and too much potassium can—"

"Stop the heart."

Anna nodded. "Exactly. Now, I know you're fond of your bugs over there, but honey, I'd suggest you throw them into an incinerator 'cause I don't believe I can counteract what their toxins do."

"Seriously?"

"On Earth, there's little that can be done, and they have almost any type of antitoxin you can think of. But us? We're far more limited."

Clark nodded. "I understand. So we don't have any way to help Roy?"

"'Fraid not. All he has is hope, but I don't think there's even enough of that."

"Thanks for analyzing it."

Anna forced a smile. "Glad I did. Now we know what we're dealing with. A better solution is figuring out how to get our asses on a shuttle to Earth. I don't like the idea of living anywhere near them."

"You mind if I keep this data to show Jonas?"

"Help yourself."

"Thanks."

She placed her hands on her hips. "And when you talk to him, ask him if we're going to get a chance to shuttle to Earth before things get even worse around here."

Clark gathered the data sheets and nodded. "I'll ask."

He walked to the door.

"And *don't* forget your bugs. I'm no bug-sitter."

JONAS, Boony, and Derek stared at the satellite map on the large screen. Four dots were visible.

"I thought there were eight?" Boony said.

"They have stealth technology," Derek replied.

"Meaning they turn invisible?"

Derek nodded.

"Shit," she said in a near whisper.

Jonas pointed to the four robots' position. "They're less than a few hundred yards away."

"I know," Derek said. "They seem to be following my path."

"Then they'll reach us in less than an hour or so?" Boony asked.

"At their current pace," Jonas said. "Faster than that."

Derek stared at Jonas. "Grayson said there are no kill switches?"

Jonas nodded. "And no deactivation codes."

Derek sighed. "There has to be something we can do. Our laser rifles and plasma pistols won't harm them."

"You're certain?" Jonas asked.

"Quite sure. And regular guns... bullets flick right off the robots' armor. It's a shame we don't have a tank."

Jonas offered a slight grin.

Boony frowned. "You think that's what it'd require? That kind of force?"

Derek shrugged. "I honestly don't know. They're powerfully structured with the hardest metals. I imagine it'll take something incredibly strong to destroy them."

"We don't have a lot of time," Jonas said.

"I know. I'll head to the engineering department and do some brainstorming. Maybe I can figure out what else can be done before it's too late."

Chapter 45

Matthews entered the infirmary. Dr. Sheung and Dr. Lee stood at the side of Roy's bed, studying the medical chart. Fluids flowed through the I.V. attached to back of his left wrist.

Sheung narrowed a harsh glare when she noticed Matthews. "What do you want?"

"What's wrong with him?" Matthews crouched, studying Roy's skin and breathing.

"Did Jonas send you?" she asked.

Dr. Lee seemed to shrink smaller and eased away from her.

Matthews didn't like her attitude. He crossed his arms and frowned back.

"You need to leave," she said. "Unless Jonas sent you."

"Then maybe I should speak to Jonas. He's the one in charge anyway." Matthews turned to walk out.

"Wait!" she said without urgency but still sternly demanding.

Matthews faced her with anger burning in his eyes. He hated for anyone to address him with such a condescending tone. The challenge in her voice infuriated him. Regardless of anything else she'd ever say to him, he'd always view her as an enemy and find a way to put her in her place. The fear in Dr. Lee's eyes clued him to her reputation as well.

"What do you want?" she asked.

Matthews gazed from her to Roy. Rumors had already spread to the guards about what had happened in Mineshaft Fifteen. Whatever poison these insects possessed was something Matthews could use to his advantage, provided he found a way to collect it. "Have you determined what placed Roy into this state?"

Dr. Lee shook his head but didn't verbally reply.

"No," Dr. Sheung said. "We're still waiting for the lab results to come back. Why? I'm certain Jonas will get the information before we do."

"So he's been unresponsive to any medicines or steroids?"

"I don't see how that's any of your concern."

Matthews placed a hand on his laser pistol and cocked his head to the side with his brow raised. "Because I'm a guard?"

For the first time since he entered the room, she looked nervous. Her eyes focused on the pistol. "Jonas didn't send you?"

Matthews shook his head.

"Then why are you here?"

"We're in near crisis and will be if the guards are unable to seal off the shaft where those insects are. I, for one, don't believe Jonas is capable of keeping us safe."

The hardness of her face faded. A relieved smile curled her lips, which looked foreign to her facial features. "And what do you propose?"

Matthews grinned. "For me to take his place."

"I'll gladly assist you in such an endeavor."

"You need to understand," Matthews said, "*I'm* in charge. Not you."

She nodded. "That's fine, as long as it isn't Jonas."

CLARK ROLLED the data sheets and tucked them under his arm. He carried the cage in his right hand and walked down the corridor. He thought about Anna's remark of how dangerous it was to keep these insects alive. In many ways, he agreed.

But out of the thousands of insects, why had these three surrendered? They seemed eager to communicate and were almost social, or was it a ploy? Did they intend to act docile until an opportunity arose for them to signal the rest of their horde to emerge in full force?

Clark stopped midstride, closed his eyes, and shook his head. As intelligent as these creatures were, he'd inadvertently been giving them vital information and knowledge of how their headquarters were set up. If they didn't actually intend to aid the human population, these insects had plenty of necessary information they could relay to the hive. Even though they communicated by spelling words, he didn't know what other ways they could relay messages to one another. For all he knew, they could be reporting the layout of the facilities.

The Olympus Mons encampment possibly had a Trojan horse comprised of three super intelligent insects.

He remembered Shad's death and hurried to get to the security office.

The insects displayed an incredible military strategic pattern when they surrounded Shad. It indicated their ability and knowledge to quickly maneuver and box him in so he couldn't escape. While these three exhibited peaceful behavior, they were armed with the same toxin.

Clark considered incinerating them, but what if they were actual allies? How could he know with certainty they weren't enemies? He couldn't ever truly know. If they were allies, they didn't have any reason to be concerned. But as enemies? The longer he kept them alive, the more danger the human population faced.

He entered the security department.

Jonas glanced at the door. "Did you get a toxin analysis?"

Clark nodded.

"And?"

"It isn't good."

Boony's eyes widened. "Why not?"

Clark explained what Anna had shown him on the data sheets and the comparison of the insect toxin to that of the box jellyfish on Earth. "No anti-toxin is known."

Jonas took a deep breath. "Then we have no choice but to find a way to kill the hive before they attack and kill us."

Clark put his index finger to his lips.

"What?" Jonas asked.

He pointed to the caged insects, set down the cage, and walked to Jonas and Boony.

"What's wrong?" Jonas asked.

Clark whispered, "After what Anna told me, I'm worried that maybe I've placed too much confidence in these three being hospitable."

Jonas frowned. "You think they'll become hostile?"

Clark shrugged. "Is there any way we could ever know?"

"What was her suggestion?"

"Toss them in the incinerator."

"That's a bit extreme," Boony said.

Jonas shook his head. "I don't know, Clark. You might be getting a little paranoid. After seeing Shad killed and some of the prisoners dying, you might be succumbing to inner fears?"

"I know. But the more I've thought about the situation, the less inclined I am to think they might not be allies."

Jonas placed a firm hand on Clark's shoulder. "The container they're in seems strong enough to prevent their escape. If you're not comfortable keeping them near you, let me keep them here."

Clark shook his head. "No, you see, that's more my worry than these three actually killing us."

"What is?"

"Giving them further access to any of our facilities."

"You think they can somehow transmit that information to the rest of the hive?" Jonas asked.

"You've seen what they can do. Their intelligence is phenomenal. Who knows what else they can do? I'm not an entomologist, but insects on Earth do communicate in various ways. Pheromones, tapping antennae, and other ways, but on Mars... who knows?"

Jonas offered a slight nod, more from kindness than actual belief. "Look, let me ask you something."

"Sure."

"We know from your account how they killed Shad, and we saw the one dead prisoner. Both were drained of their blood. What are the ones inside the hive eating?"

A bewildered expression came to Clark's face. He shook his head, trying to find an answer. "I don't have any idea."

"What would be your guess? I mean, there are thousands of them on the other side of that wall. They've had to eat something. What's your best guess?" Jonas asked.

"I'd say they must eat the weaker ones, but really, we've no way to know unless we were spent a lot of time watching their behavior."

"Which is something we cannot do," he replied.

"I agree."

The office door swung open. Jonas and Boony turned quickly. Gary was helping an exhausted miner stand. The older man looked like he could collapse any moment.

"What's going on?" Jonas asked.

"Sir," Gary said. "You might want to sit down and listen to what this gentleman has to say."

"He's a prisoner. Did his chip malfunction?"

Gary shook his head. "He's dressed like a prisoner, but he's actually a guard."

Jonas frowned. "What?"

Gary nodded and helped the man to a cushioned swivel chair where he promptly plopped down. Boony rushed to the man with a bottle of water.

"Yeah. This is Norm Schrader. After his Sleeper Chip malfunctioned, and when he was brought to me, I recognized him. He was aboard the shuttle that brought one of Grayson's sworn enemies to Mars."

"Who?"

"Steven Matthews."

"Where's he?" Jonas asked.

"He's posing as one of the guards."

Jonas glanced at Boony. "Find every file on Matthews so we know who we're dealing with."

"Yes, sir."

Norm swallowed a big gulp of water and sputtered afterwards. Gary patted the man's back. Norm's face was flushed. His eyes were weak. He was exhausted. "When you find that bastard, I'm going to kill him."

"I understand your reasons for wanting to do so," Jonas replied.

Norm shook his head. "No, you don't have *any* idea."

"Perhaps not."

"No. I read his files. Matthews is a very dangerous man. According to Grayson, he has only one goal."

"What's that?" Jonas asked.

"To take everything he can away from Grayson. Look what he did to me. Psychologically, he's a monster, worse than Grayson. If you go after him, you'd best go with the intent to kill him. Don't even consider trying to take him into custody."

"Why not?"

Norm's eyes narrowed. "Because he's a desperate man. He'll kill everyone he can before he allows anyone to take him into custody. But you know what I'm betting?"

Jonas shook his head. "No, what?"

"He plans to find and kill you first since you're the man in charge. That's his objective and how his mind operates."

Chapter 46

Derek returned to the engineer department to see Bradbury standing beside Isaac.

"*Welcome back,*" Bradbury said.

Isaac's head spun in Derek's direction. "*Good evening, Derek.*"

Derek stared with surprise. Isaac was rebuilt and fully functional. "You've been busy, Bradbury. You already have Isaac in working order?"

"*If anyone should know how to reassemble one of us, certainly it would be easier for me than you, would it not? After all, I know how I function and what part connects to which component and so on. We have built-in repair manuals, too.*"

Derek smiled. Indeed the AI program was continuing to evolve. "Those Chinese robots are headed here."

"*I expected as much,*" Bradbury replied. "*Which is why we've been working on this.*"

Derek looked at the long metal table where the two robots were building something. "What's that?"

"*We've comprised a weapon capable of utilizing a strong electromagnetic pulse to incapacitate those robots,*" Bradbury replied.

"That'll work on them?"

"*Not certain. Do you have any other suggestions?*" Isaac asked.

"No."

"*Their exterior armor's resistant to lasers, fire, and metal projectiles,*" Bradbury said. *"That leaves nothing effective in your arsenal's weaponry to destroy them."*

Bradbury was right. They didn't have any weapon capable of destroying these robots except the turrets, but those were at the Phobos Crash Site and not hooked up. An EMP wasn't something Derek ever considered building. It held the potential to work though, but only if they were set it up in time.

"How close are you to completing this?" Derek asked.

"It's ready," Bradbury replied.

Derek marveled.

"You look surprised," Isaac said.

Derek nodded.

"You needn't be," Bradbury said. *"We are in sync with all of the computers. Information's readily available within a microsecond. We don't need to browse and search databases. We are databases."*

Derek studied the EMP device. It wasn't much larger than an average microwave oven, but as EMP devices went, it was a good-sized one. The electromagnetic pulse could short the circuits of any computerized mechanism within its radius, which presented problems in addition to its actual benefits.

Most pulse devices not only damaged computer components the weapon was aimed at, they tended to destroy similar devices in a full circle around it. This meant a human must fire the weapon. If a robot fired the weapon, it would be immediately short-circuited.

The locked steel doors that opened to the Martian terrain rattled hard. The sound came like a heavy hammer or battering ram being slammed against the door. A few seconds passed and the doors shook again.

Derek looked at Isaac and Bradbury. "Our enemy robots are here."

"YOU REALLY THINK Matthews will try to kill me?" Jonas asked.

Norm shrugged. "Who else is in charge? Any final decision that needs to be made is yours, isn't it?"

"Yeah. I suppose so. But I don't see how killing me makes him more powerful. There isn't much he can do. He's a fool if he thinks he can succeed with a revolt on Mars. We're a colony of Earth, reliant primarily on the shipments that Grayson sends. Without them, we die. We cannot support ourselves with food, paper supplies, and other necessities."

Boony brought up Matthews profile and picture on a large screen. "Here he is. We have two identification photos. The one on the right is after he underwent major plastic surgery to redefine his appearance. He looks nothing like the original."

Jonas looked at her. "Send his profile picture to the guards via their hologram visor screens. If anyone sees him, Matthews needs to be taken into custody immediately."

She typed quick commands on the keyboard. "Done."

Norm finished the bottle of water. "That's not all you're going to tell them, is it?"

Jonas frowned at him.

"He's *not* going to peacefully surrender to you. Grayson hired a woman to kill Matthews, but then changed his mind and decided it was more entertaining to ship Matthews to the mining pits. Now, he should've let the woman shoot Matthews between the eyes. Your best option, sir, is to issue a *kill-on-sight* order to your guards."

"I appreciate your advice, Mr. Schrader," Jonas said. "But let me handle this. I'd rather question him for information. If he's dead, I can't do that."

"Sir, guards will die. And if he finds you, he might kill you before you even get a chance to question him."

"Noted!"

Boony pointed to the screen. "I combed through the HR records of Grayson Enterprises and found when Matthews was hired. Grayson listed every sinister encroachment Matthews performed to undermine Grayson and how Matthews tried to steal top-secret property and scientific technology from the company. His I.Q. is substantially high."

"But not too high to prevent being captured," Jonas replied.

"He's no longer in custody, is he?" Norm asked with frustration.

Jonas glanced at Gary. "Take Mr. Schrader to the infirmary and have a nurse evaluate him."

Gary nodded. "Come with me, sir."

After Gary exited with Norm and the door closed, Boony said, "I think maybe you should take Norm's warning more seriously."

"Oh, Boony, not you, too?"

"Jonas, with everything that's happened, don't you think—"

Alarms wailed through the corridors.

"Shit," Jonas said. "What now?"

A red light flashed on a computer monitor, indicating where the alert had been initiated.

Mineshaft Fifteen.

DEREK STOOD near the steel doors. The robots battered with such fierceness they were denting and bending the metal inward.

Three engineers grabbed laser weapons and joined Derek at the doors. Isaac and Bradbury held their EMP device between them.

"Don't fire that at the door. You'll only incapacitate yourselves," Derek said.

Both robots tilted their heads at him with a silent stare.

Even Derek knew he had stated the obvious. *Of course, they'd know that!* He felt foolish for even addressing the comment.

The alarms wailed. Red lights flashed along the perimeters of the engineer department.

"What's that?" Adam asked. "Is that for this?"

Paul tapped his visor and then shook his head. "No. Mineshaft Fifteen. Should we go?"

Adam glared. "Do you need to ask?"

Derek shook his head. "This is top priority. We cannot allow the outside robots entrance or we're all dead."

"Then what's going on in the mineshaft?"

"My guess is the strange insects," Derek replied.

Paul lifted his visor. His eyes widened. "You mean the ones that put Roy into a coma?"

"Yes."

"Shit."

Derek shrugged. "I don't know which situation is worse. The Chinese robots or the poisonous insects, but I don't think it matters."

"Why not?"

"Because we're stuck in between."

Chapter 47

By the time Jonas and Boony arrived at the mouth of Mineshaft Fifteen, three guards were dead. They lay facedown on the gritty floor next to a stack of steel plates on a forklift. The insects were gone, but it was obvious what had killed the men. Little holes were encircled with blood on the back of their suits.

Jonas looked at two guards standing about fifteen yards away. "What happened? Where are the insects?"

One of the nervous guards walked to him. "They ran back down the shaft."

"How many?"

"I'm not certain. These guys were in the tunnel trying to cover the hole at the drilling machine. Next thing we know they're running at us screaming."

"You ran?" Jonas asked.

"What was I supposed to do? Only the flamethrowers kill them, right? I don't have one."

Jonas nodded. "You did the right thing. I thought the guards brought flamethrowers."

The guard pointed at the three dead guards. "They did. They had them down the tunnel."

Jonas shut his eyes and winced. "The flamethrowers are in the tunnel?"

"Yes."

Damn.

Jonas looked at the guard. "Barry, what were you doing when you noticed the attack?"

"We brought the stack of steel plates to seal off the tunnel."

"I'm afraid we're left with few options now. If the only flamethrowers we have are down there, the tunnel has to be sealed. Call together the architectural engineers and carpenters and seal it off. Make certain each plate's flushed with the next. Leave no gaps. Don't leave any holes where they can squeeze through. Should they reach the general population, we're doomed."

"What about the other prisoners down the shaft?" Barry asked.

"They're dead."

"You sure?"

Jonas nodded. "I'm quite certain, but if you'd like to go check it out?"

Barry shook his head. "No, sir. I'll take your word on it."

"Good. Get that corridor closed off as quickly as possible."

"On it, sir."

Jonas looked at Boony. "We need every available guard to work on sealing this opening."

"How can you do that?"

"I'm shutting down the mines until the corridor is closed. It's top priority. We cannot afford to lose more guards. From the miners' appearances, they could use a few days of rest."

"You think it'll take that long?"

He sighed. "I hope not, but I'd rather them do it right than rush it."

Boony nodded.

"The only downside is it might become harder to locate Matthews."

"Why's that?"

"What's to stop him from hiding with one of the prisoners while the other guards are here?"

"You think Norm's assumption's correct?"

"That Matthews will make an attempt on my life?" Jonas shrugged. "It wouldn't be the first time. But like I said in the office, Matthews would be foolish to take over the operations here. Grayson could starve us to death by refusing to send any shipments to Mars."

"Maybe, but if Matthews wants to hurt Grayson financially, all Matthews has to do is offer China or Russia or any foreign power free access to Olympus Mons in exchange for goods. They'd probably jump on such an opportunity."

"Perhaps. But those countries are far behind what Grayson possesses. Who's to say they could even successfully reach us?"

"Their robots did," Boony said.

"Yes, but that's not the same. They're not humans."

Boony nodded. "So should we focus on finding Matthews now?"

"I'd rather send all the guards and staff to Earth since we have no way to combat those insects."

A gentle, beautiful smile curled her lips. "I'd vote to do that."

"Between you and I, if the dangers continue to increase at this pace, I see nothing else better to do. We go home and tell Grayson where he can stick it. I doubt he'd find crew members willing to face these dangers."

"I've had my limit, too. I'll alert the guards to escort the prisoners to their cells."

"Thanks."

GARY WALKED Norm to the infirmary, but as much as Norm leaned against Gary for support, Gray was almost carrying the older man.

Gary was surprised Norm had survived the mining pit as long as he had. Norm's exhaustion was not surprising. Although he knew Norm, Gary was a patrol guard and never worked the pits. Otherwise, he'd have recognized Norm well before his chip malfunctioned. Norm's age should have keyed any perimeter guards at the mining pit that he wasn't one of the prisoners. But, with working conditions as they were, and the overall lack of enthusiasm, most guards didn't give a second thought to what should be a prominent warning flag until it was too late.

The receptionist gave Gary an odd expression when he led Norm to the desk. Prisoners were always taken to a separate office for medical treatment, not that there really was any specific need to have two offices. Most of the staff and guards were more comfortable not being around the prisoners, regardless of their Sleeper Chip implants.

Gary had spoken with other guards and female staff members at The Vortex. He found it comical how others viewed the chipped prisoners. While some were grateful to know the violent prisoners were fully controlled by the chips, they still couldn't handle being near the convicts. The prisoners' blank hypnotic stares unnerved people, like live storefront mannequins. Besides, no one liked being stared at. Several staff members expressed how they feared the prisoners might awaken and brutally attack them.

"Why'd you bring him here?" she asked in a disgusted whisper.

"Because he's not a prisoner. He's a guard."

Her facial expression became odder. "What?"

"You heard me. Now, he needs an I.V. to rehydrate and—"

"Sir, you're *not* a doctor."

Gary glanced at her name tag. "And you're not much of a receptionist, either, Cindy."

Her eyebrows rose, and her face flushed red.

"Look at him," Gary said. "We don't station prisoners this age. There's a reason for that. They could never keep up the pace."

"Then why was he mining?"

Gary frowned. "That's confidential."

"How's that?"

"You have any questions, ask Jonas. He's the one who told me to bring Norm here."

Cindy took a sharp breath. "Very well. Make him sit over there. A nurse will get him in a few minutes. What's his name?"

"Norm Schrader."

She wrote down the name on the sign-in sheet.

Gary headed to the door.

"Where are you going? *I'm* not touching him. Where's your CAM-L?"

"He's *not* a prisoner. He's not being controlled by a chip."

Cindy appeared nervous. "He doesn't have a chip?"

"He's harmless, Cindy. An exhausted old man who needs rehydration and a few days of sleep. If you don't believe me, search his name in the database. He's a guard. I need to report to Jonas ASAP. We have other urgent situations going on right now." Gary opened the door.

"Wait, Gary," she said nervously.

He turned and looked at her. She motioned him to come around the desk. "What is it?"

Cindy pointed at the computer screen. "That's the picture for Norm Schrader. Not this man you brought in."

Gary shook his head. "No, that picture's Steven Matthews. He swapped places with Norm *before* their shuttle reached Mars. He must've hacked the files and switched their photos. He's a dangerous criminal."

She tapped the computer screen. "So that's the real prisoner?"

He nodded.

She swallowed hard.

"What's wrong?"

Cindy whispered, "He was here earlier."

"Is he still here?"

She nodded. "I think so. He went back to talk to the doctors, but I never saw him leave."

Gary drew his laser pistol. "Where?"

She pointed. "Through that door. Dr. Lee's and Dr. Sheung's offices are back there."

"Stay here."

Chapter 48

Paul and Adam trained their rifles on the battered steel door, even though Derek stressed the weapons were useless against the enemy robots. They held their rifles like a child clung to a security blanket.

Derek's main concern was how they could possibly defend themselves. Once the Chinese robots broke through the doors, which seemed inevitable, Isaac and Bradbury could effectively use the EMP one time. In such tight quarters, his robots couldn't shield themselves from the electromagnetic pulse. To defend Derek, they must sacrifice themselves.

Were all eight robots at the door? If only one came through, forcing his robots to prematurely use the EMP, the other seven robots remained functional. The satellite map indicated four had reached the locked door. Were the other four in stealth mode outside the doors or elsewhere?

"Suit up," Derek said.

Adam gave a nervous glance. "What?"

"We cannot let them come through."

"Then why do you want us to suit up?"

Derek smiled. "We're taking the EMP to them."

Paul's mouth dropped. "Are you crazy?"

Derek shrugged. "If we wait until they've come through the door, they'll kill us. My robots have only one shot inside this enclosed area. The pulse will short them out, too. To us to survive, my robots need to be functional."

"Exactly how do you plan to take the weapon to them? If we open the door, it's no different than them charging through. They'll kill us," Adam said.

"Not if we plow through the door with one of these Caterpillar dump trucks. You two get into the cab of that truck and crash through the door. The impact should flatten the robots pounding on the door. It won't destroy them. It might not even dent them, but it should knock them down."

"What good does that do?" Adam asked.

"I'll back that flatbed truck through the door with my robots and the EMP on the bed and hope for the best."

Paul shook his head. "It's suicide."

"So is waiting."

Adam nodded. "That's true. Let's suit up. I'd rather die fighting than running."

"Me, too," Derek said.

GARY STOOD with his back pressed against the wall as he eased open the door that led to the doctors' offices. He tapped his earpiece. "Jonas?"

"Yes?"

"Matthews is in the infirmary."

"You're certain?"

"Affirmative. Heading back to where the receptionist said he was."

"Wait for backup."

"He's cornered where the doctors have their offices."

"On my way."

Gary glanced down the narrow hallway. Three doors lined both sides of the hall. Examination rooms. He guessed the doctors' offices were at the far end of the hall and to the left. At least that was what he determined by the hallway's shape.

Six rooms didn't seem like a lot for the number of people on Mars, but since the prisoners weren't able to complain about injuries, they seldom were examined. Most guards and staff members only suffered from one common ailment: severe hangovers.

As Gary neared the first door, he wished he'd asked Cindy if there were any patients in the rooms. The doors were open, and he didn't hear any sounds that indicated people were waiting inside. One room at a time, he edged to the door and turned with his gun aimed into the room. He found no one, so he pressed against the wall at the end of the hallway and listened.

Soft voices spoke around the corner.

He took a deep breath and dared a slight glance. One desk was visible with no one standing nearby. He read the name plaque on the desk: Dr. Lee. The end of the shorter hall seemed to open into a larger room. Was another desk or office outside his immediate view? He hated not knowing the office's layout because that meant he approached blind. One misjudgment could become a fatal mistake.

Gary was halfway down the short hall when footsteps scuffed the floor behind him. He turned and aimed. It was another guard. Carlton Baxter. Gary placed an index finger to his lips. Carlton nodded.

Gary motioned a finger above his head, indicating for the guard to head to the wall across the hall. As he stepped into the open and slid against the far wall, Gary stepped from his hidden point as well.

Matthews noticed them, drew his gun, and grabbed Dr. Sheung from behind, placing the gun to her temple. Matthews shook his head. "Lower your weapons and back away."

"You bastard," Sheung seethed.

"Matthews," Gary said. "Put your gun down and surrender. You don't have any way out."

Dr. Lee cowered to the floor, covering the sides of his head with his arms. He whimpered and whined like a frightened pup.

"Back away," Matthews said. "Or I kill them both."

Lee burst into tears, sobbing aloud.

"Matthews," Gary said. "This can be settled in a civil manner. It does no one any good if you kill the only two medical doctors we have on Mars."

"Then do as I said."

"We cannot do that."

Jonas eased into the hallway with his gun aimed at Matthews. Boony was only a few feet behind him with her gun drawn.

Matthews smiled. "Ah, welcome Jonas! Just the man I was hoping to see."

"You might rethink your enthusiasm," Jonas said.

"Grayson's marionette has a long set of strings." Matthews laughed. "Your reputation certainly precedes you, even on Mars. I've heard so many splendid details of your work with the CIA. Never thought a man with your background could become a hired hand of one of the most notorious men on Earth."

"It's a job, not a love affair."

Matthews smiled and nodded. "Nicely put, Jonas. As I understand it, Grayson's padded your fattening wallet quite well over the years. Surely you'd like to take that money and simply... *retire?* Rest those weary old bones of yours?"

"And what?" Jonas said. "Leave Olympus Mons in your hands?"

"Ah, now, that's a good trade. I can see how we both benefit from that."

"For a lot of good it'll do you," Jonas said.

Matthews tilted his head to the side and cocked a brow. He grinned like a spoiled child. "Now, see, *that's* where you're wrong. Taking Olympus Mons for myself would be for the greater good."

"How do you figure?"

"Grayson has more money than he could ever use."

"He's earned it."

Matthews shook his head slowly. "Are you so blind to the obvious, Jonas? Grayson's corrupt to the core."

"Your list of transgressions is quite high, too."

"Yeah... I've not always been the notable, God-fearing Boy Scout most mothers favor. But hey, who's perfect, right? Here you are on Mars, as the *grand* overseer of all these wonderful slaves Grayson tricked the U.S. government into handing over into his care. Slaves in the 21st Century. My, how *that* would make the perfect news headlines back on Earth?" He paused to chuckle and gave another smug smile. He raised his free hand and tapped the air to emphasize each word of the predictive title. *"Ex-CIA Agent Oversees Corrupt Tycoon's Mining Plantation on Mars.* You think that headline would snap the attention of every civil liberties and rights activist in the world? Of course it would. Never mind that these men are ruthless psychopaths unable to conceive the slightest notion of a conscience. You know how the media runs with things? You've seen it. They'd have a field day with *this*. You'd be in their tarnished spotlight for everyone to see. You're reputation would become as stained as Grayson's already is in society's view."

"I don't agree with how he's setting up Mars," Jonas replied.

"And yet, here you are. I doubt you're rejecting those wonderful monetary deposits in your bank account." Matthews released a slow, gentle laugh. "But looking around, where will you spend it all? Such a barren wasteland, isn't it? No steakhouse establishments. You like steak? Oh, a porterhouse would be *lovely* this evening. Some red wine. It's a shame there aren't any cows on Mars or vineyards, for that matter."

Jonas eyed Matthews sternly. "By your narcissistic attitude, I'd swear you and Grayson are twins."

"Dashing out insults now?" Matthews' eyebrows rose. "There's no way I find that comparison flattering."

"No, it's not meant to be an insult. It's merely my observation," Jonas replied. "I've worked for Grayson for many years. I see great resemblance in the two of you. Your report lists you as a pompous bastard."

"Does it now?"

Boony nodded. "Word for word."

"Well, I must take the time to read that. I'm sure Grayson has added all sorts of exaggerated animating details. Perhaps a wee bit of editing on my part could summarize my profile better."

Boony shook her head. "No, I think it's quite accurate like it is."

Matthews laughed. "My, aren't you a feisty one? Much like the *lovely* Dr. Sheung here. Powerful women definitely bring life to the workforce, don't they? Why just look how crumpled Dr. Lee is sitting on the floor."

Gary frowned. "Yeah, he's afraid you're going to kill him."

"Nonsense, he was like this when I first arrived. The moment Dr. Sheung and I began talking, he started shaking. You can see his fear of her whenever she approaches, which means she's one powerhouse of a woman. Don't let the small package fool you."

"She's a bitch!" Dr. Lee said, staring at the floor with his head between his knees.

Matthews tilted his head back in a hearty laugh. "This lovely lady? Really, Dr. Lee?"

Dr. Lee frowned. His jaw tightened, but he refused to look up. "She *is*. Always hostile. Makes work environment intolerable. She's a hate-filled bitch."

"Seems the job evaluations have come a bit early this year and not so favorable for you, my dear," Matthews said, staring at Sheung. He glanced at Jonas. "Perhaps, Jonas, we should come to terms, hmm? I'm tired of this useless stand-off. Dr. Sheung's probably getting a nasty ache in her back and neck. So, what do you say? Can we reach some kind of truce? An agreement? Something you find favorable. Something I find favorable, and poor Dr. Sheung can stretch out those achy neck muscles. What do you say?"

Chapter 49

Jonas aimed his gun at Matthews but was hesitant to fire. Gary was, too. For a few moments, Boony wondered why. From their distance, accuracy wasn't guaranteed without laser sights. Even though Matthews was taller than Dr. Sheung, he held and swayed her at such an angle that he prevented an easily targeted shot.

"What do you have in mind?" Jonas asked.

Matthews shrugged. "I want to be the man in charge of Olympus Mons. Nothing less will suit me."

"Why should we hand Mars over to you?"

"There has to be balance in the world, Jonas. I suppose now we'd have to say 'within our universe'. Wouldn't you agree? Nonetheless, you could call us both giants. Grayson's one on Earth, and once I take the reins here, I'll be the giant who opposes him."

Jonas shook his head.

"You don't like that analogy?" Matthews asked.

"Giants have been slain in the past."

"Must you *always* spoil the fun? Didn't you have dreams, aspirations?"

Jonas opened his mouth to reply, but Matthews cut him off.

"Of course you have. We all have. But Grayson failed to understand when he and I worked together how everything in life has a delicate balance. For a yin, there must be a yang. Where there's light, darkness soon follows. Good, evil. You see where I'm going with this?"

"You really like to hear yourself talk, don't you?" Boony asked.

"Oh, I suppose I do. It's been a long time, after all, since I've held such a *captive* audience." He glanced into Sheung's eyes when he said it. He kissed the top of her head. The soured expression on her face wrinkled even deeper. "So forgive me if I over-embellish due to your indulgence."

Boony glanced at Jonas and whispered, "Either reach an agreement with him or I'm going to shoot myself. I can't handle much more of this."

"As much as I dislike Grayson," Jonas said, "I cannot justify handing Olympus Mons to you."

"I had the feeling that would be your answer, so I'll throw out one more detail I was holding back. Quite a surprise actually. You like surprises?" Matthews reached into his guard uniform pocket and pulled out a CAM-L. "You're familiar with these devices. As warden and overseer, I'm sure you are."

Jonas nodded. "Yeah. So?"

"Without going into all the boring details," Matthews said.

"Thank you!" Boony said.

Matthews narrowed his eyes. He released an agitated sigh and continued. "On my journey to Mars, after I released myself from the Sleeper Chip's hold—"

"How'd you do that?" Boony asked.

"Look at you? *Now* you *want* details? Sorry, but that's a secret I *won't* bother boring you with." He glanced at Jonas. "Anyway, back to this. I spent a lot of time on my journey researching every aspect of these interesting devices. I discovered a code no one else probably ever noticed."

Jonas said, "What code?"

"See? A master code, if you'll pardon the poor pun, which overrides all CAM-Ls, including yours. By typing in a few numbers, I can release every prisoner from his or her control."

"That's absurd," Jonas said.

"It works. Want to see?"

Jonas shook his head. "No, I don't doubt that it works. But if you release these prisoners, they'll kill everyone, including yourself."

"Perhaps," Matthews said, tilting his head to the side and nodding. "But I'm not so certain they'll kill the man who liberates them. Even criminals hold some allegiance, especially if they know I can reclaim them with the simple touch of a button."

"Okay," Jonas said. "All you've told us is something that benefits only you and not the rest of us. What's in it for us?"

"Are you really going to negotiate with him?" Boony whispered.

Jonas ignored her.

Matthews pretended to look at a wristwatch. "My proposal, which lasts only a few minutes before I release the prisoners, is for you to choose ten people to return to Earth with you on the next passenger shuttle out. Only ten."

"Ten?" Boony asked. "Why not all of us?"

Matthews burst into fierce laughter. "That's too foolish a question to even consider answering, but I'll humor you. I can't possibly do *everything* here. I need staff and guards to keep operations running properly. Jonas can choose ten people to return to Earth. No more."

"That'll cause a riot," Jonas replied.

"Only if you make a public announcement, which isn't advisable given the current circumstances. I'm sure you, and that young lady you're fond of, can take a few moments to discuss it. As to the guards beside you, I'll double their earnings if they decide to stay and work for me."

Gary glanced wide-eyed at Carlton.

Boony placed a hand on Jonas' elbow, but he kept his attention on Matthews.

"How can we be assured you won't kill us after we let you go?" Jonas asked.

Matthews grinned. "I'll give you an hour or so to gather your belongings, board the shuttle in the landing bay, and we'll shuttle you out. Two hours should suffice."

"That's not a guarantee."

"Jonas, I'm a scientist and occasionally a shrewd businessman, but I'm *not* a murderer."

Boony looked at Dr. Sheung. The doctor's face contorted with rage. Boony met Matthews' gaze. "And what about your threat on her life?"

Matthews offered an innocent smile. "Simply a means of negotiation. I'm sure you can appreciate how a desperate man might resort to any means to be heard? Ah, no matter, a detail that might be missing in Grayson's file on me is how I've tried to use science to help the less fortunate. Before he attempted to kill me, I was working on a genetic rejuvenation drug capable of prolonging life and healing people of their ailments. Is that in there?"

Boony shook her head.

"Of course it isn't." Matthews sighed. "See? Grayson cannot stand someone else outperforming him. He won't share the limelight if it threatens to diminish his *supposed* prominence. Time's a wasting. Give me your decision."

"If we don't agree with you, you're going to release the prisoners?" Boony asked.

Matthews nodded. "Guaranteed."

"And yet, you're not a murderer?"

He smiled. "Consequences. But I won't be the one spilling blood. They will. Tick-tock."

"Sounds more like blackmail to me," she replied.

"Must you delay your decision over semantics?" Matthews asked.

Jonas turned and faced Boony.

"What are you going to do?" she asked.

Jonas looked fatigued. "Concede."

Her eyes widened. "Seriously?"

"You said earlier that you want to go back to Earth?"

"Yes, but not like this," she replied.

Compassion reflected in his eyes when he looked at her, like a father's affection for a daughter. Her heart quickened.

"Look at what's happening on Mars, Boony. Grayson's set so much contention on Earth that the Chinese sent killing robots to slaughter us. The steel wall the guards are building won't contain the insect hive forever. Those insects crave blood. Who knows what else we'll face?"

"You're certain the wall won't hold them?"

"Boony, this is a volcano. Fissures are everywhere. It's like setting sail on a ship made from Swiss cheese and trying to plug all the holes before it sinks. It's impossible. Eventually, the insects will find another way out or we'll accidentally drill another hole into their massive hive or perhaps into an entirely different colony."

"What about Grayson?" she asked.

"What about *us*?"

<hr>

HIS QUESTION MADE Boony flinch at the possible implications. He seemed to notice her uneasiness so he redirected his answer for clarification.

"You, me, Derek, and Gary. What about us?" Jonas asked. "Are you really concerned with Grayson keeping his hold on Mars more than our own lives?"

"No. Not really, but we'll be handing these prisoners and miners to another tyrant."

"True, but then it becomes Grayson's battle, not ours. And honestly, I cannot take much more stress. Interrogating Cain had me seconds from a heart attack or major stroke, not to mention—murder. I've not been that angry and worked up in years. But there's so much more than that. I came here to work, but not to die defending a gem-mining industry. Did you sign a work contract to sacrifice your own life for this corporation?"

She shook her head, but she wanted to say that essentially she had. All of them had because their contracts allowed Grayson to treat them like they were his property.

"Well, neither did I. Boony, I almost lost Derek this week. He could've died. I brought him here because I thought we'd be safer. It was almost a costly mistake."

"But won't returning to Earth place your lives into jeopardy again?" she asked.

"After this week, it's a risk I'm willing to take. There are plenty of places on Earth where Derek and I can change our identities and hide. But, if you think fighting Matthews is the better option, now's the time to tell me if you wish to oppose his offer."

Boony glanced at Matthews. When she noticed his guard uniform, she thought of Magnus. She smiled, remembering his massive body stuffed inside a overly tight uniform. She wanted to see him again. He was only a few weeks out into space. Leaving now meant she might be able to find him on Earth and assist him in clearing his name before he found himself on the wrong side of the law for a real murder.

Besides, she'd hate to die without knowing how his story ended.

She looked into Jonas' eyes and smiled. "Let's go home."

After she voiced her decision, an invisible weight lifted. Instead of worrying about Olympus Mons, she could turn her attention to a new future and what she hoped it could become.

Jonas lowered his gun and motioned the others to do the same. "We accept the proposal but only if you'll agree to one more thing."

"What's that?" Matthews asked.

"Don't inform Grayson we've left for Earth and you're in charge of these operations for at least one week."

Matthews nodded. "Splendid. Keep him in suspense. I like that. Certainly, I can do that."

He released Dr. Sheung. She turned and started slapping at him. Matthews caught her hands and gently pushed her to the side of the desk to get out of her reach. "You can take her to Earth with you."

Jonas shook his head. "No thanks. She wasn't part of the agreement. She's all yours since I can only take ten passengers."

Dr. Sheung gave Jonas a harsh glare.

Matthews looked at her with a slight grin. "You see? They don't appreciate you like I do."

Boony placed her hand on Jonas' forearm. "Let's get out of here."

Jonas nodded.

"You taking the offer?" Carlton asked Gary.

"Not if Jonas has room onboard for me," Gary replied.

"You're welcome to join us, Gary. And you, too, Carlton."

Carlton shook his head. "Nah, I think I'll see this out. Twice my pay? Hell no. I'd never find a job like that on Earth."

"Suit yourself," Jonas replied.

Boony smiled as they left the doctor's office. She'd try to get a message to Magnus. The excitement of leaving Mars was stronger than her original joy of traveling to the red planet. She couldn't wait to be on Earth. Of course, what the mind imagined was never what reality offered.

Chapter 50

Adam drove the giant dump truck through the steel doors almost as successfully as Derek hoped. The impact slung three of the enemy robots aside but didn't deter their pursuit of the truck. The steel doors landed on top of the fourth robot and the truck ran over it. The heavy doors weighed the robot down, but it attempted to crawl out from beneath them.

The problem Adam and Paul faced was staying out of the robots' weapon range. The heavy dump truck wasn't built for speed, and regardless of how much Adam pushed the accelerator, the truck wasn't moving any faster. The vehicle's breakneck speed was approximately twenty miles per hour on the rugged terrain.

Sitting in the flatbed truck, Derek looked over his shoulder as he prepared to back the truck over the fallen steel doors. Dropping the truck in reverse, he gunned the engine. Isaac and Bradbury held the EMP between them. He was thankful for the robots, but he still grieved over the loss of the other three, and feared losing these two once they fired the weapon.

Derek couldn't have predicted the actions the enemy robots would've done when Adam crashed through the doors. He feared the robots would ignore the truck and enter the engineering department. If so, his plan would've ended.

Instead, the robots pursued Adam's truck. Were they programmed to annihilate any human they encountered? Once they targeted a human with their heat-sensors, nothing deterred their pursuit. They had located him while he worked on the radio towers and from that moment on, they encircled him and tightened their radius to prevent his escape. Even after he hid inside the rocky debris for days, they remained outside, patiently waiting. Had Derek not driven away from the crash site, they'd have killed him. But even after driving outside their range, they refused to abandon their hunt. They tracked him like predators sought prey. They followed Derek to Olympus Mons much faster than he anticipated.

Red dust and silt billowed behind the dump truck. Three of the robots were close to catching it. For robots with heavier armor, they ran incredibly fast.

The EMP device wasn't overly large. Building one didn't take a lot of components. Pinpointing range and accuracy proved to be more challenging. Often an EMP allowed one pulse to be fired, which neutralized the device itself. He hadn't had the time to question his robots about the specific capabilities this device could perform, so he didn't know what might occur.

His flatbed truck backed over the pinned robot, pushing it deeper into the compacted soil.

Derek increased the truck's speed and was gaining on the two robots behind the dump truck. The third one was at the side of the dump truck and determined to reach the passenger door.

Bradbury and Isaac could easily take out the pair, but it was doubtful the EMP could strike the electrical components of the third one.

"Fire!" Derek shouted.

Bradbury flipped the trigger switch.

The two enemy robots dropped face-first on the road.

Derek came close to cheering until he noticed the EMP struck the dump truck, too. Its speed slowed rapidly.

The third robot hurried to the passenger door, grabbed the handle, and yanked.

"Damn," Derek whispered.

PAUL LOOKED AT ADAM. "Can't you get this thing to go any faster?"

Adam shook his head. "I'm practically standing on the pedal!"

"A robot's approaching my door."

"I see it, but there's nothing I can do."

Nervously, Paul looked at the side mirror. "When are they going to use that EMP?"

"I hope soon. I don't see the other robots, which makes me nervous."

"I'm more concerned about the one coming to my door."

The loud engine silenced. The dashboard lights went out.

"What the hell, Adam?"

"The EMP took out our engine and everything."

"Shit!" Paul said, as his door came open. Red eyes gleamed a moment before the robot grabbed his right arm and yanked him from the cab.

The bones shattered in his forearm and his shoulder popped out of place from impacting the hard abrasive rocks. He wailed. "Run, Adam!"

For a moment, Paul thought the robot was going to grab Adam, too, but it didn't. It walked slowly to him. Its robot face was that of a machine, but for some reason, it looked evil and menacing.

Paul tried to crawl backwards, down the steep embankment, and hoped to get away. But with only one good arm, his progress diminished. He cradled his broken arm to his chest to lessen the tormenting pain.

Useless lasers bounced off the robot's shielded back. It ignored them. Adam jumped from the passenger door and grabbed several large rocks. He threw them like baseballs. Two smacked and thwacked off the back of its head.

Nothing.

Paul swallowed hard. Tears welled in his eyes. He kicked his feet against the loose rocky debris, pushing himself a few more feet down the embankment. The robot advanced. Its heavy weight dislodged larger rocks, pebbles, and silt, causing a cascading array of turf to slide around Paul.

Paul kicked against the debris. With the added weight of the loosened stones, he descended ten feet deeper into the ravine. He glanced over his shoulder and noticed he couldn't slide any farther or he'd plummet several hundred feet to the jagged rocks below.

He didn't want to think about death, but it was the major intruding thought rambling inside his mind. Either the robot killed him, or he plunged to his death. Neither would be pleasant.

Two more rocks bounced off the back of the robot's head.

"Run, Adam! Save yourself."

"I'm not leaving you."

"How do you plan to stop it? There isn't any reason why we both should die. Run!"

The robot raised its laser arm and aimed at Paul's face.

Paul shoved his feet against the rocks and pushed. He experienced moments of peace as his body left the rocks and dropped through the air. He felt light, carefree. The screaming of his name carried with the rushing wind around his helmet. The robot's laser split open his chest piece. A fiery sensation rushed into his chest. It was the last thing he felt, and the last thing he remembered when he struck the rocky terrain at the bottom of the ravine.

Chapter 51

Derek stopped his truck behind the dump truck. He hurried from the cab and stopped beside his robots. "You only have one shot?"

"It's charging. It'll take a few more seconds."

"Adam! Get over here!" Derek said, waving his arm. He glanced at his robots.

"Two more seconds," Bradbury said.

Adam stood near the edge of the road. "Paul went over the embankment."

The loose debris cascaded around the Chinese robot's feet. The soil was giving way beneath it, burying up to its knees. Not concerned about the threat of falling over the cliff's edge, it raised its weapon and pointed at Adam.

"Hurry," Derek said to his robots.

Adam turned and ran.

Isaac and Bradbury turned the EMP toward the robot and fired. The robot stiffened. The current of rocks and silt carried it over the ledge.

Adam stopped beside Derek. He was panting and teary-eyed.

"I'm sorry," Derek said. "There wasn't anything we could do."

"I know. If he could've waited another minute, but he kicked himself over the ledge."

"That's four robots down, leaving four more."

Adam counted. "Four? Only three are deactivated. The other one is—"

"Under the doors. I know. Come on. I know how to stop it."

Derek got into the cab of the flatbed while Adam climbed in on the passenger side. Derek drove until he reached the doors and parked the truck on top of them. "That damn robot won't be going anywhere soon."

"Derek?" Jonas said via transmitter.

"Yes?"

"Where are you?"

"Shutting down the Chinese robots."

"What? You're outside Olympus Mons?"

Derek paused a few seconds. "Yes, sir."

"What the hell for? Get your ass inside now."

"We took out four robots, but we don't know where the others are."

"How'd you destroy them?" Jonas asked.

Derek smiled. "My robots built an EMP."

"That worked?"

"I told you there had to be a way to stop them."

"You never *mentioned* using an EMP. Get back inside immediately."

"I need to find the other four," Derek said.

"It's not our problem anymore."

"What?"

"You heard me. Get to your quarters, pack up whatever you wish to keep, and get to the landing bay ASAP."

"Why?"

"We're returning to Earth."

"To Earth?"

"Yes, Derek, *home.*"

"Can I take Isaac and Bradbury?" Derek asked.

"Sure."

"What's going on? Why are we leaving?"

"I'll explain the details when you get here. I can take ten people, so if you know someone that wishes to hightail it home, bring him with you. Once we leave, we're never coming back."

"Roger that."

Derek got out of the truck and slammed the door. They were only ten yards from the open entrance to Olympus Mons. Adam hurried beside Derek. His face displayed the sadness of losing Paul.

"That was Jonas?" Adam asked.

Derek nodded and walked toward the entrance. Bradbury and Isaac followed them. "Yeah."

"What'd he want?"

"Apparently, a few of us are returning to Earth."

"Really?"

"That's what he said. He's taking ten people. You want to go?"

"In a heartbeat."

"I thought you enjoyed it here."

"Overall I have, but other than work, there's not much to do. But what about our work contracts? Has this trip been approved by Grayson? Or is this like a military leave and we'll be required to return?"

"I'm not sure. My grandfather said he'll explain the details in the landing bay."

"I'm ready."

Derek slowed his pace. He was torn about leaving Mars. If he did, this final walk to Olympus Mons was most likely the last time he'd experience the Martian terrain. Of course, he was still young, so returning wasn't impossible. He understood his grandfather would never return to Mars.

What was so urgent for them to leave?

In many ways, Derek wanted to watch Mars' evolution. He wanted to see the first buildings and homes erected. He stopped outside the entrance and looked across the terrain. A part of him wept. He stooped and grabbed a handful of the reddish soil.

"Souvenir?" Adam asked.

"Yeah."

"*Derek,*" Bradbury said. "*Enemies overhead!*"

Derek glanced up. The other four robots materialized on the narrow ridge above the Olympus Mons entrance.

"Adam, watch out!" Derek dove to shove Adam out of the robot's aim, but wasn't fast enough.

The laser struck Adam's left leg, melting through his smart suit. Adam screamed, grabbing his blistered injury. He fell hard under Derek's late tackle.

"Dammit!" Derek said. He read the pain in Adam's eyes and remembered how badly the laser burn hurt. "Come on, let's go."

Isaac and Bradbury lifted the EMP and aimed at the ridge line.

Derek rose to his feet, pulled Adam up, and then slung Adam over his shoulder. He ran to the entrance. Adrenaline gave him extra strength and speed.

A second after Derek rushed through the entrance carrying Adam, one deactivated robot crashed to the road with a heavy clank. There wasn't time to glance back and evaluate the situation. Adam needed to see a medic immediately. He tapped his helmet. "Jonas! The other four robots are at the engineer bay doors. We need a team to seal the entrance or everyone will die!"

"What's wrong with the doors?" Jonas replied.

"We have no doors."

"What?"

"It's a long story. No time to explain. Adam's been hit and I'm heading to the infirmary."

"Negative. Don't take him there."

"Why not?"

"Bring him to my office. Now! We'll tend to him."

"Why not the infirmary?"

"I'll explain when you get here."

"Roger that."

DR. SHEUNG GLARED AT MATTHEWS. "How *dare* you put a gun to my head!"

Matthews chuckled and feigned complete innocence with an amused high-pitched voice. "I wasn't *going* to pull the trigger."

"They might have fired at you and shot me instead," she replied.

"If only..." Dr. Lee said, walking down the hallway.

"Where do you think you're going?" she asked. "Get back here."

"Let him be, doctor," Matthews said. "If he stresses any more, he'll have a stroke. You wouldn't want that, now would you? Then you'd be the *only* doctor here."

"You heard what he called me?"

"Of course. You should hear the names that have been hurled at me. The list has to be a mile long. When you're a hard ass, or in my case, a *brilliant* scientist, it comes with the territory."

She crossed her arms and continued glaring at him. She was small but the look made her appear to be an intimidating, towering beast.

"Come now, Kim, how long are you going to harbor a grudge?"

"How do you know my first name? I've never told anyone."

Matthews chuckled. "I know everyone's name at Olympus Mons."

"How?"

"Research. A bit of hacking. The details aren't important."

"Are you really going to let Jonas and the others leave?"

Matthews shrugged. "Sure. Why not? They're of no importance to me, and they're another set of thorns in Grayson's side."

"I thought you were going to kill them."

"Like I told Jonas, 'I'm not a murderer'. But I think you really *hoped* I'd kill them, right?"

The sour expression returned to her face.

"What have they done to you?" Matthews asked.

"Nothing. I don't like the way Jonas parades around, all high and mighty; and that girl with him, she's always kissing up to him."

Matthews grinned. "A shame you can't train Dr. Lee to act like that around you. But going back to your question, if they had continued to resist and hoped to have a new chip implanted in me, yeah, some of us would've died."

"You'd die rather than have a new chip?"

He shrugged. "After you died, of course."

She formed fists and gritted her teeth.

Matthews placed a gentle hand on her shoulder. "Kidding! My, Kim, you really need to loosen up a bit. It's no wonder people don't want to be around you. You have no bedside manner."

"What?"

"Oh, there's a huge list of complaints about you."

"Where?"

"Online. On restroom walls. Even a few were filed with Jonas. Has Jonas ever reprimanded you?"

"Never."

"See? Maybe he's not as bad as you think."

"Won't letting them go cause you more problems with Grayson?"

"Grayson's months away. Even if he sends forces to replace Jonas and the others, it allows me ample time to prepare. But I'm certain he and I will become best of friends, *chums*, after a few months of negotiating."

"He's going to try to kill you."

"I expect nothing less in the beginning, but in time, he'll understand I'm the best asset he can ever have. The budding of a relationship is often the hardest in the beginning."

Kim grinned. The expression was foreign to her otherwise harsh wrinkles.

"You like that? See, smiling isn't that bad after all, is it?"

"I don't think you know Grayson very well."

"I know him better than he knows himself," Matthews replied.

"So you're going to let Jonas and his crew leave?"

"I am. Without them here, we have less resistance and opposition in what I plan to accomplish. Once they're in space, they cannot change their minds and try to arrest me. Besides, their return to Earth will severely piss Grayson off, and whenever he's distracted by his anger, he becomes unfocused and even though he never admits it, he makes vital mistakes that render him vulnerable. I'll capitalize on his vulnerability."

Dr. Sheung shook her head. "You know what's strange?"

"What?"

"I never imagined Jonas would be one to back down so easily. He could've easily killed you and me, but he gave up? That's not like him."

"He's old and tired, Kim. Extreme weariness makes even the most savage dog lose its bite."

She frowned, deep in thought. "No, there has to be another reason why he's willing to leave."

"If there is, perhaps we'll find out soon. But, my bet is he's preparing to board the shuttle and leave, but just in case, we'll expect the worst."

Chapter 52

Boony hurriedly packed items from her office desk drawer into a box. She glanced over her shoulder. Jonas rummaged through several First Aid kits, preparing for Derek and Adam's arrival.

"Do you think Matthews is really going to let us leave Mars?" she asked.

"I didn't discern any dishonesty in his eyes."

"But he's a sociopath. You cannot tell if he's lying."

"Psychopath. And as a profiler, I've dealt with a lot of them. His target's Grayson, not us. If I read into his goal, he believes allowing us to return to Earth is more crippling to Grayson than if he simply killed us or held us hostage. His intent is to make Grayson suffer the most he possibly can. Grayson has a lot vested in me overseeing the operations here, but with all the added dangers, I'm too old to deal with it." Jonas laughed softly. "I'm not certain Matthews has really thought this all through."

"What do you mean?"

"The insects. The robots. The malfunctioning Sleeper Chips. His threat to release the prisoners from the chips if we didn't comply was a ruse."

"You think so."

"Boony, he's not foolish. He knows for him to control Olympus Mons is to ensure those prisoners remain mindless and controlled by the chips. He wasn't going to kill Dr. Sheung."

"How do you know?"

"He kept the safety on his weapon the entire time. He simply wanted us to listen to his rambling proposal, and I obliged him that much. But I cannot watch any more people I love get killed. I can only choose ten. I wish it were a greater number than that."

Jonas set out gauze, antibacterial ointments, tape, and scissors.

The door swung open.

Derek lowered Adam to the floor.

"Damn, I could've walked," Adam said.

"I was trying to get you here quicker." He looked at Jonas. "So tell me what's going on? Have the insects scurried from the tunnel?"

"Sit down while I tend Adam's injury, and I'll explain."

CLARK SAT IN HIS ROOM. He placed the three Martian insects on his bedside table and stared at them. They gently tapped on the glass, watching him. He didn't want to leave them in the security office or the science research lab because he feared they were absorbing information to report to their hive.

"Clark?"

He tensed slightly and turned with relief when he realized it was his handset receiver. He pressed the side button. "Yes?"

"This is Boony."

"What do you need?"

"Jonas wants you to report to the security office immediately."

"Does he want me to bring the insects?"

She paused for a few moments. "No. He says it's not necessary."

"Okay. Be there in a few minutes."

The insects tapped the glass harder, trying to get his attention. He glanced at them. "I'll be back soon."

They tapped softly.

Although he feared them, he was more fearful to disregard their presence and offend them. He shook his head as he thought about that and walked through the door.

Clark hurried to the hallway. The door hissed closed behind him. Jonas wanted to see him. Why? Until he had discovered the insects, Jonas seldom spoke a word in passing, and now the Space Warden kept tabs on him constantly. In a way, he liked the recognition, and being a part of the research team to access the overall decisions deind procedures made him feel important and necessary. Unlike the way Anna and others disregarded his job title and degree, Jonas sought him for possible solutions.

He increased his pace into a slow jog. A smile spread on his face until he rounded the next corner. A long line of mining prisoners approached. They were heading to their quarters. He looked at his watch. Their shift didn't end for several more hours. What was going on?

CAIN AWAKENED in the interrogation room. His back and neck ached from the angle he leaned while asleep. Radiating pain heated his face. His swollen black eyes blurred what little vision he had.

How much longer did he have to wait before Jonas returned? How many hours had passed? The room didn't have a clock. His stomach growled.

Cain hadn't sleep peacefully. He suffered odd dreams most considered nightmares, but they weren't as bad as what Jonas would do when he returned. Was the pain and punishment worth the pleasure he'd taken with Jessica? He didn't think the excitement of being with her could be properly measured. And even now, if he could do it all over, would he? He mulled that over for a few minutes and concluded he would, but he'd be more careful and cautious and not get caught.

He tried to recall his dream, and what in that dream had awakened him. It was an odd sound, almost like someone scraping fingernails down a rough panel of sheetrock with the coarse grains embedding under the fingernails. Chills shot down his back. It grated his nerves. But that wasn't the only disturbing sound. There was something more.

Cain closed his eyes, thinking. Trying to remember. His mind carried him to the house where he'd been raised. He hated his memories of that house and the things he suffered after nightfall.

Sweat covered him. He tried to jerk free of the memories, but they clung to him, trying to pull him under the Sandman's quicksand where he couldn't escape. He could only watch in horror.

From his bedroom, he remembered those sounds. No outside light. No inside light, either. Only the tapping on the glass. Tap-tap-tap. He was only a kid, but no other sound haunted him like the neighbor tapping the glass late at night.

Tap-tap-tap.

That same noise had awakened him only minutes before, only it wasn't in his dream. It echoed in the interrogation room.

Tap-tap-tap.

Cain's eyes flicked open. The sound was close. He looked at the door and then around his seat. He stood, but his handcuffs prevented him from reaching the door. He doubted screaming would do any good, either.

Shadows crept around him.

What the hell?

The tapping sounds continued, growing stronger, louder.

Cain glanced at the LED light on the ceiling. A strange shadow, long with six thin legs, moved behind the plastic cover. It scurried, tapping on the plastic. A second later, there was another and then another. More shadows danced, until the covering came loose and crashed on the table before him. Dozens of Martian insects scurried across the table and sprang on him. More crawled through the narrow opening around the overhead light fixture, dropping on the table.

He tried to wipe them off the table, but one bit him. Then another. He wanted to scream. Couldn't. He couldn't move or breathe. The heat of their poison flowing through his body lasted a few seconds.

Dozens of insect probes bore through his skin. He couldn't move or fight. He was helpless as the insects slowly drained his blood, devouring him. He couldn't help but think that not even Jonas could've planned a better execution. Death came painstakingly slow, in spite of his paralysis. Somehow Cain believed Jonas would've been pleased.

JONAS AND BOONY tended Adam's injury. It wasn't as bad as Derek's, but Adam complained about the severe pain. Regardless of size, a burn hurt and drew attention to itself, but deep laser burns were in a different class altogether.

Clark entered the security office. Anna was already there. Several guards stood along the wall. Jonas nodded at Clark upon his arrival.

After Jonas finished bandaging Adam, he faced the small group. "Our passenger shuttle is scheduled to leave in approximately an hour. I'll be aboard, and I've chosen each of you to accompany me to Earth. Now, the choice is yours if you wish to go or stay. But if you stay, you're not to tell anyone else about the shuttle's departure. Is that understood?"

Everyone nodded.

"Any questions?" Jonas asked.

One guard raised his hand. "Why are we leaving?"

"The dangers are beginning to outweigh our safety levels," he replied.

"You're abandoning your post as Head Warden?" another one asked.

"Not exactly."

"Who'll be in charge?"

"I'm not at liberty to say at this moment," Jonas replied.

"But someone will take your place, correct?"

"Yes. Someone else has been appointed." Jonas sternly looked around the room with the fierceness they recognized. "So I suppose the next question is, 'do any of you wish to stay?'"

No hands went up, but five of them exhibited total confusion.

A young female guard with a long black ponytail raised her hand.

"Yes, Heidi?" Jonas said.

"What about our contracts? Leaving Olympus Mons is a breach of contract, unless expressly written and approved by Grayson Enterprises. Do you have updated contract forms for us to sign?"

Others nodded with concerned expressions, too.

Jonas crossed his arms and narrowed his eyes. One by one, he went around the room, making eye contact with each individual. "There are no forms."

Murmurs and groans went through the group. Several shook their heads. A couple gave perplexed stares.

"Again, you're free to remain here," Jonas said. "Nothing changes if you do, and everything proceeds as normal."

Heidi gave a wry smile. "I'd head to Earth in a second, Jonas, but the breach of contract basically screws our lives over. It's a hefty penalty."

Jonas nodded. "I agree. It is. But I think there's a way around that."

"How?"

Jonas pointed to Boony. "Care to handout their care packages?"

Boony smiled. She held a tray with eleven small drawstring bags.

"Each bag contains thirty-five carats of uncut MarQuebes, which is far more than any of you will earn serving out your contracts."

Their eyes widened.

Heidi shook her head. "Jonas, that still doesn't cover Grayson taking our pension plans. The stipulation is that a breach of contract reverts back all the money he has reserved for us. On Mars, that doesn't mean much. On Earth, hell, that's the price of a nice house."

Jonas nodded and smiled. "Two words sum it up better: Class action."

"You really think that's going to work?" she asked.

"Knowing Grayson, yes."

"Why?"

"The last thing he wants is the negative publicity of a court trial for unfair work conditions and safety regulations. OSHA might not have any jurisdiction on Mars, *yet*, but since Grayson lives on Earth, he's still subject to all the labor regulation laws, regardless of where his employees are stationed."

Several guards opened the bags and poured the gems onto the palms of their hands.

Jonas asked again for a show of hands if any wished to stay. No one raised a hand.

"Okay, folks, dismissed. Pack up and be in the landing bay in an hour. Tell no one else about this. Understood?"

Each person nodded, passing him at the door.

Clark remained behind.

Jonas gave him a curious stare. "Question?"

"What about the three insects?" Clark asked. "Take them or leave them?"

"I'll leave that up to you. I know you want credit for the discovery, and without them, you have no proof. So if you decide to bring them, we'll find a secure place to securely store them. Okay?"

Clark nodded.

Jonas smacked Clark's shoulder. "Good. Get packed. An hour isn't much time."

Chapter 53

Senator Johnson stepped meekly into Grayson's office. Henry closed the door and stood between it and Johnson.

Grayson turned from his panoramic view of the ocean and faced the senator with a harsh glare. He crossed his thick muscled arms. "I've been calling you for days and you've not returned my messages. Is the state willing to release more prisoners into my care?"

Johnson cleared his throat. "The decision was a resounding, 'no.'"

Grayson studied the senator and detected a slight, amused smile, even though Johnson didn't meet Grayson's gaze. "You think this is funny?"

Johnson straightened like he'd been shoved, and he was trying to regain his balance. "No, sir."

"I'm under the impression you didn't put forth your best effort with the prison board."

"I told you when we last spoke they weren't going to approve more prisoners until you provided definite proof of their safety and a full report of their health statuses."

Grayson frowned. "You did little to sway them. You simply agreed with them and ridiculed my project."

"That's not true."

"Oh?" Grayson said.

Senator Johnson shook slightly.

"I have a recording of the meeting. Would you like to hear it?"

Johnson met Grayson's eyes then. "What? How?"

"That's not important. What angers me the most is how you come into my office and *lie* to me, while thinking their denial of granting me more workers was humorous. How long have you known me, senator?"

"A long time."

"Over two decades, right?"

"Correct."

"What has generally happened to anyone who has gotten in my way whenever I've needed something?"

Johnson frowned and fought not to look away from Grayson. "Don't threaten me, Boyd."

Grayson chuckled softly, but his eyes blazed with indignation. "Log reports show that your son is presently aboard one of my shuttles and on his way to Olympus Mons to inspect operations. Isn't this correct?"

Johnson stood silently.

"Isn't that correct?"

"Of course," Johnson replied. "That's his normal schedule. Nothing unusual about that. You even signed the contract approving his inspections to report to the government aviation committee."

"Since your recent backstabbing and obvious avoidance of meeting me, I've taken it upon myself to reconsider that agreement."

"What do you mean?" Johnson asked.

"I've revoked his contract, and now, it seems, your son's trespassing. I've placed an order for him to be taken into custody immediately, and he'll be held in a cell when he reaches Olympus Mons."

"What?"

"Turn your hearing aid up, if you can't hear me."

"I heard you. Don't dare threaten me, especially when it comes to the welfare of my son. You cannot expect to get your demands by holding my son hostage."

"Hostage?" Grayson shook his head. "No. He's trespassing, which means he's breaking the law. He's a criminal."

"You can't change the rules after he's already left Earth's atmosphere and thereby take him into custody. That's unethical and illegal."

"Illegal by whose statutes? The U.S. holds no jurisdiction aboard my vessels and certainly not at Olympus Mons."

Senator Johnson's face flushed crimson red. "Boyd, you cannot do this."

"Seems I already have."

"That's it! I'm reporting you before Congress and you'll be under full investigation. They'll scour every transaction you've ever made. I'll make sure of it."

Grayson grinned. "Your threats are pathetic when you don't have any ground to stand on."

"You've crossed the line."

"Capital punishment no longer occurs in the U.S., but on Mars, I make the laws. Did you know that I could enact a clause for any trespasser be put to death without prejudice? That'd be on the books for months before your son even arrives, so it would be valid and not considered a spur of the moment amendment."

Johnson's lips quivered. The crimson on his cheeks paled. His desperate eyes searched Grayson's for mercy that didn't exist. "Please, Mr. Grayson. Don't do this. I'm sorry for my outburst. If you can give me another month, I can approach the prison committee and make a new request? Or I could plead with a committee in a different state? But Joey, Joe's my only child. My boy."

"The outburst's not the issue," Grayson said in a low tone that almost resembled the threat of a growl. "However, your defiant disregard is quite problematic. I thought when you left my office we had an understanding. An agreement. Do you think I spout words to hear myself talk?"

"No," he replied in a near whisper.

"No is correct. I addressed *you*. Right where you stand."

Johnson nodded.

Grayson stepped around the side of the desk and sat on its edge, still crossing his arms. His gaze was colder than an angered cobra sizing up its prey. "You have one month to redeem yourself. One hundred prisoners, as I requested. You fail, and you'll suffer severe consequences."

Johnson nodded nervously. Tears moistening his eyes. His lower lip trembled so he bit it.

"You need to realize I have eyes and ears planted all over the world in the places where you'd least expect it. I've a good mind to release that video to the public of your imprudence. Not only would that put you in new light to your wife, but I also imagine it'll draw major skepticism by your counterparts in Congress. They're like jackals when they smell fear. Regardless of what side you're on in politics, there are always those within your own party that seek to remove the weaker. So *never* step into my office making threats. Understand?"

JOHNSON NODDED.

"I don't think you do. Take a look behind you."

Johnson's eyes widened. He turned and Henry pressed a 9mm to Johnson's forehead. The cold barrel caused Johnson to take a deep breath. The senator swallowed hard and piss ran down his legs.

Grayson had made threats before, but never had one of his men ever pulled a gun on him. Johnson's eyes crossed as he stared at the gun barrel. He noticed the wide grin on Henry's face and the gleam in his eyes. There was a hunger in the guard's eyes he'd never seen before. Johnson had never seen the man smile, and now, he wished he never had.

Grayson wasn't a part of any mafia, but he was something more powerful and far worse in Johnson's eyes. Johnson questioned his decision to challenge Grayson after all this time instead of acquiescing Grayson's demands like normal.

Henry lowered the gun and stepped aside.

Slowly, Johnson faced Grayson again. Johnson's pants legs were hot with wet lines running down the inside seams. The smell of urine lofted. Grayson seemed to ignore it and the slight puddle on the carpet.

"I can make you disappear," Grayson said. "Don't think I cannot replace you with another senator. Someone younger and more power-hungry. Someone with the incentive and ambition to get the job done properly. Now get the hell out of my office."

JONAS STOOD at the shuttle door until the ten passengers he'd chosen had boarded. Oddly, Matthews never made his presence known. Jonas expected him to at least make an appearance at the landing bay, but in a sense he was relieved Matthews hadn't.

Jonas boarded and motioned the pilot to seal the door. He took a seat beside Boony.

She smiled. She wore makeup and styled her hair. She didn't look like she normally did.

"I guess you made the right decision," Jonas said.

"Why?"

"You look happier and more relaxed."

Boony nodded. "I suppose so. What about you?"

"Ask me in seven months."

She laughed and then nodded at the seat across the aisle. "Is that Norm Schrader?"

"Yes. Since he wants to kill Matthews, Norm's safer returning with us. Matthews would probably have killed him if Norm stayed behind."

"Probably."

"Besides, Norm needs a lot of time to recover from working the mines."

Boony nodded.

"Clark came too, but only if I let him bring the insects," Jonas said.

"You let him?"

"Of course."

Her eyes widened. "Really?"

He nodded. "Not to worry. These three insects eat ferret food. Derek's two robots are guarding them inside an enclosed room."

"I suppose that's safer."

Jonas nodded. "Yes. I can't deny a young scientist's ambition."

"Even if it endangers the lives of others?"

"Unraveling the mysteries of science isn't always a safe endeavor. But since it's unlikely any of us will ever return to Mars, I wouldn't want Clark to spend the rest of his life living with the regret of abandoning his greatest discovery. If these insects prove to be the only docile ones to emerge from their hive, they can contribute a vast amount of understanding about their hive and possibly give us more information about the history of Mars."

"Do you think Grayson will attempt to steal Clark's glory?" she asked.

Jonas shrugged. "It's possible, if Grayson learns Clark brought them to Earth. I won't tell Grayson. I've told Clark not to say a word, either. Countless scientific laboratories in the U.S. would secretly grant him access to their labs for secondary recognition."

"Grayson will sue once the knowledge is released to the public."

"I'm serious about the class action suit, Boony. He's going to be so tied up in court and dealing with legalities about violating human rights, the insects will be the least of his problems. If justice is served properly, he'll spend a long time in prison."

Boony grinned and shook her head.

"What?"

"People like Grayson don't get time in prison. They seldom do."

"That's true some of the time, but Grayson has a lot of enemies in the political world and with the general public. There'll be protests. People will insist he pay for his crimes, especially family members of the prisoners."

Boony laughed softly. "And all this time I thought you liked Grayson."

"I had a job and a duty to perform. I did what I had to in order to protect Derek, but even I have my limitations. No amount of money can override my true morals. What Grayson didn't know was that I've kept a journal about what he's been doing, and what the prisoners have endured. I've kept thorough documented records of their shifts, sicknesses, and the use of the Sleeper Chips. The

Sleeper Chip technology is the most damning evidence against Grayson because their use violates all human rights."

"Is this why you don't mind allowing Matthews to take control of Mars?"

"Let the two egotistical monsters battle it out. I'm too fatigued to make this my fight, and with all the evidence I can present in court, making my exit now is in my best interest as well as everyone else's."

Boony marveled. "Honestly, I never viewed this to be your stance. You seemed so devoted to keeping order on Mars."

Jonas nodded. "Keeping order? Of course. Without the prisoners being under control of those chips, everyone's life was endangered. But, Boony, at the CIA I enforced the law and protected the innocent as best I could. That's something I cannot dismiss, even after I retired. I kept the best poker-face possible. Grayson was none the wiser."

"None of us were."

"Once Grayson receives news about Matthews taking over Mars, he's going to contact me."

"Will you talk to him?"

Jonas shook his head. "No, We're going to be in Hyber-Sleep in a day or so. We could all use the rest."

She smiled. "I was apprehensive about undergoing that on my flight to Mars. Other than the intense grogginess for the first few days after being brought out, I felt better. Will we be awakened each month like before?"

"I think that's safer."

"Probably. But with us asleep, Grayson will be pissed when he cannot talk to you."

"I know. I'd love to be a fly on his office wall when Matthews gives him the news."

Boony winced. "Oh, I imagine there'll be a great deal of outrage."

"Unlike anything another human has ever witnessed. But, there's not much Grayson can do about it from Earth. He has weekly ships arriving, but more are empty ore vessels than passenger shuttles. He might send more trained guards to Mars, but it'll take seven months for them to arrive. There's no way to predict exactly what Matthews will do. He might make good on his promise to release the prisoners from the Sleeper Chips."

"You think he'd be that desperate?" she asked.

Jonas shook his head. "It's not desperation. You've read each prisoner's records, haven't you?"

"A lot of them."

"These are people who have no conscience under a madman's control. Even if Grayson sent his best tactical squad, a lot of people will die. It's a no win situation for Grayson. If his soldiers kill the prisoners, he has less miners and less work. There's a greater chance his men suffer failure rather than succeed."

Boony sighed. "You've thought this out for quite some time, haven't you?"

"I calculate circumstances all the time. I never had any reason to until the Sleeper Chips began malfunctioning." Jonas turned slightly in his seat so he could look Boony in the eyes. "Can I ask you something and get an honest reply?"

She nodded. "Sure."

"You helped Magnus escape, didn't you?"

Boony looked away.

"Look, I'm not going to reprimand you or report what happened to Grayson now, okay? I want the truth."

"I did, but I had legitimate reasons for doing so."

"I imagine you did. I've worked with you long enough to know you never deliberately act outside the law. But, if I may ask, what about Magnus led you to believe that he's innocent?"

Boony pursed her lips. After a few moments, her eyes peered into his. "Some things in his records didn't seem right."

"You think he was framed?"

"The evidence against him was sketchy at best, and the warden in Texas was hasty to offer Magnus to Grayson for the prisoner-release Mars program. Even if Magnus was guilty of murder, he doesn't have a record like the others."

Jonas nodded. "I read through his file. I agree. Something wasn't right, and I can see why Magnus wouldn't return even with my assurance that I'd see he got a fair retrial. Hell, it'd be difficult to trust anyone after you abruptly awakened in the Martian mines. I'd take the first chance to Earth myself. But I have connections on Earth. If we can find him when we arrive, I might be able to help him. The problem is they have a few weeks' head start."

"I know. I've thought about that, too."

"One more question."

"Okay?"

"Did you let him into the gem vault?"

Boony's face flushed red. "I did. I'm sorry for lying about that."

Jonas shrugged. "I thought so and that's what gave me the inspiration for giving those gems to everyone aboard. Even if a class action against Grayson guarantees we keep our pay and pensions, they deserve an incredible bonus for their service."

"And their retreat?"

Jonas laughed. "With the dangers on Mars, we're all safer aboard this shuttle than on Mars."

"What about the Chinese robots?"

"According to Derek, Bradbury and Isaac used the EMP to knock all eight out of commission."

"So Matthews doesn't need to worry about them?"

"No, not unless there are more than eight. Their biggest nightmare are those bloodthirsty insects. I hope they've sealed off Mineshaft Fifteen. It doesn't guarantee they won't be attacked later, but it keeps them safe a little while longer." He leaned back in the soft seat, rested his head, and closed his eyes. "I suggest finding something to read from the computer library or streaming a good movie."

"I've been browsing. It's hard to make a decision. Are you going to nap?"

Jonas chuckled. "Let an old man have a few moments to rest. I think with the stress I've endured, I deserve it."

Chapter 54

Matthews sat watching the security cameras in what had been Jonas' main security office. A few minutes after the shuttle departed and the landing bay doors sealed shut, Matthews spoke over the intercom system:

"Greetings to my new employees. Let me introduce myself. This is Steven Matthews and I'm proud to announce that I own the operations inside Olympus Mons. Of course, the entire Martian planet is far more accurate since we're the only ones living on this otherwise barren wasteland.

"Now, you're probably questioning who I am, and what has happened to your beloved Jonas, and how I came to be the man in charge? Jonas decided he wanted to return to Earth for his well-deserved retirement, graciously leaving me in charge, which for some of you, that's good news. But the even better news is I will handsomely increase your wages."

Matthews cleared his throat without turning off the intercom. "Yes, Grayson was the one who gave your pay raises, which was quite seldom, was it not? At least according to your records... opportunities for promotion have been scarce. That effectively changes today. I'll reward you according to your work efforts. The harder you work, the more you get paid. Fair warning, however, is the opposite is far worse. If you piddle, twiddle your thumbs and half-ass do your job, your reward will be a Sleeper Chip implant. You'll join the mining force. Not exactly one of those 'gotta-have-it' types of jobs, now is it?

"With the recent changes in the seat of power inside Olympus Mons, I need qualified employees I can count on as my right hand men and women. Over the next few days, I'll handpick those worthy of such positions since we're undergoing a revolution of sorts. You'll find your surroundings hospitable, and to those Grayson shall send, and understand, he *will* send others to attempt to overthrow us, we'll make such rivals regret ever crossing the galaxy on behalf of Boyd Grayson. Those loyal to this empire shall benefit with untold wealth, and for those who oppose, you'll suffer a severe fate working in the mines, making the rest of us wealthier with each gem you unearth."

Matthews turned off the intercom for a moment and looked at Dr. Sheung with a smug grin. "How am I doing so far?"

"You sound worse than Jonas."

Matthews' brow rose, and he quickly formed a frown, shaking his head. "Really? I'd hoped to make a better first impression."

He punched a button and turned on the intercom. "As I understand it, the prisoners have been tucked away safely inside their cells for the night while the majority of you are busy sealing off Mineshaft Fifteen. I cannot stress the importance of constructing that steel wall within the next few hours. Those nasty critters have the capability to kill all of us. So when you've completed it, I'm giving everyone a paid two-day holiday. Drinks at The Vortex are on me."

Matthews gave a rather pleased smile to Kim and pointed at the camera footage from the outside Mineshaft Fifteen. The men and women working on the metal barricade cheered. Some jumped. Others high-fived. "See? They're rather happy with our new arrangement. With enthusiasm like that, you could fortify a city in a few short weeks."

"Not if they're all drunk," she replied.

"Most seemed to have already gone that route. Have you not ever been to The Vortex?"

"No."

"You should go sometime. Mingle. Loosen up. Let people see you and realize you're one of them."

"But I'm not."

"Come now, Kim, don't tell me you're *not* human."

She scowled.

"See? There's that look again. You hold it so often I wonder if it hasn't frozen on your face. No one ever makes wine with sour grapes. You know that, right?"

"The sad truth is I'm beginning to miss Jonas."

"Really? You're pining after him when we were just beginning to become chummy?"

Her eyes narrowed. "You and I will *never* be chummy."

"Oh, Kim, lighten up. I'm starting to think you hate people, and if so, *whatever* possessed you to become a medical doctor?"

"I do hate people. The medical field was not my choosing."

"No?"

"No. Father refused to pay for my education if I didn't become a doctor."

Matthews shrugged. "I suppose a career of splitting atoms to make nuclear weapons was out of the question? Your father opposed such a career, but that seems more your line of work. Creating ways to eradicate humans on Earth."

"Such does not have to be extreme, Mr. Matthews." The coldness in her voice matched the glint in her eyes.

Matthews smiled and laughed. "Ah, I suppose not, Kim."

Her countenance didn't change. "Do you know the difference between remedy and poison?"

"The dosage."

Kim gave a slight satisfied nod at his reply. "Do not forget who administers the cure on Mars, Mr. Matthews."

Before he could reply, she turned and left the security office, leaving him alone. After the door closed, Matthews shook his head and spoke to the door. "So Dr. Lee, I see *why* you fear her as much as you do. How she ever got past the medical boards is beyond me."

Matthews turned in the swivel chair and watched the workers constructing the steel wall. He had promised Jonas not to contact Grayson for a few days, and the temptation to ignore their agreement weighed on his mind with pure agony.

Oh, how he wished he could hear those long moments of complete silence after he gave Grayson the news. But since the two of them wouldn't be standing in the same room, he'd have to wait at least fifteen minutes for the reply. That silence was far too long. However, Grayson's sharp harangue afterwards would return with quite a vicious tone. He expected no less from the muscled bullying entrepreneur. No matter, the banter would be enjoyable, all the same. Grayson would wish he'd allowed Lydia to kill Matthews.

TWO DAYS LATER:

MINESHAFT FIFTEEN WAS SEALED TIGHT. The miners shoveled dirt into the shaker machines while the hungover guards could barely stand up straight. The rattling noises had to be unmerciful.

Matthews occasionally viewed the guards via surveillance footage for added amusement. He'd gladly paid their tabs, which they obviously abused, and now their temporary bliss was shrouded by agonizing dismay.

"Live and learn," Matthews said with a wry smile.

Matthews attempted to contact Jonas but learned they had entered Hyper-Sleep.

Grayson left Jonas a message at the security office, but Matthews didn't reply, even though he strained and fought the nagging urge.

Jonas must've placed everyone in hibernation to prevent Grayson from needling him for information about the welfare of Olympus Mons. Now Matthews could take the sheer delight in telling Grayson everything.

Sitting at the computer, Matthews scrolled through the list of numbers on Earth to contact via satellite. Several numbers for different branches and departments of Grayson Enterprises appeared on the screen. He scrolled through the list until he finally found the New York number where Grayson worked when he hired Matthews. Jonas had written a note to the side of that number, which explained that Grayson could only be contacted at the California number.

"Interesting," Matthews thought. He entertained the idea momentarily that he was the one responsible for making Grayson flee to the west coast. While it probably wasn't true, it gave Matthews a tidbit of information he could use as repartee to mock Grayson if necessary.

Matthews clicked the 'dial' button and waited for the computer to upload the recorder so he could dictate his first message for Grayson.

After the device connected, Matthews said, "My dearest Grayson. How are you doing, old chum? Matthews here, delightfully enjoying my newest endeavors as the Chief Overseer of Olympus Mons. *King* would be significantly dated, don't you think? You did a splendid job with the initial transformation of this massive volcano, but it's high time I made a few modifications of my own. It's a shame we couldn't meet in person, as I'd have *loved* to join you for a mug of freshly brewed Luwak coffee. It'd certainly take away the sting of listening to the constant BS coming out of your mouth. But no matter, understand that Olympus Mons is now in excellent hands, and nothing you should concern yourself over. I'm sure you have many questions about how I'm here and not in the mines, and I'm certain you're sorely disappointed by the outcome. Oh, and please give Lydia my regards."

He hit the send button and leaned back in the swivel chair with a broad smile on his face and a fresh cut cigar in his hand.

He mused. "If Hell existed, I'd find a way to take the throne away from the devil himself. But I suppose that's what I've done here."

Chapter 55

Matthews' message played through Grayson's earphone, which was almost like Matthews intimately whispering in Grayson's ear. He pictured Matthews' smug face as he emphasized particular words.

Grayson sat frozen at his desk. He was too stunned by his disbelief to allow his inner rage to register and kick in. The painful news felt all too similar to the worst nightmare he had ever dreamt, but this was real and *not* a dream.

He replayed the taunting message, listening keenly to the gloating undertones in Matthews' complacent voice. The arrogance was still there, like it had been when Grayson worked with Matthews, which was the biggest factor for why their personalities violently clashed. He detested the condescending timbre Matthews displayed, but in his self-blindness, he never realized the actual similarities he demonstrated to everyone else were identical.

A chill rushed through Grayson. The pit of his stomach ached from a sudden rise of desperation, which was an alien sensation for him. How had he allowed himself to be bested by his greatest enemy? The worst part about the situation was Grayson could've killed Matthews, totally eliminating any future threat from Matthews.

Lydia had pleaded for Grayson to let her carry out her hired assassination to kill Matthews. Instead, Grayson chose to keep Matthews alive as a miner on Mars to prove Grayson's ultimate power and control, thinking the lifelong punishment was better than death. But Matthews would never take any threat Grayson offered seriously now.

Even if he could find Lydia, Grayson knew she wouldn't travel to Mars to finish the assignment. If his speculation about her was correct, she had a new target instead. Him.

Grayson stood and looked out the window at the crashing ocean waves. Anger still hadn't stirred within him. Dismay rose instead. Everything he'd worked so hard to earn was slipping from his grasp. How could he possibly side-step these disasters?

Jonas was the one man he trusted above all others; someone he thought he could depend on to keep Mars in perfect running order. Now, Matthews was in charge? It didn't make sense. What happened?

His mind reflected over the details of the previous messages Jonas had sent. He vaguely remembered something about deadly insects being discovered in one of the mining shafts, but due to the circumstances with the Chinese and the Russians and Parks' wellbeing, Grayson simply shrugged it off as a joke when he should've known better. Jonas never teased or joked about *anything*. He certainly wouldn't have made up these insects.

Grayson rubbed his tired eyes. He had failed Jonas. Was Jonas dead? Whether he'd died because of the insects or at Matthews' own hand, it didn't matter. Either way, Grayson was at fault.

He took a deep breath and released a long sigh, wondering what to do.

Henry said, "Is something wrong?"

"Many things."

"Anything I can help with?"

Grayson shook his head. "No, but I'd like some time alone, if you don't mind."

"Not at all."

Henry turned, opened the door, and stepped out, closing the door behind him.

Grayson's eyes heated. Burning tears blurred his otherwise splendid view of the ocean. His chest tightened. He couldn't recall the last time he'd actually cried. Perhaps when he was a child? But his tears didn't come from sadness or remorse. They flowed due to his increasing frustration and loss of control. His massive ship had been the target of his enemies for quite some time. Now they were firing at it from all sides. His vessel was hemorrhaging and leaking from numerous holes. He didn't see any way to repair the damage before the coming tsunami tossed and capsized it.

He noticed his reflection in the glass, saw the tears meandering down his cheeks, and a new resolve kindled within him. Those moments of self-despair somehow tapped into his pool of indignation, which ignited strong enough to dry his tears in an instant. He refused to be steamrolled by anyone, and espe-cially *not* Matthews.

Regardless of what Matthews might believe about his reign over Olympus Mons, Matthews was a thief. Grayson could not idly sit by and ignore this hostile takeover. However, given the situation, he couldn't enact swift actions, either. None whatsoever. The only thing he might successfully achieve was to poison his enemy with kindness until he could adequately deal with the situation appropriately.

Grayson could cut off future supplies, but he couldn't afford to lose what was left of his guards and staff inside Olympus Mons. No, he must extend a pretentious olive branch to Matthews and hope to work out a mutual agreement about the Martian settlements, but how could he make it sound authentic? With all the sludge between them, Matthews could never trust him anymore than he could trust Matthews. The skepticism between them was a thick barrier. They were too much alike and despised one another equally. Even if they truly wanted to become friends, they couldn't. They'd constantly question the motive behind every action, good or bad.

Grayson returned to his desk chair and sat. He uploaded the message Matthews sent and clicked to reply.

"Steven Matthews," he said. He began his message without any hint of hostility and used an almost comical tone. "Is there not any way I can make you vanish for good? You're like an insect immune to all pesticides. Again, you've *proven* yourself capable of outfoxing me. You must tell me how you managed to free yourself from the Sleeper Chip. In addition to being a great geneticist, I recall that you're a technological genius, and since you have such skills, perhaps you could investigate what's the flaw in my current chips? If you look at Jonas' records, you'll see how these chips have malfunctioned.

"I know we've had our differences, Steven, and you know I initially hired Lydia to kill you. But I didn't allow her to carry it out. There are reasons why I prevented her from doing so. The world, even Mars, would be at a loss if your intellect was eliminated. You're knowledge is too valuable, and I have realized that almost too late."

Grayson chuckled softly. "So why did I have you implanted with a chip and placed in the Martian mines? Naturally, that'd be my first question if our positions were reversed. I simply needed to test you. You accessed my top-secret records when you were employed in New York. The computer records indicate you read the information about the Sleeper Chips. Since you knew about them, I wanted to test your abilities to the limit, and you succeeded in finding a way to counteract the chips or perhaps defect the one implanted in you.

"Jonas was a dear friend of mine and someone I entrusted to oversee Olympus Mons. But he was old. I couldn't expect him to continue much longer. Besides, you have ambitious zeal and youth on your side. I'm certain we can both set our past differences aside and work for a productive future together in building the Martian civilization. Can we not? I offer you a high percentage of all profits, and I'm in progress of obtaining one hundred fresh miners to transport to Mars. There's no need for this contention to remain between us. Let me know your decision, and we'll keep the machine running. *Our* machine. I won't stop shipping essential supplies, and those working on Mars will continue receiving their monetary deposits. What do you say? Can we be partners? I maintain the business side from Earth and you maintain the Martian activities? I await your reply."

Immediately after he finished the message, he found his stomach so nauseated that vomiting probably wouldn't have eased the rising bile at the back of his throat. He didn't believe Matthews would take the offer seriously because he had a difficult time placing the deal out in the open.

To his surprise, thirty minutes later, he received a prompt reply from Matthews.

Matthews chuckled softly when he began his diction. "And people here told me that you and I could never become friends. Boyd, I'd be happy to work from Mars, but I have a couple of things you must approve. I realize I'm not exactly in a place of making demands, but this isn't for me, but for the workers employed here. I've offered them twice their salary to continue onward. They've endured severe hardships with these strange insects in Mineshaft Fifteen, which *is* sealed by the way. However, we lost a few prisoners and some guards during the process. From the engineering department, I have news that might interest you as well. It seems you had an unsuccessful attempt by the Chinese to eradicate the general population of Olympus Mons. The robots the Chinese commissioned have been destroyed with Derek Walker's help. That is, if the Chinese only sent *eight*.

"Anyway, if you can have an attorney draw up an agreement between us, I'm certain we can become a powerful team in the world of universal science, keeping Mars for ourselves and shutting out the other countries on Earth. While in the past, our relationship and the competition between us has often been strained, we're finally working at the appropriate distance from one another where we can remain amicable. Worlds apart... so to speak.

"But no matter, we'll attend to things as they occur by not allowing our egos to get in the way of one another. Contention crumbles any empire. Never forget that. Instead of working against one another, imagine what we can achieve by working together. Awaiting your reply."

After the message ended, Grayson sat perplexed. Was Matthews on the level or was he feeding Grayson the same kind of BS Grayson had messaged him? The latter seemed more likely, but he imagined the possibilities if they decided to work together. Surely Matthews had weighed the same aspirations. As a team, they could become unstoppable.

The news about the destruction of the Chinese robots thrilled Grayson and lessened the chance for the Chinese government to destroy his encampments and delayed their hopes for a hostile takeover of Mars.

Grayson called his attorneys and gave them specifics for drawing up a contract with Matthews and offering him a lucrative forty percent cut of the profits made from the Martian exports. It was simply a formality, which might work or sour. Only time would tell. But keeping communication lines open between them allowed Grayson to figure out if he needed to take any extreme action in the near future to secure what he still considered to be his property or not. He didn't fully trust Matthews and the feeling was probably mutual. There were at a strange impasse without either knowing what to believe or what might happen next.

Chapter 56

Percival 3000 (Month Two)

CARTER BROUGHT Sylvia and Magnus out of hibernation a few days ahead of schedule. Despite the alien's stern warning not to awaken them early, he didn't think a few days would affect them or cause any damage. His reason for the premature wakeup call was due to his loneliness and fatigue, as well as his fear of the alien returning to harass and threaten him.

His direct disobedience to ignore the alien's request to undergo hibernation was possibly the reason she visited less often. In some ways he was relieved, but in other ways, he missed her seductive, mind-melding touch. Each time she entered his mind—with the exception of her last visit—intense euphoria overwhelmed him. But since he'd angered and displeased her, he worried about what repercussions he'd suffer.

During her absence, he decided *not* to kill Grayson. His increasing determination made him bolder. He awaited the opportunity to explain his reasons to her, even though he believed Grayson was guilty of numerous atrocities against humanity. He should be punished. Carter simply couldn't be the one to deliver the deathblow.

Had he put enough distance between them to prevent her from reaching his mind? He hoped so.

Carter brought Magnus and Sylvia some juice-filled pouches with attached straws. After he gave them the bags, a tingling sensation occurred near the base of his skull.

Within seconds, the touch flowed down his spine like jagged ice. Waves of frigid tendrils whipped and crept inside his mind, numbing him.

"I'm sorry," he said to Sylvia. He winced and placed his hands on his temples.

"What's wrong?" she asked, trying to stand. Her footing faltered. Magnus caught her by the arm, and eased her into the seat.

Carter rushed down the aisle and ran to the restroom.

"EASY, SYLVIA," Magnus said. "Gradually work at walking. Brace yourself with the seats, if necessary. Eventually, we need to being training on the exercise machines."

She nodded but turned with a worried expression. "What's wrong with Carter?"

Magnus sipped his juice, thought for a moment, and shrugged. "No idea. But, judging by the dark bags under his eyes, he never went into hibernation with us."

"Seriously? Why wouldn't he?"

"That's something you could ask him."

Sylvia took a long sip from her juice pouch. "I plan to. What's he been doing all this time?"

"Another question you'll have to ask him."

She looked into his eyes, grinned nervously, and lowered her head. "I know. Sorry."

"Don't be."

"How'd you sleep?" she asked.

"I feel well rested."

"Me, too. Did you dream?"

"Some."

Sylvia glanced at him. "A lot of my dreams were odd. They were frightening and didn't make sense."

"Mine, too. But I figure it's because our subconsciouses were probably trying to determine how to jar us awake."

"Maybe. If Carter didn't hibernate, how's that going to affect him?"

"I'm not a psychologist, but my guess is it could mess with his psyche. He might suffer stir craziness."

"I hope not. He's gone through enough as it is."

Magnus nodded. "I know, but bad stuff happens to everyone at one time or another."

A tear edged in her eye. "It does."

———

CARTER LEANED against the restroom sink. He splashed his face with cold water, but the coolness didn't lessen the searing pain inside his skull. The pressure continued building.

"No need to tell me," the female alien whispered. "You've changed your mind."

"Go away!" he seethed.

"I cannot."

"Please..."

"I *am* a part of you. You cannot escape me."

Carter's body convulsed with heavy sobs. "Please, don't make me kill Grayson."

"*You promised!*"

He wiped tears from his eyes. "I know, but my rage is gone."

"You can forget her so easily?"

"Who? Wanda?"

"Yes."

"I've not forgotten her."

"But you're refusing to avenge her death."

Carter shook his head. The slight movement made him wince. "The loss has eased, but I've never stopped loving her."

"And if I die, will your want for me perish, too?"

Carter stared into the mirror. The alien's image materialized behind the glass. He refused to make eye contact, more out of spite than fear.

"You wish to forget me after all your begging and urges to have me close again?" she asked tenderly.

Pain throbbed inside his head. His ears burned. His cheeks and neck were hot. His heart thudded hard against his ribs. "I'm in so much pain."

"Would you like me to take away the pain?"

"Please?"

"Always wanting but never compensating."

His jaw tightened. He stared into the mirror and gnashed his teeth like a rabid dog. "Everything has a price, doesn't it? These headaches never occur unless you torture me with them. Forget it, okay? Kill me instead. At least I won't have to endure this any longer."

"I could never kill you," she said softly.

"And yet, you torture me."

"You torture yourself by resisting, by fighting me."

"No. That's not true. Lately, all you've done is torment me."

She was silent a few moments. Finally, she said, "Close your eyes and relax. Allow me to rid you of the headache."

Carter obeyed.

"Relax."

"I'm trying," Carter replied. The pain pounded, striking the base of his skull over and over, forcing him to shut his eyes tighter. His stomach sickened from the intensity of the nerve-grinding headache. He fell forward, catching himself against the sink. His knees buckled, but he refused to fall. Hitting the floor would cause him to lose consciousness.

"I'll take your pain, but this makes twice I've rescued you. You've done nothing in return. You think that's fair?"

"I'm sorry."

"Reconsider my first proposal."

The pain increased, forcing him to double over the sink in pain. "If you're going to torture me, just kill me."

"I've done nothing, yet."

Carter opened his eyes, but the building agony caused whirling darkness to cloud his vision. In seconds, he'd pass out, if it persisted. Was she being honest about *not* causing further pain?

"End it!" Carter snapped.

"Reconsider?"

A sharp humming rang in his ears, more annoying than a hungry mosquito on a hot summer night. Misery sought to swallow him inside its cloud of darkness. Between the harsh spike-like pains throbbing through his skull and the increased droning, he feared and welcomed death at the same time. He thought of Sylvia and Magnus. Would this alien harm them after she killed him for disobeying her demands? He feared she might, but he wasn't certain.

"Okay," Carter surrendered in a near whisper. "Stop the pain, and I'll do it. I'll kill Grayson."

He opened his eyes when a hand touched the top of his head. The mirror showed nothing. No hand, nor the alien. Warmth spread from her touch and seeped through his brain. The pain stopped. Breathing became lighter, easier, and the heat in his cheeks and neck dissipated. The sickness in his stomach lessened.

Carter wanted to thank her, but her reflection in the mirror vanished. The slightest pulse of her energy was gone, too. Relieved, he thought about Sylvia.

He washed his face and dabbed it dry with a paper towel. Composing himself, he left the restroom. Being with Magnus and Sylvia he found comfort and security. But each time he sat in solitude, the alien took advantage and worked to regain her control over him. This was why he awakened Magnus and Sylvia. He didn't dare shun their companionship for the remainder of the trip.

Perhaps by telling them about the alien, they'd help him. No. The alien would probably find that unacceptable and unleash her wrath on them. He must keep his silence about her for the time being. However, if her threats escalated, he'd *need* to tell them about her.

CARTER WALKED to where Magnus and Sylvia sat.

"I'm sorry," he said. "I shouldn't have run off like that."

"What's wrong?" Sylvia asked.

"You looked to be in a lot of pain," Magnus said.

Carter nodded. "I've had horrible headaches off and on during the last few weeks."

"You didn't set up your chamber, did you?" Magnus asked.

Carter shook his head.

Magnus frowned. "Why not?"

Carter glanced nervously at him. "Fear, I guess."

"What's to be afraid of? You're a doctor. You've been in one of these chambers before."

"I know, but things are a lot different than they were on my trip to Deimos."

"Why's that?" Magnus asked.

Carter shrugged. "To be asleep an entire month, especially when we're wanted, is a frightening thing."

Magnus frowned. "Why? We're not on Mars. Earth's still months away. We're the only ones on this ship. It's not like Jonas will send a police shuttle and pull us over."

Sylvia laughed and quickly covered her mouth. "Sorry."

Carter suppressed a grin and sat down. "While that's true, you forget one thing."

"What?" Sylvia asked.

"The ship's controlled by computers. We go to sleep and Grayson could take over the controls."

"That's doubtful."

Carter shook his head. "No, it's not."

"What makes you think that?" Magnus asked.

"When you're able to stand, I'll show you."

Magnus used the armrests for support and pushed himself to his feet. He placed his right foot forward, placed weight on it, waited a few seconds before pressing more weight, and then he raised his left foot. He stumbled but not enough to fall. He balanced until he was certain his leg muscles could sustain him. He wasn't as weak as he feared he'd be when they awakened.

After a few gingerly steps, he was confident he could walk. He turned and offered his hand to Sylvia. She clasped it, and he pulled her up. Unlike him, her legs were weaker, but after a few steps with Carter's assistance, she walked down the aisle to the pilot's cabin.

When they reached the computer control panels, Carter pointed.

"Should we be traveling this fast?" he asked.

Sylvia frowned. "That's not the speed I programmed the shuttle."

"No, it isn't."

Magnus faced Carter. "Did you do this?"

"No," Carter replied nervously. "Why would I?"

"You tell me," Magnus said, towering over the doctor.

"You can trust me."

"Can we?" Magnus asked.

"Magnus," Sylvia said. She put her hand on his arm. "Calm down."

"Sorry," Magnus said, rubbing his eyes. "Still a bit of a hangover feeling, which is making me irritable, but I still have a difficult time knowing you put us to sleep and stayed awake."

"I explained why," Carter said softly.

Sylvia typed numbers into a distance calculator. After a digital readout, she said, "Someone definitely tampered with the propulsion engines. We're going to get to Earth a couple of months earlier than we expected."

"In a way, that's good," Magnus said. "But the problem with it, is Grayson knows more precisely *when* we'll get there. So, Carter, I apologize. Grayson's probably the one that changed our velocity."

Carter waved his hands. "I know about medicine, viruses, and bacteria. A little bit about computers, but engineering is *not* my specialty."

Magnus' eyes narrowed as he stared into Carter's eyes. Carter appeared nervous but never broke their gaze. Magnus smiled. "The next time we go into hibernation, you'll be the first one to go to sleep."

The suggestion made Carter visibly uneasy. Magnus watched him for several seconds. "You really fear being put under, don't you?"

Carter nodded.

$$\overline{}$$

Chapter 57

$$\overline{}$$

The Next Day

SYLVIA PULLED UP HER PANTS. Carter hurried and zipped his pants before reaching for the restroom door. She grabbed his hand and turned him to her. She frowned but evident hurt was in her eyes.

"Is that it?" she asked.

"What?" He seemed confused by the question.

"I'm a quickie for you? After nearly a month of you being isolated and alone while Magnus and I were in hibernation, all you want is to... *relieve* yourself and walk away?"

"No, Sylvia."

Her eyes moistened and her cheeks flushed red.

"I'm sorry," he said, leaning closer.

Reluctantly her lips met his, but no passion came in his kiss, but even if it had, the moment for her was gone, ruined. She pushed the door open and brushed past him.

"You okay?" he asked.

"I'll be fine."

"I'm sorry."

"Yeah, you said that already." She glanced back. A lost, hurt expression hung on his face. For some reason, Wanda and her death came to mind. Sylvia winced. Of course, *why* didn't she even consider that? Was Carter still grieving over her? She bit her lower lip and closed her eyes, feeling like an idiot. "Carter, I'm sorry, too. I wasn't thinking. Is... is what we did too soon?"

"What?" He appeared confused.

Sylvia swallowed hard. "After Wanda?"

Carter shook his head. "I've not dwelled on her the past few weeks. Maybe it's bothering me at a deeper level."

"Is that why you didn't want to hibernate?"

He shrugged. "It could be part of it. Really, there's a lot on my mind, and I can't discuss this right now."

"You're sure I didn't do anything wrong? You know, rushing us?"

"No. Don't be silly."

She forced a smile. "If you need more time—"

"Sylvia, please, it's a combination of a lot of things. Not this. Certainly *not* this or what we have."

"Okay. I don't mean to press you, but talking about problems with a friend can help. Is it Grayson, too?"

"Yes, him, what we'll do once we get to Earth, and maybe it's sleep deprivation." His eyes narrowed. He looked away obviously angry and frustrated.

"If you need to talk sometime—"

"There's *nothing* to discuss. Okay? Please, give me a few minutes to think." He refused to make eye contact.

Sylvia nodded, fighting tears. "I'll wait for you at our seats."

She hurried down the aisle.

CARTER SHUT the restroom door and locked it. He ran his hands through his hair and rubbed his eyes, trying to gain enough courage to look in the restroom mirror. Having sex with Sylvia in the restroom was a huge mistake. The alien always visited him in this restroom. She probably watched everything.

He pumped sanitary hand cleanser from the wall dispenser and coated his hands, rubbing them together vigorously. Still, he feared glancing into the glass.

While his fling with Sylvia was quick and pleasurable, the sensations could never compare with the alien's, which he truly longed to experience again.

He took a deep breath and faced the mirror. "I'm sorry. I shouldn't have done that with Sylvia."

The alien's face didn't materialize like before, but he felt her presence. "No, let her believe you love her."

"Why?"

"So you can fulfill your duty to kill Grayson."

"She has nothing to do with that."

"No, but continual isolation from her draws more suspicions toward you and what's hidden inside your briefcase."

Carter thought about that. He agreed, but was troubled she wanted him to become more intimate with Sylvia. "What about you and I?"

"I'm always with you."

"But I need more than you inside my mind. I need what we shared on Deimos when you healed me. Our physical bond. That's what I miss. I've never experienced such ecstasy before."

"You fulfill your oath, and you'll have that again. Make certain Sylvia believes you're with her. She and Magnus mustn't ever learn about me."

Chills ran down his arms. She *was* a threat to the others. When her presence faded, he washed his face.

MAGNUS SAT with Digger curled on his tree trunk of a leg. The ferret slept with its belly exposed and appeared to have a slight smile on its face.

Sylvia approached. She looked distraught and near tears.

"What's bothering you?" he asked.

"You mind if I sit beside you?"

"Your company's always welcome."

"Thanks. I moved things too fast with Carter."

"You seemed to have taken a quick liking to him."

Sylvia shook her head. "No. I've been attracted to him since I met him nearly a year ago. But since he was stationed on Deimos and I was assigned as a landing bay mechanic on Mars, I never allowed my feelings to show. He seldom came to Mars though."

"What's the current problem?"

"His mind's overwhelmed by everything. I think he still hasn't gotten over Wanda's death."

"Losses like that take time to heal."

"I understand that," Sylvia said. "I do. But if he'd let me, I'd do anything to love away his pain."

"You still have a few months of space travel to learn more about one another. If it's meant to be, trust me, it'll work itself out."

"And if it doesn't, these will be the most awkward months of my life."

"That's true, too, but try not to focus on the possible downside, okay?"

"I'll try not to."

Carter came down the aisle holding his briefcase. She crossed her arms, frowned, and refused to glance his direction.

"Look," he said, "I'm sorry for being short with you."

Magnus cradled Digger in his hands without waking him and stood. "I'll give you two some privacy."

"Men can be regular jerks. You know that, right?" Carter said.

"He's right about that," Magnus said, heading down the aisle.

Carter feigned a smile. "Look, I was the biggest asshole ever a while ago."

"You think?" Still she refused to look at him.

"I never meant to disregard your feelings. You've every reason to be upset and hate me, but—"

"I don't hate you. I'm very turned *off* by you right now. In my mind, I had one image of you and us together as a couple, but you burst that thin fantasy bubble."

Carter nodded. "I know, and I'm truly sorry. You don't have to accept my apology or even forgive me. I don't deserve someone like you."

"You're right. You don't."

Carter turned to walk away.

Sylvia grinned and glanced at him. She pointed at the seat beside her. "Sit."

Puzzled, he met her eyes. "You're sure?"

"How else are we going to work through this unless we talk?"

"You're right." He set the briefcase in the aisle beside the seat. "I'm sorry."

"No more groveling. As much as a woman hates men who are dicks, we also hate pleaders and whiners. It's still a long trip to Earth. Let's figure out where we stand and proceed. If we're not going to work as a couple, at least we should get that out in the open right away."

Carter stared at her and smiled. "You'd really consider being with me after how I acted?"

"Let's start from this moment forward, okay?"

He shrugged. "Okay."

"I'm willing to overlook your actions as you internally struggle to cope with your losses on Deimos. I'll put it as that, for now, unless it happens again, and then, no. I'm not going through any further disrespect."

"Fair enough."

"I know little about you."

"What would you like to know?" he asked.

"What brought you to Deimos? I know you're a medical doctor, but why travel to Mars and Deimos, *besides* the money. I know Grayson pays quite well."

Carter smiled. "The money's good. No argument there. But I've worked in the most destitute places on Earth when I was with the Peace Corps. I've watched people die from horrible diseases, and I couldn't do anything to save them. I helped develop vaccines, but in the time it takes to manufacture a vaccine for an epidemic, hundreds of people would be dead. Grayson offered me this job, and I liked the idea of working on a new frontier. I figured diseases would be at a minimum. The last thing I expected was for everyone on Deimos to die. After all, the people here were healthy until exposed to a new virus we cannot vaccinate against."

She read the sincerity in his eyes, his facial expressions, and the gentleness of his voice. She slid her hand into his. For the next few hours, they talked about their likes and dislikes, hoping to find their compatibilities to lay the groundwork for their relationship.

Chapter 58

Matthews sat in the security office, reading through the legal proposal Grayson's attorneys sent via computer. An amused smile spread across his face. The offer was quite lucrative, but nagging at the back of his mind was whether the agreement would legally stand or not.

He shook his head. He and Grayson were two superpowers, like reigning Kings of distant lands. History on Earth was compiled of numerous enemy kingdoms reaching peaceful agreements in order to work together. How had they ever managed to do such a thing? Did one ever fully trust an enemy?

Grayson never seemed a man who'd bow to any sort of hostile takeover, but in this case, did Grayson have any choice? What repercussions was the tycoon planning, if any? Was the deal legitimate?

Matthews was willing to take the chance. He electronically signed the document and returned it to Grayson. The difficulty of working across the galaxy from one another was not being able to sit together at a conference table. Matthews was an expert at reading most people's flaws and tells. But setting up a webcam between one another wasn't successful, either. Everything between Earth and Mars was relayed via satellite transmission. At best, there was a six-minute delay, but on average, one might wait fifteen to twenty minutes for the response to arrive.

Dr. Sheung sat beside Matthews with her hands folded atop the table. Her sour expression hung on her face.

Matthews shook his head when he glanced at her. "I can never tell if you're in a good mood."

"You sought me for what exactly?" she asked, ignoring his statement.

"Your counsel."

"Why me?"

Matthews shrugged. "You contain a wealth of information. Your disdain for society in general almost equals mine. And I expect your dislike of me will never smooth over, so I respect you'll harshly tell me what you think without holding back."

"But you have no way to know whether I'll always tell you the truth."

"There's that as well." Matthews grinned and nodded. "But in your better interest, I think you're more apt to be honest with me than deceptive."

"And why's that?"

Matthews chuckled. "Because if anything ever happened to me, *you're* not capable of running this encampment. You know this, even though you might not want to admit it."

Sheung offered a grim smile. "No argument from me. Being a dictator has never been in my interests. I feel you wish to keep your enemy close by your side."

"Kim," Matthews said softly, shaking his head. "Why do you think I view you as an enemy?"

"Why else call me here about your negotiation with Grayson?"

"Counsel, as I said. Grayson's every bit as cunning as I am. While I find his contract easily acceptable, I have to wonder his true intentions."

"And he, you," she replied.

"See? *That's* the kind of counsel I seek."

"I'm certain you had already come to that conclusion."

"I had. But it's good to have a voice outside my own head to validate my assumptions." He slid a paper across the table to her.

"What's this?"

"A list of possible candidates I've chosen to have as high ranked officers and advisors. Most of these I think you should know, so I'd like you to choose six of them that you believe could benefit us in our Martian government."

"Us?"

Matthews grinned. "You're the head physician here. I consider you to be one of the top members of our regime."

She stared at him in silence for several moments.

Matthews chuckled and shook his head. "Kim, you've no level of trust at all, do you? Not even a smidgen. My, I hope in time you'll risk letting go of your overly suspicious nature. While I know that can be difficult, there are benefits in keeping acquaintances that lie on the fringe of friendship."

"You consider me a friend?"

"Not yet. The possibility's there, however small. Anyway, you give that list a thorough inspection and get back with me about your choices and why. Okay?"

She stood with the paper in hand and nodded as she headed for the door. After she left, Matthews formed a bridge with his fingers and rested his chin. Many ideas formulated inside his brilliant mind on how to make the most of his uncertain relationship with Grayson. Perhaps he should take the advice he'd given Dr. Sheung? He shook his head. Even he wasn't that foolish.

SYLVIA SAT in the pilot's seat. Carter and Magnus stood to the side.

"According to the computer's calculations," she said, "since someone sped up the propulsion acceleration, we should arrive a month earlier than originally planned."

"That soon?" Magnus asked.

She nodded.

"The sooner the better," he said.

"I agree," Carter said.

Magnus glanced at her. "Other than a little agitation, I didn't have any problems from undergoing the hibernation process, did you?"

Sylvia shook her head. "No. I did fine. Of course, we've no idea how Carter would do."

"Sorry."

Magnus gave him a stern stare. "This time, we're hooking you up first."

Carter sighed heavily but didn't argue.

"So we could hibernate at least four more months and awaken when we're about a month out?" Magnus asked.

Carter nodded. "We could, but if we're going to hibernate, I'd suggest we awaken two weeks out."

"Why so late?" Sylvia asked.

"In all honesty, I'll sit and worry about our entrance regardless of the amount of time we're asleep. I'd rather it be two weeks' stress than an entire month," he replied.

"He has a point," Magnus said. "I could do that provided no one increases the engines' speed again."

Sylvia shook her head. "It's highly doubtful they would. We are at the maximum level required by the safety regulation committee. If increased any higher, we could suffer severe engine malfunction or even worse. To Grayson's credit, he's never had one shuttle fatality or any crashes. He won't risk that over us, especially since this is his coveted shuttle."

"Okay," Magnus said. "Carter, get the controls set. I'll set up the pet feeder and water system for Digger. I hate leaving him alone that long. He did fine for a month. Not sure how he'll do for four months."

Carter said, "It's problematic for all of us."

"You don't think our hibernation chambers are safe?" Sylvia asked.

"I'm sure they are. Should we have any major malfunction, including loss of power, the computers bring us out of hibernation. There's a backup generator that kicks on." He smiled, still a bit nervous. "But like you mentioned, Grayson's never lost a shuttle. No one's died during hibernation."

"Good to know," Magnus said. "Let's prepare ourselves. It'll be nice to know that when we've awakened, we'll have less than two weeks before returning to Earth. Lots to do then."

Carter nodded. His eyes grew distant, deep in thought.

                                    Chapter 59

4.9 Months Later

MAGNUS AND SYLVIA sat in the shuttle cabin watching the control panel.
Carter was in the restroom. The Percival 3000 was less than half a day from
entering the Earth's atmosphere. Digger slept curled on Sylvia's lap while she
read different computer readouts.

Magnus looked over his shoulder at the cabin door. He sighed. "Carter
spends a lot of time in the restroom, doesn't he?"

"I know," Sylvia said. "He likes to sort through issues in private."

"Is that all he does?" Magnus asked with a naughty grin.

She blushed. "Since we came out of hibernation, I think I've kept him too
busy for him to want to—"

"I'm teasing." Magnus laughed deeply.

"I know. I can't ever get him to open up with me about what's bothering
him."

"I worry about him. His mental stability isn't quite on the right edge."

"You've noticed that, too?" she asked.

He nodded. "Yes."

"He frightens me at times."

Magnus looked into her eyes. "Why? Has he ever hurt you?"

She shook her head. "No. Nothing like that. But his mind drifts off for long periods. When he goes into a trance, it's nearly impossible to shake him out. Once he snaps back into reality, he doesn't remember zoning out."

"I checked his hibernation chamber's settings after he went under. He scheduled himself for the same amount of time as us this time. The deep sleep might have somehow affected his brain, but I've seen him slip into trances before then. Is he taking any medications? Being deprived of them during hibernation—"

"He's never told me about prescriptions. But I think he's still upset about Wanda's death, but he never mentions her. Of course, I don't because I don't want him to regress. But, you know, I thought my affections could make him forget that pain. If she's not the reason why he's still having issues, what is?"

He shrugged. "I've no idea."

"Nor do I," she said softly.

Magnus rubbed his hands together while watching the curve of the Earth. Seeing the world from above, the oceans, the landmasses, and the puffy white clouds, was more vivid than he could describe with mere words. The world truly was a spectacular sight to behold. Much more colorful than the rusty Martian landscape.

He couldn't wait to be on Earth again. He sorely missed the freedom he once had before his setup for murder and before he awoke on Mars. He looked away from the panoramic screen. Sylvia's eyes filled with tears. Her hope to heal Carter weighed hard on her.

"Pain of loss is hard for some to overcome," he said softly. "Some never get past it, regardless of how much others try to help."

"I know," she said. "I'm too optimistic. A bad flaw, I suppose."

"No, it isn't. As long as there's hope, you have something to strive for. Once hope disappears, death knocks. Without hope, we've no reason to live."

Her hand stroked Digger's neck while she sat deep in thought. She probably didn't even knowing she was doing so. It's why people needed pets. Comfort. Therapy. Her free hand wiped her eyes before more tears escaped and streamed down her face.

"Any idea how long before we land?" he asked.

"Within eight hours? We should circle the earth a few times as our acceleration slows."

The cabin door opened. Magnus and Sylvia turned. Carter smiled. Concern crossed his face when he saw Sylvia's red eyes and cheeks.

"Is everything okay?" Carter asked.

She nodded. "I'm fine."

"You've been crying."

"I'm homesick and a bit worried about how we're going to land without Grayson or the authorities taking us into custody."

Carter frowned and stepped to the console. "You no longer have control over the shuttle to land?"

"I've not actually tried."

Magnus stood. "See what you can do."

She typed commands into the ship's computer. A red alert flashed on the console screen: PROGRAM ERROR!

"Dammit!" she said.

Digger uncurled and blinked away sleep before dropping to the floor and crawling to Magnus.

"Sorry, Digger," Sylvia said. "Oh, I upset him."

Magnus picked up the ferret. "He's okay."

Carter watched the message flash. "What's wrong?"

"I have no control at all now. And we're entering the Earth's atmosphere."

She typed in different commands. The computer responded with the same message.

Magnus leaned closer. "Nothing works?"

Sylvia shook her head. "No. I don't understand it, either. The systems were never overridden. But now, every command is being rejected."

"Odd," Magnus said. "Keep trying."

"Okay. Not sure it'll change anything."

Magnus looked at Carter. "Come with me."

He walked out of the pilot's cabin and Carter followed.

"What is it?" Carter asked.

Magnus walked to a storage closet and slid the narrow door open. He reached inside and handed two parachute packs to Carter one by one. "We're left with few options."

"There's no way we can jump."

Magnus nodded with a serious stare. "Eventually, yeah, we'll have to."

"Aren't you afraid of heights?"

"Scared to death. But I'd rather face that fear than get arrested before I fulfill a promise I made to myself and others when I went to prison."

Carter nodded. "I agree with you on that."

"Good."

A few minutes later, Magnus and Carter returned to the shuttle cockpit with the parachute packs. They set them on empty seats.

Sylvia growled with frustration, glaring at the computer screen, as if it understood her anger.

"Still no luck?" Carter asked.

"No. Grayson has full control. I'm locked out. I've tried every access code and override command I know."

"Where are we programmed to land?" Magnus asked.

"The landing strip in California right alongside Grayson Enterprises."

Carter's jaw tightened. "Shit! There's no way to alternate the landing coordinates?"

"I'm afraid not. He's going to take us into custody the minute we land."

Magnus smiled and pointed to the emergency parachutes. "We got these."

Sylvia still didn't look hopeful. "At the rate of speed we're traveling, there's no way to jump. The wind shear will rip us apart."

"See if you can find a way to lower the shuttle's speed once we descend into the final landing orbit," Magnus said. "That's the safest way for us to escape."

"I can try, but I can't promise anything."

"We need to decrease speed once we're closer to California. Preferably a state or so away where we won't be noticed exiting the craft," Magnus said.

Sylvia forced a smile. "You only have two chutes."

Carter grinned. "There are several dozen back there."

After an hour of reading the computer archives, Sylvia turned and a smile crossed her face. Great excitement rose in her voice. "I've discovered something."

Magnus leaned forward in his seat. "What?"

"They never got access to the shuttle computer until we entered the Earth's orbit. I mean, they sped up our acceleration to make our arrival a couple of months early. But they never took full control of the ship until a few hours ago."

"Why'd that change?" Magnus asked.

"From what I've noticed, as long as Hyber-Sleep is initiated, massive firewalls prevented anyone outside the ship from gaining access. This is probably a safety preventative to keep terrorists from taking control of a vessel while the occupants are asleep. Virtually unmanned."

"But we came out of Hyber-Sleep yesterday," Carter said.

She nodded. "I know, but here's the kicker. There's an eight-hour time gap after we awakened where the computer still maintains that firewall, which expired. But the way the program's set, once we entered the atmosphere, there's less likely a chance anyone should remain in hibernation. So—" she glanced at Carter.

"Are you implying we initiate the Hyber-Sleep again?" Carter asked.

"Would that work?" Magnus asked.

Sylvia shrugged. "I'm not certain, but it wouldn't hurt to try."

Magnus stood. "And what if it does? What can you do?"

"Provided I can get back partial control, I should be able to slow the shuttle enough so we can jump at a lower elevation without injuring or killing ourselves."

Magnus looked at Carter. "Is it even possible to activate Hyber-Sleep without one of us being hooked to the I.V.?"

Carter bit his lower lip while he thought. "Not sure. Let's go see."

Magnus handed Digger to Sylvia. "You want me to stay here?"

"For now, Sylvia," Magnus replied. "Keep reading those archives. If those firewalls pop back up, give us a shout."

"Will do!"

Magnus followed Carter to the passenger compartment. For the first time in several hours, he was more optimistic they'd actually touchdown on Earth without Grayson capturing them.

Carter studied one hibernation seat. He looked at Magnus momentarily and then knelt beside the chair arm where an occupant normally rested their arm for the I.V. hookup.

Magnus watched but held his silence. Carter's eyes gleamed while he went deep in thought. Magnus didn't want to break the doctor's concentration because this wasn't something Magnus could figure out. He hoped Carter did. Quickly.

"While I might be able to hook the I.V. unit to something to start the flow, I don't know how we'd mimic a person's body temperature."

Magnus said, "Hmm."

"Wait!" Carter said, snapping his fingers. "I'll be right back."

Carter rushed past Magnus toward the restroom.

"Not again," Magnus whispered.

But instead of Carter entering the restroom, he continued running to the storage rooms farther back. Out of curiosity, Magnus followed.

Standing outside the storage room, he watched Carter grab an empty catheter bag and a thermometer. Carter smiled as he hurried out the door and into the restroom. Instead of closing the door like the doctor normally did... *for hours*, he left the door open so Magnus could observe.

Carter turned on the faucet. "This might be impossible to do, but if I can get the water to the proper temperature, it should last long enough for the computer to activate the Hyber-Sleep and, I hope, trigger the firewalls back up."

Carter handed the thermometer to Magnus. "If you don't mind?"

Magnus frowned. "What do you want me to do?"

"Hold it under the water until we adjust it to body temperature. Then, I need to figure out a way to syphon water into the bag."

Several minutes passed before they acquired the proper water temperature.

"That's *too* warm," Magnus said.

Carter shook his head. "By the time I get everything set up to activate the hibernation program, the water's temperature will probably drop a few degrees."

"What happens once the water cools down *below* body temperature?" Magnus asked. "Won't the computer alert the system that there's a problem?"

"Hopefully by that time, we'll be ready to jump. However, our body temperatures drop significantly during hibernation mode, so it won't send out an alarm right away."

"Okay," Magnus said. "That's good. But what about brainwave detection?"

"There's a mode I can use to turn that off."

Carter carried the catheter bag of warm water to a hibernation seat. He gently tucked the I.V. needle into the bag at an angle that prevented the water from leaking. There was enough empty space in the bag to allow the I.V. nutrients to flow without rupturing the bag for at least for a few hours.

After pressing a few buttons and setting the Hyber-Sleep program, the computer activation system glowed green.

Carter smiled. "It worked."

Magnus clasped Carter's shoulder firmly and patted his back. "Great job!"

"Firewall's up again!" Sylvia shouted.

Magnus released a huge sigh. Everything seemed to be turning in their favor.

Chapter 60

After the long agonizing months of waiting, the day had finally arrived. Within hours, the Percival 3000 would be landing. Grayson was prepared. He hated thieves.

During the past few months, his Martian settlement thrived, much to his surprise. He'd anticipated Matthews to sever their contract agreement, but instead Matthews somehow increased the mining output with fewer miners than Jonas had during the past year.

Because Matthews had proven his loyalty, not necessarily to Grayson, but to the prosperous industry, Grayson readily deployed the next hundred miners on their journey to Mars. Senator Johnson held true to his word and negotiated with New York's Prison Committee to recruit one hundred prisoners for the Martian Work Release Program. New York readily offered to hand over an additional two hundred miners by the end of the year.

The announcement pleased Grayson and Matthews.

To prevent a potentially massive riot from the established prisoners—controlled by possibly defective chips—Matthews designed a flawless Sleeper Chip, far more superior than Grayson's chips. He sent the design to Grayson. After Grayson approved it, he sent it for immediate production.

Grayson smiled and crossed his arms, watching the ocean. Things were looking good.

His earphone rang. Grayson tapped it. "Yes?"

"I've lost control of Percival 3000," Thomas said.

"What? *How?* You told me you hijacked back the command."

"I did."

"Then what happened?"

"The firewalls have reestablished their control and blocked my access."

"That doesn't make any sense," Grayson said.

"Actually, it does."

"How?"

"The hibernation system was reactivated."

"What? No one in their right mind would induce sleep on themselves now. Not when they're preparing to land!" Grayson bit his lower lip. A drop of blood swelled and dripped. He grabbed a handkerchief and placed it to his mouth.

"My thoughts exactly. Somehow they must've figured out the hibernation program prevents outside computer takeover."

"Override the system," Grayson mumbled, holding the handkerchief to his bleeding lip. "Get control of that shuttle."

"I'm working on it."

"Be quick. They should land in less than an hour."

"I know."

"Keep me posted."

"Roger that."

MAGNUS, Carter, and Sylvia put their arms through their parachute straps, pulled them over their shoulders, and tightened the harnesses. She watched the elevation monitor.

"This is our final orbit," Sylvia said. "The shuttle's beginning its descent."

"Where are we?" Carter asked.

"Almost over Texas."

Magnus grabbed the handle of the emergency door. "I need to jump *now*."

"No," Sylvia said, shaking her head. "It'll kill you. Our altitude's still too high."

"Grayson will certainly kill us if we don't jump," Carter said.

Magnus held the door handle. "How soon before I *can* jump?"

"Nevada?" she replied. "I really don't know. But the descent is steadily dropping. Shouldn't be too much longer."

Magnus said, "It'll have to do."

Sylvia typed in commands. On the large screen a grid came up that detailed the ship's speed and the amount of altitude descent. Beside the door was a sign indicating the emergency procedure and at what speed and altitude occupants could safely jump, should it ever become necessary.

Magnus read the sign aloud. "Once we fall to twelve thousand feet and slow enough, we can jump."

"Not much longer," Sylvia said, watching the monitor.

Magnus unzipped the front of his suit and slipped Digger inside. He zipped it back up. He gripped the emergency handle.

"Now!" Sylvia said.

Magnus didn't hesitate. He grabbed a metal bar beside the door and shoved down the handle. The door dislodged. A strong sucking force pulled at them. He held tightly and used his body to keep Sylvia from being dragged past him and out the open door. The rushing air roared.

"See you on the ground," Magnus said, looking over his shoulder with a broad smile.

He jumped.

Sylvia gripped the metal bar Magnus had held. Her knuckles whitened as she clung to it. Her insides quaked as Magnus vanished. She held her breath and wanted to scream.

"I can't do this," she said, shaking her head. "I can't."

"Yes, you can."

"No way. I'm going back to the cabin."

"You can't, Sylvia," Carter said. "We're too close to succeeding. I'm not going to let you. Let me get this briefcase situated and then, you hold my hand. We'll jump together."

Carter tucked the briefcase into his safety harness and then fastened Velcro security bands around it to prevent it from being blown out while they dropped to the Earth.

Sylvia nervously looked at Carter.

Carter took her hand in his, rubbing her knuckles with his thumb.

"You ever do this before?" she asked. She clutched his hand. Her nails dug into his flesh.

He nodded. "It was a requirement I had to perform before Grayson would hire me."

"Really?"

Carter nodded with a reassuring smile.

"Why would he require that? I never did, but I'm a prisoner."

"Grayson wanted his doctors, nurses, and techs to make at least one jump from a plane because it tested our determination of how much we wanted to work for Grayson Enterprises."

Sylvia shook her head. She was pale and turning green. "I'm glad I'm a prisoner. Only, I don't know what I'm supposed to do?"

Carter pointed to the pull ring. "Okay, after we jump and stabilize, I'll let go of your hand. When I do, pull that ring. That releases the chute and it'll jerk you up."

"Oh, God."

"You don't have to be terrified by this."

"And how can I not be?"

Carter smiled. "Do you like amusement park rides like rollercoasters?"

"No. Not really. Merry-go-rounds make me sick."

"Seriously? Okay. Remember when I let go of your hand to yank that ring. You got it?"

"I hope so."

"Here, put these on." He handed her protective goggles.

She nodded and adjusted them to fit her face.

He kissed her cheek. "You'll do fine."

He stepped ahead of her at the door. Her fingernails dug even deeper, almost drawing blood. He pulled her beside him. The terrain below seemed so far away. Roads were lines. Buildings looked like miniature toys. Thin layers of clouds resembled strange wisps of white smoke.

Carter stepped forward and pulled her with him. Together they plummeted out the door.

She screamed.

He grabbed her other hand and pulled her so they faced one another. The air rushed and roared around them. The pressing air made the skin on Carter's face ripple. His smile looked deformed. Sylvia couldn't stop smiling. Adrenaline pulsed through her, and she found herself laughing. It was the oddest sensation to be falling through the sky. She actually enjoyed the rush.

She was less worried about their descent now. Falling rapidly together, she no longer held any fear. Of course, it was too late to be afraid. This was an activity where she didn't get a second chance should her chute fail.

Carter released her hand. He motioned to his ring like he was tugging and then he pointed to her.

She tucked her chin against her chest to see where the ring was on her parachute. She looped a finger around through the ring and then she looked for Magnus. He was much closer to the Earth than they were. It appeared he was nose-diving to descend faster, and he still hadn't pulled his chute.

She pointed. "Look at him!"

Magnus' chute opened, yanking him upward quickly.

"We need to pull the rings, okay?" Carter shouted.

She nodded.

"Are you ready?"

"Yes."

She crinkled her nose and smiled before pulling the ring. Her chute yanked her into the sky above him and she screamed. But not from fear. She liked the lofty feeling and the excitement that tickled her stomach. Sylvia's heart pulsed with excitement. She felt exhilarated from the adrenaline rush.

Two seconds later, Carter yanked his cord.

They floated carelessly on the winds, exchanging smiles.

Chapter 61

Grayson stood at the end of the tarmac, awaiting the shuttle's arrival. Dressed in silver and black fatigues, his small army of guards stood with their weapons drawn. With recruited mercenaries working for him, he was at a better advantage than relying on the government or local authorities about the theft of his shuttle. He'd keep matters in-house and exact his own judgment.

Thomas stood beside Grayson and held a small computer tablet. Grayson shoved his muscled hands into his pockets. The approaching small shuttle seemed to grow larger as it descended from the sky. His jaw tightened.

"The hibernation is still activated?" Grayson asked, never looking away from the shuttle.

"Yes."

"I suppose we should check it out. If they're asleep, they'll be easier to take into custody, but be prepared for a trap."

The shuttle slowly touched down, skidding slightly as the tires met the pavement at the far end of the runway. Giant chutes pillowed out behind it, drastically slowing the shuttle. The small army readied their weapons. Their hardened faces were determined like Grayson's.

When the shuttle came to a complete stop, a motorized staircase was driven to the side door. Two guards rushed up the stairs. They opened the door and headed inside.

Grayson and Thomas walked along the runway to the shuttle.

One of the guards pushed his head out. "Shuttle's empty!"

Perplexed, Grayson looked at Thomas. "What the hell?"

Thomas shrugged.

"How in the hell is it empty?" Grayson picked up his pace.

"It shouldn't be. Unless—"

"Unless what?"

"They parachuted. The emergency door is on the other side of the shuttle. We should check that."

"What?" Grayson asked. His face flushed red. "Where would they get parachutes?"

"Most of the personnel shuttles have emergency parachutes. This one does."

"And you didn't think to tell me that?"

"I figured you knew." Thomas swallowed hard. "You insisted every shuttle be equipped with all safety precautions. Parachutes are one of them. It's a rare circumstance for anyone to need to use parachutes during reentry. I never expected they'd think of such a maneuver. But desperate people are known to do some crazy things."

Grayson nodded. "That's true. But the computer still shows the hibernation activated?"

"Yes."

"Even after landing?"

Thomas nodded and hurried up the steps to the door. Grayson followed.

Before Thomas stepped inside the shuttle, he glanced at Grayson. "Yes. I want to know why, too."

They hurried to the passenger cabin. Thomas stopped midstride when he noticed the catheter bag filled with water with inserted I.V. needles.

"I'll be damned," Thomas said. He walked to the bag and removed the I.V. needle. "I don't know who that third passenger is, but he must be the one behind this."

"Yeah, I'm curious who he is, too. Any way we can backtrack and find out *where* they jumped out?"

"I'm on that."

Grayson glanced around the shuttle. Less than an hour earlier, his three employees had been right here. He shook his head. For months, all he could think about was apprehending them to understand their motives. How had they contrived such a plan so effectively within a short amount of time? He wanted to know the specifics, so he could prevent any future attempts. The more he learned, the better he could improve security protocol.

"While you're at it, have a team dust the seats for prints," Grayson said. "Find out who the hell this other person is."

Thomas nodded. "You got it."

"Do you think they survived the jump?" Grayson asked.

"Possibly. The parachutes were placed here in case an emergency occurred during landing or glitched controls prevented a safe landing."

"Find them."

Thomas nodded. "I'll do what I can, but getting access to the satellite feed takes some time."

Grayson chuckled. "Call Donovan Taylor at the Sleeper Lab. Get him busy tracing their chips. We should have them in custody by the end of the day."

"The chips would be quicker."

Thomas stepped away to contact the forensics team.

Grayson crossed his arms and looked out the shuttle door at his armed guards. Another shuttle was approaching Earth, but Jonas and his crew were still a month from arriving. Matthews had been forthcoming in the news of its arrival because he wanted Grayson to know he didn't kill Jonas. Jonas chose to leave. Was Matthews being on the level with him? What was Jonas' reasons for abandoning his post? Jonas wasn't easily manipulated, so Grayson planned to ask during Jonas' debriefing. If there was a deeper reason, Grayson would find out.

EVEN THOUGH THE CHUTE SLOWED MAGNUS' descent, he approached the rugged terrain fast. He tried to run with the direction of the wind current, but his left knee buckled slightly, knocking him off balance. With Digger tucked inside his suit, he didn't dare fall forward. His weight would crush the little ferret. Instead, he pivoted to his left, dropped, and landed hard on his back. He groaned and winced in pain, but at least Digger was spared. Despite the two strenuous weeks of daily exercise, Magnus' legs were weaker than he expected.

"Damn, that'll hurt even worse tomorrow," he said.

The dry wind yanked his puffed parachute and tugged. Had he been a smaller, lighter man, the chute would have dragged him across the ground. Instead, he sat a giant anchor with the wind rippling the parachute behind him.

Before he sat up, Magnus unfastened the straps and slipped his arms from the harness, allowing the wind to blow the chute away. Scrubby shrubs and sharp rocks snagged the billowing material, preventing it from sailing away.

He gazed into the sky, looking for Carter and Sylvia. He located their position in the bright blue sky. They were much farther away, being as they hadn't immediately jumped after he had. He watched Carter and Sylvia floating downward, their images growing larger. He hoped their landings were more graceful than his.

The wind seemed to be carrying them his direction. A professional jumper could've maneuvered with the wind current and dropped somewhat closer. As it was, Magnus would have to walk a good half-mile to join them. Provided neither of them was injured, they could get to a small town or community and hide until they found a way to make their next move. By now, Grayson had discovered they weren't aboard the Percival 3000, which meant a search team would be dispatched to find them. They had little time to disappear.

Digger squirmed and rolled near his stomach, pushing his pointed nose against the fabric, trying to weasel out. Magnus chuckled, unzipped the suit, and Digger popped his head out and chattered with excitement.

"Easy, Digger. We're okay. Well, I'm a little cut up and bruised, but at least *you're* okay."

The harsh arid breeze kicked up layers of dust that made the air reddish brown, instantly reminding him of Mars. For a moment, he felt trapped inside a nightmare like they'd somehow returned to Mars instead of reaching Earth.

Magnus stood slowly. Every slight movement ached. He imagined that was why most three-hundred-pound men weren't interested in skydiving. The landing was excruciating for heavier individuals. Of course, it could have been worse. He could have dislocated his knee, broken his legs, or tore an ACL.

He stooped slightly, brushing off the reddish dust on his pants, not that it mattered. The wind freed the parachute and carried it upward until another set of bushes snagged it.

Magnus walked in the direction where he anticipated Carter and Sylvia to land. At first, every step brought involuntary groans from him, but after twenty yards or so, walking actually seemed to lessen the pain. Digger sniffed the air, enjoying the warmth of the sun.

"Good to be outside, eh?" Magnus said.

Magnus walked the length of a football field by the time Carter landed, took to running, and skidded to a stop without falling. Sylvia dropped behind him. Right as Carter turned, she ran straight into him. He caught her, but the impact sent him backwards with her pile-driving him to the ground.

His grimace showed his obvious pain. She planted a kiss on his lips.

Magnus chuckled and walked to them. He offered his hand to Sylvia. She accepted, and he pulled her up. She unlatched her chute while Magnus helped Carter stand. He glanced at Sylvia. "I wondered if you'd jump or not."

"Carter pulled me with him because I was terrified. But, wow! I'd like to do that again."

Magnus chuckled. "You *liked* it?"

She nodded with a huge smile. "It was exhilarating!"

"At least the two of you landed better than I did."

Carter frowned, clutching his crotch. "I don't know about that. She almost killed me."

"Sorry."

Magnus roared with laughter.

He shrugged and unfastened the Velcro straps around his briefcase.

"Where are we?" Sylvia asked.

Magnus nodded toward the road. "According to the road sign, we're in Red Rock. Either of you know where that is exactly?"

"No," she replied.

Carter shook his head, kicked away his chute, and released it before the wind caught it and propelled it like a sail. He looked to be in pain.

"You okay?" Magnus asked.

"Yeah. I'm fine. You know, it really doesn't matter where we are," Carter said. He immediately checked the latches of the briefcase to make certain the rough tumble with Sylvia hadn't jarred it open. It was still tightly shut. He sighed with obvious relief. He brushed the dirt and grit off his pants. "We need to find a change of clothes quickly. Grayson probably issued an APB for state patrolmen to look for three individuals wearing Grayson Enterprises suits. His emblem's easily identified by most people."

Magnus nodded at the suggestion. "I agree. These jumpsuits will make us stand out more."

While he stared across the terrain, Sylvia adjusted her pants and then fidgeted with her hair, shaking dust from it.

Another gust of wind churned more grit and dust into the air, forcing her to shield her eyes. She turned her back to the wind. "Where are we going to find any clothes out here? Looks like we're in the middle of nowhere. And I'm not making clothes out of leaves."

Magnus smiled and headed to the road. Digger was curled against his chest in the crook of his left arm, basking in the sun.

"Where are you going?" Carter said.

"There are some RVs and campers over there," he replied. "Looks like a campground. I'm going to check it out."

Chapter 62

Sylvia wiped dust off her face and then, finger combed her hair. "God, I hope there's a washroom nearby. I probably look like shit after crashing into you, Carter."

"Yeah? Well, I'm still trying to find my nuts."

Her eyes widened, and she placed a hand over her mouth. "Oh, I hit you there?"

With a grimace, he nodded. "Kneed them good."

"I'm so sorry."

"Probably because I didn't say I loved you when we were still on board?" he asked with a forced smile.

Sylvia blushed and looked at the ground. She wiped away a tear, and when he noticed, he hobbled next to her. He placed his finger to her chin and gently lifted. Her moistened eyes sought comfort in his.

"Don't cry," he said. "With all we've shared on the shuttle, all the intimate moments and conversations, I *do* love you. I've not been able to express it so much in words because I feared losing you the same way I did Wanda."

"I know," she replied. "That kind of loss is painful."

"Plus, I've had so much self-doubt about us successfully reaching Earth. That's worried me most of all."

She smiled. "I knew you had a lot going through your head, but I thought you really didn't like me."

"No," he said softly. "It's never been that."

"I guess it was everything else combined?"

He nodded and gave a charming, reassuring smile. "I'm over that now. After we take care of what needs to be done, we can start our life together."

She studied his face. His facial expressions and voice indicated his sincerity. He looked relieved, happy, unlike any time since their journey to Earth. The misery haunting his features was gone. He was the energetic and enthusiastic Carter she remembered before the Deimos tragedy.

"You're serious, aren't you?" she asked.

Carter leaned forward and kissed her. He kissed her with a passion that surprised her. It wasn't one of his gentle, but yet cold, kisses. The hungered need in this kiss made her ache deep inside. Her body leaned against his and had they been in a secluded place, she'd have given herself to him.

When he pulled away, he said, "More serious than anything I've ever known in my life. More than what I thought I had with Wanda. I know what I have with you is what I hope to keep."

Sylvia wrapped her arms around his neck and squeezed, otherwise her weak knees might have allowed her to fall. When she glanced into his eyes once more, he smiled. He held an air of sovereignty about him. The burden controlling his soul had crumbled. But a part of her remained skeptical. Seldom did people drastically change when it came to affection. It slowly built over time. While his passion didn't seem forced on his part, it didn't seem completely genuine, either.

With his free arm, he embraced her.

Magnus stopped on the edge of the road, arched his back, and then turned to face them. "All right you two lovebirds, let's get moving! The longer we're out here, the better chance Grayson's people have in finding us."

Sylvia released Carter's neck and lowered herself, looking into his eyes.

Carter didn't break eye contact with her. "Unfortunately, he's right. Let's go."

He took her hand in his and hurried alongside her. They caught up to Magnus who was moving quickly for a man his size.

Carter was moving faster, in spite of his pain.

"Are you okay?" Sylvia asked.

"Ah, yeah," Carter replied. "It hurts, but not as badly."

"Keep walking," Magnus said, "to work out the soreness. The ground wasn't too friendly with my arrival, but the more I walk, the better it's gotten."

Sylvia held an embarrassed smile. "His isn't quite the same thing."

Carter shook his head and placed a finger against his lips.

Digger's little nose crinkled as he eagerly sniffed the air.

"He seems happy to be here," she said.

"In a way, I think we all are."

Carter nodded. "I feel like a different person already."

Sylvia smiled. He seemed different, but why the sudden transformation? He kept a tight guard on the briefcase, even now. At the first opportunity she got, she was going to see what was inside the case. She should have done it months ago, but he never left the briefcase out of reach.

Another sign came into view as they walked. Magnus pointed at it.

"Las Vegas is only twenty miles away," Magnus said. "If we can get there, it'll be nearly impossible for Grayson to find us."

GRAYSON SAT BEHIND HIS DESK. Frustration creased his facial features. The anger pulsing through him was almost unbearable. Never one to suffer from high blood pressure or anxiety, the combined events on Deimos and Mars had accumulated more psychological stress than he'd ever experienced before.

At least he and Matthews were at what seemed a profitable, mutual work relationship. He had never imagined capturing the ones who had stolen his shuttle would have been difficult, which was why he never had given it a second thought. In his mind, the worst possible outcome was the shuttle crashing or the passengers dying before they got to Earth. But, other than those issues, everything else seemed set. Destined. The shuttle would land and the passengers would be apprehended immediately. Nothing could've been easier.

What disturbed him was someone staying ahead of him every step of the way *before* and *after* they stole the Percival 3000. For ordinary people to pull off such a theft so effortlessly was more than Grayson's narcissistic mind wanted to accept. He desperately wanted to know who was behind the major insubordination, especially since he personally reviewed all applicants' files before allowing the final acceptance in hiring. Not only that, he watched and monitored their interviews via video or through a mirrored glass from an observation room.

When his billions of dollars might be at stake, he wanted to ensure as little risk as possible with whom he hired.

This person was cunning and somehow had slipped under Grayson's unique radar for reading people's personalities. That intrigued him even more. Thinking through the most brilliant employees he'd hired over the years, none came to mind that possessed the shrewd, calculating qualities like this unidentified employee. *How* had he missed this?

Donovan entered the office. Grayson rubbed his eyes and motioned Donovan to take a seat.

"Have you traced their chips?" Grayson asked.

Donovan sighed as he sat down. "No. Magnus' chip had malfunctioned on

Mars. In fact, they were preparing to take him to the lab to have a new one implanted and that's when he attacked the guards and escaped."

"I received the report about that, but I thought that maybe you could still trace it."

Donovan shook his head. "No. His tracer's part of the chip, so it's shorted out."

"Does that happen often?" A curious frown furrowed his brow.

"About ten percent of the previous chips were defective with unfavorable side effects."

Grayson frowned. "Like what exactly?"

"The chips melted and caused such severe pain that several prisoners killed themselves or the injuries caused irreparable damage to their nervous system. But only two have occurred like Magnus' where they shorted out."

"Who was the other prisoner?"

"Steven Matthews."

Grayson took a sharp breath and ground his teeth. "Any idea why theirs were different?"

Donovan shrugged. "I can't know without examining one of the chips."

"Damn."

"Well, if you find Magnus and capture him, I can examine the chip."

"I thought the burden of finding them on you."

Donovan grinned. "We're looking to see when they popped open the emergency door. Once we have that information, I'm sure we can narrow down where they might have landed and have a radius of where they might flee next."

"Good," Grayson replied.

"You could call the authorities," Donovan said.

Grayson shook his head. "No. This stays in-house."

"Why? It doesn't hurt to have some outside help."

Grayson sighed. "The fact I never reported the theft of my shuttle will raise red flags. They'll suspect what I had intended anyway."

"I see your point."

"Not to mention how embarrassing the entire situation would be. Naysayers would be dancing on the news and in the streets," Grayson said.

"Yeah. I've never understood why people like to see successful people fail."

"Jealousy."

"That's probably accurate."

"You said ten percent of the original chips were defective?"

Donovan nodded.

"That means at least ten prisoners should have suffered chip malfunction.

We never had that many reported on Mars. Was the percentage higher for the prisoners on Deimos? Do you know how many of theirs were bad?"

"On Mars, it was a minor technicality. The defective ones are scheduled to be replaced on Mars with the ones Matthews designed. Until we have upgraded the prisoners on Mars to the new design, you might have several more malfunction. At least the hundred prisoners on their way to Mars all have the new chips implanted. That's less you have to worry about."

Grayson nodded. "What about on Deimos?"

Donovan shook his head slowly. "We've not been able to make contact."

"I know. I've not been able to contact anyone since the shuttle from Deimos landed inside Olympus Mons. Isn't there any way we send a damn shuttle back to Deimos?"

"We tried, sir. Whoever left Deimos for Mars messed with the landing bay gates at the Deimos Life Station."

Grayson's jaw tightened, and he folded his hands together. "How?"

"By enabling a computer program to block outside access. We've tried to hack the system and every time we've gotten close, the code changes again."

"To the best of my knowledge, we didn't have any techs on Deimos with that kind of programming knowledge, did we?"

"No, we didn't," Donovan said. "All the techs worked directly under Jonas and Derek's supervision. They relayed information to the Deimos computers. The techs only went to Deimos if an emergency absolutely required it because the Deimos base is so small."

"Have you checked for the last time the techs visited Deimos before the shuttle left the life station port?"

"Yes."

"And?"

Donovan scanned the details on his computer tablet. "Approximately two weeks prior to the shuttle leaving Deimos and landing at Olympus Mons."

"Did they notice anything unusual?"

"Not according to the documented reports," Donovan replied. "Since Jonas and Derek are heading to Earth, you can debrief them when they arrive. Maybe they can tell you something not listed in the reports."

"Do you think maybe the chips malfunctioned on Deimos and the prisoners rioted and killed the guards and staff?"

"Until we find the pilot that landed at Olympus Mons, your guess is as good as mine."

Grayson sighed. "Okay, so we can't trace Magnus' chip. What about Sylvia's?"

"Hers has been deactivated."

"What? How?" Grayson stood, shoved his hands into his pockets, and walked to the large tinted windows overlooking the ocean. His face heated.

"My guess is one of them found the implant devices the guards have access to on the shuttle. There is a magnetic device that deactivates Sleeper Chips."

"This complicates things," Grayson said.

"How?"

"The person responsible for this entire situation has some kind of computer knowledge never disclosed to me. The person went to great lengths not to include this information on his resume or during the interview. This isn't something a novice would know, right?"

"No. The person behind all this has an incredible understanding of computer programming and hacking. Shit, you'd have been lucky had you'd hired him or her as a computer technician instead of whatever job the person was hired for."

"Damn," Grayson said. "I don't know whether to be incredibly angry or flattered."

"Flattered?"

Grayson turned and grinned. "Ruthless masterminds enthrall me."

"But the person stole your shuttle that's worth billions of dollars?"

"I know. What's impressive is *how* he or she managed to do it without me ever suspecting the person was capable in the first place."

"Don't tell me you'd consider having this person continue to work for you after you find him?"

Grayson shrugged. "I hired Matthews a second time, and that seems to be working quite well at the moment."

"The chips he developed are certainly a great improvement."

"I agree."

"I do have a bit of good news," Donovan said, looking at his computer tablet. He grinned. "It's just been sent to me."

"What?"

"We've pinpointed the exact moment the emergency door popped loose."

"Good. Then we should be able to find them."

Donovan winced. "Might be more difficult than you think."

"How's that?"

"At the altitude they dropped, the wind current may have carried them for miles before they finally landed."

"Any guess to where that might be?"

"Not exactly *where*, but we're pretty sure where they'll head."

Grayson's eyes beamed with interest. "Where's that?"

"Vegas. That's the quickest access to an airport."

"Then we find and stop them before that happens."

Grayson tapped his desk intercom. "Olivia, get Michaels on the phone."

"One moment." A few seconds later, she said, "He's on the line."

Grayson pushed the button for the loudspeaker. "Michaels?"

"Yes?" he replied.

"Get a covert team together and get to the Las Vegas airport immediately. Donovan will send you pictures of two people I want captured and taken into custody. Find and bring them to me unharmed."

"Yes, sir."

"There's a third person with these two. We don't have any idea who this person is. This man or woman is the one we need even more than the other two. Don't let him *or her* escape, understood?"

"Yes, sir."

"Above all else, keep the person alive."

"Roger that."

Chapter 63

Magnus, Carter, and Sylvia approached the central building in the Red Rock Canyon Campground. They were drenched in sweat due to the overbearing sun and rising heat.

"Why are we hiding?" Sylvia asked.

Magnus whispered, "In case Grayson reported us to the media."

Carter wiped sweat from his brow and leaned against the wall.

Magnus peered around the corner of the building. He held Digger and stroked the ferret's neck. "There's a gift shop across the way there. They should have T-shirts and shorts. Anyone want to volunteer?"

"I'll go," Sylvia said. "Besides, I need to pee."

Carter shook his head. "None of us have any money. And we sure can't sell MarQuebes here."

"I don't need money to get clothes," she said.

Magnus turned with a stunned look. "Then how?"

"Shoplifting."

Carter said, "No. If you get caught, we're all caught."

She smiled. "I *won't* get caught. I've done it before without being seen."

"You ended up on Mars—"

"For bank fraud, dear. *Not* shoplifting."

Carter shrugged and grumbled under his breath.

Magnus smiled. "Be careful."

"I will."

Sylvia crept from the building and cautiously made her way into the restroom. She was thankful to be on Earth and off the space shuttle; however, she missed being housed deep inside Olympus Mons because she liked the sheltered feeling it had. She never liked dealing with a lot of people. Before being incarcerated and especially right *after*, she often wished she was invisible, and that's why she enjoyed the thrill of shoplifting. Because if she could take items without people noticing, even though they were standing a few feet away, it made her feel like she could turn invisible.

"Here, hold Digger," Magnus said, handing the ferret to Carter.

"Why? What are you doing?"

Magnus wiped sweat from his brow, unzipped his silver jumpsuit, and stepped out of it. Glistening sweat rolled down his muscled back, chest, and arms. He sighed. "I'm losing the suit. This heat is murder. Besides, taking a piss sounds like a great idea."

"You're going to walk to the restroom in your underwear?" Carter asked.

A gust of warm wind flowed past. Magnus closed his eyes. "Now, that's much better."

"For someone not wanting to attract attention, standing outside in your underwear sure will."

Magnus chuckled and shrugged. "The showers and laundry room are in that building. I won't look too weird. I'd like a nice cold shower about now, anyhow."

"What about Digger?"

"I'll take him with me. He'll play in the water, which will make him feel better, too. He's probably thirsty."

"God knows I am," Carter said, wiping away more sweat.

"I'm sure there are plenty of showers and you can drink water from the sink."

Carter shook his head. "No, I'll wait for Sylvia. She might get in trouble and need my help."

Magnus took the ferret, rounded the building, and entered the restroom. Seeing no one, he placed Digger in an empty shower stall and turned on the water. Digger rolled in the cool water spray and washed his face. While the ferret played, Magnus relieved himself at one of the urinals.

A couple of minutes later, he returned to the shower and laughed at the playful ferret. Digger splashed and jumped and then slid to Magnus' feet. Magnus slid off his shorts, rinsed them, and hung them on a hook outside the stall. He stepped inside and pulled the thin shower curtain closed.

The cold water struck his chest, making him give a slight *Woot!* Chill bumps pimpled his flesh. The ferret splashed around his feet.

Magnus didn't have a washcloth, so he rubbed his hands over his arms, chest, and legs, trying to remove as much sweat and mud as he could. The water around the drain was rust colored. He turned his back to the shower, letting the coldness soothe his cuts and abrasions from the harsh landing. After several minutes, he finally shut off the water, even though he could've easily stood there an hour.

Water dripped off his body. Digger continued rolling around on the wet tiles after the water had drained.

Magnus dripped dry for several minutes, flinging his hands and shaking his body back and forth, attempting to get more water off. He reached from the shower, grabbed his shorts off the hook, and pulled them on. With the humidity, he'd dry fast.

The ferret looked at the giant of a man. Magnus leaned and picked Digger up. The ferret nuzzled his hand, content with the cold water. Magnus sighed and stepped outside the stall.

"Oh, cool!" a young boy exclaimed. "A ferret!"

Magnus looked over at the door, startled to see a boy and man staring at him. Magnus assumed the man to be the boy's father.

The boy wore a white T-shirt, brown shorts, and flip-flops. His hair was a tinge red, his face freckled, and he wore glasses. The man's hair was a dark brown, but he and the boy both had similar noses and identical dimples tugged at the corners of their mouths.

"Can I hold him?" the boy asked.

Magnus, dressed in his boxers, didn't know how to react. He felt uncomfortable standing in his underwear with a teenager talking to him.

"Now, Troy," the man said. "You don't need to bother—"

"But Dad?"

"If you don't mind him holding the ferret," Magnus said, "I don't mind. Is that okay with you, sir?"

The man nodded. "I guess so. The boy's been begging for a ferret for several years now."

Magnus handed Digger to Troy. Troy's face lit up with a broad grin. He gently rubbed Digger's neck.

Magnus extended his huge muscled hand. "I'm Magnus. Excuse how I'm dressed. Was doing some laundry and decided to take a shower while waiting."

"I'm Mick," the man said, shaking Magnus' hand.

Troy scratched behind Digger's ears and looked at Magnus. "What's his name?"

"Digger," Magnus replied.

Troy smiled at his son and looked at Magnus. "Would you sell Digger?"

Magus felt a tinge in his gut and winced. He'd grown attached to the ferret and truly hated the thought of not keeping Digger with him. But he was also concerned about the situations he, Carter, and Sylvia might encounter. Should something happen to Magnus, he wasn't certain either of them would properly take care of Digger. Seeing the excitement in Troy's eyes, he knew the boy would be attentive to the ferret's need. Digger would have a loving owner.

"Actually, Mick, I've been thinking Digger needs a good home. I'm afraid I'll be too busy in the near future to take care of him like he needs."

"How much do you want for him?" Mick asked.

"Actually, my friends and I are in need of a ride to Vegas. I'd trade him for a ride."

"Great," Mick said, smiling. "We're headed that direction ourselves, but we're in a pickup truck, if you don't mind riding in the back."

"That'd be great. We don't mind at all. Where can we meet you?"

Mick pointed. "We're parked near the tourist information building. We did a short hike earlier, but the heat's a bit more than I expected."

"I know what you mean," Magnus replied.

"I'm driving a yellow Toyota."

"Okay. Let me tell my friends, and we'll meet you there."

***

SYLVIA HURRIED around the building where Carter stood, holding the briefcase. She had clothes draped over her arm.

"You got all that from the gift shop?" he asked.

"No. The shop owner watched me like a hawk. I found these strung between an RV and a utility pole."

Carter shook his head. "Another reason why people should use a laundry mat and not a clothesline."

"I hope the overalls are large enough to fit Magnus."

"It might be difficult to find his size."

"Where is he anyway?" Sylvia asked, looking around.

"He went to the restroom to take a shower."

Magnus came around the corner with a huge grin on his face. He scratched between Digger's ears.

"What are you so happy about?" Sylvia asked.

"I got us a ride to Vegas," he replied.

"Great," Carter said. "I'll be glad to get out of this heat and not walk any farther."

"How'd you find a ride so quickly?" she asked.

Magnus shook his head, sighed, and brimming tears reddened his eyes. "I sort of traded Digger for the ride."

"Why'd you do that?" Sylvia asked, reaching to pet Digger.

"A boy's father offered us a ride in exchange for him," Magnus said.

"Aww, you didn't need to do that," she said. "We could have found another way."

Magnus shook his head. "I'm not sure how things are going to turn out after we get to Vegas and once I return to Texas. Besides, there's always the possibility Grayson will find us. I need to know Digger's safe regardless."

"I understand. Here," Sylvia said, handing the overalls to Magnus. "I doubt they'll fit, but I didn't find anything else that was even *close* to your size."

"It'll have to do."

Magnus pulled the tight overalls on, but she didn't have a shirt to fit him. She got out of her jumpsuit and pulled up a short skirt. She put on a boy's shirt that cut off at her midriff.

Carter put down the briefcase and held up the clothes Sylvia handed him. He winced. "You've got to be kidding?"

The shirt was bright green with a dark-eyed alien face spread across the front. He shuddered.

She shook her head. "We're in no place to be choosey."

"I suppose not."

Magnus said, "After we get to Vegas and sell these gems, we can buy better clothes."

Carter shook his head. "I can't wait."

"Come on," Magnus said. "Let's get to the truck before they change their minds."

Chapter 64

Riding in the back of the pickup, Magnus stared at Troy in the cab with Digger. The boy's smile was a greater reward than what money they'd get from selling the MarQuebes in Vegas. No amount of money bought happiness like that. Although Magnus smiled, his eyes were sad.

The hot wind blew over their faces. The roar of the highway beneath the truck was almost a lulling comfort.

"You going to be okay giving Digger away?" Sylvia asked.

"I gotta be. Besides, it's for the best."

"What do you mean?" Carter asked.

"You and Sylvia now get to Vegas quicker where it'll be a lot harder for Grayson to find you. With my business in Texas, at least Digger has a good home now."

Sylvia frowned. "So you're leaving us?"

"Your affairs with Grayson don't concern me. After we sell the gems in Vegas, we divvy up the money and part ways."

Carter forced a smile and stared at the briefcase. "I hate to see you go. I thought maybe you'd help me, and I'd return the favor."

Magnus shook his head. "Nah, Grayson's *your* demon to wrestle. I've demons of my own."

Sylvia placed her hand on Carter's and squeezed. "Carter, why don't we forget about Grayson and help Magnus?"

Carter cocked his head to one side and stared straight ahead. A frozen expression controlled his face. It appeared he was deep in thought or listening to someone else.

"You okay, Carter?" Magnus asked.

Carter shook his head, his eyes widened, and he looked at Magnus. "Yeah, I'm fine."

Magnus peered closer at Carter's eyes. "Are you sure? This heat can mess with your mind, make you see things, especially after everything else we've gone through."

Carter glanced at Sylvia. His pupils were dilated. He cleared his throat and shook his head. "I'd love to help Magnus, but Grayson needs to be held responsible for what occurred on Deimos."

Sylvia squeezed his hand tightly. "*You* don't have to be *that* messenger."

A strange smile crossed his lips. "Yes. Yes, I do."

Fear surfaced on her face. Her eyes widened because of the sudden coldness in his voice. She looked at Magnus momentarily and then returned her attention to Carter. "No. Report him to the authorities or government officials."

"That won't do any good," Carter said.

Frustrated, Sylvia sighed. She nodded at Magnus. "I'm sure Magnus would testify about the cruel punishment the prisoners undergo in the mines being controlled by one of those Sleeper Chips. Once Magnus finishes with his business in Texas, that is."

Magnus nodded and placed his huge hand on Carter's shoulder. "Sure, Carter, I'd be happy to do that."

Carter's hands tightened on the silver briefcase. Anger stirred in his voice. "I doubt the government would grant me an interview, much less actually *do* anything. Rich people are seldom held accountable for their actions, and if judgments come against them, it's always minor infractions or a short time in prison. That's why the sooner I strike, the better."

Sylvia's eyebrows rose. "*Strike?* Exactly *what* are you planning to do?"

Carter looked away. "It's best that I don't tell you."

Sylvia looked at Magnus with great concern. Her mouth opened to speak but no words came.

Magnus shook his head. "Sorry, Sylvia, but he's right."

"How can you take his side?"

"If his plans incriminate him, it's best you don't know what he's going to do. Then you're innocent of any charges."

Her eyes narrowed. "Do you know what his plans are?"

Magnus shook his head. "No. And I plan to keep it that way. I suggest you do the same."

The truck slowed. Magnus smiled and pointed at the road sign.

"Welcome to Vegas!" he shouted.

Sylvia didn't share his enthusiasm. Instead, she stared at Carter in disbelief. Hurt and betrayal weighed her gaze. Magnus wanted to tell her that things might get better, but that was a lie she'd easily detect. Anything he said at this moment was nothing more than deceptive hope, and he didn't want her wrath on him after all the dealt hands played out. Las Vegas was where people wagered on luck, but in the reality of the real world, the stakes were much higher and the payout a lot less.

Lessons in life were often learned through the gambling of one's emotions, heart, and soul. Those stakes were higher than any money lost in a casino. He truly hoped Sylvia weighed her hand, called, and accepted whatever outcome she received. Good, bad, or totally devastating, she needed to move forward with her life.

Others he'd known never got that chance, and when his opportunity to right the wrongs presented itself, he'd tilt the scales of justice in the proper direction, even though the one that had lost his justice would never know.

GRAYSON ENTERPRISES SECURITY OFFICE

DONOVAN SAT and busily typed commands on his laptop while Grayson looked over his shoulder. Donovan's mesmerized eyes focused on the screen while he accessed vital information between various screens.

"Can we find them?" Grayson asked.

Donovan shrugged slightly. "If they head to Vegas, we'll be alerted the second a camera captures their images. Provided they head to Vegas."

"It seems the most plausible choice."

"I agree. Anyway, if they do, I've hacked all the casinos' security cameras." He pointed at the screen. "And I'm working on a link to the traffic cams along the streets. With facial recognition technology like it is, the results should be instantaneous."

Grayson smiled. "Good. That's good. I've sent a twenty man TAC team. They're ready to dispatch the moment we locate them."

"Want me to contact Vegas police, too?"

Grayson shook his head. "No. It's best that they're not involved."

"Still keeping it in-house?"

"Always. You know that. The last thing I want is for the U.S. and the U.N. to think my operations are vulnerable. I've worked too hard and invested too much time and money for an outside group to try to stake premature claims on my establishments."

"They'd do that?" Donovan asked, peering over his shoulder.

Grayson turned to the large window and clasped his hands behind his back. "They're already *trying* to do that." He chuckled and shook his head. "These other countries expect to use my landing bays and operations in order to help start their own settlements."

"Essentially you've paved the way for others to do so."

"No. Not on *my* millions I haven't. I took the risks and proved it could be done. They want a piggyback ride, and I'm not carrying their dead weight."

"I don't blame you. Merely my speculative opinion of what they want."

Grayson nodded slowly, watching the bright sun glisten off the rolling ocean waves. He sighed. "I'm glad that you see what I do. They're too blind to recognize that they expect me to roll out a welcome mat with open arms and invite them to share my wealth."

"Perhaps they see what they're doing, and are hoping *you'll* ignore it."

"Donovan, I'm an only child. I never had to grow up fighting with others over what toys I wanted to play with. Needless to say, I've carried that into adulthood. I don't play well with others. I've a hard time sharing something that's already mine. If I invite them to my party, I'll gladly share the pie, but I've not given invitations to anyone and I never intend to."

"I understand. I get it. That's why you're so hard bent on capturing Magnus and Sylvia."

"And their unknown accomplice. Especially him. They stole from me. Liars and thieves I cannot tolerate. But I believe he's the true mastermind and started it all. Once we find them, they'll wish I held a bit of mercy. But justice will be served. *My* justice."

Donovan wanted to reply, but he didn't. Chill bumps rose on his arms. He gently rubbed them for quick warmth and then immediately turned his attention to tapping into the traffic cams data feed. He often worried he might be working for a ruthless madman, and Grayson had done little to convince him otherwise. Donovan was certain he would do everything possible to find Magnus and Sylvia because doing so prevented Grayson's wrath from raining down on him.

Chapter 65

Mick stopped the pickup truck along the Vegas main strip. The rough engine sputtered while Carter, Magnus, and Sylvia climbed out. Troy rolled down his window as Magnus stepped to the side of the passenger door.

Magnus smiled, reaching inside, and rubbed Digger's head. "Take good care of him, Troy."

"I will," the boy replied with a broad smile.

Magnus made eye contact with Mick. "Thanks again for the ride."

"Not a problem. I appreciate the trade. I can tell the ferret means a lot to you."

Magnus nodded. He ruffled Troy's hair. "He does, but Digger's in good hands. I've no doubt Digger and your son will have great times together."

Mick put the truck in drive and slowly pulled away. Magnus looked at Sylvia with sadness.

She rubbed his arm. "Where to now?"

Magnus sighed. "Let's find a pawn shop."

"Shouldn't be hard," Carter said. "They're all over."

"I know, but we need one with little traffic and away from the main street. Discretion's key."

Glancing at the edge of the sidewalk, something caught Magnus' attention. He reached down and picked it up. "I'll be damned."

"What's that?" Sylvia asked, stepping closer to inspect it.

"A casino chip."

Stamped on one side was 'Lady Luck Casino'. On the other was its value: $1000.00.

"It's really worth a thousand dollars?" Sylvia asked.

"That's what it says."

"Wow," she said in a near whisper.

Magnus studied the chip. "Vegas is the city for Lady Luck, but not that often."

Carter said, "Maybe it's a sign of good fortune?"

"Not for the person that lost it," Magnus replied.

Carter laughed. "I suppose not."

Magnus said, "But my Mama always said that everything glittering isn't always gold. Here, Sylvia, you take it."

"Why?" Her eyebrows rose as she took the chip. "What do I do with it?"

He nodded at the building across the street. Within all the flashing lights displayed the casino with the same name. **Lady Luck**.

"That's the casino it came from. Take it to the cashier's window and cash it in. Use the money to get you and Carter a suite. Live a little before he confronts Grayson. It's been a long trip, so reward yourselves."

"You sure?" Carter asked.

Magnus grinned. "What's a thousand bucks compared to the value of these stones?"

"That's true."

"What about you?" Sylvia asked.

"I've other things to take care of," Magnus replied. "Simply leave word at the desk to inform Carter of your room number. But don't use your real names."

"Why not?" she asked.

"Grayson's looking for us," Carter replied.

Sylvia glanced at Carter. "What name would you like to use?"

He thought for a moment. "Rick... Davenport."

"Okay. I'll be Tory Jones."

Magnus tapped Carter's arm. "Perhaps you should let her carry the briefcase."

"No," Carter said, shaking his head adamantly.

"By you holding the briefcase, it'll make talking to the pawn shop worker more difficult."

"No, it stays with me."

"You don't trust me?" Sylvia asked.

Carter released a frustrated sigh. "It's not that, Sylvia. Really. I don't trust letting this leave my sight at any time."

"Why not?" Magnus asked, folding his arms and looking at him.

"It's personal."

"What's inside the briefcase?" Magnus asked. "You've been overly protective of it ever since you landed on Mars."

Anger flickered in Carter's eyes. "Neither of you have any idea what I endured on Deimos. It was horrible. What happened there was... I don't have the words to describe it, okay?"

Magnus nodded. "I've lost people close to me, Carter. It happens. We have to move on."

"Sometimes moving on isn't easy."

Sylvia wiped tears from her eyes. She gently rubbed Carter's shoulder, and he turned away. "Don't shut us out, Carter. We're your friends."

"We are," Magnus said. "Whenever you're able to open up to us, we're here."

Carter shook his head. "I know you both want to be closer to me. I sense that by your words and actions. I did the moment I landed on Mars. But it's hard to let anyone get close to my heart. I'm sorry. I've lost too much."

"And that prevents you from trusting us with your briefcase?" Magnus asked.

"What I carry in this case is *my* burden."

"It doesn't have to be," Sylvia said.

Carter gave an even smile, ran his free hand through his hair, and his eyes became cold. "It always will be, Sylvia. Look, this much I can tell you, okay?"

Sylvia and Magnus nodded. Their eyes reflected immediate interest.

"I brought back the badges of all the people I worked with on Deimos," Carter said. "I want to show Grayson they were people, not inventory, not his property. They were people who sacrificed their lives by leaving Earth to help him advance the new frontiers on Mars. They had *names. Dreams.* And because he didn't take the proper precautions, they're all dead. That's why I'm so protective of this case. If someone stole it, I've failed my colleagues and friends. I'd have no physical record of their names and identities."

Magnus nodded and extended his hand. Carter shook it. "Thanks for sharing that with us, Carter. It makes perfect sense. Sorry for the intrusion."

Sylvia wrapped her arms around Carter's neck and squeezed. She kissed his cheek. "Thanks, Sweetie, for opening up. It explains everything so much better. I want you to know I truly love you."

Carter smiled. Tears moistened his eyes.

"Look, we're wasting valuable time," Magnus said. "The longer we're out here in the open, the easier Grayson can find us."

"Do you really think he could find us here?" Sylvia asked.

Magnus nodded. "Of course. Never underestimate him. With his wealth and power, he has people in every major city, but my guess, *especially* here."

"I believe it," Carter said.

"See you soon," she said to Carter with a hopeful smile.

Sylvia crossed the street to the casino. While she walked away, Magnus and Carter detoured down a narrow side street. The bright lights faded. Both sides were drab and looked more like an alley than an actual street.

A small pawnshop named, 'Down on Your Luck?' was less than half a block away. Magnus grabbed the suspenders of his overalls and winked. "I can't look anymore down on my luck than I do right now. Hell, I can even tell 'em I lost the shirt right off my back."

Carter grinned. "Certainly looks like it."

"Maybe the owner will feel sorry for me."

"Every little bit helps."

AN ALARM BEEPED sharp and quick on Donovan's laptop. Grayson turned from staring out his large window.

"We have a hit," Donovan said with a broad smile.

Eagerly, Grayson hurried to the desk and stared at the screen. He pointed. "Pull it up. Who is it?"

Donovan brought up the facial recognition image on the large wall screen. Sylvia's face displayed. Her eyes were nervous and uncertain.

"Where is she?" Grayson asked, stepping around the desk.

"Location?" Donovan asked the computer.

'She entered the *Lady Luck Casino*.'

Sylvia glanced around the casino floor like a timid mouse. Afraid to move, she stood examining her surroundings.

"What about the others? Where the hell are they?"

"We don't have anything on them yet. But if she's there, they shouldn't be far away."

"We can't be certain of that," Grayson said.

"Sir, they're on the run. It's in their best interest for them to remain together. Even if she entered by herself, the others are nearby. It's only logical."

Grayson shoved his hands into his pockets. His jaw tightened. "You're right. To have gotten this far, they've shown remarkable brilliance. They're stronger as a team."

"Not to worry, sir. If the facial recognition found her, it won't be long until we find her accomplices."

Grayson squeezed Donovan's shoulder. "Great work."

"Thanks."

Grayson tapped his earpiece. "We have a visual on Sylvia. She's inside the Lady Luck Casino. Get into position. Stand ready until the other two are located."

Chapter 66

Magnus and Carter peered through the front glass of the 'Down On Your Luck?' pawnshop. The inside perimeter was lined with glass counter displays that housed expensive watches, rings, necklaces, and other silver and gold collectibles. Another counter was filled with shelves lined with 9mm handguns.

Rare, lavish paintings hung on the walls behind the counters. Even though the pawnshop was filled with luxurious items, Magnus didn't see any customers milling around.

"This looks like the safest place to sell these," Magnus said.

"Why?"

"We'll have our privacy. The less people that know about these MarQuebes, the better."

Carter shook his head. "Looks like the name of the shop is appropriate. The owner seems down on his luck."

"Well, his luck and ours are about to change."

Magnus pushed the door open. A set of bells rattled against the top of the door. Only one man stood behind the counter. Boredom couldn't have been sketched any better. The bells aroused his interest. His eager eyes clued Magnus to believe the man's afternoon had been dead, and perhaps, at last, he might make some money.

Magnus and Carter approached the counter, and the man's eagerness turned to suspicion while he watched them. Of course, Magnus' apparel didn't lead anyone to believe he'd be worth the time to talk to, and Carter's shirt led one to believe he was a devoted Roswell fanatic, which meant he probably wasn't a high roller in the casinos, either. The shop owner's clothes definitely displayed a man down on his luck. He wore a denim jacket with the sleeves ripped off. Loose strings hung from where the sleeves had once been sewn. The blue tattered threads intertwined with the his hairy arms.

The man's hand moved out of sight beneath his overhanging jacket to his belt. Magnus assumed he was armed, as any pawnshop owner should be, because desperate people often performed the most unexpected crimes.

"How are you doing this evening, sir?" Magnus asked.

The owner's frown narrowed. When he swallowed, his bulging Adam's apple bobbed. "The only person around here to be addressed as *sir* would be my father."

"Is he around?" Magnus asked.

"No, but I'm in charge until he gets back from vacation."

Magnus sighed. "I see. And you are?"

"Call me Eli," he replied.

"Looks like business is slow today," Carter said.

Eli shrugged. "It varies day to day. Today's been an *extra* slow one."

"It happens, I suppose," Magnus said.

"What can I help you boys with?" Eli asked with slight agitation. "You don't seem to be toting much, except that briefcase, so I'll assume you're interested in buying somethin'? But from the looks of it, you ain't looking too well off on the money side, either."

"As a matter of fact, I think we can work some sort of a deal." Magnus slid his hands into his pockets.

Eli's hand moved and the front of his denim jacket opened to reveal the butt of a .45 revolver. His eyes narrowed. "Exactly *what* kind of deal are you talking about?"

"Easy," Magnus said. "No reason to become alarmed. Show him the gems, Carter."

"Gems?"

Eli glanced at Carter's silver briefcase, expecting Carter to open it and retrieve the gems. But instead Carter tucked the briefcase under his arm, and pulled the small envelope of MarQuebes from his back pocket. He slowly and carefully poured the stones on the glass-topped counter. They rattled softly like a small bag of shaken marbles.

Eli's eyes widened. "Don't move. Stay right there."

Magnus' heartbeat increased. He was certain this man was going to call the authorities.

Instead of taking out a cellphone, Eli hurried to the door, flipped the open sign over to 'closed', and locked it before he rushed to the countertop. A hypnotic gaze set in the man's eyes as the stones shimmered from ruby red to purple.

"Are these genuine MarQuebes?" Eli salivated and drool beaded at the sides of his mouth.

Magnus smiled, seeing the glow in the man's greedy eyes. He and Carter were about to sell the gems without much of a problem. "Yes, sir, they are."

"And *uncut*. Damn!"

Magnus and Carter nodded.

"How the hell did you boys get this many of these gems? Cut ones are damned near impossible to find. But to get *uncut* ones?"

Magnus folded his thick, muscled arms. "I'm afraid we can't tell you that. Are you interested? Or shall we look elsewhere?"

Eli placed both hands on the counter and shook his head. "Oh, no. I'm sure we can reach an arrangement that makes us both happy. What's your price?"

Carter looked at Magnus and shrugged.

"Sixty thousand," Magnus said without any hesitation. Although he could probably get more than a hundred thousand at a larger pawn shop, to avoid unwarranted attention from others, he decided to settle for far less.

Carter swallowed hard and in disbelief, he whispered, "Sixty thousand?"

Eli took a handkerchief, wiping sweat from his brow. "I... I don't know."

"Once you cut and set these, you'll make ten times that. Easy. Since they're uncut, no one can trace them. You know how high the demand is. Hell, you said it yourself."

"I know." Eli eyed Magnus and Carter shrewdly. "You two are cops, aren't you? Trying to set me up. Dammit! I knew something like this was too good to be true."

"No, sir. Far from it," Magnus said. "But, hey, I understand your skepticism. If it's too rich for you—" Magnus scooped the stones into his massive hand and turned to walk away.

Desperation quivered Eli's voice. "Wait. Now, I didn't say, *no*. Give me a few minutes to get the money together, okay? It's in my safe. I'll have to go get it."

"That's fine. But only under one condition."

"Oh? What's that?"

"We stay in the same room with you at all times in case you get the urge to call the police."

Eli shrugged. "Hey, that's not a problem. The damn police are the last people I want inside my establishment. It doesn't look good for potential customers along the strip to see cops hanging around."

Magnus smiled. "I understand. We don't want the cops here, either."

"Come on. Follow me to the back."

Chapter 67

Sylvia timidly walked through the casino, avoiding eye contact with anyone. The room seemed to close in around her, and she realized she was entering the early phase of a panic attack. She seldom suffered them before she went to Mars and was fortunate enough while in the landing bay to never succumb to one. But now, tightness squeezed her ribcage. Breathing hurt. Dizziness made the room spin.

She took a quick breath, closed her eyes, and slowly exhaled.

Noises magnified around her. Slot machine handles clicked downward, followed by the whirling computerized beeping as the rows of various pictures spun. The roulette wheel ticked. A marble bounced. Some people cheered while others groaned or swore obscenities.

Her hand tightened around the thousand-dollar chip. When she opened her eyes, she fell forward and grabbed the side of the nearest slot machine. She steadied herself, turned, and placed her back against the machine for stability. Although no one noticed her dilemma, she felt like everyone was staring at her with hot, piercing glares.

Sylvia closed her eyes. Perspiration dampened the back of her neck, beneath her arms, and trickled down her spine. She'd never feared crowds, as these were places she could slip into and disappear. Had she been locked away so long that she feared stepping into a public place? Most of her interactions inside Olympus Mons Landing Bay were with a few mechanics and an occasional guard. Any time she encountered a prisoner, she never experienced the possibility of a threat, mainly because the Sleeper Chips controlled them. Their eyes were frozen without judgment or any leering. The prisoners were nothing more than machines, obeying whatever commands the guards programmed. But here, in this bustling room of gambling hopefuls, they had the free will to gaze however they chose, but fortunately most were too busy counting their chips or rationing their tokens to give her the slightest second thought.

Those seated at the slot machines whispered, prayed, and cursed while a few of the crazier ones chanted, rubbed their lucky charms, and busted. In what most considered faint noises and rhythms, to Sylvia the commotion was thunderous and aggressive. Would she ever be able to blend in with society without this sickening anxiety?

"Miss?" a woman asked.

Deep in her mental prison of desperate fear, she didn't hear the waitress.

The woman nudged her. "Miss, are you okay?"

Sylvia jerked and her eyes opened. She almost screamed but clamped her hand over her mouth to muffle her cry.

"I'm sorry," the topless hostess said, setting down her empty tray. She combed her blonde hair from her blue eyes while she studied Sylvia with a concerned expression. "Are you okay?"

"I'm fine. I... I'm just overwhelmed by everything."

"It's okay. Is there anything I can help you with?" The woman straightened the hem of her emerald-studded miniskirt, which barely covered the V of her green panties. She wore fishnet stockings and emerald high heels.

Sylvia read the waitress' sticker name tag and nodded. "Yes, thank you, Marti. I need to cash this chip in, but I don't know where to do that."

"A thousand dollars? Wow, dear, I see why you'd be overwhelmed. Lady Luck shone full blast on you, eh?"

Sylvia blushed and nodded. "I suppose so."

Marti smiled. "They'll cash it at the cashier's window. Follow me, and I'll show you."

"Thanks."

"Are you sure everything's okay?" Marti asked. "You look a bit frightened."

"Crowds make me uncomfortable."

"You do look out of place," Marti said with a gentle smile.

"It's never bothered me before."

"Perhaps the excitement of winning is partly to blame?"

"Maybe."

Sylvia followed Marti, but she kept her attention on Marti's shoes to prevent making eye contact with anyone she walked past.

"Here you are," Marti said, waving her hand at the window.

"Thank you."

Sylvia walked to the bulletproof glass window and placed the chip through the small window. The cashier was a young man with tanned skin. His jaw was firm, and his brown eyes, piercing. His endearing smile caused her to blush.

"Can you cash this for me?" she asked.

The man behind the glass took the chip and nodded. "Certainly. How would you like it? Large bills or different denominations?"

"I need a room, so it doesn't matter."

"I can put it on an in-casino card if you plan to use it here. Will that work?"

She nodded.

"Okay, what's your name?"

Sylvia hesitated, trying to remember what name she told Carter. Then she said, "Tory Jones."

The man adjusted his black tie, smiled, and typed in the name. A second later he looked at her.

"Do you have some identification, Tory?"

Sylvia patted her pockets and nervously shook her head. "No. I lost my purse."

"Okay, in that case, I'll give you large bills." He licked his thumb and counted out ten one hundred dollar bills. After she took the money, he pointed. "Take the money to the registry desk over there. Casey can help you get a room for the night."

"Will I need identification?"

"Usually," he said, "but if you, erm, *tip* her, I'm sure she'll make an exception." He grinned. "Tell her Burt sent you."

Sylvia returned the smile. "O-okay, thanks."

She hurried to the desk where a heavyset older woman stood. Her silver hair twisted upward in a strange bun design. Casey wore more eyeliner and rouge than most stage girls. Her red lipstick made the woman look cheap and childish. She chomped on stale chewing gum, much like a cow chewed its cud.

"I need a room," Sylvia said in a near whisper. "I don't have identification, but Burt said you'd help me, provided I give you a decent tip?"

The woman glanced at Burt. He waved and grinned. "Sure, honey. Let me see what I can do. How many nights will you be staying?"

"Tonight."

"And your name?"

She hesitated in giving her name. Her mind went blank. Her eyes looked up, and she bit her lower lip while he searched her memory. "T-t-tory... Jones."

The fake name didn't flow smoothly, and the expression on Casey's face indicated a lot of people probably made up names for discretion's sake.

"I see. Will you be staying alone, Tory?"

Sylvia shook her head. "No. My friend will be here soon."

"Oh, your *friend*." Casey rolled her eyes. "Does your friend have a name?"

"Yes. Rick Davenport." Sylvia thought it odd she remembered Carter's fake name better than her own.

"So how much money do you have?" Casey asked.

"One thousand dollars."

Casey slid a coded door key to her.

"How much?" Sylvia asked.

"One thousand, honey."

"All of it?"

Casey nodded and winked. "Welcome to Vegas, honey. You have a penthouse suite since I had a cancellation."

"Really?"

"Yes," Casey replied. "Unless you'd like something a bit more modest?"

Sylvia shook her head. After what she, Carter, and Magnus had experienced, she'd like to pamper herself.

Sylvia slid the money across the desk. Casey eagerly took it. "When your *friend* gets here, I'll send him to your room."

"Thank you."

Casey grinned, counting the money. "No, my dear, thank *you*."

Sylvia's heart plummeted, thinking of spending the entire amount of money for one room, but then she thought about the MarQuebes. Those stones were worth much more than the casino chip. Carter would return with possibly more money than she'd ever seen before she went to prison.

She smiled and took the room code key. She wanted to take a hot bath before Carter returned. The quick, modestly lukewarm showers on the shuttle hadn't made her feel clean. She wanted to fill the tub up to her neck and soak for as long as she could. Life, she hoped, was about to get much better.

Subtlety of life has often never been what the imagination built. True lessons in life were usually paid with a heavy, unexpected price.

Chapter 68

Eli glanced over his shoulder at Magnus and Carter while he tapped the code for the electronic security door lock. Beads of sweat formed on the pawnshop owner's brow, which made Magnus wonder if Eli was extremely nervous about their deal or if he planned something more sinister. Either way, Magnus refused to take his eyes off Eli until the money and gems were exchanged. Once they were safely outside the pawnshop, he'd forget about Eli and Vegas forever.

The door lock changed from secured to green. The lock clicked. Eli smiled and pulled the door open.

"Seems everything's all electronic these days, eh?" Eli said, stepping into his small office.

"More than you know," Magnus replied, rubbing the back of his head.

A small desk set on the far side of the room. Several rusted filing cabinets, covered by a thin layer of dust, lined the wall behind the desk.

"I suppose you don't spend much time in here, do you?" Magnus asked, trying to keep a polite conversation going.

Eli shook his head. "No. It's just me and another person working most days."

"Why not hire more people?" Carter asked.

"Less profit and more paperwork. Besides, I don't trust people that much."

"And your father?" Carter asked.

Eli rolled his eyes and shook his head. "Never around since he married a stripper a few months ago. *Always* on vacation."

"It happens sometimes," Magnus said.

"I guess. I always thought that midlife crisis crap was made up, but hell, you should see the young woman he's with. He drives a Corvette convertible. His money's the *only* reason she's into him. Hell, my stepmom's younger than me."

"Maybe you should flash money around, too," Carter said.

"Believe me, I've thought about it."

Eli walked to a filing cabinet and knelt at the floor safe. After fidgeting with the combination lock, he lifted the small metal lid. A second later a loud click broke the silence. Before Eli stood and turned to aim the gun, Magnus hit him hard. Eli dropped to the floor. The gun scraped across the grimy floor out of their reach.

With one hand, Magnus grabbed the front of Eli's jacket and hefted him eight inches off the floor and pinned him against the wall.

Eli grimaced as Magnus pressed against the man's throat. "I had a bad feeling about the two of you. Take what you want, okay? Please don't kill me."

Magnus looked at Carter and nodded to the open safe. "Carter, count out sixty thousand from the floor safe."

Carter walked to the safe. Magnus frowned at Eli and pressed harder against his throat. Carter found an empty gym bag and pulled it to the safe.

Magnus glared into Eli's eyes. "Your bad feeling was you didn't pull your gun fast enough. All we wanted was the trade. Nothing more."

"Sorry," Eli said softly.

Carter placed the bundles of large bills in the gym bag beside his briefcase. "That's sixty thousand, but he doesn't deserves the gems."

Magnus shook his head. "No, a deal's a deal, no matter how badly greed controls him."

Eli's face was nearly purple.

When Magnus eased his grip, Eli said, "I'm sorry. I honestly thought *you* were going to hold me up, keep the gems, and take the money. Honest. I've been robbed many times. Besides, my father's almost bankrupted us."

"*That* you need to work out with him," Magnus said.

Eli nodded nervously.

Magnus released him. Eli dropped to the floor and backed against the wall. Magnus took the envelope of MarQuebes and tucked it inside Eli's jacket pocket. He picked up the gun and the gym bag filled with money. Then he nodded at the door adjacent to the desk.

"Is that a back way out?" Magnus asked.

"Yes."

Magnus smiled. "We'll see ourselves out."

He tossed the gun across the room, and opened the door that led to the quieter alley. Before Magnus stepped outside the door, Carter grabbed the gun, stood over Eli and pointed it at Eli's head.

"Carter, what are you doing?" Magnus asked.

In a low, almost hypnotic tone, Carter replied, "We can't afford any witnesses."

Eli covered his face with both hands. "Please, *don't* kill me."

Tears streamed down Eli's face as he peered through opened fingers. He whimpered like a pathetic spoiled child.

"You were going to rob us, possibly kill us," Carter said in a hypnotic tone.

"I'm sorry!" Eli shouted. "Okay? Please?"

Carter steadied his aim. His eyes became distant, cold, and black. The cold expression on his face reminded Magnus of the hardened prisoners he'd seen in the Texas prison. Those people were heartless and killed for pure sport. He understood Carter had some issues with possible post-traumatic stress after what happened on Deimos, but he never expected to see this kind of callousness in the medical examiner.

"Carter," Magnus said. "We have what we came for, so put the gun down."

Carter's eyes narrowed. He inched the gun closer to Eli's face. His hands didn't shake, but from what Magnus knew about Carter, the doctor didn't know how to use a gun. Or at least that's what Carter implied on Mars.

"Carter! This man's not Grayson. We got what we came for. Now, let's go!"

Carter shook his head. "No. Sorry, but I can't. He's seen us. He has to die."

Carter squeezed the trigger, Eli winced and screamed, but the safety prevented the gun from firing. Carter squeezed harder. Still nothing. Magnus lowered his head and charged at Carter like a giant linebacker determined to tackle a quarterback. Magnus hit Carter and lifted him off the floor, and then landed on top of him. The gun slid even farther across the room.

Carter blinked in surprise and groaned, clutching his ribs. "Damn! What was that for?"

"What the hell's wrong with you? We have the money. Now let's get the hell out of here."

Magnus rose and yanked Carter to his feet. Carter grabbed the briefcase with one hand while clutching his ribs. He checked to see that Magnus' tackle hadn't jarred the case open. It was still closed.

Magnus grabbed the money, shook his head in anger, and stormed out the door into the alley. A small growl rumbled in his throat as he walked ahead of Carter, not looking back. The coming night darkened the alleyway where several dumpsters rested against the rough walls alongside the alleys.

"Wait up!" Carter said, sprinting to catch him.

Magnus huffed. His muscular jaw tightened, but he held his anger, refusing to answer. His huge hands tightened into thick fists.

"What happened back there?" Carter asked, running around in front of Magnus to stop him.

Magnus shoved him aside, and Carter stumbled to keep from falling.

"You best get away from me, Dr. Carter."

"Please, Magnus, what did I do? Why'd you tackle me?"

Magnus glared into Carter's frightened eyes. The doctor looked completely different than he had inside the pawnshop when he held the gun on Eli. The darkness in his eyes had faded.

"You really don't know?" Magnus asked.

"Honest. I don't."

"Don't be bullshitting me," Magnus said in an angered growl.

Carter shook his head in defeat. "I don't remember anything other than when I counted out the money while you were choking Eli."

"If that's true, Carter, you need to take part of your share and seek medical help. A good psychological examination would be in your best interest."

"Okaaay?" Carter said. "Why?"

"You aimed the gun at Eli's head and tried to pull the trigger twice. If the safety hadn't been on, you'd have blown his brains out."

"Seriously?"

"Hell, yeah. Why would I start lying to you? You need to get your shit together before you go on a killing spree or something, man."

"You're right. I need a mental evaluation. I black out from time to time."

"You keep going into some kind of trance."

"I feel fine though."

"That's the danger. You've no forewarning of slipping from your present reality and zoning into *whatever* crazy state of mind you veer to. Come on. We need to get out of this alley before Eli calls the cops."

Carter frowned and looked over his shoulder. "You think he'd do that?"

Magnus shrugged. "Depends on how pissed he is that you tried to kill him. The best you can hope for is he's too scared to call them. Afraid we'll come back if he does."

A half block away, Carter said, "Thanks, Magnus."

"For what?"

Tears formed in Carter's eyes. "Thanks for stopping me from killing him. That's the last thing I'd ever want to do."

"I won't be around much longer to stop you when you shift into a different psychological zone. You'd best get some medical help soon. I'd hate to get the news that you killed Sylvia. She's been good to you and deserves a better fate."

"I'd never hurt her."

"If you ever hurt her, I'll find you and mess you up. Understand?" Magnus held a fierce unyielding stare.

Carter nodded.

"Good. Now, come on."

Chapter 69

When the elevator opened on the penthouse floor, Sylvia slipped off her shoes. Her bare feet sank into the lavender plush carpet with its golden patterned designs. The soft fibers hugged the rough bottoms of her feet. The comfort was a pleasurable amenity she'd not experienced in a long while. Tired and stressed, she pictured stretching out on the carpet and falling asleep more comfortably than any time over the past two years.

With carpet this nice, she couldn't imagine what luxuries awaited in the penthouse suite.

She hurried to the door and slid the key card through the electronic reader. After the light turned green, the door lock clicked. She pulled the door handle downward and opened the door.

To the left was a polished, walnut dinette table with six high-back chairs. A small basket of fresh fruit set in the center. Sylvia grabbed a shiny Macintosh apple, took a big bite, and made her way to the open bedroom. The cloth wallpaper wasn't appealing with its clashing stripes, but she ignored it after seeing the king-size bed with a half dozen plush pillows layered against the headboard.

Sylvia walked to the large bathroom and flipped on the light switch. The clawed foot tub was surrounded by three mirrored walls. More mirrors covered the ceiling. Folded, plush body towels rested on two shelves. Near the tub was an intimidating glassed-in shower with a massively large shower head fastened overhead, which could mimic a waterfall, if she had her guess. All the faucets in the sinks, tub, and shower were gold-plated.

She stepped on the cold tile floor and headed to the tub. After turning on the hot water, she poured jasmine scented bubble bath from a hotel bottle. A smile crossed her lips, and she closed her eyes.

The gentle splash of running water filling the tub relaxed her. She stood and slipped out of her stolen clothes, letting them fall to the floor. She hated the thought of ever wearing them again. Once Carter returned with the money, she'd order new clothes from a local store and have them delivered to their room. It would be nice wearing something colorful and fancier than the mechanic jumpsuit.

Looking in the mirror at her nude body, she bit her lower lip. She was still athletically built, but her ribs showed more than she remembered. Space travel and Carter's stressing behavior prevented her from maintaining a healthy appetite. Of course, the food packets on the spaceship weren't delicacies. No one ate those for the taste. They simply ate to get enough adequate calories for survival. Nothing more.

Now that she was on Earth, she savored eating richer foods and working out in a full-size gym. She wanted to return to her place in the world and live a better life than before her prison sentence.

Sylvia rubbed her dry hair between her index finger and thumb. As much as she favored bathing, she wanted a decent haircut at a hair salon to trim off the frazzled ends. A spiral perm would be a nice change, too. Makeup and sweet perfume was something she'd buy once Carter returned. It'd been forever since she spoiled herself with a shopping spree.

Not a *shoplifting* spree, she thought and laughed. Her thieving days were over. Buying items instead of stealing them was what she'd have rather done years before. Taking things that didn't belong to her wasn't worth the penalty of jail.

When the tub was three-fourths filled, she turned off the water and slid into the white bubble coated water. The heat of the water seeped through her. She sighed. Never had a bath felt so good.

Sylvia gathered the bubbles around her and rested the back of her head against the tub. "Carter, you're going to be in for a treat when you get here."

A sly grin spread across her face while she thought of how she'd make love to him when he arrived. She wanted to give him a massage and help release his tensions. He'd suffered enough loss, and she hoped she could replace his pain with love and let him know he could heal.

ALBERT BENNETT STOOD in the lobby of the Lady Luck Casino. He wore khakis and a light sport jacket. Beneath his jacket was a Glock 9mm, neatly holstered so the gambling patrons couldn't see it. He wore dark shades with chrome rims, which indicated his cockiness and a charade to pass as hotel casino security.

Being tall and athletically built, he caught the eye of most females as he walked past. His charming smile sent a heated blush to a lot of the women who came to Vegas for more than the gambling, but he never approached them, even after recognizing their interested gazes.

Albert seldom came to the casinos, except during the times when Grayson held meetings with potential clients who liked to gamble. Grayson never gambled his money on the various card games or machines, but often during negotiations, he'd slide a few thousand dollars to someone he hoped to seal a deal with, telling them to enjoy the tables. Funding another's potential to increase their wealth or their gambling addiction was a temptation that made his clients wonder how much more working for Grayson benefited them.

Even though Grayson wasn't a gambler except in the risks he took as a businessman, the casino owners knew him and his security entourage. They knew Albert and his team members, so Grayson's TAC team was never relieved of their weapons whenever they entered a casino. They were considered trustworthy by casino security teams, and should any inadvertent damage ever occur, the owners knew Grayson would readily compensate for more than the cost of repairs.

Albert walked past the one-arm bandit machines and stopped beside Morgan Phillips, a tall brunette with long wavy hair. She wore tight jeans with a snug, white tank top, which exposed her muscular arms. Morgan never carried weapons. With her martial art skills, she *was* a weapon.

She noticed Albert's approach and glanced at him. Her eyebrows rose in question.

He simply shook his head.

Another man, Lars, joined them. He was bald, muscular, and abnormally pale for someone living in Vegas. He was a rugged individual with his gun tucked behind his back. His long-sleeved shirt draped over the back of his pants, concealing his weapon.

Albert tapped his earpiece. "Yes?"

"Sylvia's in the penthouse suite," Grayson said. "Move in. Take her. If she resists, you know what to do."

"She's alone?" Albert asked.

"Yes."

"What about the others?"

Grayson was silent, but Donavan could be heard in the background. "Mr.

Grayson, please reconsider. Give this a few more minutes. Magnus and their partner must be nearby."

"It doesn't matter, Donavan. Once we have her, the other two might be persuaded to turn themselves in,"

"With them on the run," Donavan said, "they aren't likely to come to one another's aid."

Albert glanced at Morgan and Lars, rolling his eyes. "Apprehend or stand down?"

"Apprehend her," Grayson said firmly. To Donavan, Grayson said, "Can you unlock her door so they don't have to burst through?"

"Uh, yeah, give me a few minutes," Donavan replied.

"Albert," Grayson said.

"Yes?"

"Get your team into position. By the time your elevator reaches the penthouse floor, maybe he'll have hacked her lock. Hold position until I give the okay."

"Roger that," Albert said. He motioned the other two to follow.

They crossed through the center of the gambling tables until they reached the hall with the elevators. Morgan pushed the UP button. They stood in silence while they watched the floor numbers descend. When the doors opened with a loud chime, they stepped inside.

After the doors closed, Morgan asked, "How many are there?"

"Only the female," Albert replied.

"And the others?" Lars asked.

Albert shrugged. "Donavan seems to believe they're nearby."

Morgan sighed. "So are we waiting for them, too?"

Albert shook his head. "No. Grayson wants Sylvia taken into custody. From what he told Donavan, they're hoping the other two turn themselves in."

Lars grinned. "She must be something if two escapees would simply turn themselves for her."

Morgan's eyes narrowed. "Now we see why you're single all the time."

"Not *all* the time," Lars said.

"I've never seen a woman on your arm," she replied.

"I don't allow myself to get attached."

"Perhaps it's the other way around. They don't want you attached to them."

Lars laughed. "No. I get what I *need* and move on to the next one."

"Is that so?" She asked, crossing her arms.

"Quiet," Albert said with a frown. "Focus on the job. We apprehend and take her to Grayson. We don't know if the other two will show up as we exit. So, stop the useless prattle. Keep your eyes open."

"They have weapons?" she asked.

"I've not been told if they've gotten guns or knives, but always expect they do. Never underestimate a convict. You both know that."

Lars nodded.

The elevator stopped at the penthouse floor. The doors opened, and they stepped out quietly, gazing down the empty hall.

Albert tapped his earpiece. "We're here. Getting into position."

Albert placed his back against the wall, pulled his 9mm, and slid his back along the wall as they neared Sylvia's room.

"Okay," Grayson said. "He's unlocked the door."

Albert placed his left hand on the door handle and pushed downward. The lock clicked softly. He eased the door inward and listened.

Morgan glanced at him. "You sure she's in here?"

He nodded. He motioned her to go to the right and he went left.

Lars walked through the living room and toward the bathroom. Water splashed softly. He smiled and licked his lips, quietly approaching the half-opened door. His heartbeat increased, and he swallowed hard. He neared the door with nervous excitement; not because he feared her, but she was nude. He waited until Albert and Morgan slipped into different rooms before he placed his hand against the door and gently pushed it wider.

Soap bubbles covered the surface of the bathwater, up to her chin. Her eyes were closed as she rested her head on the edge of the tub. Earbuds were tucked in her ears. The music was slightly audible, so he anticipated she'd never hear his approach until after he pulled her from the tub.

He took a deep breath, slid off his shoes, and eased the door closed.

Chapter 70

Soft piano music flowed through Sylvia's earbuds like gentle raindrops on a summer afternoon. The meditation music from the hotel's wall stereo, combined with the heat of the bath water, made her drowsy. Drifting on the edge of sleep, her head tilted side to side. For the first time in a long while, she felt totally at ease, no worries, and for once, her future seemed brighter than ever.

The entire time she was confined inside her cell on Mars, she missed taking a bath. Showers were better than nothing, but it was impossible to relax while standing.

Her head bobbed slightly forward. Bubbles clung to her chin. She opened her eyes and noticed the man's reflection in the wall mirror. Before she could scream, he dunked her under the water.

Sylvia thrashed her arms and held her breath.

The man released her for a moment. When she pushed herself out of the water, he slid his hands around her, yanking her against him. Water sloshed on the tile floor. His rough hands firmly cupped her breasts as he held her. She tried to pry his hands off, but she couldn't budge him.

Adrenaline pumped through her. Rather than scream, Sylvia placed her feet on the side of the tub and pushed hard. Her unexpected thrust knocked the man off balance. He loosened his grip, trying to find footing, but the soapy water dripping off her body made the tile floor more slippery. His wet socks held no traction, and he fought to correct his balance.

She swung a swift elbow into his ribs, drawing a sharp groan from him. He released her to clutch his pain. She turned to see the anger stirring in his eyes, but then his eyes swept over her nude form. A smile curled on his lips.

"Who the hell are you?" she asked, trying to cover herself with her hands.

"Don't worry your pretty head about it," he replied.

Sylvia turned, grabbed a towel, and covered her front.

"Ah, baby, don't do that. I like the view." His crackling voice was rough and annoyingly nasal when he spoke, grating her nerves.

"Who are you?" Her face flushed red.

Lars lowered his hands and took a step toward her. "I'm taking you into custody."

"What?"

He nodded. "Grayson sent me. Who else? But, for a few little favors, I'll let you escape. He wouldn't need to know." His hands rested on his belt, near the buckle.

Sylvia frowned. "No, thanks."

"That's the way you want it?"

She nodded.

Lars grinned. "I like it rough, too."

He took another step closer. She backed against the wall, and he came even closer, cornering her. His smile didn't lessen and the lust in his eyes increased.

"Please, don't," she said, tightening her grip on the long plush towel.

When Lars was within arm's length, he reached and grabbed the towel. He yanked with such force that her fingers ached. His roaming eyes sickened her.

The door opened.

Sylvia looked past Lars and noticed a woman enter. "Help?"

"Lars!" Morgan said. Her hands formed tight fists.

Lars glanced over his shoulder, and Sylvia planted a swift knee to his groin. He clutched himself, and she raked her fingernails down the side of his face. Angered, he reached for her, but she moved to his side, inches out of his reach. This time he slipped, and dropped to his knees. Blood filled the sharp grooves carved down his cheek. He rushed and grabbed her arm, but she tugged free. He lost his balance and slipped forward. She rammed a fist into his nose. Bones cracked. He groaned and blood flowed over his lips.

"Stand down, girl," Morgan said.

Sylvia stared at her for a moment and noticed the woman didn't have a visible weapon. The intimidating woman looked stronger than she. Sylvia couldn't afford being taken into Grayson's custody. She worried that Carter and Magnus had been caught. Had they traveled so far, simply to fail?

Lars wiped blood from his nose. He looked at Morgan. "Step outside and close the door. When I'm done with her, this bitch will become less hostile."

Morgan shook her head. "Based on her breaking your nose in front of me, she'll kill you if I left you alone with her."

"Five minutes, Morgan," he replied, "and I'll prove otherwise. Twenty minutes is preferable, but that's me being greedy."

"Not happening, Lars." Morgan said. She tossed another towel to Sylvia. "Sylvia, come quietly with me and we'll get your clothes. Lars won't touch you. I promise."

"You don't know what Grayson will do to me," Sylvia said. "Please, just let me go."

"I gave you a great offer so you won't have to," Lars said.

Sylvia ignored him and wrapped the towel around herself. "Grayson will have me killed."

Morgan shrugged. "I don't know what Grayson will do, and frankly, I don't care. We were hired to bring you in. All I'm interested in is getting the money."

"Please?"

Morgan shook her head. Her defiant eyes dared Sylvia to give her a reason to physically restrain her. The muscled woman stood partway inside the bathroom door. The door was open far enough, Sylvia reasoned, that if she rushed Morgan, she might shove her way through the door and make a run for the outside hallway. If she reached the elevator or stairs, she might escape.

Lars wiped away more blood with the back of his hand and water splashed as he stood. He advanced and stood behind her.

She looked at Morgan. She'd rather make the bold attempt to forcefully thrust her way past Morgan than for Lars to place his grubby hands on her again. In strength Sylvia was at a disadvantage and outnumbered. What she needed was some kind of distraction, but nothing useful came to mind.

Sylvia turned slightly, so she could keep an eye on Lars and Morgan at the same time. Lars took another step. Sylvia pointed a stern finger. "Back the hell away."

"Lars," Morgan said in a cold, threatening tone.

While Morgan's eyes and finger were trained on Lars, Sylvia bolted for the door. Morgan lowered and braced herself with her legs spread shoulder length apart. She held her hands out to both sides in a grappling pose. Sylvia lowered her shoulder and head and struck Morgan full force.

Both Sylvia and Morgan tumbled into the hallway. Morgan's eyes narrowed with rage, she bore her teeth, and with a viselike grip, she clamped a hand around Sylvia's left wrist. Sylvia rolled and noticed Lars hurrying behind her. Being sprawled while fighting to pry herself free of Morgan's hold, Sylvia realized she was fully exposed, giving Lars a show she never intended. In desperation, she tugged her left arm and pivoted, but Sylvia couldn't break Morgan's grip.

"Hold her," Lars said, steadying himself inside the doorframe. He simply stood and watched, not offering to help assist Morgan at all.

"*Pervert*," Sylvia thought.

Sylvia rolled, pulling Morgan over her, but Morgan didn't release her. Sylvia slugged the woman in the face twice; still Morgan didn't let go. Instead, Morgan gripped both hands around Sylvia's left wrist, pulled Sylvia to her feet, and swung Sylvia all the way around, crashing her into the wall. Morgan pressed her weight against Sylvia.

"You've got spunk," Morgan whispered in Sylvia's ear. "But you're no match for me. If Grayson hadn't insisted we not hurt you, you wouldn't be walking out. We'd be carrying you."

Albert stepped around the corner with his 9mm raised.

"Where the hell have you been?" Morgan asked.

He gave her an odd glance. "I was setting the bugs and spy cameras for when the others show up. I figured the two of you shouldn't have any problem taking her. Besides, Grayson was talking to me."

"Handcuffs?" Morgan said.

Albert reached to his back pocket and handed the handcuffs to Morgan. Lars wiped pouring blood from his crooked nose. Albert shook his head. "Look, let her get dressed before you cuff her."

"You going to behave?" Morgan asked Sylvia.

Sylvia glanced at Albert and saw the gun. She nodded.

"You'd best," Morgan said, "because I'm hoping you give me one reason to get even."

Morgan backed away from Sylvia. She turned with a swollen lip.

Albert winced. "She did this to the two of you? Or did Lars piss you off again."

Morgan rolled her eyes. "Lars is still standing, ain't he? Remember the last time?"

Albert nodded. "Yeah. He didn't wake up for a few hours."

"What else did Grayson want?"

"He asked us to see what belongings she had, but I couldn't find anything," Albert replied.

"That's because I don't have anything. I didn't bring any belongings with me," Sylvia said.

"Really?" Albert asked.

She nodded.

"Then how'd you manage to afford this suite?"

"Got lucky."

Morgan laughed. "Lucky? Honey—"

Albert said, "Grayson's under the impression you pocketed some MarQuebes. Is that true?"

Sylvia shook her head, but her eyes indicated her fear and proved she was hiding something.

"Okay. Lie if you want," Albert said. "But Grayson has ways to find the truth. It's really much better if you tell me where you stashed them."

"I don't have any MarQuebes. I never took any, either."

"How else could you afford this room?"

"I told you. I got lucky. I found a thousand dollar chip on the edge of the street and cashed it in."

"Likely story," Morgan said.

"It's the truth," Sylvia said, while she hurriedly dressed.

"So your accomplices have the gems?" Albert asked.

"I've told you all I'm going to say. Take me to Grayson and let's get this over with," she replied.

Morgan held up the handcuffs with her right index finger, letting the cuffs dangle. "Turn around. If you're lying, Grayson will become even angrier."

Sylvia turned and placed her hands behind her back. Morgan tightened them around her wrists. She wanted to cry, but she wasn't about to give these three bounty hunters the satisfaction. She'd face her punishment, but she refused to give Grayson any information that'd aid him in finding Carter and Magnus.

Chapter 71

Grayson turned to Donavan and smiled. "Sylvia's in custody."

"One down. Two to go," he replied. "But you may have screwed your chances to catch Magnus and his mystery accomplice."

"She'll talk."

Donavan shrugged. "Perhaps. Perhaps not."

"You're generally more optimistic than this."

Donavan chuckled. "I offered you my advice."

"So you're mad I didn't take it?"

"Not mad, but... it seems you don't hold much confidence in my suggestions."

"I do, actually. Your idea for hacking the street and casino cameras to use facial recognition was a great one. You found Sylvia. I can't see how we're going to find the man from Deimos."

"I received an email a few minutes ago from Shelly in the computer tech office. She's been reviewing the footage of when the man from Deimos arrived at Olympus Mons."

Grayson put his hands in his pockets. "Did she find something we've missed?"

Donavan nodded. "She's found something of great significance."

"What's that?"

"Come here, and I'll show you."

Grayson walked to where Donavan sat and watched over his shoulder.

"When he got off the shuttle, he was holding that briefcase. She's sent multiple still-frames from various cameras throughout his routes while he was at Olympus Mons. He never left that case out of his sight, apparently."

"Wonder what's inside it?" Grayson asked.

Donavan shook his head. "I don't know, but it must be worth quite a bit."

"Gems!" Grayson said. "He must have stolen MarQuebes."

"It seems the most likely thing," Donavan said. He tapped his earphone. "Give me a second, Mr. Grayson."

Donavan listened to the message and then looked at Grayson. "Shelly's on her way to your office."

"Why?"

"She'll show us when she gets here. It's quite urgent."

"It had better be," Grayson said.

"She's near my equal in computer analysis and hacking, so if she says she's found something of great importance, she's not exaggerating."

A quick rapping came at the door.

"She must've run," Grayson said.

"Up the stairs," Donavan said, nodding. "She dislikes elevators."

Grayson nodded at Henry. Henry opened the door. A thin blonde walked into the office with a laptop tucked under her arm. She was pale, almost a reflective white, wore no makeup, and looked like a ghost trapped in human form. Her eyes were slightly pink. An albino.

"What'd you find?" Grayson asked.

She walked to his desk and set down the laptop. She opened it and typed for several seconds. Afterwards, she grabbed his remote control off the desk and aimed at the large computer screen attached to the wall.

"When I found this footage, I knew you'd want to see it immediately," Shelly said. "Really, there's not any decent way to describe it in words."

Grayson nodded. "Go ahead."

She clicked the 'Start' button and talked while playing the footage. "I received this video transmission from Deimos Life Station a few minutes ago."

"The Deimos Life Station?" Grayson asked. "We've not been able to make contact with them for months."

Shelly smiled. "There's a reason for that."

"What?"

"Well," she replied, "Dr. Carter on Deimos somehow manipulated the computer feed of the cameras to prevent us from getting footage."

"Dr. Carter?" Grayson crossed his arms. "He's the medical doctor on Deimos. He's not a computer tech."

She shrugged. "He apparently has some knowledge because it's his identification number used to log into the computers and alter the codes."

"You managed to override his codes?" Donavan asked.

"No," she replied. "He delayed our access to the cameras and apparently to our means for communications."

"Why'd he do that?" Grayson asked.

Shelly pointed to the screen. "Watch."

On the screen, Dr. Carter's working with a dying patient. Behind him are sheet-draped bodies on gurneys.

"What the hell happened?" Donavan asked.

"An outbreak?" Grayson asked, walking closer to the large screen.

"That's what it looks like. Lots of bodies on the beds behind him. But I can't answer that," she said. "Watch."

Another clip showed Carter seated on the edge of a bed with a syringe in his hand. He placed the needle close to a swollen vein on the inside of his left elbow. His face was flushed. Beads of sweat covered his forehead. A shadow spilled over him, and the footage paused and pixelated. Static blurred the visual.

"What was that?" Grayson asked.

Shelly sighed. "I've no idea. But it's like someone deliberately cut the footage of the person who entered the room."

"What was he doing? Shooting up?" Grayson said.

"No. He looked sick. He might've been preparing to overdose on something to kill himself. But watch where the next footage picks up."

In the next scene, Carter stood at a laboratory table. Numerous vials, pipettes, a centrifuge, and microscope slides littered the table.

Donavan stood and walked to stand beside Grayson. "He's not sick there."

Grayson frowned and looked at Shelly. "Are you sure the date and time stamp of these clips are accurate?"

She nodded. "These are chronologically correct. I can't explain the missing footage, or if these were the only things Carter wanted us to view."

"What's he doing?" Donavan asked.

"Looks like he has isolated a virus or a disease-causing agent and is beginning to propagate it," Grayson replied.

"He's growing it?"

Grayson nodded.

"Why would he do that?" Donavan asked.

"Revenge."

Dennis glanced toward Grayson. "Revenge? For what?"

"I think I know," Shelly said.

She clicked the rewind button on the remote and backed through the footage to a scene before Carter started to inject himself. The scene was when

Carter kissed Wanda's dead lips only moments before shoving her corpse into the incinerator.

"Girlfriend?" Donavan asked.

Shelly shrugged. "That'd be my guess. This is before the film pixelated. Now, let me forward to the last few minutes of the footage."

Carter stood in the laboratory and held up two sealed glass vials. He smiled. Carefully, he tucked them into a cushion, which was inside a silver briefcase.

"Shit," Grayson said.

"What?" Donavan asked.

"That briefcase," Grayson said softly. "He carried that everywhere. Carter's the unidentified man that arrived at Olympus Mons."

Shelly stopped the screen. "He brought the briefcase to Earth?"

Grayson shook his head. "Love-smitten fool must blame me for the woman's death. That's touching."

Donavan said, "So Carter brought back whatever virus killed the people on Deimos?"

"We really don't know what he packed, but we need to speculate that he brought a deadly virus to Earth," she replied.

"You want me to call Homeland Security?" Donavan asked.

Grayson shook his head. "No. We handle this ourselves."

"How?"

"We have something Carter might want," Grayson said.

"Sylvia?" Shelly asked. "You think they're a couple?"

"We'll find out once we make contact with him," Grayson said.

Donavan looked uneasy. "If they are, you're proposing a deal to trade her for the virus?"

Grayson nodded.

"Why do you want the deadly virus?"

Grayson smiled. "The man who owns that virus rules the world and possibly, the universe."

Chapter 72

When the elevator opened on the ground floor, Albert tapped his earphone. "Yes?"

They stepped outside the elevator. Sylvia's hands were cuffed behind her back. Lars held a blood-soaked washcloth to his face. Morgan kept a firm grip on Sylvia's left elbow.

Albert looked at Morgan. "It's Grayson."

Morgan rolled her eyes.

"Mr. Grayson, we have Sylvia. Morgan will drive her to your headquarters and then Lars and I—"

"Stand down on the two men," Grayson said.

"Why?"

"Get Sylvia here immediately. The man with Magnus is Dr. Carter. Do not engage. Understood?"

"Yes, sir." Albert looked confused. "But why?"

"Do *not* engage. Get Sylvia to my office ASAP. Where's Team Two?"

"On the street outside the casino, looking for these two men."

"Inform them to stand down and observe. Inform us whenever Magnus and Carter are spotted."

"Roger that."

"We're sending you all his most recent profile photo." Grayson ended the call.

"What does he want now?" Morgan asked.

"To bring her in," Albert said.

"What about the others?"

"Nothing yet. Only for us *not* to engage them."

"Shit," Morgan said, pushing Sylvia to walk. "I guess a third of our bounty is better than nothing."

"A third?" Lars asked. Fury burned in his eyes.

Albert shook his head. "Grayson never said that. Right now, he wants her. He's never shorted us before."

"I wouldn't put it past him," Morgan said.

Albert motioned to the right. "Take her out the back, in case the two men enter through the front. I'll notify Team Two to observe and stand down."

"Grayson believes we should be that apprehensive of them?" Morgan asked.

"Maybe we should be asking Sylvia *why*," Lars said, easing close to her.

Sylvia stepped uneasily away from him.

They walked through the casino, passed the barred cashier windows, and headed down a carpeted hallway. An exit sign led to the the parking garage.

"Lars," Morgan said. "I'm warning you for the last time. Leave her alone."

Albert glanced at Sylvia. "Any reason why Grayson wouldn't want us to approach your two friends?"

"Other than Magnus beating the crap out of you?" she replied.

Lars snorted an odd laughing sound. "I'd like to see him try."

Sylvia grinned. "Maybe you'll get to meet him soon. You'd be minus a face."

Morgan smiled at her. "There's always room for improvement."

GRAYSON SAT BEHIND HIS DESK. "Shelly, do you have anything else we need to see from the Deimos archives?"

"Where the film pixelates, there are large areas that are deliberately blacked out. With your permission, I can try to recover what was lost."

"By all means," he replied.

"That could take some time, preventing me from working on anything else."

"With what Dr. Carter has brought to Earth, I need to know *everything* that occurred on Deimos. It's not only for our safety, but also for the entire population. We cannot underestimate Carter and his intentions."

She nodded. "Yes, sir. I'll get right on it."

CARTER WALKED alongside Magnus in the alley. His eyes roamed as he tried to remember.

"I tried to kill the pawnshop owner?" Carter asked.

Magnus nodded.

"I honestly don't remember doing that."

"Sylvia and I have worried about you for quite some time."

"Why?" Carter asked.

"Your erratic behavior and memory lapse indicate much deeper problems. Maybe it's due to the long space flight? Or it might be something worse."

"But I feel fine."

Magnus frowned. "You didn't look fine. I cannot count the number of times since we met when you've zoned out. Neither of us could get your attention."

"Seriously?"

"Yes. You survived the virus on Deimos, Carter, but have you ever considered it might've altered your brain chemistry?"

Carter frowned. "I've never thought about that, but you could be right."

They stopped at the edge of the alley, near a dumpster. Magnus counted out the money and took his cut. Then he gave Carter forty thousand dollars. He kept the gym bag since he needed to be on the move. Otherwise, he'd have stuffed the stacks of bills into his overalls pockets. Still not certain about Carter's briefcase, he figured if Carter needed, he could always put his money inside it.

"I took a third of the money," Magnus said. "The rest is for you and Sylvia to divide."

"You sure you'll have enough money?" Carter stuffed the stacks of money behind the waistband of his pants and stretched his shirt down to hide them as best he could. "After all, you've done so much to help us."

Magnus nodded. "Yep. What I need to do won't require a lot of money. I hope you know Sylvia's more than fond of you."

"I know. We spent a lot of private time aboard the shuttle, as I'm certain you're aware."

"Carter, to her it's more than sex. Her eyes reveal her love for you. Don't abandon and hurt her."

Carter looked stunned.

"After seven months aboard the ship, I still get the feeling your heart's elsewhere. You don't hold the same affection for her as she does you. It's more than evident in your actions when you're with her."

Magnus extended his hand to Carter.

Carter stared at Magnus for several moments before accepting it.

"Carter, I wish you the best of luck. Please look after Sylvia."

"I will," Carter replied.

Magnus smiled and gave a nod. "This is where we part ways."

Magnus turned and headed to the edge of the street where he hailed a cab. One stopped. When he got inside, he didn't bother to look Carter's direction.

Carter felt alone and worried. He tightened his grip on the briefcase. Fear swept through his mind as he studied the passersby, wondering if any of them were hired by Grayson to apprehend him. He'd have felt safer if Magnus stayed because Magnus was an intimidating person in appearance, but oddly more gentle than most pups... unless provoked.

He noticed the hotel across the street where Sylvia waited. It was best he hurried. There was great comfort in being with a close friend. At least, the alien had not tapped into his mind. He hoped he was outside her mental reach now. But with the strange episode in the pawnshop that he couldn't recall, he feared what she might do next.

CARTER ENTERED the front doors of the Lady Luck Casino and Hotel. He clung to the handle of the briefcase so tightly his knuckles whitened. Walking with all the money tucked at his waistline was awkward. Each step shifted the money stacks and he feared a bundle might hit the floor and draw immediate attention. He kept his movements sure and steady as he crossed the floor. When he approached the registration desk, a young blonde with too much makeup smiled.

"Can I help you?" she asked.

"I'm here with Tory Jones. She should already be in our room."

"What's your name, sir?"

"Rick Davenport."

The young lady typed information into the computer, beamed a smile, and slid a keycard to him. "Yes, she's in the Penthouse suite. Here's the key."

Stunned, Carter placed his hand atop the keycard and palmed it.

"Is there anything else we can do to make your stay more pleasant?" she asked.

Carter shook his head. "No. No, thanks."

He turned and looked around until he saw a sign with an arrow pointing to the elevators. He smiled. He never expected Sylvia to use the chip's entire value to get a room. Magnus' assessment of her feelings for Carter was right. How had he missed the obvious? Unexpected surprises like this made his fondness for her so much stronger. But not all unexpected surprises were worth receiving, as he would soon discover.

Chapter 73

When Carter stepped out of the elevator on the penthouse floor, he glanced both directions. The hall décor was phenomenal. He couldn't wait to see the suite.

He read the room number and walked in the direction for the suite. As he neared the room, the door was partway open. Something wasn't right. He sensed it, stopped walking, and searched the hallway. Not hearing anyone inside the room or along the far end of the hall that connected to another hallway, he returned his attention to the door.

Carter eased to the door, leaned across the threshold, and listened. No music, television, or any sounds were audible. What had happened? Was Sylvia okay? She was apprehensive of Grayson finding them like he was. She would never leave her door open or unlocked.

He pushed against the door, opening it wider before he finally took the courage to step inside the suite. He tucked the keycard in his front pocket. Out of instinct, he closed the door. He felt safer with it closed and self-locked.

After walking through the spacious living quarters with plush seats and small tables, a sidebar, and a sofa, he walked in the huge master bedroom. He set the briefcase on the bed and sat beside it.

"Sylvia?" he called out.

No reply.

Other than his briefcase and the cash Magnus had given him, neither he nor Sylvia had personal belongings, so he didn't have any idea if she'd left voluntarily or by force. His guess was the latter. Had Grayson found her? Of course,

Vegas was the most likely place anyone would have chosen. But, it seemed the safest because they could blend into the crowds.

DONAVAN SAT in the cushioned chair across from Grayson's desk. His eyes were captivated by what was on the screen. He looked at Grayson and grinned.

"What is it?" Grayson asked.

"Albert set up the cameras in the penthouse."

"Are they working?"

Donavan nodded. "Yep. Carter's there now."

Grayson stood. "Really?"

"Yes."

"Does he still have the briefcase?"

"Right beside him."

"What's the room number?" Grayson asked.

"You're calling him?"

"Time to begin negotiations."

CARTER LEFT the briefcase on the bed and went to the bathroom. Puddles of soapy water and streaks of blood covered the floor. Someone had taken Sylvia by force. He backed away from the bathroom door.

The phone rang.

His heart hammered.

Carter let the phone ring and hurried to the bed to grab the briefcase. If they'd taken Sylvia, they were coming for him next. Once he reached the bed, the phone continued ringing. The sound grated his nerves.

Finally, he answered. "Yes?"

"Dr. Carter?"

Carter swallowed hard. Even though he assumed it was Grayson on the other end, he still asked. "Who's this?"

"Boyd Grayson. I'd have readily given you a welcome back to Earth, but since you broke our contract and *stole* my shuttle, I'm afraid I cannot offer any words of endearment."

Carter took a deep breath. His hands shook.

"However," Grayson said, "I believe we can reach a threshold of agreement."

"About what?"

"I have something of yours."

"Sylvia?"

"Yes."

"Is she okay?" Carter asked.

"She's fine, for now. But you have something I want."

"What's that?"

"The briefcase you've been carrying."

Carter placed his hand on the briefcase and rubbed it. Sweat beaded his brow.

"Carter, you give me the briefcase, and I'll release Sylvia to you. I'll even forget about the MarQuebes you and Magnus stole."

"I'm afraid I can't do that."

"What?" Grayson paused for several moments. "Seems I've overestimated your affection for this young lady.

"No. I care about her a great deal, but I'm not stupid. If I hand you this briefcase, I'm dead. You'll kill me."

"Dr. Carter, I'm a lot of things, but I'm not a murderer."

"Do you have any idea what's in this briefcase?"

"I suspect whatever killed everyone else on Deimos."

"You know?" Carter asked. His stomach tightened.

"Little occurs on my properties without my knowledge. Eventually, I find the information I need."

"You obtained the video footage on Deimos?"

"Yes."

Carter said, "It should've been destroyed."

"Parts of it aren't viewable, but I saw enough to know you propagated something in the lab. Possibly a virus?"

"It's worse than anything this world has ever experienced." Carter placed the briefcase on his lap.

"Did you find a cure?" Grayson asked.

"There isn't a cure. At least nothing I tried ever worked."

"And yet, you brought it back to Earth? Carter, you're a brilliant doctor and as a scientist I'd have thought you had more intelligence than to do something so stupid."

Carter's jaw tightened. "You should be held accountable for the deaths of those who died on Deimos."

"You're blaming me?"

"Yes."

"Dr. Carter, I had nothing to do with their deaths. Nothing. Explorations always have risks. Hell, that was even in the contract you signed. Settling Mars and Deimos posed great risks for everyone involved. Those risks you signed waivers for. Did you forget what you signed on for?"

"No, I—"

"You want me to suffer? Okay, let's say you infect me with this virus and I die. I suppose you'd garner some satisfaction about it. Then what? If it's as contagious as you indicate, everyone else inside my building will catch it and die. Once it spreads outside my facilities, it has the potential to kill millions more, right?"

"Yes. I didn't really think about that."

"Damn right you didn't think! But even though your anger and hostility have been directed in the wrong direction, I admire your passion. I wasn't wrong in hiring you."

Carter frowned, cradling the briefcase against his chest.

"Carter," Grayson said, "you're exactly the type of person I need. Ruthless and cold-hearted. I'm willing to put this behind us and offer you twice the amount you made if you continue working for me."

"What? You still want me to work for you?"

"Yes."

"No, I can't do that," Carter replied.

"This is an offer you need to take some time to consider. You've already admitted that your possession of the virus isn't in the best interest of the human population. The world's much safer if I have it."

"Safer how?" Carter asked, frowning. He held the phone between his ear and shoulder.

"My facilities have the securest storage units in the world. There's never a chance the virus will become pandemic. Are you able to make such a guarantee?"

Carter wiped sweat from his brow. "No. I can't."

"Neither can the CDC. And then there's Sylvia. I'll make a deal with you. Okay? You give me the virus and you can continue working for me. Or if you don't want to work for me, you and Sylvia are free to go. Now, do we make a trade?"

"Under one condition," Carter replied.

"What's that, Dr. Carter?"

"You and *only you* bring Sylvia to me. The virus is yours if you agree to that."

"By all means," Grayson replied. "Set a time and place."

"I'll get back to you," Carter said, slamming the phone into its cradle.

Chapter 74

Grayson tapped his earphone and shook his head.

Donavan gave him a perplexed stare. "You're really going to let him go?"

"Hell, no. Once I get that virus, I'll turn him over to Homeland Security. He'll wish he died with the others on Deimos."

"Does it sound like he's going to cooperate?"

"He said he'd get back to me. He's not concerned about Sylvia like I'd hoped. I need more leverage."

Beatrice spoke over the intercom. "Grayson, Hodges from Team Two called and said they found Magnus."

"Thanks," Grayson replied. He glanced at Donavan. "Looks like this day's getting better all the time."

MAGNUS RODE in the rear of the cab. Up ahead at an intersection two black Jaguars with dark-tinted windows were parked catty-cornered, blocking a yellow pickup on a narrow side street. He recognized Mick's pickup.

Two men pinned Mick against the side of the truck. A third man held Troy's arms tightly behind his back. Troy was in evident pain.

He tossed the driver a hundred. "Stop here."

The cabdriver hit the brakes.

Magnus hurried from the cab and slammed the door. Magnus ran in a slow jog and as he approached, one of the men said to Mick, "Where's the man who gave you this ferret?" The three men were dressed in black fatigues, sported crew cuts and were possibly ex-military.

"I swear I don't know," Mick replied.

The large man pressed his arm tighter against Mick's throat. "He just gave it to you?"

In a strained whisper, Mick replied, "For a ride... to Vegas."

Digger chattered inside the truck.

"For some reason, I'm finding that difficult to believe."

Mick's eyes stared past the militant man and widened. The TAC leader turned and was greeted by Magnus' huge right fist. The impact caused the man's grip on Mick to loosen. He spiraled, grabbed for the side of the truck, but instead, he hit the ground.

The second man holding Mick turned, and Magnus punched the man in the gut. The man dropped on his hands and knees, gasping and wheezing for air. The man holding Troy punched Magnus in the stomach. The man grabbed his hand and rubbed it in obvious pain. Magnus smiled.

Magnus struck the man in the stomach several times. The side of the truck prevented the man from falling. He leaned over, holding his stomach and Magnus struck the man's jaw with a swift knee.

Mick grabbed Troy and moved to the rear of the pickup.

Magnus kicked the second man in the gut when he tried to get up. The leader with the crew cut scrambled to his feet and reached for his gun. Magnus charged him. The gun fired but the bullet struck the pavement. Magnus grabbed the man's wrist and slammed his hand against the hood of the truck several times until he released the gun. Magnus grabbed the gun and pressed it against the man's ribs.

"Why are you bothering them?" Magnus asked.

"We're trying to find you."

"Well, you found me. Was it worth the search?" He pressed the gun harder into the man's ribs and glanced at Mick. "You two okay?"

"No thanks to you. Take your damn ferret and get the hell away from me and my son."

Magnus frowned. "I'm sorry. I don't understand."

"Ask that asshole," Mick said, pointing at the man Magnus held the gun on. "The whole reason they stopped us was because they were tracking Digger. Now take the ferret and go, so we can get out of here."

Magnus gripped the man's shirt and shoved him against the truck. He noticed an I.D. patch on his shirt. "Hodges?"

Hodges nodded.

"Is what he said true? Digger has a chip?"

"Yeah."

Magnus shook his head. "Dammit. I never even thought to check him. So why do you want me?"

"Why do you think?"

"Grayson?"

"Yep. He sent us to bring you in."

"Not going to happen," Magnus replied.

With the gun trained on Hodges, Magnus backed up and retrieved the two unconscious men's guns. Partially kneeling, he removed the earpiece from one man and tucked it into his front pocket.

"Cuff your partners. One wrong move and I'll drop you right here. I've nothing else to lose, now do I?" Magnus said.

Hodges kept his left hand raised and removed plastic zip-ties from his belt. He cuffed both of his partners. Magnus took a third plastic zip-tie and fastened it around Hodges hands.

"Which vehicle's yours?" Magnus asked.

Hodges nodded to the one closest. "That one."

"Let's go."

Mick grabbed Digger from the truck to give to Magnus. Magnus shook his head. "No. He's yours."

"I don't know what kind of trouble you're in," Mick said, "but we want no part of it."

"Sir, I assure you it's not what you think, but none of these men will ever bother you about Digger again. I can promise you that."

"Whatever it is, you've put our lives in danger. I don't appreciate it one damn bit. Now, here, take him."

"Da-a-ad," Troy said.

"Digger belongs to Troy," Magnus said.

Mick looked at Magnus with suspicion. "You're certain they won't bother us again?"

"Trust me. They won't. It's me they're after."

Troy hurried to his father and took Digger.

"Let's go, Troy," Mick said.

Magnus said, "For what it's worth, I'm sorry."

Mick slammed his door. Neither of them looked back as they rode away.

Magnus opened the passenger door of the black Jaguar. "Well, Hodges, get in."

Hodges sat and Magnus took another zip-tie and tied Hodges' cuffed hands to the handhold above the passenger door. Magnus shut the door and then opened the trunk. He dragged both unconscious men and tossed them inside the trunk, and then he slammed the trunk lid shut.

Magnus got in the driver's seat and started the vehicle. "I suppose finding me wasn't the best thing for you, was it?"

"You came up on my blindside or things would be a lot different."

Magnus shrugged and laughed. "Doubtful. You talk big for someone rough-housing a thin old man back there."

"You didn't knock me out, did you?"

"No, you can take a punch, I'll give you that."

Hodges smiled. A bruise was swelling on his face. "And you can deliver one, too."

"To be honest, I was holding back."

"Yeah, right."

"You can't talk if you're unconscious, so trust me, I'm being honest. I could've hit you a *lot* harder."

"I'm not all for chit-chat, so you'd have done yourself a better service if you had knocked me out."

"I don't want to talk to you, but you're going to do some talking. Or else."

Hodges gave him a confused stare.

Magnus adjusted Hodges' earpiece. He placed the other one in his ear but snapped off the mouthpiece. "Tell Grayson you have me in custody. Nothing more or..."

Hodges eyed the gun and swallowed hard.

"You understand?" Magnus asked.

"Perfectly."

"Good. Because I don't need this gun to hurt you."

"I said I understand."

GRAYSON TAPPED HIS EARPHONE. "YES?"

"Hodges calling in."

"Okay. You have news for me?"

"We have Magnus in custody, sir. What do you want us to do with him?"

"Any sign of Carter?"

"That's a negative, sir."

"Then bring Magnus in."

"Roger that."

CARTER SLIPPED into a trancelike state for several hours. Methodically, he worked on the silver briefcase. Using a small toolkit and some hardware he'd delivered to his room, he connected springs, buttons, and screws near the handle. After he fastened the final button in place, he grabbed the phone and punched numbers without any real thought. When the phone rang on the other end, he shook his head and awakened from the trance.

"Yes?" Grayson asked over the phone.

"I'm ready to meet," Carter said.

"Great!" Grayson said. "Where?"

"2010 Valley View Road in the abandoned parking lot in an hour. Bring Sylvia. No one else. If I see any of your security team, the deal's off."

"Have you considered my job offer?"

"Let's see how the exchange works out."

"Fair enough."

Chapter 75

Grayson smiled at Donavan. "It'd be a lot easier if Carter would've chosen to stay with the company."

"Why? You'd really want him working for you?"

Grayson nodded. "Of course. It's a valid offer."

"I heard rumor Steven Matthews is in charge of Olympus Mons."

"That's not a rumor."

"Seriously?"

"Yes."

"Everyone thought you hated him."

Grayson shrugged. "At one time I did, but he's proven to be a valuable asset with his IQ equivalent to mine. Some of his great ideas will aid Grayson Enterprises to greater advantages in technology within the next few years. So, here's the thing, Donavan. Sometimes you have to be forgiving, even if you can't stomach being around the person."

"How can you trust Carter and Matthews?"

"It isn't really a matter of trust. I'd always know where Carter is. Matthews is on Mars, and should he attempt to do anything there, I shut down supply lines for a year, and he's doomed. He knows that."

"But it's not the same with Carter."

Grayson smiled. "The biggest reason I need Carter is because he's apparently immune to the virus."

"So? What good's that?"

"His blood has antigens we need to develop vaccines to immunize people before the *chance* of an outbreak occurs on Earth. That's the real reason I offered him such a ridiculous amount of money to stay."

"And if he declines?"

Grayson shoved his hands in his pockets and turned to face the sun on the horizon. "There are other means for negotiation. We'll reach an agreement one way or another."

"I hope so."

"Have some faith," Grayson said, walking to his desk. He pushed the intercom button. "Beatrice, have them prepare my helicopter."

"Yes, sir."

Grayson pushed another button on the intercom. "Is Sylvia ready?"

"Yes, sir."

"Have her escorted to my helicopter on the roof. We leave immediately."

MAGNUS LISTENED to Grayson give instructions to Hodges via the earpiece.

Grayson said, "I'm scheduled to meet Dr. Carter in an hour at 2010 Valley View Road. Get your team in position but make certain you're not visible. Understood?"

Hodges glanced at Magnus. Magnus aimed the gun at Hodges' head.

"Roger that," Hodges said.

Magnus reached over and removed the earpiece from Hodges.

What are you up to, Carter? Magnus thought.

DUSK WAS SETTLING over the parking lot. Carter stood between a dumpster and a graffiti-covered wall. He held the briefcase while scanning the parking lot. He glanced at his watch and shook his head. He kicked loose gravel and grumbled curses.

A stretch black limo drove slowly across the parking lot toward him. After the limo stopped, the rear tinted window lowered. Grayson motioned Carter to approach.

Carter frowned. "I was beginning to think you weren't going to show."

"You realize my office is *in* California? I had to fly and rent a limo. That takes some time."

Carter nodded. "Where's Sylvia?"

"Right beside me."

With the approaching darkness of night, he couldn't see. He leaned closer, squinting. Grayson flipped on the inside lights. Sylvia sat beside him.

"Sylvia?"

Sylvia didn't respond or move. She sat, staring straight ahead.

"Is she okay?" Carter asked.

"She's fine."

"Sylvia?" Carter said. "What's wrong?"

"Here, let me move out of your way." Grayson rose from his seat and moved to the seat opposite her. "Look closer."

Carter leaned partway through the lowered window. "Sylvia, look at me. You okay?"

In an instant, her hand moved. The cold metal of a gun barrel pressed against his temple. She faced him. Her eyes were glazed over. Carter swallowed hard.

"One word," Grayson said. "I give one simple command and she squeezes the trigger."

"You bastard. You implanted a Sleeper Chip in her?"

"As a precaution," Grayson replied. "That's all. I made you a generous offer, and I'd like your answer."

Carter's thumb slid atop the button at the side of the briefcase handle. "Looks like I'm going to turn it down since this transaction didn't go smoothly like we agreed."

"I hate to hear that. I looked forward to keeping you on staff. Now I suppose Sylvia will carry out her assignment now."

"Before you make any hasty decisions, you might want to look out the window."

"Why?"

"I've rigged the briefcase to shatter the virus vials and pop open. Unless Sylvia lowers the gun, I push the button. Maybe you'll escape with your life today, but eventually this virus will kill you."

Grayson laughed. "You're more shrewd than I thought. Sylvia, put down the gun."

Sylvia obeyed. Carter took a deep breath and backed from the window.

From the opposite side of the parking lot a black Jaguar sped at Carter and the limo.

"Driver, go!" Grayson yelled.

The rear window rose and the limo sped away. Carter turned and stared in horror at the Jaguar coming straight for him. The car screeched to a stop. When the window lowered, Carter was stunned. Magnus smiled.

"Is everything okay?" Magnus asked.

"What are you doing here? I thought you were leaving the city."

"It's a long story. Are you sure you're okay?"

Carter nodded. "I'm fine, but Grayson has Sylvia. She has a Sleeper Chip now."

"Dammit! Hop in."

Carter opened the back door and sat behind Magnus. "We have to get her chip removed. She can't be at Grayson's mercy."

"We'll make it right, but it'll take some planning."

Hodges glanced at Magnus. "You'll never get past Grayson's security."

Magnus chuckled. "You weren't much of a challenge, Hodges, so you might want to keep your opinions to yourself. We'll find a way inside somehow."

Magnus drove the car to the parking lot entrance.

"Shouldn't we go after Grayson?" Carter asked.

Magnus shook his head. "Not yet."

"Why not?"

"Never run into a situation without preparing first. We need a plan. Going in blind will get us killed."

Carter sighed with frustration. "I suppose you're right."

MAGNUS GLANCED in the rearview mirror. Headlights came on from a parked car he'd driven past. Another set came from a side street and both vehicles sped to catch him.

"Shit!" Magnus said, pressing down on the accelerator. He turned left and narrowly missed an oncoming car.

Carter turned uneasily in his seat and looked at the two speeding cars behind them. "What the hell's going on?"

"Apparently, Grayson dispatched another team besides Hodges' to take you into custody. He doesn't give up easily."

Hodges laughed. "Did you expect any less?"

Magnus gave a side-glance to Hodges. "You're really beginning to piss me off. You know, you're not a passenger I need. How about if I drop you off at fifty-five miles per hour if you say another word?"

Hodges looked away and became quiet.

"Good," Magnus said. "That's much better."

Chapter 76

Bullets chipped across the trunk of the Jaguar Magnus drove. Magnus swerved back and forth in the lanes, trying to avoid the gunfire. He glanced in the rearview mirror at Carter.

"I'm not liking our situation one bit, Carter."

Carter lowered in the seat. "Me, either."

At the next intersection, Magnus took a sharp right, cut through an alley, and discovered it to be a dead end.

"Dammit!"

The two vehicles screeched to a stop at the end of the alley behind him. The drivers pulled their cars across the alley to block it. Magnus looked over his shoulder, shook his head, and dropped the car into reverse.

"Hang on!"

Magnus pushed the gas pedal to the floor. The tires squalled and spun as the car sped in reverse. The tail end of the Jaguar smashed into the two stopped cars. Metal crunched and the impact knocked both vehicles with enough force to allow the Jaguar to speed through.

He cut the wheel sharply, put the car in drive, and hit the gas. Both drivers stepped from their cars and began firing at the Jaguar, but Magnus made the next intersection and turned. Then he remembered the two guards in the trunk, winced, and shook his head. He hoped they were alive but they'd known the risks when they took the assignment. If they survived, they wouldn't be harassing anyone else for a long time.

SENATOR JOHNSON SAT at a table with Justice Watkins and the leader of the California Prison Committee, Lee Tidwell. Johnson was drained. Fatigue had aged his face fifteen years.

For the past several months, Johnson remained at Grayson's every beck and call. He had no other choice since Grayson had taken Johnson's son into custody aboard the shuttle. When Joe Johnson arrived on Mars, Matthews ordered a chip implant for Joe. As long as Senator Johnson complied with Grayson's orders, Joe wouldn't be sent to the mines. At least that's what Grayson had told Johnson. He didn't have any proof otherwise.

Johnson was helpless. At his age, he'd never survive a space flight to Mars, even if he got past Grayson's security to board a passenger shuttle. He was at Grayson's mercy, which essentially wasn't any mercy at all. He reminded himself each morning when he looked in the mirror that he should've retired from the senate several years before Grayson gained such a powerful hold over him. But money,—more money than he could ever have acquired doing honest work—was the lure that snared him. In hindsight, all his gains weren't worth his losses, which included what little dignity he possessed as a politician.

Lee Tidwell finished flipping through the stack of paperwork on the table. His short grayish-silver hair was sparse. His glasses rested halfway down his thick nose. He gathered the papers into a neat stack and clacked them atop the table to straighten them. Looking up, he pressed his glasses against the bridge of his nose and stared a Johnson with a slight smile. "So Grayson wants another hundred prisoners to transport to Mars?"

Johnson nodded. "Could that be arranged?"

"This makes three hundred prisoners over the past six months."

"I know. It's asking too much—"

Tidwell laughed. "Are you kidding, senator?"

Johnson frowned and sat back in the high-back chair.

Tidwell shook his head. "I'll gladly dispatch two hundred *more* prisoners if Grayson wants them. I appreciate what he's done for our prison systems in California. He's lessened the overcrowding problem we've endured for years. We're better able to care for a smaller population without worrying about inner prison riots from opposing gangs. Hell, I'd like to shake his hand, senator. I truly would. I simply don't understand how he's prevented massive riots on Mars. Has he, by chance, had uprisings?"

Johnson shook his head. "To my knowledge, and from what he's told me, he's never had any problems at all."

Justice Watkins was tall, slender, and sported a deep California tan. He gave Johnson a stern stare. "You're sure of that, senator? Everything Grayson does is so tightly sealed. No one outside his enterprises even has a clue as to what his Martian mining operations are like. From my tally sheets, he has nearly five hundred prisoners?"

"Most are in transit to Mars, your honor," Johnson said.

"How's he capable to attend their needs?"

"Food supplies are sent weekly. Vast amounts," Johnson replied.

"Do you have the paperwork to verify this?" Watkins asked.

Johnson leaned forward and opened a manila folder. He slid several papers across the table. "Here's the past month's shipping invoices."

Justice Watkins scanned the invoices. "Impressive. How about medical records? Do you have any of those? Death certificates? I imagine with such a large operation on Mars, there must be fatalities. Injury reports?"

Johnson sighed. "Right now, Mr. Grayson has only the health screening clearance sheets from where the prisoners have been given physicals prior to boarding shuttles bound to Mars. He said he should have monthly reports soon. Within the next week or so."

"I have to admit," Watkins said, "I never thought anyone could benefit our society like Grayson has while building a new civilization on another planet. This gives me hope for the future of mankind. Of course, given the population occupying Mars right now, I'd never make travel arrangements to go."

Johnson and Tidwell laughed softly.

"But why does he need so many so soon?" Watkins asked, becoming more serious.

"He's expanding."

"When you speak to him again," Watkins said, "can you get him to submit blueprint layouts of his mining operations and the housing facilities these prisoners reside in?"

"I can ask him, but it's doubtful he'll share that information," Johnson replied.

"Why's that?"

"He's stated it's confidential information to prevent others from stealing his patented designs."

Justice Watkins formed a finger bridge and leaned back in his chair. "In some ways, I kind of get a picture of a massive slave operation taking place on Mars. With Grayson remaining so secretive about what's going on there, the more inclined I am to think maybe something isn't right. Perhaps we should temporarily deny any future prisoner transfers into Grayson's custody."

Johnson's hands shook. He nervously straightened his tie. His face flushed red.

Watkins noticed Johnson's intense nervousness. "Is there a problem, senator? Are you okay?"

"Yes, I'm fine."

"You look quite nervous," Watkins said. "Has Grayson ever threatened or bullied you in any way so you'd become more supportive of his operations?"

Johnson wanted to tell Watkins everything, and if Grayson didn't have Joe in custody, Johnson would've spilled every corrupt detail of what he believed Grayson was doing. But he knew if he did, Joe was dead. Although Grayson never directly threatened to kill Joe, he'd been rather blunt, implying that *accidents could occur inside Olympus Mons.*

Johnson shook his head. "No, sir."

Tidwell frowned and looked at Watkins. "Wait, are you saying this deal isn't going through today? I'd like to clear out more prisoners."

Watkins gave an even smile and stood, facing them. "What you two have agreed inside this room today will be granted. But nothing more after today, not until Grayson's ready and willing to disclose the proper paperwork to my satisfaction. I hope I'm not making a huge mistake in granting this current agreement."

Tidwell and Johnson stood.

"Thank you, your honor," Tidwell said.

"Yes, thank you," Johnson said.

After the justice left the room, Tidwell shook Johnson's hand. "Tell Grayson how much I appreciate his help in relieving our overcrowding situation."

"I will."

Tidwell left the room.

Senator Johnson sighed and sat down. He leaned over the table with his hands clasped together. His mind reflected his life's decisions and he found he had far more regrets in life than positive memories. He didn't know how to redeem himself or how to save his son's fate from whatever Grayson planned to do.

Chapter 77

The next morning Magnus awakened in the cheap rundown hotel room he'd rented on the outskirts of Vegas. Carter snored, sleeping on the other twin bed. Magnus shook him awake.

"We'd best get moving," Magnus said.

Carter rolled over and slid his feet over the edge of the bed. "I could use a shower."

"Be quick. We can't afford to stay in one place too long."

"You think Grayson will find us here?"

"You never know," Magnus said. "He seems overly fond of using tracer chips. That's why we abandoned the car and took a cab here."

When Magnus ditched the car, he left the trunk slightly ajar so the three men could call for help when they awoke. They were bruised badly from Magnus' getaway, but none were shot.

"Since it was a company car, you're probably right." Carter opened the bathroom door while holding his briefcase. "I can shower quickly."

Magnus nodded, sat on the edge of the bed, and used the remote to turn the small television on.

WHILE WAITING for the water to warm, Carter examined the dark stubble on his face in the mirror. He wished he could shave. As he leaned closer, a shadow stirred behind him in the mirror's reflection.

Carter turned but saw nothing.

He looked around with panic swelling inside him. "Where are you? I know you're here. I sense your presence. Show yourself, please?"

A sensation rushed through him like a surge of electricity. His eyes rolled back. To prevent falling, he gripped the edge of the sink.

The alien's voice echoed softly. "Kill Grayson. Stop him. If you don't, Sylvia will die."

Carter lowered to his knees with sweat beading his brow. After a few seconds, he no longer sensed her closeness. He wept. He thought he was outside her reach, but she'd never stop torturing him until he did what she demanded.

Once the shakiness left his legs and he could stand, he stepped in the shower. He thought about what the alien had said about Sylvia and recalled how lifeless she seemed being controlled by the chip. The alien was right. Grayson must die. It was the only way to save Sylvia, and he hoped by obeying, he could rid his mind of the alien's invasion.

MAGNUS SAT WATCHING the news when Carter stepped outside the small bathroom.

"I can't believe this," Magnus said.

"What?"

"California's handing another hundred prisoners to Grayson for deployment to Mars."

"Seriously?"

Magnus nodded. "Yeah. A committee met yesterday and granted Grayson custody. That makes nearly three hundred prisoners in the past few months, according to the news report. And that man right *there*... he's the man we need to talk to."

Senator Johnson's image appeared on the screen. He was answering press questions as he walked past.

"You think Senator Johnson would help us?" Carter asked.

Magnus shrugged. "I don't know, but it wouldn't hurt to contact him. He needs to know how corrupt Grayson is."

"He's a politician. He probably knows what Grayson's doing. Besides, he's probably more corrupt. Never have I seen an honest politician."

"I know it's a long shot, but I could testify against Grayson's prison operation. Grayson might get charged and put in prison for what he's been doing. My participation could get me pardoned or open an investigation into arresting the men who framed me."

Carter nodded. "You've never told me exactly what happened. Why'd you end up in prison?"

Magnus chuckled. "I was in the wrong place at the wrong time. My girlfriend's cousin got messed up on meth from the neighborhood drug dealers. I wanted to help, so I told her I'd find the scumbag that sold him the shit."

Magnus turned off the television. "So I followed her cousin, but I never thought he was a member of a drug-pushing gang."

While he explained, his mind carried him back.

Magnus rode his motorcycle and followed his girlfriend's cousin, Davis, as he drove his junky hatchback. Davis turned and parked at a closed metal roll-down door at an old warehouse. Magnus drove on past and parked near some dumpsters.

Since Davis was wired on drugs all the time, Magnus thought he was buying more drugs, and that mistake changed everything.

Davis was a skinny black teen with ratty clothes. He rapped his fist against the door beside the rolled-down one. It opened a crack and then wider, allowing Davis to enter. The door closed quickly.

Magnus said, "I wanted to help him, but he was too deep. Too hooked. As I neared the warehouse, someone followed me."

"What happened?"

Magnus closed his eyes, recalling the scenes. He had hurried to the narrow alley near the front door. He reached for the handle, but a gun pressed against the back of his head. Magnus raised his hands.

The man with the gun knocked in a code-rapping manner. When the door opened, the man pressed the gun against Magnus' ribs, telling him to step inside. Magnus obeyed without hesitation.

Davis saw Magnus. "Why are you here, man?"

The gang leader looked from Magnus to Davis. "You know this man?"

Davis nodded. "Yeah, Tyler, he dates my cousin."

Tyler frowned at Magnus. "Why you here, big man? You need a job? I sure could use some extra muscle."

Magnus shook his head. "I don't work with garbage and this cesspool could definitely benefit from a major cleanup."

Someone struck him from behind with a blunt object and knocked him unconscious.

Magnus shook his head. "I was awakened by the police sometime later. Davis had been shot dead. The gun had my prints on it. A dozen bags of meth were shoved in my pockets."

"So they killed Davis and framed you?" Carter asked.

Magnus nodded. "Yeah."

"So that's why you want to go back to Texas?"

"Yep. I have to. Those men are the ones who need to be in prison. Well, actually, they deserve much *worse* than prison. But I won't be satisfied until they receive what's due them."

"What about your girlfriend? What happened to her?"

"She believed the police report and all the bad press I received. Ever since, she's never had anything to do with me. She wouldn't accept my phone calls from prison or even answer my emails. She's moved on but I won't until after these men are in prison. I owe her cousin that much."

"That's a good incentive," Carter said. "I don't blame you. In fact, it's how I feel about Grayson, especially now that he has Sylvia. Maybe after you've gotten vengeance for Davis, your girl will have a new outlook."

Magnus shook his head. "If she didn't have enough faith in me to believe my innocence back then, I sure as hell don't need her now."

"So we should contact Senator Johnson?"

"It's the best thing we can do at the moment."

"How do we find him?"

Magnus stood. "If we had a computer, we could find out a way to contact him."

"There's a computer in the lobby."

"Might as well use it before we check out."

Magnus waited for Carter to exit with the briefcase. Magnus slung the gym bag over his shoulder. "As soon as we get to a decent place to shop, I need to buy some nice clothes."

Carter nodded. "I want to burn this alien head shirt."

Magnus laughed. "I don't know, man. For some reason, it kinda suits you."

Carter soured at the comment.

Inside the hotel lobby, Magnus sat in front of an old computer. He typed a search for Senator Johnson's contact information and the cursor spun endlessly.

"This damn thing's nearly older than me," Magnus said. Finally, the cursor stopped spinning and the information appeared in a long menu. He clicked the top choice. "Ah, good. Look. The senator's scheduled to speak at a luncheon in three hours. You think we could get there in time?"

Carter looked at the county map tacked on the wall, which pinpointed the best places for vacationers to see the local attractions. "There's a small airport not far from here. We might be able to hire a pilot to get us there."

"My cousin Benji flies a small commuter plane," the desk clerk said.

Magnus and Carter turned.

"Can he get us to L.A. in less than two hours?" Magnus asked.

"Sure. You want me to call him?"

"If it's not a problem."

"No problem at all. My son could drive you to the airport, if you need trans-portation? I noticed you had a taxi drop you off."

Magnus smiled. "I'd pay you quite handsomely for your help."

The man nodded. "Okay. Give me a few minutes."

Chapter 78

Two hours later, Magnus and Carter landed at the airport, took a cab, and arrived a few blocks from the convention center where Senator Johnson was scheduled to appear. They stopped at a Men's Wearhouse and bought leisure suits. They hid stacks of money in various pockets in their jackets and slacks.

Magnus straightened his tie and smiled at his reflection in the mirror. "Carter, I'd enjoy having a job where I dressed like this every day."

Carter nodded, staring at his own reflection. He picked up his briefcase. "Makes you feel a lot different in how you dress, doesn't it?"

"Definitely."

They stepped outside the store and headed down the sidewalk to the convention center. People stood in long lines outside the center.

"Even if we can get in, how will we get a chance to talk to the senator personally?" Carter asked.

Magnus noticed the people holding tickets. "Damn, I don't know. They already have tickets. We don't."

"Tickets? Why would you need tickets?"

"Must be election year or a fundraiser."

"So we've wasted our time?"

"Maybe not," Magnus said.

"But we don't have tickets."

Magnus smiled. "No, but we have a *lot* of money."

Magnus scanned the people as they walked. He noticed a young couple holding VIP tickets. Political fanatics. Convenient, if he could get them to part with their tickets. Magnus smiled at the man and approached.

"Excuse me, sir," Magnus said.

"Hey, no cutting," the man replied.

"I'm not cutting. I'd like to buy your tickets."

"What? Why?"

Magnus gave his best smile. "We really need to talk to the senator. Do your passes give you an opportunity to meet him in person?"

"Of course, but we paid several hundred dollars for them."

"I'll pay you five thousand dollars for the pair."

The guy's eyebrows rose, and he looked at his girlfriend. She smiled. "For real?"

Magnus nodded.

"But why?"

"Political reasons. We weren't able to arrive earlier to buy tickets, but we'll pay you far more than you did." He pulled out a wad of hundreds and counted.

"Damn," the man said. He glanced at his girlfriend. "Want to sell them?"

She eagerly nodded.

The man handed the two VIP ticket passes to Magnus for the money.

"Thanks," Magnus said. He turned and handed one ticket to Carter. They watched the excited couple hurry down the sidewalk. The VIP line moved much faster than the other lines, and they were inside the center within a few minutes.

An usher directed them to a roped off section to pick their seats.

***

SENATOR JOHNSON DELIVERED A RATHER dry speech to the audience that didn't deserve any applause, but he received it all the same. He didn't have any energy or enthusiasm in his words. His humdrum monotone and lack of facial expressions indicated a defeated man who wished to part ways with the political arena, and one who hoped no one voted for him.

After Johnson finished the speech and headed off stage, Magnus and Carter hurried to follow him behind the stage.

Carter said, "Senator Johnson, may we have a moment?"

Two security guards stepped between Johnson and Carter.

"I'm sorry, gentlemen," Johnson replied. "I'm very busy. Thanks for your support."

The senator started to turn away.

Magnus cleared his throat. "What we need to discuss has to do with your involvement with Boyd Grayson."

Johnson's eyes widened. "To what exactly are you referring?"

"For starters," Magnus said. "The prisoners you've been releasing into Grayson's custody for the miner prisoner release program."

Johnson became nervous. "What of it?"

Magnus smiled. "Mind if we speak in a place more private?"

"Like I said, I'm very busy."

Carter frowned. "Too busy that you're willing to ignore the fact that you're aiding and abetting Grayson's abduction of my girlfriend?"

"Come on, Carter," Magnus said. "There are reporters all over the place. Let's give this information to them and the Feds. I'm sure their investigation will produce enough evidence to implicate the senator's role in this scandal as well as Mr. Grayson."

"Wait!" Johnson said. "Come with me. We might be able to help one another out. Forgive me for this. Bill and Jake, check them for weapons."

The two security guards patted them down. "No weapons. Lots of cash though."

One guard looked at Carter. "We need to check your briefcase."

Carter hugged the briefcase to his chest and shook his head. "No. This is top secret. It never leaves my side but you have my word I won't open it."

"Then we'll have to ask you to leave," one guard said.

"Carter," Magnus said.

Carter shook his head. "No. It cannot be opened."

"How about if one of the guards holds it while we talk with the senator?" Magnus asked.

"As long as he doesn't open it," Carter replied. "I'd rather he lock it in the car trunk while we talk."

"We can do that," Johnson said.

"Thanks," Carter said with a sigh of relief.

Johnson shook his head. "We'll go to my limo. We'll have privacy there without the press nosing their way into our conversation."

"Works for me," Magnus said.

When they reached the parked limo, one guard opened the rear door and let them inside with Senator Johnson. The guard took the briefcase and locked it in the trunk. The other guard climbed inside with them.

Senator Johnson sat back and exchanged glances with Carter and Magnus for a few quiet moments. "So, what information do you have that proves Grayson's holding your girlfriend against her will?"

"He's holding her for ransom," Carter replied.

"I work with Grayson a lot," Johnson said.

"So we've noticed," Magnus said.

Johnson's face reddened. "He's done a lot of underhanded things but he's never kidnapped anyone. At least not on Earth."

"He has her," Carter said. "I went to trade with him last night."

"Then why didn't you?"

"Things didn't go exactly as planned."

Johnson shook his head. "With Grayson they never do. What do you have that he wants?"

"A deadly virus from Deimos."

Johnson's eyes widened. "You're Dr. Carter?"

"Yes."

Magnus glanced at Carter with pure skepticism. He looked like he wanted to say something but held back.

Johnson flicked his gaze to Magnus. "And you're Magnus Knight?"

Magnus nodded.

"So, Dr. Carter, Grayson's holding Sylvia?"

"Yes, sir."

"Grayson has ranted quite often about you. I could see aiding Dr. Carter in getting Sylvia released, but Magnus, I cannot justify helping you since you're an escaped prisoner."

"I was framed."

Johnson nodded. "Of course, *all* prisoners are framed."

"I'm serious."

"Well, explain something to me. This is something I recently learned that Grayson kept hidden from me for quite some time. Apparently he's been using some kind of mind control computerized chip that prevents the prisoners from rioting. Is that true?"

Magnus nodded.

"So how'd you get free of its control?"

"Mine malfunctioned."

"Does that happen frequently?"

"From time to time. In severe cases, the prisoners have died."

Senator Johnson winced and looked out the side window, wringing his aged hands. "I was afraid of that."

"Why does that trouble you so much?" Carter asked.

"Grayson implanted my son with one of those chips. He showed me video footage and my son's nothing more than a zombie-like person that's controlled by a computer remote control." Johnson fought tears.

"Look, senator," Magnus said. "We can help one another."

"How's that?" he asked, not looking at him.

"I'd be happy to testify before Congress about what Grayson's doing. It's unethical. He's using the prisoners as slaves. They don't work willingly. They don't have eight-hour shifts. I worked several twelve hours shifts without a working chip. Some prisoners work in the mines until they drop from sheer exhaustion, only they don't feel or realize it. But, I could testify on behalf of their mistreatment in return for—"

"Your freedom? A pardon?" Johnson asked.

"No, sir. The crime I was charged with wasn't something I did. I want a new trial and a good attorney not appointed by the state. I want my name cleared. In short, sir, I want justice."

Johnson looked Magnus in the eyes. "I see. Well, your testimony could be quite useful in bringing Grayson's corruption to light. A lot of government officials would love to have this information. They've been building a case on him for years but have never been able to get conclusive evidence that could stick in court."

Magnus smiled. "I'm glad to do whatever's necessary to help."

"Dr. Carter," Johnson said. "Where's the virus Grayson wants?"

"It's hidden in a safe place."

"And if I can arrange a meeting with Grayson, can you produce the virus?"

Carter nodded. "Yes, but Grayson should never be allowed to get his hands on it. There isn't a cure."

"So we're talking about a potential epidemic situation here?"

"With this virus in his possession, he holds leverage over the world. He'd become far more dangerous than he already is."

Johnson nodded. A grave expression formed on his face. "I'll make certain Grayson never gets the virus. It needs to be destroyed."

"Of course."

Johnson turned in his seat slightly, facing them. "If you two would indulge me, I need to stop by my office. It won't take a few minutes. While I'm there, I'll contact Grayson and set up a meeting. I think I can convince him to let Sylvia go."

"How?" Carter asked.

"I arranged for him to receive more prisoners. That's a huge bargaining chip. I'll threaten to deny the deal if he refuses to remove the chip and let her go."

Magnus shook his head. "Regardless of what he does, senator, you cannot allow him to get those prisoners. The work conditions on Mars are inhumane, and not one of them will live long enough to fulfill their contracts. Ask Carter. He's a doctor. The workers are aging at an alarming rate."

"That may be," Johnson said. "But we must do one thing at a time if we wish to keep Grayson from suspecting we're setting him up."

Chapter 79

Outside his office, Senator Johnson got out of the limo. He walked to his receptionist's desk and motioned Carter and Magnus to take a seat.

"I'll be right back," Johnson said.

Johnson walked past the receptionist and entered his office, closing the door behind him. Magnus rose and looked around.

"What are you doing?" Carter asked.

"Time to part ways," Magnus replied.

"What? *Why?*"

"You have the senator to help you. Besides, he didn't act like he wants to assist me. I'm still a prisoner in his eyes."

"Nonsense."

"Carter, I've been around enough people to know when a man doesn't believe me. He thinks I'm guilty. It's best I head to Texas and get things settled properly."

Magnus extended his hand and shook Carter's.

"Magnus, I wish you'd stick around."

"Tell the senator I'll testify against Grayson. But for right now, I need to go."

Carter nodded. "Good luck."

"And to you."

JOHNSON SAT at his desk and pressed a saved number on his cellphone list.

"Yes?" Grayson said. "What is it, Senator Johnson? I saw the news report. Good job. I'm quite impressed."

"I have even better news, sir."

"What's that?"

Johnson chuckled softly. Something he had not done in quite some time. "Dr. Carter and the escaped con are outside my office."

"Really? Why are they with you?"

"They've requested my help."

"Help? With what?"

"They want to stop the prisoner trade. Dr. Carter wants Sylvia released. Magnus wants to testify in court against you."

"Is that a fact?"

"Yes, sir."

"Senator Johnson, can you bring them in?"

"I can do a lot of things, Mr. Grayson, provided you do something for me."

"Joe?"

"Yes," Johnson replied coldly. "Let him and Sylvia go. I want video proof that Joe's been released from the mind control chip. You do that, and I bring these two in for you."

"Consider it done."

"I need proof, Mr. Grayson, or I swear I use these two men to bury you beneath piles of legal actions. Money cannot buy your way out of a Congressional Hearing. You understand that?"

"Finally growing a backbone, Ralph?"

"You crossed the line with my family. When I have proof Joe's free of that chip, send me video via my phone." Johnson didn't wait for a reply. He ended the call. For the first time in a long while, he felt powerful and in control. He wished he'd stood up for himself years ago.

SENATOR JOHNSON STEPPED outside his office and noticed Magnus was gone.

"Where's Magnus?"

"He had some personal business to take care of."

Johnson shook his head. "No. That's not good. No. We need him. Maybe we can find him if we hurry."

"He said he'd testify in court against Grayson."

Johnson stormed past Carter and out the doors.

"Did you contact Grayson?" Carter asked.

"Yes."

"And he agreed to meet?"

"He did, but he won't be happy Magnus left."

"We don't need him to get Sylvia."

Johnson shrugged. "Maybe not, but Grayson will be suspicious that Magnus isn't with us."

As they neared the senator's limo, they noticed both of Johnson's bodyguards unconscious on the sidewalk.

"Dammit!" Johnson said. "I should've kept a guard on him."

"He's not violent. He didn't even take one of their guns."

"It's obvious that he doesn't *need* a gun. He's probably more dangerous than you ever gave him credit."

"No, I've been around him seven months. He's a gentle giant.

"Yeah, well, tell that to my men. Mars was probably the best place for Magnus to have remained." Johnson headed to the limo and opened the rear door. "Come on, Dr. Carter. Grayson's patience is less than my own."

Carter looked at the rear door nervously.

Johnson sighed. "Well, do you wish to free your sweetheart or not?"

"Coming."

<hr>

AFTER AN HOUR, a short video arrived on Johnson's phone. He hit 'Play'. Joe spoke and informed Johnson he was okay. He seemed groggy and believed he had just arrived at Olympus Mons. Grayson kept his word. Johnson relaxed with an internal sigh of relief.

"Where's the virus?" Johnson asked.

"As soon as I know that Sylvia's okay and no longer under the chip's control, I'll hand it over."

The driver drove the limo into the rear parking lot at Grayson Enterprises. Two of Grayson's large guards approached the rear of the limo. Carter noticed the sudden nervousness in Johnson's eyes.

"What's wrong?" Carter asked.

"Nothing. Let's get this over with."

"I need my briefcase," Carter said.

Johnson picked up the phone and told the driver to pop the trunk. Then he and Carter exited the rear of the limo. "Get your case and let's hurry."

Carter leaned into the trunk and opened the briefcase. He grabbed the badges of his former coworkers on Deimos and shoved them into his left coat pocket. He carefully slipped the two vials into his right pocket and then he pulled out the briefcase.

* * *

THE TWO ARMED guards escorted Johnson and Carter inside Grayson's high-rise office and then they stood beside Grayson. Carter held the briefcase handle with both hands, resting it in front of himself. Sylvia stepped from behind the desk and walked around to face Carter.

Carter looked at her. "Are you okay?"

She nodded.

Grayson grinned. "As you can see, her Sleeper Chip's deactivated."

"Good," Carter said. "The senator and I are here to negotiate the trade."

Grayson smiled at Senator Johnson. Johnson looked at the floor as he stepped away from Carter. Both guards pointed their guns at the doctor.

"Sylvia's free to go," Grayson said. "But I must insist you continue working for me, Dr. Carter."

"That wasn't part of the agreement," Carter said.

Grayson nodded to Henry. "Take the briefcase."

Henry did so.

Grayson glanced at Carter. "It's the best offer you're going to get."

"That's where you're mistaken." Carter removed the virus vial from his pocket. He held it up and squeezed tightly. His eyes grew cold and narrow. His voice altered. "Sylvia and I both leave or you die."

The guards tightened their grip on their guns.

Furious, Grayson flicked his gaze at Johnson. "You let him take the virus *out* of the briefcase?"

Johnson raised his hands in surrender. "I didn't know where he had it. He told me it was stored elsewhere."

"Let us go," Carter said. "Or I swear I'll crush it."

"Don't be a fool," Johnson said.

Grayson smiled. "Listen to the senator, Carter. You break that vial and Sylvia dies as well as all of us. Is that what you want?"

Carter looked at Sylvia. Tears formed in her eyes. His hand shook.

"Why are you doing this, Carter?" she asked.

"Because too many people have died because of Grayson. It needs to end now." He reached into his other pocket and took the ID badges and flung them in the air. "This is what remains of my coworkers on Deimos. That's why I'll crush this if you try to force me to stay."

Perplexed, Sylvia stepped toward Carter. She glared at him. "You'd allow my death to do that? I thought you loved me."

Sweat beaded on Senator Johnson's forehead. "Carter, put down the vial. Please."

"You betrayed us," Carter said to the senator.

"No," Johnson replied.

"That's how it looks to me. No wonder you got worried when Magnus left."

Johnson pointed at Henry. "Take Grayson into custody."

All three guards looked at one another with strange glances.

"My men don't answer to you, Johnson. You should know that."

"They had best, Mr. Grayson. If they don't, and Carter bursts the vial, we're all dead. There isn't a cure. From the look in Carter's eyes, he's not bluffing."

"What makes you so certain he's not bluffing?" Grayson asked.

"Because he had the same look as you do whenever you blackmail me. That ends today, by the way. Justice will finally be served. Your reign over Mars and this enterprise ends, too. Either they cooperate and take you into custody, or they're looking at life sentences."

Henry took a set of handcuffs and approached Grayson. "Sorry about this, sir."

"Don't worry about it. Johnson has no idea what kind of payback he's facing now. You know what to do."

"Enough with your damned threats!" Johnson said. "I'm sick of catering to you."

Grayson's jaw tightened. "Senator, you've made the worst mistake of your life. Trust me, this isn't something you want to do."

"No, it's something I should've done a long time ago."

With tears, Sylvia looked at Carter. Hurt and betrayal softened her eyes. "I really thought you loved me."

"I do."

"No, if that were true, you'd *never* have made such a threat in my presence."

"I came here to make certain Grayson released you from his custody," Carter said. "My threat was a bluff, nothing more. Magnus has promised to testify against Grayson and I will, too."

"I'd really like to believe you, but I can't."

"I'm sorry, Sylvia."

"Me, too." She walked past him to the door.

"Please, wait," Carter said.

Sylvia stood with her back to him. "No. I never want to see you again."

Senator Johnson turned to Carter. "I need that vial, okay?"

Carter looked at Johnson and then at the vial.

"Carter," Johnson said. "Don't worry. I'll make certain it's incinerated before we leave the building."

Carter shook his head. His eyes grew distant and his voice changed. "No, I can't. I came here for one reason. I can't leave until Grayson's dead. I must do it for her."

Sylvia turned with a strange look on her face. "What?"

"For Sylvia?" Grayson asked. "She's free."

"No, not her. For the female alien that healed me. She ordered your death and I promised to carry it out."

Grayson frowned at Johnson. "Can't you see that you're dealing with a lunatic?"

Johnson nodded. "So it appears."

The intercom on Grayson's desk beeped. Grayson nodded at the guard closest to his desk. The man pressed the button.

Shelly said, "I've finally decoded the block placed on the Deimos video footage. Uploading it to your big screen now."

Henry pressed the remote and the screen glowed to life. The footage showed Dr. Carter injecting sick patients with needles and the patients stiffening in death. In other clips, he chased healthy staff members down corridors and battered them to the floor with a broom handle before injecting them with poison. Some of them he killed by slashing them repeatedly with a scalpel.

In the last clip, Carter, obviously ill and deranged, sat on his bed with a syringe. His door opened and a nurse stepped to the side of his bed and placed her hand against his forehead, checking his temperature. Carter became enraged and choked her until she fell limp in his grasp. He lowered her to the floor and injected her with the needle. It was Wanda.

Chapter 80

Senator Johnson, Grayson, Sylvia, and all the guards were stunned. Their mouths hung open.

Finally, Johnson said, "My God! You killed all those people."

Sylvia stammered, clearly in shock. "All this time... and it was you who killed Wanda?"

Carter stared at the screen in disbelief. His arm lowered and his hand shook. Sylvia covered her mouth and rushed out the door and down the hall.

Carter shook his head. "I didn't kill them. The virus did. It killed them all."

Johnson pointed at the screen. "The footage indicates otherwise."

"No," Carter said. "She came. She healed me. The alien. She was there. She wants Grayson dead."

"You're delusional," Johnson said. "Insane. There was no one else. You killed them."

Grayson shouted, "Guards, take Carter down!"

Henry fired, striking Carter's shoulder. Carter toppled backwards and the vial spiraled into the air.

Johnson dove as the vial dropped. It landed in his outstretched hand. He carefully enclosed his hand around the vial.

Grayson smiled. "Good catch, senator."

Johnson rose slowly with his eyes closed. His hand shook. He released a long sigh.

Henry stood over Carter with the gun aimed between the doctor's eyes. Carter blinked and shook his head. Blood seeped through his jacket.

"What happened?" Carter asked.

Johnson motioned the guards. "Take Grayson and follow me."

"Grayson, you've violated too many codes of ethics. It's time you answer for your crimes against humanity. Money cannot buy your way out of everything."

"What occurred on Deimos wasn't my doing. Carter's the obvious madman. I didn't cause a viral outbreak. Hell, I'd be willing to bet there's never been any virus at all."

"No, perhaps not, but you did try to hide it. Had the people that died on Deimos all been hardened criminals, I could dismiss your indifference. But some of them were doctors, scientists, and nurses. Their lives held meaning."

"You're right, and I'll make it right with their families."

"I'm afraid the cost is much more than money this time, Mr. Grayson."

"Is it now?" Grayson asked.

Johnson nodded.

"Shelly? You still on the line?" Grayson asked.

"Yes, of course."

"Seems Johnson thinks he can usurp authority over me. Unless these hand-cuffs are removed in the next few seconds, I want you to release CD-943 to the press immediately."

"Yes, sir. Uploading the video file now," she replied.

Johnson loosened his tie. "What video's that?"

Grayson smiled. "Need you ask? You know what it is."

Johnson's face paled. "Shelly, send it to the press ASAP."

Grayson frowned. "What?"

"My wife and I had a long talk this week. I told her all about my affair. At first I thought she'd divorce me, but after serious thought, she actually forgave me. So, go ahead, give it to the press. I don't give a damn. This is my last term in the senate. I've never worried about having a legacy, but you on the other hand? You've got a lot to answer for."

Johnson took the vial and held it up to the light.

Grayson shook his head. "You can send that to my laboratory for analysis, but I've the feeling there's nothing except air inside the vial."

"No, Mr. Grayson," Johnson said. "This is safer in the hands of the CDC."

Henry grabbed Carter and yanked him to his feet. Carter cried in pain.

"Where's the other vial?" Johnson asked.

"My pocket."

Henry pressed his gun against Carter's temple. "Hands where we can see them."

Carter obeyed and Johnson retrieved the second vial, placing the vials in his jacket pocket.

A group of men in military fatigues entered the room. Johnson addressed the squad leader. "Take Carter to a military hospital and keep him under twenty-four hour surveillance. Once his injury's healed, transfer him to a mental ward for full evaluation. From the video we watched earlier, he's a dangerous man and a serial killer."

"Yes, sir."

Grayson frowned. His face flushed red. Henry placed his hands on Grayson's shoulders, trying to calm him. "When are you going to release me?"

"Henry," Johnson said. "Escort Mr. Grayson to the sleeper lab, or whatever the hell it's called. Grayson should receive the same dose of medicine he gave Sylvia earlier."

"Henry," Grayson said in a low threatening tone.

Johnson glared at them. "Either Henry obeys, or these military men will take him in custody as well. Of course, if your guards decide not to stand down, it might get quite bloody here."

"Henry," Grayson repeated.

"Sorry, sir."

"No, do what I told you earlier after you take me to the lab."

"I will, sir," Henry whispered.

Once they reached the Sleep Lab, Grayson was sedated by a military doctor while several National Guardsmen stood nearby. Once the chip was implanted and programmed, Johnson told the men to make certain Grayson was on the next shuttle to Mars. He told them if they had questions about the orders to call Justice Watkins. They nodded.

Johnson left the room and headed for the elevator.

Senator Johnson smiled as he exited the front doors of Grayson Enterprises. Finally, he held the sense of triumph over Grayson that he'd long hoped to achieve. Joe was freed from the Sleeper Chip, and Grayson was being sent as a miner to Mars. Freedom never seemed better, nor tasted sweeter. He made his way down the winding sidewalk steps, enjoying the cooler breeze as the sky became overcast and hinted of rain.

When he rounded the last curve of the stairs, two men approached him. They weren't massive men like the goons Grayson kept for bodyguards. Both men wore nice leisure suits, and for a moment, Johnson assumed they were federal agents to assist in Grayson's apprehension. He stopped at the bottom of the steps. His limo was less than ten yards away, but too far for a man of his age to sprint to.

"Good evening, senator," the older man said. His face was pocked and wrinkled. "Let's, how do you say it in dis country? Go for a little stroll."

The other man pulled back the front of his jacket and revealed his gun.

Johnson gulped and glanced around the parking lot, hoping to see someone to call to for help. No one else was in sight. "Who are you?"

"Senator, what are names at dis point? But if it makes you more comfortable, I'm Viktor and dis is Parks. Let's say dat Grayson has asked us to place you into early retirement."

"Permanently," Parks said.

"Grayson's no longer in charge," Johnson said sternly. "I've seen to that."

"Have you now?" Viktor said. "Is that any way to show your loyalty?"

"Loyalty? Grayson's always been underhanded and deceptive. He's a ruthless man."

"He paid you well, did he not?" Parks asked.

"I had no choice but to take the money."

Viktor laughed. "There are always choices, senator."

"He'd have killed me if I didn't do what he asked. Death wasn't one of the choices I favored."

"It has come to you all the same," Viktor pulled his gun with its silencer from inside his vest.

"Wait," Johnson said. "Isn't there something I could do for you?"

"The vials?" Parks asked. "Where are they?"

Johnson patted his jacket pocket.

"Hands up," Parks said, reaching into Johnson's pocket and retrieving the two vials.

Viktor smiled and fired two shots into Johnson's chest.

Johnson winced and placed his hands over his heart. His knees struck the sidewalk heavily. He fell forward with wide eyes as death claimed him.

GRAYSON ENTERPRISES (Two weeks later)

JONAS SAT at Grayson's desk, looking through various files, and approving work orders.

Boony entered the office. "Is everything going okay?"

Jonas looked up and nodded. "I suppose. The last thing I ever expected was for the leadership of Grayson Enterprises to be dropped in my lap."

"I imagine Grayson had his reasons?"

Jonas offered a slight shrug. "He's always trusted me."

"I suppose it's a good thing we left Mars then?"

Jonas laughed. "That's probably the reason I was at the top of the list to oversee his operations."

"So let me get this straight. He still owns Grayson Enterprises and all the operations he set up on Mars, but he was sent to Mars to work in the mines like the other prisoners?"

"Sadly, yes."

"The irony has to be painful."

"Not if he's under control of the chip. He's not going to remember a thing."

"How long's his sentence? Won't the government try to take everything away from him?" she asked.

"That's some of what I've been reading through this morning. They'll try, but Grayson has a ruthless team of attorneys that'll find every loophole possible to have the charges against Grayson dropped. Senator Johnson was the only reason Grayson was sent to Mars without a trial or judge's order. The charges can't stick, but the shuttle took off before the authorities ever got a chance to open the investigation. And then, of course, Johnson was *mysteriously* killed."

Boony shook her head, taking in all the information. "Matthews is in charge on Mars. Even if the attorneys manage to get these charges dropped and grant Grayson freedom, do you think Matthews will ever honor such orders?"

"It's hard to say, Boony. Grayson's powerful on Earth, but like you said, Matthews is calling the shots there. It'll be interesting how this plays out. The good news is Carter never had a deadly virus, so that potential threat's gone."

"Is it?" she asked. "Who tested the vials?"

"I understood the vials were sent to the CDC."

Boony shook her head, reading a different report by one of Grayson's guards. "According to this, Johnson left with the vials."

"What?"

She handed the paper to Jonas.

"Damn," he said. "Just when I was beginning to think everything was settling down. Nothing in the police report states vials were found on Johnson's body."

"So they're still out there?"

"Seems so. I'll make some calls to the NSA and Homeland Security, letting them know the potential danger. For the world's sake, let's hope Grayson's assumption that there wasn't a virus to begin with."

Boony sighed. "It's a shame Carter killed everyone stationed on Deimos. At least he's out of the population now."

Jonas held a grim smile. "Sometimes the prisoners are the least of our worries. It's the ones who haven't yet committed any heinous crimes that are troublesome. You never know when they'll strike."

"What about the strange insects Clark brought back?"

"They're in a highly secure lab here."

"That's safe?"

Jonas nodded. "Safer than any university lab. I'm certain by the time Grayson returns to Earth, if he ever does, Clark will have all his research data on the insects and won't need to worry about Grayson stealing his thunder. Clark will have his moments in the scientific spotlight."

"That's good for him."

"It is."

Boony stood in silence for several minutes. She looked like she wanted to say something but held back.

"What's on your mind, Boony?"

"I've a favor to ask," she said.

"Sure. What is it?"

"I'd like your permission to take a few days to go to Dallas and see if I can find Magnus. I have a good idea where he is. Nothing's been reported in the news about him getting revenge on the gang that killed his girlfriend's cousin. I'd like to help if I can."

Jonas studied her for a few moments. "You still believe he's innocent of the charges."

She nodded. "I do. If I held any doubts, I'd let it be. But, all the evidence not admitted into court was damning to the prosecution and the judge's overall decision, which is why I think it was all discredited."

"You think they were in league with the gang?"

"It's very possible."

Jonas shook his head and frowned. "If there's one thing I cannot stand, it's corrupt judges, attorneys, and police. Go. Keep me posted. But promise me something."

Boony smiled. "What?"

"If you need anything, call me immediately. I have a lot of contacts, and I definitely will be calling Texas' Attorney General, informing him of the corruptness in that court. Be careful."

"I will, Jonas. And thanks."

Chapter 81

Dallas, Texas (24 hours later)

MAGNUS SAT IN HIS RUNDOWN, one bedroom apartment. He studied a
city map spread out on the floor. Empty Chinese food and pizza boxes cluttered
the small coffee table. Someone knocked.

He turned his attention to the door and frowned. To the best of his knowledge no one except his landlord knew he was there. He stood and pulled his
9mm from the back of his belt and eased to the door.

"Magnus?" Boony asked from the hallway. "You in there?"

"Boony?" He tucked the gun behind his back.

"Yes."

Magnus swung the door open. She beamed a wide smile, rushed, and
jumped to hug his neck. He caught her and wrapped his arms around her
narrow waist, holding her a couple of feet off the floor. "Why the hell are you
back on Earth and how'd you ever locate me?"

After he lowered her and invited her inside, Boony explained the reasons for
why she and Jonas, along with the others, had returned to Earth. "And as far as
finding you? You know me and surveillance cameras." She winked.

"Ah, you've been spying on me?"

"Not really, but I thought you might need some help. I didn't want you to do
something that'd land you real jail time. I was afraid since you arrived on Earth
a couple of weeks earlier than me that I was too late."

"No need to worry about that. Apparently the gang members who killed my ex-girl's cousin have long gone."

"Tyler Malcolm?" she asked. "Was he the leader?"

"Yeah," Magnus said with a slight curious frown. "How'd you know?"

"I told you I'd look into your case. When they arrested you, his name was the one you gave to the police to search, but they ignored your request."

"I guess it was easier to charge me since I was less of a threat than Tyler's entire gang."

Boony smiled. "I think some of the officers, the prosecutor, and the judge were in cahoots with Tyler Malcolm. Instead of bringing charges and arresting him and his gang members, they received a large cut of the money from drug sales."

"I've thought about that, too. But hell, there's no way to prove it, and even if I could, we haven't any idea which officers we could trust to turn them in."

"Jonas said he has ties higher up at the state capital."

Magnus looked at her and shook his head. "Jonas is willing to help me? Nah, I know better than that."

"If we get the proof, he will. I've never known him to go back on his word."

"Like I said, T.M. isn't using the warehouse where he set me up."

She smiled. "No. Now, he's using one several blocks away."

"For real? You found that out?"

"It's not difficult when you have computer access to the Dallas City Records, which Jonas does and allowed me to snoop around."

Magnus chuckled. "That's definitely something I don't have."

"So what's your plan?"

Magnus sat and pointed at the map on the floor. "Where's the warehouse he's using now?"

Boony knelt to the side of the map and after a few minutes of tracing the city grid, she pointed. "There. So what do you want to do?"

"With some of the money I got from selling those MarQuebes, I bought some spy-tech cameras and bugs, hoping to uplink whatever I could capture on film and audio to get enough evidence to have them all arrested."

"So you're not planning to kill Tyler yourself?"

Magnus' brow rose. "Lord, no. His time in prison would be a greater punishment. How can death punish him? It's instant. I want them behind bars without the possibility of parole, which based on our judicial system is a long shot."

"You need some help?" Boony asked. "Setting up the cameras and bugs?"

He shook his head. "No, I can't have you putting your life on the line for this."

"Okay," she replied. "How about an extra set of eyes? I could be your lookout."

Magnus smiled. "That'd be something I could use. I have binoculars."

"Great. So we should probably check out the warehouse and figure out how to set the devices."

"My motorcycle's in the parking lot."

"Motorcycle?"

He nodded.

"You're settling in pretty good already."

"Ah, this place, nah, I don't intend to stay here. It's a weekly lease, but a good place to blend in. Say, have you heard anything about Sylvia and Carter?"

"You didn't hear?"

Magnus looked worried. "No. Is Sylvia okay?"

"She's fine, I suppose. She's been released from her contract with Grayson and from what I can figure out, she went to live with family. But Carter—"

"What'd he do?"

Boony rose to her feet and rested her hands on her hips. "He killed everyone stationed on Deimos."

Magnus' mouth dropped. His eyes widened. "I suspected he was a bit messed up in the head because he kept going into weird trances, but I never thought he'd do something like that. And to think Sylvia and I traveled from Mars with him."

"He's not going to ever get out of prison."

"It's a shame his fate turned out so badly."

"Count your blessings. You're lucky he didn't kill you and Sylvia aboard the shuttle home."

Magnus nodded. "The first month we went into Hyber-Sleep, he stayed awake. I noticed while I was going under that he wasn't preparing to sedate himself to get into his chamber. It was frightening because there wasn't anything I could do."

"You're safe now."

"Yep. Come on, let's go scope the warehouse."

IN ORDER for Magnus to get inside the warehouse, Boony became a major distraction to lure the two gang members guarding the warehouse from their posts while the rest of the group were out on their bikes.

She wore short shorts and stood bent over the side of Magnus' motorcycle acting frustrated that she couldn't get the engine to fire. Of course, the two men offered to help, and while she feigned helplessness, they combed over the bike, trying to identify the reason for it not starting.

Magnus hurried inside and concealed cameras in every corner of the warehouse. Then he planted a few bugs where he guessed Tyler might negotiate terms for major drug deals. When he finished setting up the devices, he slipped out through the rear side door into an alley. Once he was at a safe distance where the two guards wouldn't see him, he texted Boony.

She then pointed to a loose wire, connected it, and got on the motorcycle. She started it, smiled, and then rode away.

After a week of recording video surveillance from the rooftop and the inside of the warehouse, which was forwarded to Jonas, he made contact with the state attorney general who sent a SWAT team to raid the warehouse at the most convenient time. Three local officers were inside in the middle of a trade when the armed police forced everyone to lie facedown on the floor.

Magnus and Boony sat on the roof of a neighboring building, watching everything as the SWAT officers took the gang members, including Tyler Malcolm, and several police officers into custody. Every major television news station was present, as were countless newspaper reporters.

A few days later, the national news reported the arrest of the prosecutor and the judge from Magnus' case. Jonas had pointed higher ups in the right direction as he had promised. Charges against Magnus were later dropped, and he declined the offers from attorneys wishing to represent him in a suit against the city.

Magnus treated Boony to dinner to celebrate the good news. Magnus tipped his bottle of beer at Boony and she clinked hers to his in a toast.

"Thanks for not spoiling the ending, Magnus," Boony said.

Magnus grinned. "Ending? Baby, this is just the end of a chapter. Who knows what the next chapters of our lives will gift us?"

She nuzzled up against him. "As long as it's us moving forward together."

"I'm for that."

Chapter 82

Olympus Mons: Six months later:

The passenger shuttle entered the landing bay of Olympus Mons. Steven Matthews stood near the landing pad with two guards and a medic. After the engines shut off, the door opened.

Guards rushed inside with CAM-Ls and commanded the new prisoners to exit the shuttle. Grayson was the last prisoner through the door. He was a massive man compared to the others. Matthews smiled as Grayson walked to him.

Matthews stared into Grayson's absent eyes and shook his head. "Welcome to Mars, Boyd. So, my friend, the tables have finally turned, haven't they? I imagine the last place you'd ever expected to find yourself was on Mars, as a mining prisoner, nonetheless." He chuckled. "Fate can be such a nasty bitch sometimes. Those who sentenced you to come here are probably quite tickled to entertain their thoughts of your demise as you waste away in the very pits where you sent others to slave until they died. However, how they view your fate is much different than mine."

Matthews nodded at the medic. The medic placed the chip deactivator against Grayson's implanted Sleeper Chip. Several minutes later, Grayson shook his head and blinked. His eyes darted back and forth as he tried to comprehend where he was. Finally, it dawned on him and Matthews smiled. "I shall repeat it. Welcome to Mars, Boyd."

Grayson stood with an incredulous stare. He frowned.

"You look surprised, Grayson," Matthews said.

"It's because I am. You released me from the chip?"

Matthews nodded with a broad grin spread on his face. "I did."

"Why? I don't understand. You could've allowed me to die in the mines like Senator Johnson had hoped."

Matthews laughed. "Senator Johnson's no more a threat to our establishment, if I could be so bold to assume we still have an equally vested interest in keeping Grayson Enterprises alive and well on Earth?"

"We do."

"Good. Glad to hear it."

Grayson rubbed his temples. "Forgive me. My memories are a bit distorted."

"That tends to be a side effect of those chips, Boyd, but your memories will resurface shortly."

"How can we be certain Johnson won't cause further problems?"

Matthews leaned slightly forward with a sly grin and whispered in Grayson's ear. "The senator ran into some misfortune and, let's just say, he's permanently retired."

"From the Senate?"

"From *everything*."

Grayson's eyebrows rose. "You mean he's dead?"

"*Very*."

"Who killed him?"

"You don't remember?" Matthews asked with a curious frown.

"No."

"Viktor and Parks. You requested their assistance immediately after Johnson took you into custody and ordered you to be implanted with a chip. Viktor and Parks were more than happy to oblige. And the senator's son?" Matthews patted Grayson's shoulder. "You'll find this ironically funny. He's back in the mines, slaving away. Gasp! Perhaps due to these recent humanitarian allegations, we shouldn't allude to any term about slaves. But nonetheless, as you can see, I've honored my contract with you."

"Above and beyond," Grayson replied.

"I'd have it no other way, Boyd. I recognized the power we each held prior to our first meeting, but I've also recognized how much more powerful we are as a team. The governments on Earth will soon shudder when the enlightenment of our union seizes them."

Grayson extended his hand to Matthews. "I'm indebted to you. I don't know how to repay you."

Matthews grinned and vigorously shook Grayson's hand. "Half of everything has a nice ring to it."

"Half?"

Matthews shrugged. "Equal partners. Besides, we both have far more wealth than either of us could ever spend in dozens of lifetimes. And, I think Grayson and Matthews' Enterprises is rather catchy. Don't you?"

Grayson grinned. "I'm not thrilled about it, but it's livable."

"Great!"

"What about Carter and the virus?" Grayson asked.

"Oh, yeah, that. Before Johnson's demise, Viktor and Parks took the two vials from the senator, and let's just say that those pesky National Guardsmen who arrived with the senator to arrest you, the whole group should received Oscars for their convincing performances."

Grayson frowned. "What? Why?"

"I hired them from the actor's guild. Marvelous performance, from what I hear. So, instead of taking Carter to a padded cell, he's in an induced coma."

"Why?" Grayson asked.

"Turns out, Boyd, the virus is very real, and Carter's the only one immune, so, for now, he's in a suspended state." Matthews lowered his voice to a whisper. "A drug induced coma. We're farming his antigens to develop a powerful vaccine should ever that nasty virus escape our laboratory."

Grayson nodded.

Matthews smiled. "Now, let us find a suitable way to return you to the U.S., so you can continue to be the pressing thorn in the side of those who hate you most."

"I always thought that was you."

"Once upon a time, my good man, but no longer. Let bygones be bygones." Matthews reached into his suit pocket. "Cigar?"

Grayson accepted it. "Who's currently overseeing Grayson Enterprises on Earth?"

"Jonas. Apparently you informed Henry to have Jonas take the reins for a while, but that's another reason I cannot afford for you to be a miner here. Jonas and I... well, we'll never see eye to eye on things. He's too ethical in ways you and I are not."

Grayson nodded. "I agree, but he's the only person on Earth I'd have trusted until I can return."

"I totally agree, but your team of attorneys are quite busy fighting off all the attempted fines and seizures of properties on Earth, and I expect they'll do one damn good job in preventing the government from prying anything from our grasp."

"That's why they make the big money."

"Indeed," Matthews said, striking a match off the wall.

Grayson lit his cigar off the rising flame. "Thanks."

"Of course, Jonas knows nothing of Carter and the real virus, so let's keep this between us. You know how he's a stickler for the rules, eh? Do we have a deal?"

"Sure," Grayson said. "Thanks for bringing me up to speed."

Matthews grinned. "Any time. Now, since this is your first time to visit, let me show you around. I'm sure in a few months you'll be more than ready to return to your throne on Earth. I may, in fact, accompany you. Mars has a cold way of settling on you, and as I'm certain you'll agree, 'there's no place like home'. And that's on Earth, *not* Mars. Besides, with the bizarre bloodthirsty insects locked inside the mineshaft—"

"Insects?" Grayson frowned.

Matthews nodded and explained the insects in detail. "I ordered a large supply of flamethrowers and napalm since extreme heat seems to be the only thing capable of killing them. These weapons should arrive any day, but I'd rather not be around when they reopen that mineshaft."

"I agree," Grayson said.

"Ah, to Earth it is, eh, ol' chum?" Matthews asked.

Grayson nodded and followed Matthews through the corridors to see what his Martian facilities actually looked like. Enemies can become the best of friends whenever their end goals are the same.

THE END

About the Author

Leonard D. Hilley II grew up a quiet, shy kid with an inquisitive mind. Learning to read at an early age, he fell in love with books. He read every book he could get his hands on and stacks of dark comics about ghosts, monsters, and creepy things that stalk the night.

Like a lot of boys, he caught beetles, wooly bears, butterflies, and had an ant farm. When he was ten, his interests in science increased even more after seeing a professor's insect collection. Soon he set out on his quest to build his own collection. He also learned to rear butterflies and moths to obtain perfect specimens. He learned botany, gardening, and set his goal to become an entomologist.

At eleven, he saw Star Wars. His imagination soared. Soon after, he discovered Roger Zelazny's Chronicles of Amber. Six months later, he had written the first draft of a novel. A novel he later discarded, but the characters stuck with him. Years later, these characters came to life in Shawndirea, which Hilley intended to be a novella for Devils Den. The characters, however, refused to be ignored and took the opportunity to unveil Aetheaon in their first epic fantasy. Lady Squire: Dawn's Ascension was quick to follow.

Shawndirea was Hilley's farewell to butterfly collecting, and those who have read the novel understand why. He has taken Ray Bradbury's advice to heart: "Follow the characters." He does. He follows, listens, and take notes—often never knowing where they're going to take him, but he's never been disappointed in the results.

Hilley earned a B.S. in Biology and an MFA in Creative Writing to combine his love of science and writing.

Sci-fi Titles: Predators of Darkness: Aftermath, Beyond the Darkness, The Game of Pawns, Death's Valley, The Deimos Virus.

Epic Fantasy: Shawndirea (Aetheaon Chronicles: Book One), Lady Squire

(Aetheaon Chronicles: Book Two), Frosthammer (Aetheaon Chronicles: Book Three), Shadowfae (Aetheaon Chronicles: Book Four), and Devils Den.

UF/PR: Succubus: Shadows of the Beast (Nocturnal Trinity Series: Book One), Raven (Nocturnal Trinity Series: Book Two), A Touch of the Familiar

YA UF/Paranormal: Forrest Wollinsky Vampire Hunter; Forrest Wollinsky: Blood Mists of London; Forrest Wollinsky: Predestined Crossroads.